WILD WOMEN AND THE BLUES

WILD WOMEN
AND THE BLUES

DENNY S. BRYCE

THORNDIKE PRESS
A part of Gale, a Cengage Company

GALE
A Cengage Company

GALE
A Cengage Company

Copyright © 2021 by Denny S. Bryce, LLC.
Thorndike Press, a part of Gale, a Cengage Company.

Thorndike Press® Large Print Black Voices.
The text of this Large Print edition is unabridged.
Other aspects of the book may vary from the original edition.
Set in 16 pt. Plantin.

LIBRARY OF CONGRESS CIP DATA ON FILE.
CATALOGUING IN PUBLICATION FOR THIS BOOK
IS AVAILABLE FROM THE LIBRARY OF CONGRESS.

ISBN-13: 978-1-4328-8785-8 (hardcover alk. paper)

Published in 2021 by arrangement with Kensington Books, an imprint of Kensington Publishing Corp.

Printed in Mexico
Print Number: 01   Print Year: 2021

To my mother, Daisy Mae
I wish you were here to read it

PART 1

Part 1

CHAPTER 1
SAWYER

On the fifth floor of the Bronzeville Senior Living Facility, I stand outside the smallest room in the world, doing my best to ignore the dropped ceiling and square linoleum tiles, stoking my claustrophobia.

No windows. No air. No natural light. Just stark-white walls out of focus like cheesecloth over a camera lens.

The old woman in the bed adds to my anxiety, as does the fact that I'm almost out of cash. But nothing will defeat me. Not this go-round. Not with the help of the old lady in the bed — Honoree Dalcour, my last great hope.

The backpack digs into my shoulder. I check the time on my cell phone, eight hours until my connecting flight to Paris. Six hours (fewer if I take a shuttle back to O'Hare) to coax the 110-year-old woman

9

in the bed (who could die at any second or who could be dead now) into telling me a story to fix my life or more likely help me finish my film project.

You see, I'm a graduate student chasing a doctorate in media studies. My documentary thesis focuses on the legendary Black filmmaker Oscar Micheaux in 1925. The project, however, has a gaping hole, smack in the center. A hole I haven't thought about in over a year. Not since my sister, Azizi, was killed in a car crash with me behind the wheel.

Fifteen months and a lot of tequila later, I need something normal to aspire to, something ordinary and reasonable like finishing the damn film. God knows, something other than talking to my sister's ghost, a conversation that unquestionably doesn't constitute normal, ordinary, or reasonable.

"How long are you planning to stand in the doorway?" A young woman in navy-blue scrubs, pushing a medicine cart, stops next to me. "If you want to talk to Miss Honoree, you should go inside."

Her no-nonsense style makes me wonder: Does she sense my fear of small spaces, which annoys her, or does she merely want me out of her way?

"Excuse me?" My version of indignant is

10

a pitch too high for a man with my usually deep baritone.

She tilts her head and frowns. "I said if you have something to say, you should stand next to her bed. Then you're not some faceless stranger, quizzing her from the other side of the room."

I can tell she doesn't like me. She's looking at me as if I were a wad of gum on the bottom of her shoe.

"I'm giving her a few minutes to wake up," I explain.

Blue Scrubs folds her arms over her stomach as her large brown eyes casually damn me to hell. This erases any hope of our having a future together.

By the way, this is my vivid imagination at work. She's beautiful and my age. Midtwenties. Super-short natural hair. Dark skin and those luminous brown eyes. The color of midnight and stars. Also, I'm a romantic, and if I were normal, I'd have her number by now.

Blue Scrubs sighs impatiently. "Don't ask her insipid questions about her secret to living such a long life. She hates that."

I smile, but her contempt is soul-crushing. "I promise I'm only here to ask her non-insipid questions. I have some photos from 1925, and if she remembers where they were taken or can confirm who was in the photos with her, it could make all the difference for my film project."

"Yeah. That is the reason you're here, or the reason I overheard you babbling about at the front desk." Her judgmental gaze skims over my perfectly groomed dreadlocks, my stylish but plain white tee, my faded jeans, and my expensive loafers. My shoulders tense. The examination feels too thorough. Can she tell I'm not wearing socks?

"You're from Hollywood." The sneer in her voice is buzz-worthy.

I wiggle my fingers. "Comme ci, come ça. I'm more Los Angeles, well, Santa Monica, to be precise, than Hollywood," I say in my defense. "What tipped you off to my roots?"

"I told you I heard you at the front desk." Turning slightly, she peers into the room. "At least you're not one of those obnoxious people from the networks who visit once a year to gawk at her."

"Once a year? Why?"

"On her birthday. They come to see if she can still eat, talk, or hear." Blue Scrubs gestures with an angry flip of her wrist.

I wince. "I want to talk about her life in 1925 and show her some photos. I may also record her, take an oral history of sorts?"

12

Her gaze is resolute. "As long as you remember, she's not a freak show. Just because she's lived longer than most and kept her wits about her, doesn't mean people like you should use her as a ratings boost or clickbait."

I sigh, exasperated by all the negativity directed at me, and I don't even know her name. "I should introduce myself. I'm Sawyer Hayes. The *Ugly American* film-maker." I smile. She doesn't. My obscure reference is just that — obscure — but I had hoped for a smile or a less pained expression. "It is a 1963 Marlon Brando flick. I'm a classic-movie buff."

"I'm Lula Kent." She extends a hand, and we awkwardly shake, touching fingertips only. "I'm a nurse's assistant here."

"Ms. Kent, or may I call you Lula?"

The go-to-hell expression answers my question.

"Okay, then, Ms. Kent. I only need a few minutes of her time."

Her side-eye is a steel blade cutting across my face into my chest. Now, what did I do?

"Who gave you permission to visit Miss Honoree? I missed that part when I was eavesdropping at the reception desk."

I like her for admitting to the flaw of nosiness, but I need a second to think. Truth is, my grandmother isn't aware of my trip to Chicago, let alone my visit to the Bronzeville Senior Living Facility. Or that I borrowed a few items from her long-ago box, my nickname for the storage bin she keeps in her attic.

From the look in Lula's eyes, I can't dodge the question. I have to say something. I nod toward the woman in the bed. "My grandmother has been paying her expenses since 1985. I think the receptionist felt obligated to let me in."

Lula cranes her neck. "Mrs. Margaret Hendrickson is your grandmother?"

"Yes, and Honoree's guardian angel, you might say."

Lula visibly grits her teeth. "Her name is Ms. Dalcour or Miss Honoree. It is disrespectful to call your elders by only their first names, especially when you've never been introduced." She returns to her cart and wraps her fingers around the handlebar, thinking about my throat, I imagine.

"Don't stay too long," she orders. "Miss Honoree needs her rest."

CHAPTER 2
HONOREE

Friday, October 23, 1925
Chicago

Honoree Dalcour sashayed into the basement of Miss Hattie's Garden Cafe a little after seven o'clock in the evening. A squirrel-collared coat hung over her arm, and a box purse dangled from her wrist. Weaving through crates of bootleg whiskey and burlap bags of sweet potatoes, she swung her hips with an extra oomph. It made the rhinestones on her drop-waist dress crackle — just like she wanted them to and with good reason.

The proprietor of the Dreamland Cafe, the ritziest black-and-tan nightclub on the Stroll, was holding a midnight audition at his establishment on State Street. Only girls Mr. Buttons had seen dance with his own eyes — and wanted to hire bad enough to risk a beef with another club owner — received an invitation. Rumor on the Stroll was an invite guaranteed a spot in the Dreamland chorus.

Honoree was no dumb Dora — and didn't believe every note of chin music she heard — but this once, she ab-so-lute-ly, positively believed. And why not? An invitation had been pushed under her front door that very afternoon.

Hot diggity dog!

After three years of dance lessons, tap classes, practicing all day, peeling potatoes all night, and selling policy player dream books (a pamphlet of lucky numbers for gamblers) while keeping her boss, Archie Graves, and his fat fingers from creeping too far up her shift, and, well — just like that — she was on her way to the Dreamland Cafe.

All she had to do was stay clear of Archie, which shouldn't be too tough. It was Friday, and he spent every Friday through Saturday morning in his office with an alderman, a madam, and, of late, an automobile dealer from Kenosha, playing poker, guzzling hooch, and smoking marijuana.

With Archie preoccupied, Honoree could skip the midnight show without too much trouble — and she'd had her share of trouble with Archie Graves. A small bone in her jaw still ached from the last time she

16

was on the wrong side of his troublesome left hand.

Soon, she wouldn't have to worry about the goons at Miss Hattie's. A better class of coloreds patronized the Dreamland Cafe. Educated. Proud Black people. Fearless people. People who spat in the face of Jim Crow, not just getting by but *living* their lives.

The late Booker T. Washington had written the book *A New Negro for a New Century*, and Honoree kept a copy in her shopping bag. It was a gift from her childhood sweetheart, Ezekiel Bailey, given to her three years ago, before he disappeared.

She was sixteen at the time, and, of course, Ezekiel broke her heart. She didn't cry the blues like most of the flappers in the neighborhood because her man ran off. She was better than that. Better than any of the chorus girls at Miss Hattie's who wept over a man, good or bad, for months.

Honoree was a sharecropper's daughter, accustomed to hard work and hard times. She had no desire to have a man for the sake of having one, and not for better or for worse, and she made no apologies for her independent mind. Just like she had no qualms about dancing at a ghetto speakeasy every night of the week, except Sundays

17

because she had plans.

She glided over the sawdust floor, moving effortlessly down the hall toward the dressing room. Light as a feather, she twirled by the freshly stoked coal furnace, sweat dripping down her back, but the heat couldn't stop her feet from dancing: step, shuffle, ball change, step, shuffle, ball change.

With a swing of her hip, the dressing room door opened, and the woodsy, damp smell of sawdust and talc powder filled her nostrils.

A dim bulb in the hallway bathed the sawdust floor in pools of light, and a tune came to Honoree's mind from *Shuffle Along,* the all-Negro Broadway musical she planned to headline in one day, when it returned to New York City.

The rhythm took hold of her limbs.

She grabbed the strand of pearls around her neck, gave them a sassy twirl, and belted: "I'm gonna dance at the Dreamland Cafe!"

A shadow stepped from the darkness.

Honoree gasped. "Archie?" Her knees turned soft as tissue paper. She pushed the button on the wall, lighting up the room.

"For crying out loud!" Honoree yelped.

"Sorry to interrupt, ma'am." A brown-skinned girl with big brown eyes stood, shaking like a skinned cat in winter.

"You scared the heebie-jeebies out of me." Honoree crossed to the opposite side of the dressing room. The ragamuffin might be one of them crazy colored girls from down south. Only the other week, Honoree had a fearsome episode when one of 'em tried to grab her purse on State Street.

"I'm sorry." The girl kicked at the sawdust, worn boots ready to fall apart. "Didn't mean no harm, ma'am."

Judging from her mud-caked clothes and bruised jaw, Honoree guessed the girl had fought her way from the Mason-Dixon Line to Chicago. "You're supposed to make a sound when someone enters a room she thinks is empty."

"I thought you saw me. I was sittin' right there." She pointed a shaky finger at a stack of burlap bags.

Honoree's mind had been so full of the Dreamland Cafe, she would've missed Jack Johnson in a prizefight. "I didn't ask where you were sitting."

The girl's eyes grew as round as Moon-Pies.

"You best hightail it outta here before Miss Dolly shows. She doesn't tolerate no squatters."

"I'm no squatter. My name is Bessie

Palmer. I'm the new chorus girl Mr. Graves hired."

Honoree's throat pinched as if someone had grabbed her by the tonsils. Why would Archie hire a new girl? Had he heard the rumors about the audition? "Archie didn't hire you."

"Yes, he did. I can prove it." Bessie dug into her coat pocket. "This is my contract. This is Mr. Graves's signature."

Honoree glanced at the papers. "I don't care what you're holding in your hand. Your legs are too short. Nose too broad, and you're two shades too dark."

Ugly words. Honoree expected to draw a slew of tears for her trouble, but Bessie raised her chin.

Honoree snatched the paper from Bessie's hand and stared at the crumpled page. "These are the same paragraphs Archie called a contract when I signed one two years ago. When did he hire you?"

"Last week."

Honoree handed her the contract with a sigh of relief. Archie had hired Bessie days before Honoree had heard squat about the audition.

"Don't you believe me?" Bessie's voice was as shaky as Jell-O.

Honoree shrugged but did not reply. The

ragamuffin could stew for a few minutes — the price to pay for scaring Honoree half to death.

The other chorus girls would arrive soon, and this might be her only chance, without curious eyes watching, to pack up her costumes, makeup, and new coral-pink gown, a gossamer silk number, with rhinestones and tassels hanging from the hem.

She sat in front of the mirror, but Bessie stood behind her, chewing on her lip like a meal.

"What are you staring at?" Honoree demanded.

"I wanna ask you a question," the girl said in a small voice.

"Go on, then. Ask."

"I need a costume."

"Goodness, gracious. Didn't Miss Dolly give you a costume?"

"I never met Miss Dolly."

Honoree removed her makeup pouch from her shopping bag. "Then who taught you the dance numbers?"

"I — I been rehearsing by myself."

"Alone? How?"

"Don't worry." Bessie's tone hardened. "I can dance."

Honoree faced her, intrigued. The girl's brown eyes were angry slits. "Miss Orphan

Annie, you have a claw."

"Why you wanna go and call me a name?"

Honoree arched an eyebrow, grudgingly impressed with her sass. "If Miss Dolly didn't teach you, who did?"

Bessie opened her mouth, but Honoree interrupted before she could say a word. "Forget I asked."

This was likely Honoree's last night at Miss Hattie's. What was the point of listening to a new girl's story?

"I need a costume," Bessie said, staring at her reflection in the mirror. Again, she was standing too close, right behind Honoree.

"Lord, stop sneaking up on me."

"I don't sneak." Bessie pulled a piece of string hanging from her sleeve. "Been standing right here. Not moving since the first time."

Honoree sighed. "Okay, then."

She reached into her shopping bag and handed Bessie a pair of ruffled bloomers and a rhinestone-covered muslin bodice. "Now, stop pestering me."

Bessie's face lit up like a Christmas tree. "Thank you!"

"It's a hand-me-down and won't fit. So don't get too excited. I'm quite a bit taller than you."

Bessie's large eyes blinked back tears as

her lips quivered.

"Don't have a conniption." Honoree eyed her up and down. "I'm taller than you, but we're about the same size in the hips and bubs."

"That's what I thought, too."

"After you're done with the outfit, you give it back washed and ironed. You understand?"

"Yes, ma'am." Bessie hugged the clothes to her chest, grinning like a Cheshire cat.

Honoree squeezed her eyes shut and groaned. She felt sorry for the child but also wanted to strangle her. She reminded Honoree of hard times. Plus, the bruises on her face turned Honoree's stomach.

"Come here," Honoree said gruffly. "I don't like seeing anyone onstage, even at a brawling speakeasy like Miss Hattie's, looking like they just took a doozy of a beating." Honoree rummaged through her makeup. "We need to cover up those black-and-blue marks."

"How would I do that?"

Honoree organized her makeup: face powder, black pencil, a small black brush, lipstick, and cake mascara. "Have a seat."

Bessie grabbed a nearby crate and sat, fidgeting like her rump had landed in the electric chair with the warden's finger on the switch.

"Sit still and pay attention to me." Honoree dipped the pink puff into a powder tin and patted her cheeks. "Now, you do the same over your bruise."

Bessie put more face powder in her lap than on her face.

"I swear, you gonna give me apoplexy." Honoree picked up a cloth and dabbed it in a jar of hand cream. "Turn toward me."

Holding Bessie's chin, she wiped her brow, her cheeks, her chin. "Learn how to do this for yourself, and don't mention I let you use my makeup. I'm not known for my generosity."

After a few minutes, Honoree turned Bessie to the mirror. "See. Makes a difference."

Bessie grinned at her reflection. "We have the same shape mouth."

"I'll admit a slight resemblance," Honoree said begrudgingly, not wanting to burst Bessie's bubble. "Though it won't make you the next Queen of Sheba."

Bessie winced. Honoree rolled her eyes, but a tinge of sympathy ran through her. "I guess we do have similar mouths," she conceded. "Our lips are too thick for Clara Bow's heart-shaped lips." She picked up the lipstick. "Colored girls paint their mouths

24

differently."

Bessie puckered her lips.

"Stop acting up and watch me." Honoree coated her lips with a dark red color, the shade of sunset. "Are you watching?"

"Yes, ma'am," Bessie said eagerly. "May I ask you another question?"

Honoree nodded.

"What's your name, or should I call you ma'am, or is it miss?"

"Don't miss or ma'am me. We save that for Miss Dolly out of respect 'cause she's been here since before Miss Hattie died. My name's Honoree, spelled with two *e*'s but pronounced Honorray."

"You sure have a pretty name."

"Yes, it is. And French. My father was Louisiana Creole." She raised an eyebrow at Bessie and her bruised but young face. "How old are you?"

"Sixteen —"

"You look younger. Not old enough to do much of nothin'. Where are your parents?"

"Ain't got no parents. Been on my own for a while."

Honoree knew about being on her own. "Who beat you up?"

Bessie stared at the floor as if she were counting splinters.

"Go on, you can tell me; I won't say

anything."

"A man I met who I thought would treat me better, but I was wrong."

"You should leave him," Honoree said, putting away her makeup. "I never get my bloomers in a bunch over a man, in particular when the man doesn't treat me right."

"I ain't as pretty as you, and I don't — I don't have much to say." Her voice softened. "I gotta take what I can get if I wanna man."

"Then don't want a man so bad."

Bessie's jaw fell like a poorly stitched hem. "Can't help myself."

"You're sixteen years old. Sure you can."

"My mama married my pops when she was fourteen."

Honoree had fallen in love with Ezekiel when she was twelve, but what good had that done her?

"A woman who doesn't leave a man who beats her is a fool." Honoree applied another coat of lipstick. "I would never stay with a man who hit me more than once." She patted her lips with a tissue. "I'll never marry, neither. Those are my rules — rules a girl like you should keep in mind."

The door banged open. The mirrors shook. Ms. Dolly James stood at the top of the steps, a hand on her hip, her generous bosoms heaving. "What are you two jabbering about?"

Honoree put down her lipstick.

Bessie grabbed her arm. "Who's she?"

"Miss Dolly. The blues singer in charge of the chorus girls."

"Lord almighty," Bessie muttered. "She looks something fierce."

A gloriously healthy woman, Miss Dolly was impressive if for no other reason than the breadth of her backside and the size of her bubs — which drew as much attention as her rugged alto.

"I asked a question." She thundered down the steps, dragging her beaver coat behind her and waving her prize possession, a silver flask, like a pointer. "Is anyone gonna answer me?"

Honoree signaled Bessie with a nod. "Go on over there."

Bessie moved from Honoree's side and turned toward Miss Dolly. "Evening, ma'am."

"Who the hell is she?" Miss Dolly asked Honoree. Bessie eased into a corner.

"Speak up," Miss Dolly ordered. "What's your name?"

"Bessie Louise Palmer."

"Bessie, you say?" Miss Dolly flung her fur coat over her chair, the only chair in the room, and sat in front of her piece of mirror. "The two of you need to get dressed," she said, pulling a Victorian hatpin from her cloche. "Where are those other witches?" She lit a cigarette. "I'm still waiting to learn what you two were gossiping about."

A busybody, Miss Dolly always wanted to be in-the-know, but before Honoree could speak, Bessie had stepped up to the plate. "We were only wondering what would happen if we got discovered at Miss Hattie's by — by Eubie Blake."

Honoree hid a smile. She liked a girl who could weave a quick lie.

"Nobody's coming to Miss Hattie's to take neither one of you to Broadway." Miss Dolly aimed her flask at Bessie. "You: too dark-skinned. And you" — she aimed at Honoree — "you might pass a brown-bag test, being high yellow with good hair and all, but you're always daydreaming."

"I don't daydream. I make plans," Honoree said, her voice firm. The blues singer had talent but no ambition other than to work at Miss Hattie's and drain a flask of hooch every hour and wait for Archie Graves to love her back.

The Archie business made Honoree feel almost sorry for Miss Dolly. Honoree had fallen for his charms briefly, too. Oddly, he was capable of showing kindness, and even some wit now and then. Drunk on his behind, he could give you plenty of reasons for the man he had become. Almost lynched at twelve and orphaned a year later, after burying his parents, he found his way to Chicago and raised his younger brother, Dewey, best he could. By then, life had ruined him, left him angry, greedy, and willing to do anything to survive.

"Ain't nothing wrong with daydreaming," Bessie was saying. "I ain't that black, neither. If I were, Mr. Graves wouldn't have hired me."

"I got no idea why Archie hired you." Miss Dolly popped a cigarette between her teeth. "Must've owed somebody something."

"I'm an excellent dancer." Bessie had gone from cowering in a corner to looking Miss Dolly dead in the eye. "Florence Mills or Josephine Baker might come in here one day — see us perform and —"

Honoree snapped her fingers. "Just like that, we'd be on our way to Broadway or Paris, France."

Miss Dolly unscrewed the lid on her flask. "And I'll be singing at the Palmer House while y'all be dancing right here until the day you die." She laughed. "Unless Archie doesn't like what he sees tonight and fires you on the spot. By the way, he'll be watching all night long."

Honoree's leg twitched hard, kicking over her shopping bag beneath the table. "All night long? Archie ain't playing poker tonight?" With Trudy filling her spot, slipping away would be twice as hard with Archie roaming about. "He never cancels his poker game. What happened?"

"I ain't no postman." Miss Dolly held the flask to her lips. "You want to know why he ain't playing poker tonight — ask him yerself, if you dare." She took a swig. "Anyways, you should be smarter than to nose around in his affairs."

Virginia and Edna Mae, two of the other chorus girls, entered the dressing room laughing and cursing, and chatting like children in a playpen until they set eyes on Miss Dolly and clammed right up.

"Where's Trudy?" Miss Dolly asked.

Edna Mae shrugged. Having worked at Miss Hattie's since before Prohibition, the tough-talking blues singer didn't ruffle her. "I ain't got no idea."

Pressing rouge into her cheek, Honoree could only guess at Trudy's whereabouts; the bleach-blond chorus girl could be anywhere. Gary, Indiana. Detroit. A North Side juice joint — anywhere partying with anyone, including Hymie Weiss and his

30

North Side gang.

She was the only chorus girl who could dance Honoree's solos without Archie having a conniption.

"Trudy'll be here soon enough," said Edna Mae, the cafe's burlesque dancer. Naked from head to toe, she lifted and tugged at her bare breasts, comparing one to the other — her usual routine. Once she finished playing with her bubs, she strolled toward Honoree's crate, smacking Wrigley's Spearmint gum.

"She'll come falling through the door at the last minute, raring to go." Edna Mae stopped next to Honoree. "Don't worry. She'll be here."

"She better show." Miss Dolly lifted her skirt and slipped her hip flask beneath her garter. "I ain't explaining a missing girl to Archie. Not tonight."

She clapped her hands twice. "Y'all hurry up, get dressed, and get up them stairs. And don't forget to throw a robe on over your costume. King Johnny and the band are winding down." A cigarette dangled from her lips. "Come on now. It's showtime, ladies."

Chapter 3
Sawyer

Friday, June 5, 2015

Lula Kent walks away from me, straight-backed and righteous as hell, pushing her medicine cart of indignation. Quite the cross to bear for a girl her age, but she is not my concern.

I take a deep breath and step into Honoree's room (excuse me — Miss Honoree's room) and tread across the linoleum to the foot of one of those sturdy hospital beds, cranked two feet off the ground.

This close, Honoree Dalcour is all angles, thin arms and legs, jutting from beneath stiff white sheets. Propped up with pillows behind her head and under her elbows and knees, she reminds me of one of the broken dolls my sister used to bury in the backyard.

"Ma'am. Excuse me? I don't mean to disturb you, but —"

Honoree opens her eyes. "Who's there?" Her voice booms, bold and vigorous.

My chest tightens. I expected a weak whisper.

"Do you understand me? Speak up."

"Good afternoon, my name is Sawyer Hayes." I remove my backpack and place it on the floor. "How are you doing today?"

She stares at me as if there's food in my teeth. Then again, she may not be able to see me with her 110-year-old eyes.

"My name's Sawyer Hayes," I repeat. "I'm a film student from California. I'm here to talk to you about Chicago in the 1920s."

Pushing aside my phobia as best I can, I circle to the side of the bed. "Margaret Hendrickson, or Maggie White, the name you knew her by, had old photographs of you in her attic. On the back of each photo was this address and the name Honoree Dalcour and the year 1925 — I assume the year the photo was taken."

I don't mention the other items in my grandmother's long-ago box, including the most important find — a reel of film I sent to a restoration company in LA. From the scribbling on the canister, it could be a lost Micheaux — I am holding my breath because it is almost too much to hope for — but if it happens, my interview with Honoree will be the second most important thing I do this summer.

My documentary about a lost film would be a significant contribution to film history. How wild would it be if my thesis includes an exclusive interview with one of Micheaux's performers? I might even make my dad jealous.

Honoree clears her throat, not a pleasant sound. "How'd you get in here?"

I nod toward the hallway. "I checked in at the front desk."

"Don't mean you can walk into my room, happy as you please."

"Margaret Hendrickson gave me permission."

"She's the same person as Maggie White, huh?" Honoree's tone is not so much surprise as irritation.

"Sorry, I forgot to mention: Maggie is my grandmother."

Honoree gasps, a sharp inhale of surprise, or someone walked over her grave. "Well, ain't that some shit!" She lets loose a coarse, bitter laugh.

I take a step back and put a little distance between us. An old woman can curse, but the laugh creeps me out. I switch gears. "Lula Kent told me you have the memory of an elephant."

Honoree isn't looking at me. She's focusing on the space surrounding me. Maybe

34

she sees ghosts, too, but I'm not ready to swap ghost stories.

"Lula talks too much, but only when she has a reason," Honoree says. "What did you do to her?"

I raise my hand, palm out. "I swear, I didn't do anything to Lula."

"You had to do something." Her eyes slam shut, and her breathing is shallow and weird. Panic grips me.

"Miss Honoree? Are you okay?"

Her eyelids flutter open. "Maggie White is your grandmother, you say?"

My jaw slackens, and I'm gulping air. I thought for sure Honoree was a goner, but, just like that, she seems fine. Clear-eyed. Breathing better — voice strong.

"Yes, she is," I say finally. "Maybe I can jar your memory."

She nods. "Go on."

"You and my grandmother were neighbors. Her foster family lived next door." I learned this from a letter I found in the box that Maggie wrote to a friend but never mailed. "From what I understand, her being an orphan and all, and her foster parents being kind of strange, the two of you became close friends."

"Is that what she told you — that we were close friends?"

35

My grandmother told me nothing, but I don't ask a lot of questions. I knew Honoree existed because of the things I found in a crate in my grandmother's attic — a letter, a bill of sale, photos. "Yes. Close friends. BFFs. Why else would she pay your bills all these years?"

"I don't remember much about those days," Honoree said in a quiet voice. "How long ago was this, again?"

"Seventy-five years." Which sounds weird. How in the hell is she supposed to remember ninety years ago, let alone seventy-five, when at twenty-five, I can't remember yesterday? Then again, I can't forget one second of what happened one night fifteen months ago.

"Where were we again when we were neighbors?"

"Louisiana." I shove my hands into my pockets. "Baton Rouge, Louisiana."

"Come closer. I need to have a better look at you."

I move in but not too close. "Better?"

"What's wrong with your hair?"

I pull two braids away from my face and knot them behind my head. "They're called dreadlocks."

She scrunches up her nose. "You look like a girl."

"Not a girl." I point at my jaw. "Got a two-day-old beard."

"Do you have a job?"

Whoa. Déjà vu. Maggie had asked me the same question Sunday mornings when Sunday mornings were ordinary. Before the car crash. Before Azizi died.

A glimmer in the corner of my eye draws my attention as the oxygen in the room evaporates. I can't breathe. I wipe my mouth with the back of my hand and blink hard.

My sister, Azizi — excuse me, Azizi's ghost — is suddenly standing next to Honoree's headboard.

"Wake up, Sawyer Hayes! I asked you a question, boy. Do you have a job?"

My nerves are broken glass, my palms are damp, but seeing a ghost shouldn't be easy, right?

"Yes, I have a job," I say too loudly. Shit. I need to chill. The Azizi sighting has put me on edge. "Sorry. I didn't mean to raise my voice. To answer your question, I'm a graduate student at the University of California, Berkeley, working on my dissertation for a doctorate in film and media studies." I breathe in deep. "I also work for a production company, and I'm headed to Paris today to work on a film for my father."

37

"Making motion pictures doesn't sound like a job," Honoree says. "You work for your daddy?"

"This has nothing to do with my father." I try not to look at Azizi as I pace next to the bed. "I have some photos to show you, Miss Honoree. I also want to ask you a few questions."

She raises a hand to the bed's side railing, trying to pull herself upright, which I figure is a bad idea. Her arms are spindles made of bones and skin.

"You need me to adjust the bed?" I search for a lever or a button.

"Leave it be," Honoree snaps. "I can do this." She drags herself forward with one hand, but I can't watch her struggle without trying to help. I go to the head of the bed and arrange her pillows so she can sit up.

"I said I don't need your help."

"Fine. No problem." I back away, not wanting to agitate her further. "How about if we examine the pictures. You're in them." I remove a handful of the photographs from my backpack. "May I show you?"

Honoree squints. "No, you may not. Why would I talk to you about my life? I don't know you, and even if I did, I don't tell my story to just any long-haired boy — who probably smokes reefer cigarettes and tells lies. You wanna hear about me? You gotta tell me something about you to make this worth my while."

"I don't lie, or smoke weed — not in Illinois — weed is illegal in this state." I'm holding the photos she won't look at, wondering how I can focus on changing her mind with Azizi's ghost staring at me. "Miss Honoree, please, just one photo." Yes, I'm begging, but if it works . . .

"In this photo, you are with Oscar Micheaux, the legendary Black filmmaker, and in another" — I pull from the stack — "you're with Louis Armstrong, the world's greatest trumpet player, and in this one —" I break my word and show her another and then another. "Here you're with Lil Hardin Armstrong and the blues singer Alberta Hunter."

Honoree rocks back against the pillows, eyeing me with a piercing glare.

"What happened in 1925 and why it happened is my business."

Something behind me moves, and I turn. Lula is standing in the archway. Has she come to check on Honoree or me?

"Would you like Sawyer to leave, Miss Honoree?" Lula says, walking by me without a glance. "He can come back another time — or not."

Honoree smiles. "Don't you worry about him, honey. I can handle eager young men with little boy minds in my sleep."

Lula adjusts Honoree's pillows. "Are you thirsty?"

"I could use a swallow."

Lula holds a glass of water with a straw, and Honoree takes a sip, but her gaze is locked on me. "I already told him if he wants to hear my story, he'll have to tell me his first, and not some silly made-up shit. Make it worth my while."

I stretch my neck to the side. The way this woman throws jabs and blocks punches, I think she used to be a prizefighter, not a chorus girl. "What would you like to find out about me?"

"Tell me about your mama and daddy. Do you have any brothers or sisters? How about your grandmother's husband, Mr. Hendrickson? Tell me about him. Tell me everything. That's the only way you'll hear my story."

Damn. Quid pro quo? She's serious. I shove the photos into my backpack. "My dad is a historian who works in Paris, and my mother died when I was twelve."

"Mighty young to lose your mama." Honoree makes a *tsk-tsk* sound like my grandmother Maggie makes when she disapproves of something. In this instance, that makes no sense, since we're talking about my dead mother.

"You got anything else to tell me?"

"Sorry," I say. "I'm better at telling other people's stories than I am at telling my own. It's why I make films."

Honoree lifts her shoulder into a lazy shrug. "You came all this way for my stories but don't have any stories to tell me. I shoulda guessed when I saw you in the doorway — too afraid to walk inside."

I cock my head. "Should have guessed what?"

"You're a coward, Sawyer Hayes. Too much of a coward to tell me your story."

"I'm not a coward." I clench my jaw.

Honoree eases the back of her head into the pillows. "Cowardice runs in your family."

"You don't even know my family."

"You're the one who said I knew Maggie White. She's your family."

I bite my tongue because I don't want to argue with a bedridden centenarian. Why am I letting her bother me?

"I'm sorry I've upset you. I'm sure you don't mean to call anyone a coward. I'll come back later this afternoon. I have a few more hours before I am due at the airport."

41

Another nasty cough erupts from Honoree, and she closes her eyes. "I am tired and need to rest. I'll feel like talking tomorrow, I swear. So come back tomorrow."

"What?" I don't disguise my surprise, and my temper escalates, but Lula intervenes.

"Honoree tires quickly," she says. "Things come to her out of order, and she says things she doesn't mean."

Lula's voice is soothing, but my frustration can't be capped by a beautiful girl's sensible words or kind eyes.

"I won't be here tomorrow."

Honoree's eyes open. *Oh, she was pretending.* "You be careful how you talk to an old woman. I still have rights in this world, and one of 'em is respect. So don't you shout at me. Just do as I say and come back tomorrow."

I am dumbfounded. That's the word. *Dumbfounded.* Slack-jawed. Worn-out. Still, Honoree has taken the last straw, broken it in half, and flung it in my face. Why is this old woman stressing me out? It must be jet lag or Azizi messing with my head.

I need to leave. Finish my thesis and fix my life without Honoree Dalcour's help. It will be her bad when the reel of film turns out to be a lost Micheaux and I make my mark on history.

42

Honoree pulls the edges of the sheet to her throat. "I'll tell you my story tomorrow." Her voice is a faraway whisper. "I'll tell you about Micheaux and Louis Armstrong, Miss Hattie's, and the Dreamland Cafe."

I shake my head. "It was nice meeting you, Miss Dalcour. Miss Lula." Without giving either woman a chance to reply, I tip an imaginary hat and exit the room and haul ass out of the Bronzeville Senior Living Facility.

Outdoors, it's late afternoon and dense, white clouds fill the sky. The breeze from the lake makes a warm day feel cooler. I remove a UC Berkeley sweatshirt from my backpack, but my hands are trembling. Fuck.

The first shuttle to O'Hare I catch at the Palmer House hotel. I take a window seat, and the skyline rolls by, but I can't stop thinking about Honoree Dalcour.

She is not the first woman to call me a coward. Not the first woman to ask me to tell her the truth. She said some disturbing things that lodged in the pit of my stomach. Yet, in my story brain, the place where my ideas turn into films, there is one thing Honoree told me she didn't mean to tell. Something happened in Chicago in 1925.

Something she doesn't want me to know. Doesn't want anyone to know. Which means, she's the one who's afraid. She's the one who's a coward. Not me.

Not this time.

CHAPTER 4
HONOREE

Friday, October 23, 1925

Honoree hurried up the narrow stairwell ahead of Miss Dolly and the other girls, hoping to be the first to set her sights on Trudy, whenever the girl arrived.

The Friday-night patrons were already zozzled. Neighborhood flappers and floozies packed the joint, laughing and singing, and boozing, smoking, and sweating. Some nights, the stench put a gag in Honoree's throat so immense, her lungs ached and her eyes watered. Thankfully, the smell wasn't too bad yet. It was still early.

Wearing a flimsy robe over her scant costume, she pushed by handsy customers until she reached a spot near the bar. Then she rose onto her tiptoes to get a better view.

Miss Hattie's was shaped like a train car with a wooden bar the length of the cafe. Scattered around the dance floor and across from the stage were a few round tables with

45

chairs. Honoree craned her neck but still couldn't see much and circled to the other end of the bar.

This was one of those times she wished Archie had purchased some barstools. Not a tall girl, she could've used the leg up. But according to Archie, the neighborhood folk didn't come to a honky-tonk like Miss Hattie's to sit on their bottoms. They came to drink, dance, leer at the chorus girls, and buy policy dream books.

Policy. Everyone played the numbers in Bronzeville, from the most righteous preacher to the drunkest drunk. For a penny, a nickel, or a dime, a gambler bet three lucky numbers and hoped to match the wheel operator's winning draw.

Honoree detested the game. Wasting hard-earned dough on chance seemed foolhardy — just like waiting on Trudy.

She canvassed the cafe again, but no sign of Trudy or any sign of Miss Dolly or the other girls. They were still downstairs, likely quibbling over a broken shoe or a ripped pair of bloomers.

Frustrated, Honoree eased into an opening at the bar and signaled Crazy Pete. She might as well have a snort while she waited.

On weekends, there were two barkeeps, Dewey Graves, Archie's younger brother, a quick-tempered hood who punched things, and Crazy Pete, who wasn't all that crazy.

He recited poems, sometimes too loudly — poems written by Paul Laurence Dunbar, Langston Hughes, and Claude McKay. He told tall tales about his exploits in the Spanish American War, his work with Booker T. Washington, and a private meeting with President Taft. Other than those stories, calling him crazy seemed unkind. He was a dreamer, and what was wrong with dreaming as long as he didn't hurt nobody? Ezekiel used to read poetry, too. No one called him addlebrained. He was the smartest boy in Chicago — Black or white. The only thing she could say about Ezekiel — he was gone.

"Hey, Pete." Honoree raised her voice extra loud to get his attention. The cafe was noisy, but Pete was also partially deaf in one ear. Probably both. "Pete!"

He swung toward her, smiling broadly and revealing two rows of black gums. "How you doing, Miss Honoree?"

"You forgot your false teeth again, Pete."

"Damn teeth hurt my mouth." He limped toward her with a bad leg caused by a white man wielding a bat during the riots in the summer of 1919. "You lookin' mighty pretty."

47

"Are you flirting? Shame on you. You're too old to flirt." Honoree grinned. She enjoyed jawing with Pete, the only person at Miss Hattie's she'd likely miss. "Have you seen Trudy?"

"Not yet, but she always shows up."

"Not always." Honoree braced her elbows on the bar. "Make me a drink, Pete. Miss Dolly and the others are still downstairs."

He grabbed a fifth of gin from the back shelf, filled a tumbler halfway, and then added honey and a dash of lemon juice. Pete's cocktail was the only way Honoree stomached the taste of bootleg hooch.

"Here you go."

"Thank you." She lifted the glass to her lips, but Dewey suddenly shoved Pete aside and leaned forward, looming over her.

Pete grabbed the edge of the bar to keep from falling. "Watch yourself, you oaf."

"Shut your trap, old man." Dewey's broad shoulders blocked Honoree's view of everything but him. "I have a mind to string you up by the neck."

Honoree reared back; he reeked of chewing tobacco, sour mash, and spit. "Do you mind? I was talking to Pete."

"You always talking to that crazy old bastard." Dewey hunched forward. "But I know what you been up to, Miss High-and-

Mighty."

She gulped a swallow. Was he talking about the Dreamland Cafe? "I don't have any idea what you mean."

"You may belong to my brother, but you'll be sorry if you rat on me over a few crates of whiskey."

The blood stopped in her veins. "I don't belong to Archie! Where do people get such a notion?" She and Archie had been a thing for a while after he found her hiding in the trunk of his Model T, but that was a little more than two years ago.

"You tell him everything."

"I don't tell him anything." She didn't care what Dewey thought. The best news was he didn't know about her audition. He was worrying her about something else.

The week before, she had arrived to work early, and Dewey was buying hooch from someone other than one of Capone's bootleggers. It was the law in Bronzeville. Every juice joint in Chicago had to purchase hooch from Capone. Dewey cheating Capone was stupid. Dewey cheating Capone without Archie's knowledge, however, was insane. Perhaps he should adopt the nickname Crazy Dewey. There was nothing smart about putting his big brother in Capone's crosshairs.

"Did you tell Archie about my business?" Dewey slammed his fist on the bar top. "Is that why he canceled his poker game — to keep an eye on me?"

"Archie and I talk about policy dream books and dancing. I don't talk to him about you."

"Don't lie. You saw me, but Capone is stealing Archie blind." He paused, his Adam's apple protruding. "I want you to tell Archie he's being robbed, and I'm helping him get his due. He'll listen to you."

"I'm not telling him anything, but you should," Honoree said. "If he finds out you purchased hooch from Bronzeville bootleggers, he'll light your behind on fire. And he should. He can't afford to make an enemy of Capone, and you can't afford to make an enemy of your brother. So, close it down, Dewey. End it before Archie finds out and you get hurt."

Dewey's throat bulged. His face darkened with rage, and she swore smoke rose from the top of his head. He shot forward, threatening to grab her by the throat, but something or someone, Crazy Pete, had driven his shoulder into Dewey's side.

"Stop haranguing the child, boy." Pete waved a towel in Dewey's face, shooing him away. "We got customers to tend to."

"What in the hell do you think you're doing, old man?" Dewey stared at Pete with murder in his eyes.

Wide-eyed, Honoree waited for the explosion, but a group of rowdy boys from the slaughterhouse shouted for drinks.

"All right, then," Dewey said, breathing through his nostrils. "I'll bide my time, missy. I'll bide my time." He gave Crazy Pete and Honoree an ugly glare, then stalked over to the slaughterhouse boys.

Pete winced. "What's he mean by that? Biding his time?"

Honoree lifted her glass, but her fingers, her hands, her arms trembled. She placed the drink on the bar. "I don't care what Dewey's babbling about. He talks more nonsense than a cuckoo bird."

Pete frowned. "You best be careful of him. He's been acting strange lately, like a mad dog up to something."

She smiled. "That's why they call you Crazy Pete. Mixing it up with Dewey is dangerous."

"Never mind me. I told you, he ain't right in the head — you best be careful, Honoree."

"I'm always careful."

Pete tapped the bar. "I don't want to see

51

you hurt." He hobbled off to wait on customers.

Honoree brought the glass to her lips and took a much-needed sip.

"What you drinking?" It was Bessie, nudging her in the back. "Can I have one, too?"

"What did I tell you about sneaking up on me? And no, you're too young."

"I'm sixteen."

"I don't believe you."

Miss Dolly and the rest of the chorus girls were on Bessie's heels.

"What took y'all so long?" Honoree asked.

Virginia raised a girlishly thin brow. "Edna Mae was having a fit about her costume."

Honoree shook her head slowly. "No offense. But she don't wear a costume —"

A commotion kicked up behind them, coming from the direction of the entrance. The crowd opened a path, and a tawny-skinned blonde waving her arms yelled, "I'm here. I'm here!"

Bessie touched her shoulder. "Is that Trudy Lewis?"

"None other than," Honoree said with a whistle.

"How'd she make her hair that color?"

Honoree twisted toward Bessie with an eye on Trudy. "Bleach — lots of bleach."

"Why would she do something like that?"

Honoree shrugged. "Her roots are knotted so tight an entire jar of lye couldn't straighten 'em. So she bleached her hair the color of yellow cotton, a tribute to Mary Pickford, I believe. But don't ask Trudy about her hair color. You might get a busted lip for your trouble."

Bessie tugged on her springy curls. "I should do something to my hair, too."

"Have you heard of Madam C. J. Walker's products? The hair-growth ointment and the iron pressing comb."

"No. Never heard of her or those things."

"Ask Virginia. How do you think she got that spit curl to lie flat against her cheek?"

Trudy was within arm's reach, and Honoree started to pull her aside, but Virginia slid between them. "Where you been?" she asked Trudy.

"Flat on her face in an alley," Edna Mae added, leaning over Honoree's shoulder. She didn't like Trudy and took any chance to pluck a feather or two from her plume.

"I don't care where she been." Miss Dolly shoved them both aside. "She here now." Miss Dolly pivoted toward Trudy. "You got on your costume?"

"I sure do." Trudy fanned open her muskrat coat and dipped her hip like some starlet in *Motion Picture* magazine.

53

Honoree turned away, hiding the expression on her face and her uncharitable opinion of Trudy.

"Let's go. Let's go." Miss Dolly shooed Honoree and the other chorus girls toward the stage. "We're all here now. Time to put on a show."

They paraded through the crowd and toward the stage. Honoree grabbed Bessie's hand and tugged her along, but once they were near the stage, she let her go and caught Trudy's elbow.

"We need to talk." Honoree looked around, making sure no one was around to overhear them. Trudy folded her arms over her stomach as if they had all night to chat.

"You wanna make some extra money?" Honoree asked.

"I like extra money. How much and what for?"

"Cover for me tonight at the midnight show."

"How much?"

"Five dollars." It was more than either girl made in a week, but Trudy's lazy eye didn't even twitch. Greedy wench. Honoree would have to sweeten the deal. "Five dollars tonight, and another five on Sunday."

"Sunday's a long ways off."

"Take it or leave it," Honoree said, betting

on Trudy's greed.

"What do you have to do so important you have to skip the midnight show?"

"None of your beeswax," Honoree snapped. "You gonna do it or not?"

Trudy's eyes sparkled. "Patience. I'll let you know after we finish this show."

The band played Jelly Roll Morton's "Black Bottom Stomp." A lively tune that always got the joint jumping.

The hoofers and the roughnecks swarmed the stage. The tables and chairs filled, and a standing-room-only mob gathered, screeching for the show to begin.

The chorus girls shimmied into place and formed a straight line. King Johnny's trumpet blared. The girls linked arms, kicked their legs waist-high, and launched into the dance routine.

Between the music, the giggle juice, and the scantily dressed flappers, the whole whangdoodle stomped and cheered. They were shaking their behinds, losing their minds, everyone having a good ol' time.

Honoree watched from the sidelines, waiting for her cue, but a nagging nostalgia played with her heartstrings.

Besides Crazy Pete, there were some other things to miss about Miss Hattie's. The all-nighters with King Johnny and his jazz quartet. The Monday predawn jam sessions with the band. The after-hour parties with the chorus girls and blues singers. And dancing with Pete at the Dusty Bottom. Though he did more hobbling than dancing.

The things she wouldn't miss were easy — Dewey's ugly temper. Miss Dolly's mean ways. Everything about Archie.

After finding her in the trunk of his car, Archie had hired Honoree to stoke the furnace and peel potatoes, but Honoree was a quick learner. A flash of a smile, a suggestive wiggle, and soon, Archie was paying for her dance lessons, her rent, and the fabric and tassels she used to sew her fancy dresses and, eventually, her costumes. When the giggles and wiggles stopped working their hoodoo, Honoree allowed Archie the privilege of putting his hands on her. She just hadn't expected necking with him to be so unpleasant.

The music changed and jarred Honoree back to Miss Hattie's. Her two solos were coming up, fast and breezy. The first routine was mostly cartwheels, leg kicks, and back and front walkovers. She sang one song but primarily danced, ending with a tap sequence before prancing off the stage to loud applause.

Edna Mae performed her burlesque act next — naked. She had the bubs for it, too. Small, full, and high, they barely moved when she jumped. She then sashayed back and forth across the stage, the crowd watching with mouths open and eyes bulging while trying not to grab things they shouldn't grab. After she finished, the band played a few more tunes, and the hoofers danced, and Miss Dolly sang a medley of blues songs.

Honoree stood behind the partition, the muscles in her legs and arms knotted, the joints in her fingers locked. She shook her wrists and stomped her feet to keep the blood flowing. She put on the feather headdress, hooked the chin strap, and waited.

King Johnny's trumpet soared to a high C, and she rushed onto the stage, making a deliberate mess of the steps. She winked an exaggerated eye, a wide grin on her face, inviting the patrons to join in on her antics. She crossed her hands back and forth and from knee to knee, imitating Josephine Baker's Charleston and the crowd bellowed.

Her head and headdress held high, she waved her arms and rotated her hips, performing a cakewalk jig strutting to the rhythm of the banjo.

The audience clapped and yelled and begged for more. Honoree joyfully obliged. She propelled her body into a series of pirouettes, using the wall clock over the cafe's front door to anchor each turn. Her eyes fixed on the clock, she whipped her head, and her body followed as she turned and turned, but in her last twirl, someone stood above the crowd and caught her eye.

A cattail in a field of withering weeds, taller than any other man in the cafe, he took off his fedora. And for the longest beat of a drum, she saw his face.

Her heartbeat fell off rhythm, and her legs crisscrossed. She missed a spin and almost fell but found her balance and twirled into another pirouette, ending in a deep bow.

The applause and the shouts of praise were cannon fire in her ears. She snapped upright and, rising onto her tiptoes, canvassed the room. Where was he? Where'd he go? She searched, quickly and thoroughly, but couldn't find him.

One last bow, one last wide smile, and Honoree fled from the stage.

She paused behind the makeshift wings separating the dancers from the patrons. Her back pressed against the hard surface, she stared at the ceiling, struggling to catch her breath.

Maybe she imagined him. Maybe the excitement of her new job, her new money, and yeah, being a New Negro, had taken a toll. But damn, she could swear on a barrel of Bibles, Ezekiel Bailey — the boy who had vanished, the man she had imagined dead, the love of her life — had just walked into Miss Hattie's Garden Cafe.

CHAPTER 5
HONOREE

Gasping for breath, Honoree fumbled with the chin strap of her headdress.

Giggly chorus girls rushed by, barreling toward the men lining up to give them a dime to have the girls sit in their laps. Edna Mae poked her in the side, pushing her to join them. Honoree waved her off and faced the wall, praying her body would stop shaking.

She couldn't let them see her fall apart. Let them see her pain, a pain she could handle if she had a minute to think — with a minute to think, she could handle anything. Even Ezekiel Bailey returning from the grave, or wherever he'd been for the past three years.

It took another minute for her to stop trembling and remove her headdress.

She hurried through the crowd. Glad-handing without touching, nodding without blinking, grinning without smiling — until she reached the storage room behind the bar.

Then she ran.

Racing down the stairwell, speeding along the corridor, stumbling into the dressing room, she slammed the door behind her.

A stab at the button on the wall and the room lit up. She combed her fingers through her hair, tugging on the roots as she examined the room's dimly lit corners. She had to be sure she was alone.

Satisfied no one was hiding in the dark, she lowered herself stiffly onto a crate as the nausea filled her belly.

What am I supposed to do? How am I supposed to feel? How am I supposed to walk back upstairs and leave for an audition without looking for him, finding him, and demanding he tell me where he was and why he's returned?

Miss Dolly's well-worn alto wended its way from the balcony. The pain-soaked lyrics of Bessie Smith's "Down Hearted Blues" sunk into the sawdust beneath Honoree's feet.

I ain't never loved but three men in my
  life
My father, my brother and the man that
  wrecked my life

Honoree hauled her shopping bag from beneath the makeup table and removed her orchestra-length cigarette holder, enamel cigarette lighter, and a pack of Marlboros.

An advertisement in the *Tribune* claimed that the ivory-tipped Marlboro made you feel *"mild as May."* A springtime lift would be heaven. She lit her cigarette and took a long drag, but the fiery taste sat on her tongue like burnt toast.

She crushed the cigarette on top of the counter. The tiny flames flickered until everything turned to ash — except for the memories.

Ezekiel's mother, Prudence, was a member of the Old Settlers Social Club. Generations of her family had lived in Chicago since before the Emancipation.

College-educated and wealthy, she was Negro royalty and blamed the newspapers and the Pullman railroad workers for the "lowlife coloreds" who'd swarmed into the city from down south, fleeing Jim Crow. It was their fault that the whites called the colored neighborhoods in Chicago the Black Belt. It was their fault upstanding Negroes had to live alongside poor, shuffling migrants. It was their fault that roving bands of angry white boys, the athletic clubs, burned down Negro-owned houses when Blacks had dared to move into a neighborhood where they weren't wanted.

For more than a decade, the Dalcours worked for the Baileys, scrubbing floors, ironing clothes, tending the gardens and Mr. Bailey's automobiles, and cooking their meals.

"We're country Negroes, Honoree," her mother, Cleo, would say. "When we came up north to Chicago from Baton Rouge — your late father's idea, by the way — we ruined things for decent colored folk like the Baileys. So when you hear Prudence or Titus (she'd never call them by their first names to their faces) talking about ignorant, no-account niggers, they're talking about us." Those were the kindest words her mother had to say about the Baileys.

Pregnant during the journey from Baton Rouge, Cleo gave birth to a stillborn child, a girl, a few weeks after they arrived. That's when Cleo's heart and tongue turned bitter and any signs of love or kindness ceased, especially toward her living daughter, Honoree.

After her father died, Honoree became desperately attached to Ezekiel — and he to her. When he left for Howard University to become a doctor, he wrote to Honoree every week.

"An Old Settlers' son will never marry a girl whose father was a sharecropper," her mother said when she saw the letters. "You're a poor man's child, and no matter how light your skin, or how wavy your hair, or how thin your nose, Ezekiel will never want you for his wife. You need a man who shares your roots."

Honoree's mother introduced her to a boy from Mississippi. A decent fella, but not royalty like Ezekiel. He knew where he belonged — in church all day on Sundays and at the bloodiest stockyard in the city every other day of the week.

"He takes care of a widowed mother, too," Cleo explained. "What better boy could there be for you?"

On a Thursday in the summer of 1922, Ezekiel returned from Howard and arrived at Honoree's front door shortly before sunset. He greeted her mother and invited Honoree to join him on the rooftop. They crawled through the back window, climbed onto the roof, and sat in silence, gazing at the stars. Ezekiel was quieter than he'd been the last time they were together, quieter than she'd ever seen him. A veil of pain clouded his eyes. Something was wrong.

But she couldn't wait for his tongue to

loosen. She had something dreadful to say, but her nerve lost its way.

"Go ahead," he urged, sensing her disquiet. "It'll be all right. No matter what you have to tell me, it'll be fine."

He patted her knee, bolstering her courage.

"I slept with a boy who lives in the tenement building at the end of the block. My mama said he is the man I should marry."

Ezekiel's black eyes glistened with an incredible softness as his fingertip scratched an imaginary imperfection on his perfect brow. When he spoke, his voice was as calm as a river with no place to flow. "Do you love him?"

"No," she replied.

"Do you love me?"

"Since forever."

"Then there's nothing to worry about. You've never made love with me, so to our bodies, and our hearts, making love with each other would be our first time. And that's all that matters."

His words surrounded her heart, and she leaned into him, pressing her lips to his. With a hand pressed to her cheek, he covered her mouth with his mouth, and they kissed, a different kind of kiss from any other they'd shared.

Hidden beneath a translucent sky and away from her mother's disapproving gaze, they made love. Quiet, gentle love, and afterward, he asked her to marry him.

Blood pounded in her ears. A drummer sat on her shoulder, gently tapping a beautiful rhythm. "Ask me again in the daylight," she told him.

He promised he would and then left for home.

When she curled up in the cot next to her mother, she wept silent tears, joyful tears until she fell asleep.

The next morning was laundry day. Her mother left for the Baileys' house before Honoree awoke. Their usual pattern. She'd join her mother later to prepare the midday meal. That morning, before Honoree dressed, her mother returned.

"We're moving back to Louisiana." The door slammed shut behind Cleo Dalcour.

A wedge of something vile cut into Honoree's throat. "We can't up and leave town. We can't leave the Baileys with no one to clean or cook for them."

Cleo pulled a suitcase from beneath the bed. "Can't you hear, child? We don't work for the Baileys no more."

Honoree could scarcely breathe. Her vision blurred, and a violent noise filled her

head. Too loud. Too much. Too unbelievable to believe. What was her mother saying? What had happened at the Bailey house
that morning? Cleo was lying. Where was
Ezekiel? He'd promised to come back —
he'd promised.

"What did you do?" she demanded of her
mother.

"I didn't do a thing. Mr. Bailey closed his
house during the middle of the night and
moved his family outta town." A suitcase
struck the floor. "None of this was my doing."

Honoree's heart jerked inside out. "All
the Baileys are gone?"

"The mother, the father, and the three
boys." Her mother dragged another suitcase
into the center of the kitchenette. "Chicago
ain't the place for us no more. We're moving back home."

"To sharecropping?"

"And why not? Your daddy's dead. My
baby daughter's dead. The only job I had is
over. Everything we've tried to do here dies,
disappears, or laughs in our faces. I'm going back to Baton Rouge."

A storm ignited in Honoree's chest. "I'm
not leaving Chicago."

"You go where I tell you to go." Her
mother's blistering gaze frightened Hon-

oree, but this day, she'd face her fear.

The morning sun filtered into the kitchenette. The gray in her mother's braided hair shimmered. Honoree squeezed her arms around her stomach until her breath caught. "I'm not leaving Chicago, Mama. No matter what you say."

"Because of that boy?" An ugly sound came from her mother's throat. "You think I didn't notice? You think he wants more than what you gave him on the roof last night? You're a fool. He is Negro royalty, and you are the daughter of a sharecropper. Forget about him. He and his family forgot about us." Her mother's chest heaved, and her plain dark face grayed. "The Baileys are gone. And so are we."

A ringing sound went off in Honoree's head. With every breath, it grew louder and shriller. Her mother may have forgotten how to love, but Honoree hadn't forgotten. She blinked back tears, grabbed her shopping bag from beneath the bed, and picked up every piece of clothing within reach. A moment later, she was standing in front of the door, shaking in her lace-up boots. She reached for the doorknob but then turned stiffly toward her mother. "I don't believe you. Ezekiel would never leave me without saying goodbye. You're a liar."

Her mother rolled her eyes. "Go on, then. Find out for yourself."

Honoree swallowed a sob and closed the door quietly behind her. It was thirty blocks from the tenement building to the Baileys' home on Champlain Street. They lived in a big house with a bright green lawn, striped canvas awning, and iron railings.

Honoree stopped across the street from the house. Titus Bailey was an insurance man and left promptly for his office at eight o'clock. The family's Lincoln automobile wasn't in the driveway, and it was barely seven. Also, the drapes were drawn across the large bay windows. Mrs. Bailey would've tied back the lace panels to let in the sunlight, even without the help of Honoree's mother.

Honoree clawed at her muslin shirt, scratching her chest. Breathing hurt. Her legs were hard, stiff poles. She crossed the street and struggled up the concrete walkway to the porch. Leaning forward, she placed her ear against the wooden door. If the Baileys had been home, she'd hear them. If they'd been home, she'd smell bacon frying in the skillet and coffee brewing on the stove. If they'd been home, Mrs. Bailey's proper-sounding voice would break through the silence as she yelled at her boys, warning them to hurry and finish their morning chores. But the house was quiet; her mother hadn't lied. No one was home. The Baileys' house was empty.

She collapsed on the top stoop and hugged her shopping bag to her chest. Her heart broken, she cried until the sun was in the middle of the sky. Then she wiped her eyes, picked up her bag of clothes, and walked home to apologize to her mother. To tell her she was right. Horribly right.

But when Honoree stepped inside the kitchenette, her mother had already gone.

CHAPTER 6
SAWYER

Friday, June 19, 2015
(Somewhere over the Atlantic)

A sudden turbulent shift reminds me I'm inside a metal can thirty-five thousand feet up, somewhere over the Atlantic, traveling from Paris to Chicago to Santa Monica.

The Airbus A380 is a huge plane, but I'm a lean six foot two and withdrew a chunk of cash from my savings account to buy some extra legroom. Although now I'm sitting straight as a board, knees practically tucked into my chest, pretending to read a book — something about old Hollywood — while I keep the plane in the air with the strength of my will.

By the way, in case it's unclear, flying is not my friend.

My iPad rests on the tray in front of me, next to three empty miniature bottles of cheap tequila, a ziplock bag of cherry-flavored melatonin, and a small plastic bottle of H_2O.

I want to sleep without dreaming — without thinking. Sleep until we touch down on terra firma. Sleep. But my mind is cluttered.

There are things in life you don't anticipate, like having a shitty time in Paris. I had hoped that even my father would be chill in France, but anytime I think one way, another way slithers in.

My dad is the director of African American history at a prestigious university, and a walking encyclopedia on why Black lives matter. I spent two weeks in Paris at his side, editing a documentary he curated on the migration of free Blacks from Louisiana to Paris in 1803. He's always doing cool shit like that. It is his job but also his calling. A while back, when I was a kid, he introduced me to Race films, the Jazz Age, and filmmakers like Micheaux. I admire him. My father is a genius.

He's also an arrogant son of a bitch who thinks he is the brainchild of everything, including how to film a documentary, which I can almost live with, but —

He blames me for my sister's death. Not in words. Not in action. In silence. We haven't talked about Azizi since that night in the hospital. That night when the look in

72

his eyes drained the blood from my veins.

So, yeah. Paris sucked.

Another round of turbulence. The passenger in the window seat next to me is the size of a small California rosewood, ruddy-faced, and snoring. The kind of guy who sleeps through earthquakes, hurricanes, and mudslides — no bark off his beak over a little turbulence.

I bounce and swing and finally lurch forward, grabbing the sides of the seat in front of me. A moment later, the plane levels, and I release the chair, but my hands are unsteady.

I chew on my cheek, open my iPad, and scroll through my documents. Flipping through files distracts me from the bumpy sky, the frozen clouds, and the noise of the engines.

I find the film clip I was looking for. Just before I boarded, I'd received word from the restoration company that they were still verifying the 35mm nitrate film reel. There's still hope that the canister I found in Maggie's long-ago box, buried beneath a pile of papers, an old blanket, several heart-shaped wicker baskets, and a stack of photos, was a lost film by Oscar Micheaux. I'm cautiously excited, but it means I must see Honoree again. I have no choice.

I jerk sideways, and the turbulence reminds me of where I am. Shakily, I put in my earbuds, tap the iPad screen, and press Play on the short video.

Three chorus girls dance onto a stage in front of a jazz band. Several men in fedoras stand off to the side, half in the frame, some halfway out. One of them is Micheaux and the other Louis Armstrong, I believe. One of the chorus girls has to be Honoree.

Suddenly, there's a glimmer in the corner of my eye. Azizi is standing behind the flight attendant, helping her push the booze cart down the aisle.

She looks righteously pissed, too. Who can blame her? Dead over a year, a nineteen-year-old girl, a ballerina in pink tights and pointe shoes, she loved to dance, laugh, cry, tease, and give her big brother a hard time.

Where did she come from? My imagination, of course, but again, why is she here? What am I doing? Thinking about my film project, my father, or did Azizi appear because of Honoree?

The muscles in my back seize up, and breathing is a strain. *Don't be a coward, Sawyer. Don't be a coward. Promise me that much. Please.*

I pop a five-milligram melatonin, lean back in my seat, and close my eyes.

As soon as I step off this tin bucket in Chicago, I'm heading to the Bronzeville Senior Living Facility.

CHAPTER 7
HONOREE

Friday, October 23, 1925

Virginia and Edna Mae rambled into Miss Hattie's dressing room, yapping like hens in a coop, sharing tales of railroad boys, and dollar bills stuffed into their brassieres, and hooch guzzled by the pint.

No one paid attention to Honoree, which suited her just fine. She wiped her eyes and breathed in deep, settling her fractured nerves, but then Bessie galloped across the room.

"Are you okay? What happened?" she asked, panting with concern. "You almost fell off the stage in the middle of your routine."

Sure, she'd stumbled. A falling-off-the-Statue-of-Liberty-size stumble, but it was Ezekiel who had caused her to lose her footing. He was to blame for her mistakes. He was the problem — not her. "I didn't fall. I barely tripped." Honoree snapped the hook

76

of her bodice so hard she ripped the seam. "Damn it."

"Are you sure you're all right?" The worry in Bessie's damp eyes bothered Honoree as much as the girl's persistent questions.

"Who are you to say anything to me about dancing?"

Bessie's eyes welled with tears.

"Don't you dare start crying. I don't have time for you and your tears."

"I'm sorry, Honoree. I didn't mean to insult you. I was just worried."

"I'm supposed to excuse your clumsy words and your awkward attempts at being friendly. I'm not in the mood for your kind of friendly." Honoree reached under the makeup counter and rooted around, searching for what she couldn't rightly say. Her thoughts were upstairs at the bar, thinking about Ezekiel, the man she hadn't seen in three years.

Bessie stood nearby, sulking. Honoree glared, wishing she'd hightail it back on over to her crate. But before she blasted into the child, Honoree remembered she could use some help. "If you're so worried about me, how about you do me a favor."

Bessie's expression changed from bleak to eager to please. "Sure, what do you need? I'll help any way I can."

"Take a seat." Honoree nodded at the crate next to her. "A man I haven't seen in a long while came into the cafe tonight. He should be upstairs. Likely at the bar. I want you to find him and tell him to wait for me." She touched Bessie's knee. "Let him know I'll be upstairs as soon as I change."

"Yes, ma'am. I can do that." Bessie rose and spun toward the door but quickly spun back. "How will I know him? There are a hundred men upstairs."

Honoree tapped a Marlboro from her pack. "He's wearing a brown wool topcoat and holding a fedora. He'll be the only man in Miss Hattie's, other than Archie, wearing a fedora. Men who come to Miss Hattie's don't own hats, or if they do, they're one of those newsboy caps."

Bessie nodded.

"He has black hair, wavy but not processed, and he's very tall."

"What's his name?"

Honoree paused. The question stumped her for a moment. It had been some time since she'd spoken his name aloud. "Ezekiel. Ezekiel Bailey."

Bessie bounced on her heels. "Don't worry. I'll find him, and I'll hurry." She darted toward the door but whirled around, again, tugging at the waistband of her

78

pantaloons. "Can I go upstairs, dressed like this?"

"Of course you can. None of the other girls are down here changing."

"I'm down here." Trudy stood at the top of the stairs, holding a cigarette between her fingers and blinking smoke from her lazy eye. "I'm changing my clothes. Maybe you should, too."

Bessie looked at Honoree. Her round brown eyes had filled with panic.

"Go on now," Honoree said. "Don't pay her no mind."

Bessie angled by Trudy, muttering an *excuse me* before fleeing into the hall.

Trudy descended the stairs. "She's an eager beaver, isn't she?"

"Did you decide?" Honoree asked, stepping out of her pantaloons.

"You gonna ignore my question?" Trudy strutted over to her crate but didn't sit. "Ten clams? How about you sweeten the pot?"

Honoree gritted her teeth. Double-dealing and Trudy were like bacon and eggs. "I'm not changing anything. The deal is the deal."

Undressing, Trudy eyed Honoree's dress, hanging on the wall. "That is pretty. One of your better designs."

Honoree might not be Coco Chanel, but she knew her way around a Singer sewing

79

machine. "You need to take your eyes off that number, Miss Anne."

"No need to insult me." Trudy stood naked with a hand on her hip.

Honoree giggled. The moniker Miss Anne was a name Black folks called an arrogant, sex-crazed, uppity white woman who liked to mess around with colored men. It applied in reverse to Trudy.

"I was only complimenting the dress. I like the rhinestones." Trudy slipped into a short silk robe. "What if Archie asks where you are?"

"Tell him I went home sick."

"Why don't you tell him yourself?"

"I'd rather avoid him." People already knew about her and Archie's past, but what they didn't realize was how much she still feared his temper. "If he sees you instead of me on that stage, he'll figure I must be sick, and we won't have to fight about it."

"Still ain't enough cabbage for me." Trudy put her other hand on her hip. "You know what — I'll do it, if, and only if, you do something for me."

Honoree couldn't stop the I-should-have-known sigh that parted her lips. "Go on."

"Deliver a package to the bartender at the Dreamland Cafe."

Honoree gulped. Heaven help her. How

did Trudy know about the Dreamland? "I'm not going anywhere near the Stroll."

"Don't bushwa me. Every chorus girl on the Stroll is talking about Mr. Buttons's invitation-only audition. And when someone like you talks about missing a performance, I can add two plus two."

Honoree was boxed in. What choice did she have but to do as Trudy asked? "Okay. Fine. I'll deliver your package."

"Here." Trudy handed her an envelope.

It was an ordinary thing, not thick or thin, just brown, and sealed. But gooseflesh formed on her forearms as if she'd reached into a block of ice. She dropped the envelope into her purse. "What's the barkeep's name?"

"You don't wanna know what's inside the envelope?"

Honoree slipped a seashell-pink shift over her head and hips. "I'm only the postman. The less I know, the better."

Trudy shrugged. "Houdini. The barkeep's name is Houdini."

"Will he know I have the envelope?"

"He's aware somebody's going to deliver it. Just mention my name, and he'll know what to do."

"What's he look like?"

"Don't you ever get uptown?"

Honoree shrugged.

"You won't have any trouble finding him. Everybody knows Houdini. Most popular barkeep on the Stroll. Jolliest man you'd ever meet. Big belly. Big smile. Big bald head."

Clearly Trudy liked the man. Houdini must be a saint to make someone like Trudy bubbly.

There was a noise in the doorway and Honoree pivoted just as Bessie charged in, huffing and puffing as if she'd run from the Tribune Tower.

"I found him!"

"Who were you looking for, Miss Lady?" Trudy asked.

"None of your beeswax." Honoree turned to Bessie. "Will he wait?"

Bessie met Honoree's gaze. "He's tall and very handsome."

"I told you that much already." Honoree beckoned Bessie closer. "Will he wait?"

"Yes, ma'am, he'll wait. He promised."

Honoree gathered her things, the shopping bag, and her box purse, but halfway to the door, she turned to Trudy. "We made a deal. I'll do my end, but you better do yours. And my friend, the new girl, will keep an eye on you. Won't you, Bessie?"

"Yes, ma'am. I sure will."

"So don't try and screw me over."

"I don't need a watchdog," Trudy said, powdering her armpits. "I'll keep my word, and you keep yours."

Honoree pulled five one-dollar bills from her box purse. "Here."

Trudy snatched the money from her hand.

"Okay," Honoree said. "You'll get the rest on Sunday."

CHAPTER 8
HONOREE

The cafe was crowded, but Honoree pushed through the swarm without a single *pardon me, excuse me, please,* or *thank you.* Coat over her arm, shopping bag and purse in hand, she had to reach Ezekiel, look him in the eye, and ask him her questions. Simple questions. Easy questions. Questions that had stomped across her mind every day, every hour, every minute that first year, like a record on a phonograph playing over and over:

Why did you leave?

Why didn't you write?

Why didn't you see me before you decided to go?

They were separated now by only a handful of Miss Hattie's patrons. He wasn't looking in her direction, but his profile was familiar and strange at once. He was gazing off into the distance as if the walls were glass and he could see through time.

Six foot three — lookin' like Joe Brooks, fashionably dressed in a brown-and-gold pin-striped suit. Broad shoulders. A tweed overcoat on his arm. A felt fedora in his hand. He looked different, hard-boiled, but also the same — the same handsome boy she had once loved desperately.

His wavy black hair was shiny with po-made, and a thin black beard covered his brown skin, and he had a mustache. But unlike the ridiculous Charlie Chaplin tooth-brush patch Archie wore, Ezekiel's full mustache suited his mouth and straight nose perfectly.

As she studied him, this new Ezekiel, she thought back to when they were children — so close, so connected, they sensed the other's presence sight unseen. Did that invisible thread still exist between them?

Her feet inched forward, as he suddenly turned. His gaze was cold, passionless, and her breath caught on the barbs in her throat.

"Hello, Ezekiel."

"Honoree." His voice carried not the slightest sign of longing. "Would you like a drink?" He raised his hand at the nearest barkeep, who happened to be Dewey. "We'll take two bourbons."

The heel of her shoe ground into the sawdust. Ezekiel hadn't said hello and said her name as if calling a cab. And why ask her if she wanted to drink and then not wait for her reply?

"I don't drink bourbon. I drink gin."

"Bootleg gin is never as good as bootleg bourbon. But if you want gin —" He put two fingers in his mouth and whistled. Half the bar jumped out of their skin, including Honoree. Both barkeeps turned, too, but Dewey walked over with a killer's scowl on his face. "Was that for me?"

"Make that two gins instead of bourbon," Ezekiel said to Dewey. Then he offered her a Chesterfield. "Would you like a smoke?"

"No, thank you." She placed her shopping bag on the sawdust next to her feet. When she straightened, Dewey had delivered the drinks.

Ezekiel knocked down his gin before Honoree touched her glass.

"Why didn't you write?" she asked.

"You're a good dancer."

They'd spoken at the same time.

"When had you seen me dance before?"

"In my mother's kitchen when you were a kid." He loosened his tie. "It was a Saturday afternoon in the spring, I think. Your father took you in his arms, and the two of you danced the turkey trot."

Daffodils were blooming in the garden,

she recalled, but it had been a long time since she'd thought about dancing with her father, or his touch, or how his voice softened when he'd hum a melody in her ear.

It was a hazy, blurry memory, a memory that made her heart ache. But the memory didn't belong to her. It belonged to Ezekiel.

She stared at the bottles of whiskey on the shelves behind the bar. "I wanted to believe you were dead."

"I'm not dead."

"I know, since I'm standing here talking to you. But where have you been?"

Studying the bottom of his empty glass, Ezekiel clenched and unclenched his jaw. Words seemed caught in his throat — the answers too hard to give.

When he finally spoke, he said the unexpected. "Aren't you happy to see me?"

"Am I happy to see you? You left town without an explanation, without leaving word. *Glad to see you* hadn't crossed my mind."

"Then why'd you send that girl to ask me to wait for you?"

An understandable question that needed an explanation if she were so inclined. She swallowed her gin, but the taste made her gag. Dewey hadn't put honey or juice in the drink the way Crazy Pete did. And now, she was choking.

"You okay?" Ezekiel placed a hand on her back and patted lightly. "You need some water?"

She gulped, attempting to make room in her windpipe for some oxygen.

Ezekiel spread his large hand over her back, massaging her with strong fingers. "You sure you don't need some water?"

She shook her head, dabbing tears from her eyes. It took a few moments, but finally she was able to swallow. "Three years, Ezekiel," she said hoarsely. "You could've let me know if you were alive or dead."

His hand fell from her back. "I wanted to write. I even tried, but —"

"Don't do that. Don't start to tell me something and stop."

"Why not?" He squeezed the still-empty glass in his hand. "If an explanation were all it would take for your forgiveness, I'd tell you everything there was to tell. Everything about every second, minute, hour, day, and night I was away from you —" He placed the glass on the bar and tapped a cigarette from his pack. His second. "Telling you where I was or what I was doing won't bring back those past three years. Life doesn't work like that."

She thought she heard a crack in his voice.

Was he angry? In pain? Frustrated? Those were her feelings. She couldn't trust his. "Is that it? Nothing else? Because if that is all you've got to say, I have to go."

"Not yet. Please. I didn't expect to see you tonight, and I —"

"You didn't come to see me? You weren't even looking for me. So why are you here?"

"I have business at Miss Hattie's." He fiddled with the band on his fedora. "Then I saw you onstage."

"You found me by accident because you had business." She covered her mouth to hold in the words. She didn't like to curse, rarely did, but at this moment, it was an effort to keep from sounding like a street wench. "What kind of business and with whom?"

"Does it matter? I know you'd rather I tell you a story, but sorry, I don't have one."

"*Sorry?* You toss out the word like it means something to you. *I'm sorry* should've been the first words out of your mouth. Not asking what I want to drink!" She couldn't pull in her temper. It burst from her pores. "What turned you into someone else? Someone who doesn't have the decency to give me an explanation. Someone callous and coldhearted. Someone I don't want to know."

He glanced up at the ceiling and seemed to count to ten before he looked at her again. "It wasn't what happened after I left that changed me. What happened just before was the problem, Honoree."

Every bone in her body went rigid. She feared she'd break into jagged pieces, falling to the floor like shattered glass. "Are you saying that making love to me is what changed you? Changed you into a beast instead of a man? Someone who says cruel, hateful things and doesn't think to apologize."

He rubbed a hand over his face. "Honoree, of course that's not what I meant. I wasn't talking about our night together. Something else happened. My leaving had nothing to do with you."

"And it seems neither has your return." Honoree spun away from the bar, looking for an exit, desperate to be on her way. She'd wasted too much time. She wouldn't be late for the audition. She bent forward to pick up her shopping bag, but her coat fell off her arm, the bag came next, and sawdust rose between her and Ezekiel.

"Let me get that." He rescued the coat, but the shopping bag had opened, and her costumes, audition outfit, and makeup bag lay scattered on the sawdust floor.

The item on top of the pile caused her the greatest concern. It was the book Ezekiel had given her, *A New Negro for a New Century.* Ezekiel probably thought she'd kept it as a souvenir, his last gift, a reminder of the night they'd spent together. Just this once, though, she wished she'd left it at home. But maybe he wouldn't remember the gift, if heaven was on her side.

"Isn't that the book I gave you?"

Of course he remembered.

"Yes."

"And you've read it?"

A hundred thousand times. "Once. Twice. Maybe."

He handed her the bag and smiled, a bright smile, and in that instant, he was the handsome boy she used to know.

Holding the book in his large hands, he examined the worn pages, the faded ink on the cover. "It's the same copy I gave you three years ago. We were on the roof."

Unable to find any words, she merely nodded.

"Have you read Du Bois's *The Souls of Black Folk?* I'll buy you a copy. Du Bois has a different perspective on the path to equality for the Race than Washington."

She took the book from him and shoved it into her bag. "What do I care about the difference between Booker T. and Du Bois?"

"Possibly nothing." His iron gaze sunk into her flesh. "You used to enjoy talking about such matters to me."

"That was before."

"Yes. It was." His smile faded, and his shoulders hunched. She hadn't noticed how exhausted he looked, how he'd aged a decade in the three years he'd been gone.

Then Ezekiel touched her forehead.

A chill rode through her, Ben-Hur at the reins. "Why'd you do that?"

"There was a strand of hair on your —" He lowered his arm. "I couldn't see your eyes."

"Don't ever do that again."

He reached for her coat and shopping bag. "Let's dance."

The shock had to show on her face because her eyes felt like they'd popped. "Why would I want to dance with you?"

"One dance." His smile was sweet and tender and squeezed her chest.

"I thought we were fighting."

"We can fight while we dance," he said as if the words made sense.

"Don't be silly."

"You told me dancing was never silly." He leaned in, his lips brushing her cheek. "Dance with me."

Every muscle in her body tensed. Had Ezekiel lost his hearing or his mind?

"I said I didn't want to dance."

Ezekiel moved closer to the bar, talking to Crazy Pete. "The young lady and I are going to dance. Would you hold on to these items for her, sir?"

He passed Pete her coat, purse, and shopping bag, which he'd somehow removed from her grasp.

Pete appeared confused, mirroring her own emotions. "Are you sure you want to dance with him, Miss Honoree?"

"No, I don't want to dance with him. I said no. Twice."

Dewey walked over and stood next to Pete. "You having some trouble with this man?" He glared at Ezekiel, and his body seemed to expand with rage. Ezekiel countered Dewey's dangerous stance with one of his own.

"Everything's jake." Except it wasn't. She feared the next move by both men would include pounding fists.

"When did my dancing with this young lady become your business?" Ezekiel's voice had dropped an octave, and he'd moved closer to the bar.

Honoree hooked her arm into Ezekiel's elbow and pulled. She'd drag him to the dance floor if she had to. But moving him was not easy. He was a mountain stuck in the mud.

"If the barkeep has a problem with us dancing" — Ezekiel's voice vibrated dangerously — "he should explain why."

"I don't have to explain shit to a piece of driftwood like you." Dewey braced both hands on top of the bar, shoulders bunched. "If you don't agree, we can step outside to discuss it."

They were well matched. Both muscular men, except one was long and the other stout. Ezekiel was the Tribune Tower, and Dewey was a milk truck. If the boys fought, Honoree's chance of leaving Miss Hattie's unnoticed would disappear. All eyes would be on the fight, and the girl at the center of the brawl, which everyone would assume was her.

"Stop making such a fuss over a dance. You're behaving like madmen." Honoree smiled sweetly, hoping to dampen the violence in the air. "It would be my pleasure to dance with Ezekiel. So mind your business, Dewey."

She tugged at Ezekiel's arm and felt a flood of relief when he moved, albeit slowly, toward the dancers in the middle of the cafe. "Come on. You wanted to dance. Let's dance."

Still eyeing Dewey, he wrapped a possessive arm around her waist, pulled her to him, and took the lead in moving them away from the bar.

A slow blues tune played, and Miss Dolly's soulful wail filled the cafe. Dancers surrounded them, moving skin on skin, heat rising from their bodies like smoke in a bonfire.

Honoree looked up at Ezekiel. "You've changed more than I thought possible for someone to change. How could you let the likes of a Dewey Graves rile you into a fight? Have you lost your mind? Or are you just drunk?"

"Takes more than a little panther piss to get me soused."

"You never used to drink. You never dressed in a fancy suit. You certainly would never start a fight in a bar."

"I didn't start it."

Had he just dared to disagree?

"Hush your mouth. Too much about you has changed." The crowd pressed in, pushing them closer together. She felt his arm tighten around her waist, and firm fingers pressed into her side.

Was he protecting her? She didn't need

95

him to do that. "How long have you been in the city?"

"You won't like what you hear."

"I've grown accustomed to not liking things you say."

He stopped dancing, or whatever they'd been doing and, extending his arms, held her away from him. "I returned to Chicago two months ago."

The air rushed from her lungs, but she kept enough breath to yell. "Two months! You've been in Chicago for two months?" She twisted out of his arms. "Where? Where have you been staying? Where do you live?"

"The house on Champlain Street."

That house. That damn house. "I went there every day for a year, praying that maybe — maybe, you'd be back. Or leave some sign, anything to let me know where you'd gone — but nothing." She jerked out of his grasp. "I've got to go."

She cut through the crowd, waving at Pete behind the bar. She was in a hurry, and he had her things ready as soon as she reached him.

"Honoree, we need to talk." Ezekiel had followed her.

She whirled. "You've been in town for two months and didn't come to see me until tonight? Didn't send me a note to let me

96

know you'd returned. Left town without saying goodbye. Didn't write for three years." Her breathing was fast, and the air burned her lungs, but nothing would stop her. "I'm late for an appointment." The roar of the crowd dulled, and the only sound in her ears was the roar of blood and anger. "And now you want to talk. No. No. I'm done."

He scrubbed a hand over his face. "I — I had no choice, Honoree."

I had no choice. I had no choice!

This whole deal was rubbish. He had a choice — a choice to leave. A choice to come back. A choice not to tell her what had happened or why. Nothing but a whole heap of bushwa summed up Ezekiel and his choices.

She raced through the cafe, heading toward the front door. In a few more steps, she'd leave behind Miss Hattie's — and Ezekiel — forever. But her life was a series of ups and downs, pushes and pulls. As one path opened, another slammed a fist into her chest.

And there it came, above the din of music and laughter and cigarette smoke — a familiar voice shouted her name. "Honoree! Hold your horses, missy. Stop right where you are, girl!"

She turned, and there was Archie Graves, barreling toward her.

"I know you heard me, Honoree." Wearing a fancy pin-striped suit (always pin-striped) and a fedora on his head — set at an angle over his left eye — he looked like a photo of Al Capone she'd seen in the *Tribune.* Except Archie wasn't a round white man or a big-shot mobster.

"Where do you think you're going, Honoree?"

"Why, Mr. Graves, what are you doing here on a Friday night?" She smiled a flirty smile, showing her girlish charms. Archie liked it when a woman acted sweet and vulnerable, whether she was or not. "Isn't this your poker night?"

A fat pink tongue slid over the edge hairs of his mustache. "Had to cancel. Had more important business to tend to." He peered down at her shopping bag and the coat draped over her arm. "Aren't you due back onstage in a few minutes?"

He stepped aside for a couple of drunks who had stumbled toward them. But he didn't take his eyes from her face. "Need to see you in my office after the midnight show. I've got some papers for you to read."

It wasn't an unusual request. Archie

couldn't read. Honoree had read the *Encyclopaedia Britannica* from *A* to *Z* by the time she was twelve. Ezekiel had taught her, which was neither here nor there with Archie staring her down.

"Did you hear me? Are you listening, Honoree? Or is your mind wandering?"

"I'm sick."

"Sick?" His nostrils flared. "Okay. Sorry to hear it," he said, not sounding sorry at all. "Then don't dance in the midnight show, but I need you to do some figuring for me."

Getting out of this wouldn't be easy. Archie had that helpless puppy-eyed look, which would change into an ugly bulldog if she said no.

"My head hurts bad. I couldn't add one plus one. Can't it wait until tomorrow? I'm feeling poorly."

She touched the collar of his shirt, fingering the edge of the lapel. "I'll tell you what. Tomorrow, I'll teach you how to read. Then you won't have to depend on me."

Archie grabbed her wrist and jerked her to him, holding her firmly against his wide, soft chest. Her feet scurried backward, but she couldn't break free of his fleshy grip.

"Don't try and fool me," he spat. "I have papers for you to read and numbers for you

99

to figure — now."

"Archie, you're hurting me."

"Don't act like a baby. You're used to roughhousing."

"Back off, Archie." Another baritone came from behind her. "She said she was sick."

Archie loosened his grip but pulled her possessively to his side. "Ezekiel, my friend. This is none of your beeswax, boy."

Honoree's stomach lurched. Had she heard him right? "You know each other?"

The expression on Ezekiel's face didn't contradict her words.

"How?"

Archie held her wrist. "Come to my office, and I'll explain."

"Let her go," Ezekiel said.

Archie spread his fingers, letting go of her wrist. "Don't get turned inside out, boy. Me and this girl go way back. She's not worried about me. I would never harm a hair on her pretty head."

Honoree rubbed her sore wrist, but confusion took her breath as she looked from one man to the other.

Archie had done what Ezekiel had told him to do without hesitation. She'd never seen Archie do anything another man asked him to do, not without a fight. "How do you two know each other?"

Archie's chest puffed up. "Ezekiel is my new business partner, my policy wheel operator. I'm opening a policy betting station right here at Miss Hattie's. My own concern, or I mean, Ezekiel and my business concern."

Drawing air into her lungs was a struggle. Honoree couldn't believe her ears. "Ezekiel, you're not a doctor?"

Archie laughed. "Why would you think this boy was a doctor? He's one of the best wheel operators in Harlem, come home to Chicago to make his mark."

"So you're mobsters?"

"No, Honoree," Archie said sharply. "We're racketeers. On our way up the ladder to policy kings. We don't kill people."

Honoree's head hurt, and her eyes burned. Ezekiel was a policy wheel operator, and Archie was opening a policy station at Miss Hattie's. Ezekiel Bailey and Archie Graves were partners.

"I'm going to vomit."

"Don't you dare." Archie grimaced. "Already got enough puke mixed in with the sawdust." He pointed at the door. "If you're that sick, go on, scram. Get yourself home."

She covered her mouth and nodded goodbye. A block away from Miss Hattie's, she leaned against a brick wall, but she didn't vomit. There wasn't anything in her stomach but shock and surprise.

The wind stirred, and an icy breeze too cold for October threatened to freeze her where she stood. She put on her coat, almost forgotten on her arm, and ran.

At the first intersection, she hailed a Checker cab.

"Where you headed, ma'am?"

"The Dreamland Cafe."

CHAPTER 9
SAWYER

Saturday, June 20, 2015

"I won't make it back to California this week, Mitch." I'm on my cell, lying in bed at the Freehand, a hostel in Chicago's River North neighborhood, convincing my man in LA to chill. "I'll send you your money in two weeks or the week after. Promise." Mitch's reply is loud, profane, and, frankly, justified. I booked his production studio two months ago, and he's waited a bunch of weeks to get paid. And yes, I avoid his calls. Usually miss them altogether, but he caught me this morning.

"Man, I'm telling you, this trip to Chicago — dude, the woman is amazing," I say. "You'll see. I'll send you some footage on Friday. I'm seeing her later today."

Mitch is good people, and I owe him an explanation. I need him to understand why I've chosen to return to Chicago (instead of giving him his money). But I'm not sure how to explain it. My sister's ghost is to blame, but that won't fly with Mitch — or anyone sane. I could point to the 110-year-old woman I suspect of hiding a mysterious past. But what if I don't get what I need from Honoree? Between her age and temperament, it's a crapshoot. If the reel of film is a lost Micheaux, Mitch will wait until hell freezes over to be part of this project. But I won't know the deal about the film for two weeks.

"Come on, give me a little more time to sort this out," I say. Mitch complains about how he'll never work again with another wannabe Spike Lee. I start to explain that I'm not so much Spike as Lee Daniels, but that would only confuse him. Referencing Spike was a hat trick for him.

"She's one hundred and ten years old and only stays awake an hour at a time. Getting what I need from her may take a week or two." (Or until my money runs out and I have no place to stay.)

Silence. I wait, eyes closed, fingers crossed, hoping he'll reconsider cutting me off. If I don't have the studio, color me sunk. There is muttering on the other end of the line.

"Two weeks, Sawyer," Mitch says, minus the high-volume, pissed-off tone that nearly eviscerated my eardrums. "That's all I can give you. Then, I'm booking your slot. Understood?"

"Thanks, man. Much love. Much love."

I get off the phone quick — I don't want to give Mitch a chance to change his mind. I sit up in the bed and make another call — this one to the Bronzeville Senior Living Facility.

It takes less than a minute to learn Honoree is refusing to see me. She must've been mad when I didn't show, but I have a backup plan — Lula. The girl in the blue scrubs. She has influence over Honoree and will appreciate my recognition of her power. She also will be surprised as hell to hear from me, especially if I'm begging her for permission to see Honoree again.

Checking the facility's website, I find an email address for Lula Kent and send her a professional-sounding message ending with a plea: *Please, give me another chance with Miss Honoree.*

If the email doesn't work on its own, I will be forced to mention my grandmother, strategically implying some punishment for not granting me another chance with Honoree. A threat that would be more meaningful if Maggie knew I was here.

Fifteen minutes after I hit Send, I receive a reply from Lula. Fifteen minutes later, I am showered, dressed, and on my way to the Red Line L train for the six-mile ride to the Bronzeville Senior Living Facility.

CHAPTER 10
HONOREE

Saturday, October 24, 1925
Shortly after midnight, the cab stopped in front of a three-story, block-wide building where a colored fella in a tuxedo, tails, and a top hat stood beneath a black awning. Still as a statue, his face an expressionless mask, the doorman guarded the entrance of the Dreamland Cafe as if it were Buckingham Palace.

Clutching her belongings, Honoree ran from the taxi toward the entrance, but two feet from the front door, the "statue man" blocked her path.

"Excuse me, but I need to get inside the Dreamland Cafe," she said, playing tag with his beefy frame. "I'm late for an audition."

"Not gonna happen through this door, girlie."

He widened his stance and folded thick arms over his chest, his body a wall.

"Why can't I come in this way? The cafe's

a black-and-tan. Negroes allowed to come through the front door just like white folks."

He grabbed her arm at the elbow. "You ain't dressed well enough to come in the front door unescorted. Go 'round back."

How dare he say such a thing. Her hand-made fur-collared coat and the newly made dress looked better than anything sold at Marshall Field's.

Rude son of a gun had no sense of fashion — just a pigheaded bully dragging her by the arm away from where she needed to be.

"Someone in the kitchen will help you." He shoved her toward the alley.

Heat sped down her spine. She never liked being jostled by a man. Made her temper step in front of her common sense. But she forced some cool night air into her lungs. It was too soon to be on the wrong side of anyone at the Dreamland Cafe.

"So, I should go this way?" she asked, using her most proper-sounding voice.

The doorman looked at her like she'd spouted a horn between her eyes. "Yes. You go that way." He nodded toward the alley.

"I appreciate your help. Thank you, sir."

She retreated, moving away from him, smiling, but she'd remember his face. When she was a big star like Florence Mills or Josephine Baker, she'd pay him back for his rudeness.

The rear entrance was less than half a block away, and she covered the short distance in a dead run. Bounding up three steps, she reached the landing and pushed open the kitchen door. The room was three times the size of Miss Hattie's kitchen and crammed with waiters, cigarette girls, cooks, and a line of men washing dishes.

There was plenty of food, shelves with bowls of fresh-baked rolls and vanilla pudding, and small plates with chocolate cake and cherry pie. Slender black waiters in starched white shirts and red bow ties stood in an orderly line waiting to load up their trays and whirl into the dining hall. They were like racehorses at a derby, rushing about carrying silver trays with plates of sizzling steaks and steaming potatoes and buttered beans.

Honoree had had a boiled egg and a cup of java for a late breakfast, but not one bite of food since. Her mouth watered.

A waiter strolled toward her. An older man, sixty or more, judging by the loose skin sagging from his jowls and the shoe-polish black hair that attempted to hide his silver roots. "You here for the audition?"

How did he know? Perhaps it was the way she stood, regal, like a dancer.

"You stay here, and Zelda will find you."

"Who's Zelda?"

"You'll know her when you see her. She gets excitable when Mr. Buttons calls an audition. But she's a good woman, and she won't hurt you."

"Mighty nice of you to let me know."

"Keep up with her, though. She won't wait for you again."

The old man's kindness eased some of her nerves. "Thank you, sir. Thank you."

A second later, a large, mostly round woman, swooped into the kitchen. Wearing a red taffeta gown, the hem dragging on the floorboards, she was about as wide as she was tall, and her lace collar appeared too snug. Her coal-black hair was eye-catching, piled high on her head like a nest of long-winged birds taking flight in every direction.

A small handbell appeared in Zelda's hand, and she snapped her wrist. The bell rang through the kitchen, stopping every cook and waiter in their tracks. The only sound left in the room was the pop and sizzle of the meat in the fry pans.

"Who's here for the audition? You?" She gestured to Honoree.

"Evening, ma'am. Yes, ma'am. Absolutely, ma'am. I'm the one here for the audition."

"You're late." With those words, the woman was on the move.

"Ma'am." Honoree hurried after her. "Ma'am!"

Zelda pushed through the kitchen doors and barreled up a nearby flight of stairs. "Stay close," she said over her shoulder. "I don't want to lose you between here and the rehearsal room."

She moved like snow on a hot stove, and it was hard to keep up. A menagerie of hallways and doors, most closed, some open, passed by, but Honoree scarcely had time to look left or right.

When Zelda disappeared around another corner, Honoree thought for sure she'd lost her until she heard the woman's heavy footfalls climbing up a flight of stairs. Racing up the stairwell, Honoree arrived at the archway leading to a long hallway. Halfway, Zelda held a door open. "Change in here."

Honoree stepped inside, and her heart sank. If this was the dressing room, it wasn't what Honoree expected. She'd wanted something bigger, better, different, but the room was small and shabby, like the one at Miss Hattie's.

"You're lucky we got a telephone call about you," Zelda was saying. "Otherwise, you'd be outta luck."

Honoree wasn't sure she'd heard her correctly. "A telephone call. About me? From who?"

"Never you mind who. Now you better hurry and change quickly. The audition will start at any moment."

As soon as Zelda shut the door, Honoree stripped out of her street clothes and dressed in her audition outfit — dance pants, tap shoes, and a loose-fitting blouse. All the while, part of her mind was thinking about the phone call Zelda mentioned.

Honoree couldn't think of anyone she knew important enough to stop Mr. Buttons's audition. Maybe Zelda would give her a name if she asked nicely if she got the job.

She glanced in the mirror, put on a fresh layer of lipstick, pinched her cheeks, and she was out the door. Zelda was waiting down the hall, holding another door open. "Come on now. We ain't got all night."

All the girls looked alike in the rehearsal room. A dozen of them with the same light brown skin, dark red lipstick, and bobbed hair. Wearing short skirts the length of step-in pantaloons, and thin cotton blouses tied at the waist, they whispered in small groups, stretched legs against a wall, and flipped cartwheels.

Most of them acted as if they'd run into a long-lost friend, and likely had. Chorus girls on the Stroll knew one another. Honoree didn't know a soul.

She tied the tails of her loose-fitting blouse at her waist and sought a spot to stretch. A few girls had lined up near an upright piano. The expensive kind with plain square pillars and trim moldings. Nothing like the broke-down keyboard at Miss Hattie's.

A girl with a polka-dot bandanna stood alone near the piano, giving Honoree a bubble of hope that she wasn't the only one who didn't know everybody. Honoree approached, lips parted, prepared to say hello, but the girl turned her back and started speaking to another girl.

Honoree felt sheepish and pivoted, trying to squelch the notion that she'd been slapped.

She placed her hands on her hips and twisted her torso from side to side, limbering up her muscles like the other girls. Except judgmental eyes were everywhere. She sensed them watching, criticizing, whispering, but Honoree refused to shrink from the attention.

Stretching her arms to the ceiling and shaking her hands limply at the wrist, she then wiggled her hips, jutting forward and backward in a suggestive fashion. It was a step she'd seen Edna Mae perform that always earned a chorus of howls. Now the eyeballs watching her were filled with awe instead of disdain.

Adding to the show, she bent at the waist, folding in half like a Chinese noodle, and hugged her knees, showing off her flexibility. But then, a hard nudge in the hip sent her flailing. Suddenly, she lay on the floor, sprawled facedown, tipped over like a clumsy cow.

"Damn it!" she yelped.

One of the girls had pushed Honoree in the backside. She scrambled to her feet.

"Why'd you do that?"

The girl with the polka-dot bandanna grinned. "Your butt was in my face."

Honoree stepped to the girl. Chest to chest. Nose to nose. "You didn't have to knock me down."

The ribbons of the girl's scarf flopped over her eyes like a puppy dog's ears. She blew them out of her face. "I barely touched you. You lost your balance. So, back up. The dance master could walk in here any minute, and he doesn't like seeing his girls fuss."

Honoree frowned. "Dance master? Who's that?"

"The choreographer," said a girl with narrow eyes. "He makes up the steps and shows us the routine."

"Most importantly, he chooses the girls to hire," said Polka Dots.

Honoree's heart tripped. "Doesn't an invitation from Mr. Buttons guarantee a job in the chorus?"

"You've been listening to the rumors," Polka Dots said. "It doesn't always work that way."

"I've been in this room on three separate occasions and didn't get hired," said the girl with finger waves so evenly laid they appeared drawn in with a paintbrush.

"Quite a few have left this room disappointed," Polka Dots said.

"The dance master makes the final decision," Finger Waves added. "He rehearses the dancers and stages the routines. He ain't gonna hire someone he can't work with."

Honoree wanted to throw up. She had counted on this being a sure thing. She turned to Polka Dots. "Are you sure the dance master decides? At Miss Hattie's, the owner hires the chorus girls."

"Miss Hattie's?" Polka Dots turned, and the ribbons of her bow covered her eyes again. She swiped them away. "Never heard of a Miss Hattie's. It's not on the Stroll, is it?"

The other girl looked at Honoree with new curiosity. "How'd you get an invite to this audition? Nothing but the best chorus girls on the Stroll got an invitation. You must be damn good, or someone made a mistake."

A slender man entered the room, tapping the tip of a cane on the floorboards. He didn't introduce himself. The way the girls cowered, he didn't need to say his name. They knew who he was.

Wearing suspenders over a blindingly white shirt with the sleeves rolled up, the dance master had an ageless face. His blue-black skin had no lines, no sagging flesh, no dark shadows beneath the eyes, although he was not a young man.

"Line up," he said, using his cane as a pointer for emphasis.

Everyone sped to a spot and formed rows and divided into even groups. Polka Dots grabbed Honoree's wrist and tugged her to the side.

"Stay close to me. You hear?"

The dance master stood in front of the room, facing a wall-length mirror. "We'll start with the opening routine." He flung his newsboy cap on top of the piano and demonstrated the steps. Then he tapped his cane on the floor again and pointed at three girls at the far end of the line. "You there. Go see Zelda."

The girls gasped. Immediately tears streamed down flushed cheeks.

"Go on now."

Gulping down sobs, they fled the room.

Honoree jabbed Polka Dots in the shoulder. "What did they do wrong?"

"Born too short. They'd mess up the line."

The dance master pointed to the tallest girl in the room. "You go with them. And ask Zelda about selling cigarettes and cigars."

She left with a startled yelp but no tears — only a wide grin. Again, Honoree didn't understand. "Now what?"

"Zelda will make her a cigarette girl. And if she knows how to work her bottom, she'll make twice as much money as any of us."

"And spend ten times as many hours on her feet, too," added Finger Waves.

The dance master snapped his fingers. "Eyes front."

He went over a series of simple steps: a routine Honoree already knew. Step, shuffle, ball change. High kick. High kick. Shimmy. Next was a more complicated combination, including fancy arm movements and a series

117

of pirouettes. Once he repeated the sequence, however, Honoree had it nailed.

So far, the audition was a breeze, but then the master started tap-dancing — fast, too. Honoree's ankles were loose. Speed and rhythm had never been a problem. Honoree kept up with him at first. Until he lowered his torso to the floor, chest to the ceiling, and held himself up with his hands, but when he added the alternating scissor kicks, she was lost.

Honoree almost wept.

Breathless, she turned to Polka Dots. "These steps are impossible."

Polka Dots landed hard on her bottom and looked as confused as Honoree felt.

Honoree scanned the faces of the other girls in their row, but they were all smiles and giggles. Everything appeared jake to everyone but her and Polka Dots.

So be it. To earn a spot in the chorus, she'd have to push her nerves aside. And if the dance master wasn't slowing down, neither was she.

Next, he added another sequence to the routine. It began with leg kicks, and then a knee lift, a cartwheel, and a back walkover into a split. "First three girls." He tapped his cane on the floor. "Let's take it from the top."

Polka Dots pulled Honoree into the second row. "Let them show us the rough spots."

The first row made several mistakes. Then it was the second row's turn.

Twirling into the last spin, Honoree swallowed a squeal of joy. She hadn't missed a step. Indeed, the second row even had the dance master raising an impressed brow.

He brushed the group aside with a wave of his hand. Honoree wiped her brow and grinned at Polka Dots.

"Too soon to relax," she warned. "We'll be doing this for another hour before he makes up his mind."

Polka Dots had spoken half a truth.

Two hours later, the dance master had shown them a dozen new routines.

"Take it from the top, ladies."

His gaze moved back and forth, up and down, scrutinizing each row, each pair of feet, each shoulder shake and shimmy.

Sweat ran down Honoree's back and soaked her throat. Her palms were slick, her hair matted. If the audition didn't end soon, she'd surely topple over in a dead faint.

Then the dance master clapped his hands. Once. Twice. The room silenced.

He hooked the cane onto the edge of the piano and folded his arms, his black eyes scanning the room. Then his jaw clicked.

Honoree held her breath.

"Jonah" — the piano player had a name — "play a song from *Shuffle Along,*" the dance master said. "Scales, ladies."

Honoree's jaw dropped.

He must've been watching her. "Yes, girlie. You've got to sing, too." He retrieved his cane and tapped out the rhythm. The song was "Love Will Find a Way."

Honoree knew the words and the melody. Every entertainer on the Stroll knew the tunes from *Shuffle Along.*

Honoree stepped forward and let the lyrics fly. Then another girl sang until one after another — everyone had a chance to sing.

The dance master tapped his cane on the floor, and Honoree closed her eyes. This was it. He was about to pick the new chorus girls.

"You, you, and you."

Honoree struggled to catch her breath but bravely opened her eyes. Who, who, and who?

"Colethea Johnson, Hazel Reeves, and Honoree Dalcour. See Zelda tonight. You'll be the trio in the Egyptian number." He made one last tap of his cane, then exited the rehearsal room with the piano player on his heels.

Every muscle in Honoree's body had gone numb.

Had he called her name? Yes.

Hot diggity dog!

You bet he called my name.

Jeepers.

The butterflies in her belly had new wings. What should she do? What should she say? What does one do when her dream comes true? What had her mother said?

Never mind her mother.

All Honoree knew was the dance master had called her name. She was gonna perform on the same stage as Lil Hardin Armstrong and her husband, Louis Armstrong, and the Dreamland Syncopators.

The best piano player on the Stroll. The best trumpet player in the world. And the best band in all Chicago — and the new chorus girl, Honoree Dalcour!

Honoree and the other two chorus girls had spent an hour in Zelda's office signing contracts and another hour listening to a lecture on the proper behavior of young women in the employment of the Dreamland Cafe.

"When you work here, you show up on time. This is a decent establishment." Zelda gently tugged on her taffeta neckline. "We don't tolerate lateness, whoring, smoking weed, or drinking bootleg whiskey on the job. I also dislike uncleanliness and fighting. If you gotta beef with another girl, settle it outside or come see me, and I'll handle it."

Honoree liked Zelda. She spoke like a rough-and-ready street preacher, looking to save the sinners in the back pew. But she had an easy laugh, which didn't burst Honoree's eardrums the way Miss Dolly's did. She also smelled like rosewater and Ivory soap, and not one drop of sweat marred her brow, despite the thickness of her high-collared taffeta gown.

"Y'all get dressed and get out of here," Zelda said when she'd finished her lecture.

They hustled out of Miss Zelda's office toward the changing room, but before they'd made it halfway, Zelda called after them: "Your first rehearsal is Monday morning at ten o'clock. Don't be late."

The threesome entered the changing room, and straightaway, Honoree spoke up. "My name is Honoree," she said, with a friendly wave and a smile.

"I'm Hazel," replied Finger Waves.

"My name is Colethea," said Polka Dots.

"It's a pleasure to meet you both." Honoree dressed quickly and headed for the door.

"What's your hurry?" Colethea asked.

"I want to see the main dressing room."

"Why you wanna do that?" Hazel asked, putting on her coat. "We'll be here every night of the week, including Sundays."

"You don't have to join me, but I've spent two years in a basement dressing room with my feet dodging rats and other crawly things. I just want to see what a real dressing room looks like."

A friendly smile parted Colethea's lips. "I'll go with you." She grabbed her coat.

Hazel exhaled a defeated sigh. "I'll go, too, I guess, but only because I hate being left out."

The dressing room had incredibly high ceilings with crisscrossed wood beams and a skylight and marble tile, polished wood furniture, and painted glass panels. It looked like a parlor in the king of England's castle.

"My goodness. It's grand!" Honoree exclaimed, gaping at the finery from the entrance.

"Resembles the dressing room at Lincoln Gardens, if you ask me," Hazel announced, walking by her.

"I've never been inside Lincoln Gardens." Honoree walked to the center of the room.

"Look at all the makeup."

A long vanity counter lined both sides of the room. There were oval mirrors and high-backed chairs with cushioned seats, and trays of cosmetics, cleansing creams, combs, and brushes, even pressing irons. The wall hooks had costumes and undergarments — lace-up bodices, tiny skirts, and brassieres, and flatteners made of silk, satin, and cotton. All were bright and colorful in swell shades of red, orange, peach, and polka dots. Baskets of rhinestones and pearls were as plentiful as in the aisles at Marshall Field's.

Honoree fingered the loose beads and tassels strewn on the countertop. "This is gorgeous." She slipped a small ruby bead into her coat pocket.

Hazel smacked her lips disapprovingly. "What are you doing?"

"No one would miss a couple of beads," she insisted as she put the bangle back in its basket.

"Give it a week. It'll look like any other dressing room." Colethea pulled a chair into the middle of the room and kicked off her shoes. "Take a load off and stop gushing about everything. It's just a dressing room."

Hazel sat in a high-backed chair and lifted her black-stockinged ankles onto the makeup table. "You wanna sip?" She removed a flask from her bag and unscrewed the cap.

Colethea nodded enthusiastically. "I would."

Hazel passed the flask to Colethea, who gave the flask to Honoree. "I understand how you're feeling," said Colethea to Honoree. "When I got hired at Lincoln Gardens, I was over the moon. But I've been in the business for a minute or two since."

"I'd say more than a minute or two," Hazel snorted.

"Buzz off." Colethea turned to Honoree. "Don't think this is the be-all and end-all. You're young. Give this a year, two years tops, and wiggle on to Broadway. Harlem. New York City."

"She doesn't have to leave Chicago to be a star," Hazel said, rubbing her ankles. "Look at Lil Hardin."

"You mean Mrs. Louis Armstrong," Colethea said.

"She was Lil Hardin, Queen of the Stroll, before she married him," Honoree said. "That's why I think she's in charge of that parade."

Colethea unwrapped her headband and scratched her head. "How old are you?"

"Nineteen," Honoree replied.

"Same age as Josephine Baker."

"I know." Honoree blew a smoke ring. "But she started in showbiz a lot —" The dressing room door creaked open and stopped Honoree short. "Who's there?"

The old waiter with the black-shoe-polished hair shuffled into the room, grinning and holding a large silver tray. "Good evening, ladies." He looked from girl to girl, brazenly eyeballing their gams and bubs.

"What do you want, old man?" Hazel asked.

"Leave him be. He's a nice man," Honoree said, tugging her shift over her knees. "What have you got there?"

"A bottle of good gin and some cheese, sliced steak, buttered rolls — a little cold, though — and apple pie."

Colethea reached for the gin. "This is mighty nice."

"It's the best hooch in Chicago." Still getting an eyeful, he placed the tray on a side table. "Stole it from Mr. Buttons's office just for y'all ladies."

"Sure, you did." Hazel grabbed a roll. "Like you'd go through that trouble for three girls you don't know."

He grinned, still ogling Hazel's gams.

Colethea grabbed a piece of cheese. "What's your name, old man?"

"Chester. Maximilian Chester."

"Or Chester Maximilian." Colethea laughed. "Your name works forward and backward."

Hazel poured some gin. "We need to be on our way outta here soon." She chugged her drink.

"Don't be rude," Honoree said. "Chester Maximilian was awful kind bringing us this treat. The least we could do is say thank you."

"Thank you," the three girls said at the same time.

Honoree picked up a piece of cheese and a roll and kissed the waiter on the cheek. "Thank you, sweetie. You're the bee's knees."

An hour later, the food had been eaten, the bottle of hooch empty, and the old waiter had left with a much lighter tray.

Colethea yawned. "I need to go home. How about you, Honoree. Ready?"

"I had too much to drink." Honoree swayed.

"I'm ready." Colethea put on her coat. "Though I'm feeling a bit cross-eyed, too."

They left the dressing room and trekked toward the kitchen. But Honoree had trouble negotiating the hallways. Indeed, seeing, thinking, and moving was a problem.

"Ouch!" A sharp pain zigzagged across her elbow. "Damn!" How had she missed that table? She grabbed her elbow as numbness moved down her arm to her fingertips, paralyzing them. She couldn't hold on to her bags, and they dropped to the floor. "Damn."

She scooped up the purse, but as soon as she touched it, she remembered — the envelope Trudy had given her for Houdini was still inside.

PART 2

CHAPTER 11
SAWYER

Saturday, June 20, 2015

The city is a blur of tall buildings, green grass (lots of parks in Chicago), and busy roadways. People clog the sidewalks, jostling from one storefront to the next, from one high-rise to another.

The L train leans into a curve. The shrieking sound of metal on metal, train wheels on hot-rolled steel tracks, recedes into the background as white noise fills my ears, and the memories ride into my mind.

Thirteen years ago, I made my first trip to Chicago and disappointed my grandmother for the first time.

A month after my mother died in 2002, Maggie White, then seventy-six, was to receive an award at a black-tie gala at the Ritz-Carlton. I was twelve and understandably screwed up after my mom's long illness and death. Grandma needed an escort and thought I could use a trip away from

Santa Monica and my grieving dad, who seemed to tolerate the company of only his daughter.

On a Friday afternoon a week before Christmas, Grandma and I hopped on a flight to Chi-town.

She used that word, too. *Chi-town.* Said she was hip for an old lady. And she *was* hip — hipper than hip. A poet and an artist, her paintings celebrated and hailed as in the style of African American painters like Archibald Motley and William Henry Johnson.

I was her favorite grandchild, but also an odd child who cried watching cartoons. Honestly, the Road Runner was a Shakespearean tragedy. And let's not mention Charlie Brown. When my mother got sick and died, and with my passion for tragedy, I got mean. My grandmother was the only person who understood my grief masked as rage.

Then one afternoon at the Ritz-Carlton in Chicago, I bolted. Ran as if the hounds of hell chased me.

Later, I realized what had spooked me at the Ritz — the sound of the Christmas carolers.

The hotel lobby's ceiling reached to the sky, and the moldings and railings were bright gold and extra shiny. The choir's voices came at me from everywhere, climbing the sides of the walls, landing on my head with the weight of an anvil. "God Rest Ye Merry Gentlemen."

A church song my mother sang to me every year during the holiday.

Grandma turned her head for the briefest of seconds, but it was long enough, and I fled.

It took hotel security and the Chicago police five hours to find me. Where was I? Where did I spend those hours alone in a big city a week before Christmas, a month after my mother died?

Lincoln Park Zoo.

Grandma was livid. I had never seen her that mad, never seen anyone that mad in my life. She made it clear she didn't mind missing her event. She hated worrying about me.

I got an earful right in front of the cops.

"So, now you're a man and can walk off and not tell your grandmother where you're going? Don't you care about my feelings?" She didn't wait for me to answer. Not that I had anything to say in my defense. "Well, if that's the kind of boy you are, then that's the kind of man you'll grow up to be." She inhaled. "From now on, you call me Maggie."

I didn't protest. From then on, she was Maggie, which shouldn't have changed what we meant to each other. But, somehow, it did.

"She doesn't want to see you, Sawyer."

"I thought it was okay, Lula. Your email said —"

"I can tell what kind of man you are. Impatient. In a hurry, and you don't read carefully, do you?"

"Ouch." I wince a smile. "That smarted."

"I don't mean to be rude. I just know what I wrote."

I remove my phone from my pocket and scroll through my emails, not a time-consuming task. I don't receive that many.

"Look." I show Lula her email.

"It says — *might* see you." She taps my phone for emphasis. "Stop by when you can, but no promises." Her nail polish is red, and her fingers are long, tapered, and elegant. "That's what I wrote."

Could be I believe what I want to believe rather than what's actually there. "Miss Honoree is mad because I had to be in Paris and had a plane to catch and a job to do — but I'm back and here now."

"It doesn't work like that, Sawyer. Her world is smaller than yours or mine. Things we think are reasonable aren't that way for her."

We are at the reception desk on the fifth floor of the senior-care facility. I stop talking, distracted by the general absence of color everywhere. The walls are pale, the furniture gray, the drapes a lighter shade of gray, and the metal carts a dull chrome in need of a polish. The only splashes of color are the uniforms worn by the staff: green, red, purple, and Lula's pretty blue scrubs against her dark brown skin.

"Did you hear me, Sawyer?"

"I do. I did. Sorry. I know what you mean." I know what I need. "Come on. She can't be that mad at me."

Lula holds a clipboard to her chest. "Yes, she can be that mad."

Hands shoved into my pockets, I wish I could come up with something to change their minds. Not that I need their permission. The threat of Maggie, although exaggerated, is alive and well. I don't want to play that card again —

"Oscar Micheaux had an office in Chicago in the 1920s, run by his brother Swan."

"What does that have to do with Miss Honoree?" Lula steps away from the counter with an irritating little stomp. "She admitted knowing Micheaux the day you left. What more do you need from her?"

"She never looked at the photos." I raise my hand in a friendly gesture. I don't want her to leave. "Micheaux made countless films. Many of them, the early ones, are gone, lost forever. But I think I found a lost Micheaux in my grandmother's attic." I pick my words. I don't want to jinx it. "I'll know for sure in a few days. The restoration company in LA has the reel now. If things pan out and the film is a lost Micheaux, it's a big deal, and Miss Honoree, this nursing home, you, and everyone, could be part of it."

"Part of what?"

"The documentary film I'm making on Micheaux."

"Isn't she already part of it?"

"Because of the photos, she is. And if she's also in the film — that puts a spotlight on her story, too. Perhaps, even more of a light than on Micheaux's. For sure, I'll record our conversations, taping an oral history."

Lula raises an eyebrow, which I take as a good sign and continue.

"I digitized a few frames of the old reel, and I swear Miss Honoree is in the film, dancing."

"You have footage of her dancing in 1925?"

"Blurry footage, but once I get the complete reel restored — even if it isn't a Micheaux, it could be significant to film historians."

"I'm listening," she says; her lyrical voice sounds intrigued.

I can't seem to open my mouth.

"It can't be that awful," Lula says, noticing my hesitation. "Tell me."

"It's not awful, just embarrassing." I shrug. "I spent the last of my money to get here and to get a room for a couple of weeks." I can't believe I'm bearing my soul to a stranger — but I need her to let me in Honoree's room. "I should've finished this project a year ago, but life happens, and frankly, fate helped me find my grandmother's long-ago box, and Honoree —"

Lula winces at my blunder.

"Sorry, Miss Honoree is the last person alive in the city — shit, in the USA — who met the people she met and can talk about Chicago history the way she can. So if this film is also a Micheaux —"

Lula chews her lower lip, studying my face, and all I can think is: *Come on, Lula. Help a brother out.*

She starts down the hall toward Honoree's

room. "I shouldn't do this," she says over her shoulder. "But if I don't, I have a feeling you'll stand here all day bothering people."

I smile. "Look how well you already know me."

We stop outside the room.

"You should go in. Miss Honoree's resting her eyes, but she'll sense you're there and wake up. Ready to answer your questions."

CHAPTER 12
HONOREE

Saturday, October 24, 1925
(Sometime just before dawn)
"Damn. Damn. Damn."

"What's wrong with you, Honoree?" Colethea propped a hand on her hip. "What are you cursing about?"

"I need to go back to the dressing room. I left my lucky cigarette holder." A small lie. She may not know what was inside the envelope, but it wasn't something she would share with anyone. Even drunk, she had that much sense.

Colethea opened the kitchen door to the alley. "Lord. I'm cold as hell."

Hazel held her coat collar to her throat. "I'm taking a cab."

Honoree called out, "I'll catch up with y'all at rehearsal on Monday."

Colethea placed a finger on puckered lips. "Shush! Keep your voice down. And don't forget to close the door tight when you

139

leave. Should be someone around to lock up."

"I won't forget," Honoree said quietly before raising her voice. "Y'all have a swell weekend."

Soused, Colethea stumbled toward the street, barely able to place one foot in front of the other. But she was no drunker than Honoree.

She shut the kitchen door and wobbled toward the hall. It had to be five o'clock in the morning — or close to it. The envelope would burn a hole in her bag if she didn't get rid of it quickly. With a hand on the wall to steady herself, she reached the archway outside the dance hall without having to crawl.

A musician played piano softly in the balcony. Not jazz, but some other kind of music. Something with less rhythm and long, lazy riffs. It was too dark to make out the face of the piano player, but the tip of a cigarette blazed like a firefly buzzing in the night. On the other side of the hall stood the barkeep, but he was not alone.

Two men, white men, were with him. They appeared to be customers, but the large Black man behind the bar had to be Houdini.

Honoree started to call his name, but she

didn't want to startle anyone. She also couldn't recall the last time she had spoken a word in front of a white man — and with a belly full of hooch, tonight was not the night to spread that particular wing.

Another bout of spinning vision and she leaned against the nearest wall, but something struck her about Houdini. He wasn't as cheerful as the man Trudy described. The big smile was missing, and the way he hopped from one foot to the other, panicked and fearful.

The white men wore fedoras and long wool coats, and one held a newspaper under his arm. She couldn't quite figure out what made them scary, other than being white men in a black-and-tan at five o'clock in the morning. But the more she watched, the more she realized they were not the type to welcome an interruption from a Negro chorus girl.

Even a New Negro had her limitations when it came to white men.

Maybe it was not such a good idea, delivering the envelope. Houdini was caught up in something that looked incredibly unpleasant, possibly dangerous. She inched backward, thinking it best to retreat, but her footing was unsteady. She crumpled to the floor, landing on her knees.

God, she hoped she hadn't made any noise and attracted their attention. She lifted her head, praying they weren't looking her way. Relief fell over her like cool rain. *Nothing to worry about.* Whatever they said to one another was more important than her drunken clumsiness. They weren't paying attention to her, and besides, she was in the dark.

A ceiling light hung on a chain over the bar. The two white men were visible, but suddenly the conversation exploded, and their words were coarse and angry.

Every bone, muscle, and thought in Honoree's body begged her to flee, but curiosity and too much gin locked her to the spot.

One of the white men planted his elbows on the bar and leaned forward — nose to nose with Houdini, whose face glistened with sweat.

"You're a goddamned lie, nigga."

No mistaking those words — trouble was coming.

Honoree crawled behind the nearest table, using the floor-length tablecloth as a shield.

Houdini yelled, swearing he had no clue what they were talking about.

A loud whack. The sound of fist on flesh burst through the hall. Honoree leaned sideways to get a better view.

The taller of the two men reached over the bar and took hold of Houdini's shirt collar. The barkeep wailed, "What do you want? Why do you want to hurt me?"

The man holding on to Houdini's shirt shoved him away, cursing and pacing, stalking Houdini as if he were prey. He said something she couldn't understand. The other man said something, too.

Then they screamed at Houdini.

"Move your ass! Fat boy! I said move your ass!"

Honoree's palms sweat, and her heart pounded in her ears. What did these men want from him? Why didn't they just leave him be?

One white man lifted his arm; the newspaper fell to the floor. He had a tommy gun; the barrel pointed at Houdini.

Honoree's hand flew to cover her mouth and stop the scream crushing her windpipe.

Houdini's features twisted. She should stand, let the white men know she was there. If they knew, they would leave Houdini alone and go back to where they came from.

No. If she made her presence known, they'd kill her, too. She crouched lower.

"I swear I don't have it. I don't have nothin' that belongs to you!" Houdini still stood behind the bar. "I don't know nothin' about that. I swear. Lord Jesus. I swear."

"You're lying to me, boy."

"I ain't! I don't know what you're talking about." Houdini shook his head hard and couldn't stop shaking it. "Dear God. Don't shoot me. Don't shoot me. Please."

The corners of Honoree's eyes burned, but she was unable to look away. The white man waved the tommy gun's barrel at Houdini like he was teasing him with death.

The barkeep raised his hands above his head, his face a twisted mask of fear and sweat. "I'll make you a deal. I'll get you what you want. I'll square it with you. I swear."

The white men turned their heads, glancing at each other. The gun barrel stopped waving. "You should've done what you were supposed to do in the first place, barkeep."

Gunfire shredded her eardrums.

Houdini staggered backward. The blood on the front of his shirt spread across his massive chest. Somehow, he pitched forward and grabbed the edge of the bar. His lips pulled back in pain, his eyes wide, and in a final furious stance, he stood erect, daring them to shoot him again.

The white man didn't shoot him. He struck Houdini in the head with the butt of his weapon over and over and over.

The bartender groaned, a gut-wrenching sound of a man's last breath, and then he fell to the floor, and silence filled the room.

Gin rolled in Honoree's stomach.

Don't scream. Don't scream. Don't scream. They'll kill you, too, if you scream.

The man who bumped off Houdini turned in her direction, eyes narrow and searching. Had he heard her breathing? Could he see her?

The other man grabbed his arm. "We gotta go. We gotta go now."

The man still holding the gun shook free of the other man and stepped toward the main dining hall and stood beneath the light shining down from the ceiling chandelier.

Every line, every inch of his face, from his beak nose, small cold eyes, and white man's skin, Honoree would never forget. No matter how hard she tried.

He picked up the newspaper and, along with the other man, walked out of the Dreamland Cafe.

Shades of blue and orange brightened the horizon as dawn approached. Rain fell as clouds of smoke rose into the sky. But silence reigned in the alley behind the Dreamland Cafe, except for the sound of

Honoree's heart knocking a hole in her chest.

She raked her fingernails over her knuckles. Where were her gloves? Had she dropped them in the dance hall? Did she even have gloves? Did it matter?

She wanted to run. She needed to run — run the hell away from the Dreamland Cafe. Except she stood frozen on the landing outside the cafe's back door. Unable to silence the *bang, bang, bang* inside her head. Unable to unsee the face of the goon who had killed the barkeep. Unable to breathe, she was a witness — a witness to a killing. A man had been shot in front of her.

God. Why didn't she wait a day? Why not deliver the envelope another day? She would've missed the whole damn thing.

Honoree closed her fingers around the wood railing. Thank God. A part of her body had moved.

She regarded the alley and her choices. Once she made it to the street, if she turned left, that was the way home. If she turned right, the police station was a few blocks away. She could go there, tell the coppers about Houdini — if she could trust them. She was a colored girl, and a chorus girl, and a witness to a Black man's murder by a white man. Would the cops care about what she had to say?

Maybe the piano man in the balcony would go to the police — another witness to the barkeep's murder. Or he was like Honoree — too afraid or too smart to let anyone in on what he'd seen.

Honoree placed a hand lightly on her rib cage. She was breathing so fast and hard, it hurt to the touch, but she took the pain as a warning. Don't be a dumb Dora. It would be foolish to trust the coppers in this city. The piano man would be a fool to take such a risk.

She looped the scarf around her head, covering her mouth and her nose, and rushed down the steps into the alley, tripping toward State Street.

She reached the end of the alley, her gaze moving from the storefront tabernacles to the speakeasies to the whores lined up on either side of State Street. Preachers shouted hell and brimstone, and automobile horns put an ache in her eardrums.

State Street: always busy, always jumping, always something going on.

She turned down a less jammed block, her footsteps gaining speed. Soon, she was running, racing toward home, running faster than she had ever run in her life.

■ ■ ■ ■

Breathing hard, legs weak, Honoree stumbled into her home. The one-room flat, a kitchenette with a cot. A small room with no bathroom. No hot water or heat. Only two ways to escape — a front door and a rear window that led to a porch and then the roof — her home since she and her family arrived in Chicago. It had kept her safe for most of her life. Could it keep her safe now? She bolted the door behind her.

Strips of light flashed in front of her eyes. She rested her forehead against the door's raw wood and trembled. A man had been shot to death in front of her. Not the first man she had seen die; her father was the first, but the police called his death an accident. The end of Houdini's life was an execution. She slowly lifted her head but kept her palms pressed flat on the door, fingers splayed.

Steady. Steady. Steady.

She didn't trust her legs to keep her standing. Still. She was at home. Safe in her kitchenette.

Shaking, she dropped her shopping bag on the floor and placed her box purse on the kitchen table. Closing her fingers into a

148

fist, she stared at the purse, wishing it could speak and tell her what to do next. But that was make-believe, and her life was not a dream.

The envelope was in her purse. A box of matches sat on the counter next to the sink. She should burn the envelope. Tell Trudy she'd handed it to Houdini. The man was dead and unable to contradict her. And if Trudy called her a liar, Honoree would call her a liar right back.

She removed the envelope and held it in her hands, but her fingers kept tugging at the corners, picking at the edges of the seal. She lowered herself into the chair, holding the envelope with the grip of a curious child. Breathless, she peeled away the edges of the seal and poured the contents on the table.

Honoree had seen policy betting slips before. Everyone played the numbers, and every other person in Bronzeville ran the numbers. Even Miss Hattie's would soon be a policy betting parlor, according to Archie and Ezekiel's new job.

On the kitchen table, she stacked a small pile of betting slips: green paper; simple, ordinary pieces of paper. Honoree counted them.

Eighty-seven. And on each slip, the same

three digits.

Had Trudy been running numbers, too? Taking bets for the white boys on the North Side? That would surprise Honoree. Trudy liked to keep her worlds separate. Those boys didn't have to travel to Bronzeville to gamble. Policy gambling parlors were in white neighborhoods, too. They came to the Black Belt for the jazz clubs, the black-and-tans, and the whorehouses, and the Plantation Cafe, a nightclub owned by Al Capone himself, or so Honoree had heard.

The shrieking *aoogha* of a car horn blared, and Honoree nearly leaped out of her chair. She hugged her shoulders and sat very still, listening and praying that no footsteps would stomp up the stairs or travel across the wood planks and reach her front door.

Panic set fire to her insides. She stuffed the pieces of paper back into the envelope and marched over to the sink. She shouldn't have anything in her possession that connected her to a murdered man, especially when a white man had killed that colored man. Only Trudy knew about the envelope. No one else would unless Honoree told them.

Burn it. Set it on fire. Watch it turn into ash.

She picked up a match and struck it on

the edge of the counter.

The smell of sulfur filled her lungs as the flame flickered red and blue. What if the smartest thing she thought of would be the worst possible thing to do?

She dropped the match in the sink. She would make a decision about the envelope after she got some sleep and cleared her mind.

She returned the envelope to her box purse, slipped off her coat, and stepped out of her shift. Wearing only her cotton chemise, she lay on the cot and closed her eyes, but she couldn't rest. The murder played in her mind like a motion picture at the cinema. Except in her movie, she could hear Houdini speak, and his words rang in her ears: *I swear I don't have it.*

What did he mean; what was he talking about? What didn't he have? *What if. What if. What if.*

Her throat closed, and her stomach churned. She was going to puke.

What if the white men had come to the Dreamland for the envelope?

No. That couldn't be what Houdini meant. No man would kill another man for eighty-seven betting slips.

Honoree hugged her arms around her shoulders, gently massaging the fear cramping her muscles. What if Houdini had been killed because of the envelope? What if his death was her fault? Oh God.

No. No. This was Trudy's doing. Honoree had no reason to feel guilty. No reason. Except. Oh God. If she had only given Houdini the envelope an hour earlier, he might still be alive, and if he still ended up dead, it would be none of her concern.

Stop. Stop. Stop. She needed to sleep and stop worrying. First, she had to hide the envelope. There was a stack of baskets next to the Singer sewing machine. She rose from the cot, took the envelope from her purse, and stuffed it into a heart-shaped basket. Then she went to the cabinet beneath the sink and removed a jug of hooch. Laura Lee, Honoree's next-door neighbor, the mother of five of the loudest children in the tenement, gave her a jug of bathtub gin as payment for mending her children's raggedy clothes.

Honoree uncorked the jar and poured herself a cupful, swallowed, and tried not to gag. Then she poured another and another. By the third cup, her vision blurred. She struggled to stay on her feet.

She put the jug away and wrapped herself in her mother's quilt. The good Lord willing, she'd close her eyes and fall into a blissful sleep. A dreamless sleep. No gunfire. No blood. No dead barkeep to haunt her.

ful sleep. A dreamless sleep. No gunfire. No blood. No dead thug to haunt her

CHAPTER 13
HONOREE

Saturday, October 24, 1925
(Around ten o'clock in the morning)
Bang! Bang! Bang!

Honoree jerked upright in the cot, and her fingers clawed at the neckline of her cotton chemise. What was that noise? Where was it coming from? Her gaze swept the kitchenette, seeking the origin of the sound banging inside her head.

"Open up, Honoree!"

No. Not in her head but knocking on her door, yelling — and the voice knew her name.

She swung her feet from beneath the quilt. The raw wood planks sent a shiver up the back of her calves.

Please, don't let it be the man who shot Houdini. Please, not him.

Fear weakened her legs, and she crumpled to her knees. Fear was also a weapon. Lying flat on her stomach, she patted the floor beneath the cot. The broken broom handle was where she had left it. She pushed herself to her feet, holding the weapon in hand.

"Honoree!"

Her spine went rigid.

"I know you're there. Open the damn door."

"Ezekiel?"

"Let me in."

She hurried forward, unbolted the lock, and, still holding the broom handle, opened the door. "What do you want?"

He glanced at her hand and the front of her cotton chemise.

"I asked you whaddaya want?" She crossed an arm over her breasts.

"Are you alone?"

Her lips parted, and she hissed an indignant gasp. "Of course I'm alone."

He started to walk by her, but she stepped in front of him, blocking his path. "Just because I live in a hovel doesn't mean you can stroll into my home uninvited."

He peered down at her, dark eyes raging like a dangerous storm. "Invite me in or move out of my way, Honoree."

Her chuckle was humorless and sparse. "After the night I've had, if you mean to frighten me, you'll have to do better than a rough tongue and angry eyes." She lifted the broom handle to make sure her weapon was seen. "I don't have to do anything you tell me."

He closed his eyes, seemingly seeking control over his temper. A moment later, the storm had faded. "Please. Let me in."

A dog barked. Ezekiel jerked a glance over his shoulder. Honoree looked, too, but there was nothing but rain and the daylight rising toward the middle of the sky.

"Honoree, if the wrong person sees me here, it'll bring hell down on both our heads." He jammed his hands into his pockets. "I don't want anything bad to happen to you, and I don't want to end up on the bottom of the Chicago River."

The lines around his mouth deepened, but the quiver in his chin mattered to her the most. She lowered the broom handle and moved aside. "Fine. Come in."

Ezekiel bolted the door behind him and stalked by her. "What did you see?"

"What do you mean?" Honoree followed him to the other side of the kitchen table.

"You were there." He shucked out of his overcoat and dropped it over the back of a chair. "Someone I trust told me."

She propped the broom handle in the corner, put on her sweater, and tried to come up with a story. He hadn't talked to one of the other chorus girls; they'd been long gone. Everyone had left except — the piano player in the balcony. Was that Ezekiel's trusted one? If she asked him that question, though, it would be a confession. She hugged the sweater around her. "Your trusted friend is a liar."

"He's not lying." Ezekiel was pacing like a madman in a box.

"Stand still! There's not enough space here for you to prowl about like a tiger in a cage."

He stopped, and his face twisted with emotions — hate, love, rage, and something wild and frightening. She checked the bolted door. How long would it take to unlock, open, and flee before he caught her?

"You were at the Dreamland Cafe this morning."

Her legs went stretchy like bands of rubber, but she had to stay on her feet. She had to look him in the eye and tell him more lies, although the room kept spinning. She reached for the table. Why was it so far away? She took a step and stumbled, losing her balance, but Ezekiel caught her around the waist.

"What's the matter?" He brought her to him, holding her close. He smelled of cigarettes and whiskey — which meant he likely could smell Laura Lee's bathtub gin on her.

Ezekiel's lips tightened. "Have you been drinking?"

"N— no. M— maybe. A— a l-little." Christ. She had slurred every word.

"Sit down before you fall." He guided her to a chair at the table.

She sat in the seat, her elbows landing on the table with a soft thud. "Why are you asking me about the Dreamland Cafe?"

"Would you recognize the man who shot Houdini if you saw him again?"

Oh God. "I'm not feeling well."

"I've got no time for cat and mouse, Honoree. Did you see him or not?"

She placed a hand on her stomach.

"Stop asking me questions I can't answer."

"Then tell me the truth."

She picked at the splinters on the kitchen table. "Nonsense. I had an audition for the chorus at the Dreamland Cafe." She added a small smile. "I got the job, too."

"God, Honoree. Two dozen girls showed up for that audition."

"I told you what you wanted to know. Are we done?"

He sat in the chair opposite her. "We have to be straight with each other. I can only help you if you tell me the truth."

What a foolish thing for him to say. "What do you mean, straight with each other? I don't need your help."

"You don't trust me, and I understand. But you stumbled into something that could get you hurt. I don't want anything to happen to you. But I need you to trust me."

"I'm not going to trust you just because you say so."

He tilted his head back and stared at the ceiling for a long moment. "Honoree, we're wasting time."

She stood up and paced, her feet smaller, her legs shorter, her circle tighter and faster. Why keep lying? He knew.

"Pack some clothes." Ezekiel rose. "Whatever you can fit into a shopping bag. I'll take you to Union Station. In an hour, you can be on the next train to anywhere. It doesn't matter where."

"Leave town? Why?"

"You witnessed Houdini's murder and can recognize the man who shot him."

"I didn't see —"

He slammed his fist on the table. "Enough lies! Pack your clothes. Let's go."

"The man who killed Houdini didn't see me — I have no reason to leave."

"Good God, Honoree. Don't be naive. If my man saw you, they probably did, too."

159

"Leaving town seems to be the only way you know how to deal with trouble. I'm not leaving."

He removed a Chesterfield from his pack. "You want a smoke?"

"No."

He lit up and reached for the tin ashtray on the counter next to the sink. Then he sat across from where she stood and took a long drag of his smoke. "If you're not leaving, I need something from you."

"And what would that be?"

"The envelope. The one you were supposed to give to Houdini. I need you to give it to me."

What? The room shifted. Her chest muscles cramped. Was she having a heart attack or losing her ability to hear? "What did you say?"

"The envelope Trudy gave you to give to Houdini — give it to me."

Her stomach churned, and the sickness rose into her throat, but the problem wasn't the hooch. She staggered toward the sink. His words had made her ill. Words she never thought would pass Ezekiel's lips. She grabbed the porcelain sink and waited, and waited, and waited for the wretchedness in her belly to spill out of her mouth, but nothing happened.

160

Ezekiel placed his hand on her back, and his voice whispered next to her ear. "Calm yourself, my love. You'll be okay. Just fine. I'm sorry to upset you, but I can't leave until you give me the envelope."

The envelope? He came for the envelope. *Oh God.*

Each morsel of food, drop of water, and the gin she had swallowed since the day before yesterday she vomited into the sink.

Ezekiel was at her side, holding her hair away from her face for what seemed like hours. Until finally, there was nothing left inside her. He turned on the faucet and cupped his hand beneath the cold, running water, and splashed her face gently.

Then she took over and rinsed her mouth, swallowing a handful of water to cleanse the unpleasant taste. "Did Trudy tell you I was at the Dreamland Cafe?"

"Trudy made a mistake. You never should've been involved. I'll handle her."

Sunlight landed on the windowsill, hard, bright rays of light, but the cold, dreary flat never changed. The sunshine never entered the kitchenette. Not once since she could remember.

"Honoree, I still need the envelope."

Her purse sat on the kitchen table. She moved toward it, but a fresh wave of dizziness caught her. She rested a hand on the edge of the table to steady herself. "I gave the envelope to Houdini."

The sadness in Ezekiel's eyes startled her. She splayed her hand over her chest.

"Are you sure you don't have it?"

"I gave it to Houdini." God, she hoped the lie didn't show.

"Did you look inside the envelope?"

"No, I just gave it to him. And if you don't believe me, check with the morgue and ask them to look in his pockets. Or ask the man who killed him where it is."

"I don't believe you, Honoree."

"I don't need to lie."

"I think that if Houdini had the envelope, he might not be dead. Did that cross your mind?"

She massaged the hard bone between her breasts. "Houdini's death is not my fault. If anything, I was a messenger. You and Trudy are to blame. Not me."

He scrubbed a hand over his chin. "When I came into Miss Hattie's last night, there was a part of me, always a part of me, that wanted to tell you anything about the past three years, because —" He shut his eyes and cursed. "Damn it, Honoree. What happened at the Dreamland Cafe is my business. And your involvement is a stupid mistake. Now I have to keep you safe, and to do that you need to leave town."

"I'm not leaving. Your man was playing the piano in the balcony, right? But he couldn't have seen me in the main hall, either."

Ezekiel snatched his coat from the chair and unbolted the lock on the door. When he spoke, his back was to her. "Don't mention that you had the envelope to anyone. If the man who killed Houdini finds out you had it — trouble will be on your doorstep in a heartbeat."

She folded her arms over her stomach and pushed in hard. "Do you know who killed him?"

He faced her. "Whoever it was, if they find out you were there, they'll kill you, too. And then I'd have to hunt them down and kill them, or die trying."

Ezekiel held her gaze. "If you don't leave town, if you need anything, you find me, and I will help you, but you've got to promise me, Honoree. Promise, you'll come to me and only me."

CHAPTER 14
SAWYER

Saturday, June 20, 2015

Broken beams of light reach Honoree's room from a window in the hall, softening the jagged edges of my claustrophobia. The slightest bright strip dulls the effect of the white walls, low ceiling, and monotonous tile, helping me to breathe.

Conversely, the sunshine also illuminates the angles and shadows in Honoree's face. I drift into a corner to stare.

My grandmother Maggie is eighty-nine, but age gathers everyone under one roof, and these two women look almost the same. Both are small-boned with a head full of cottony white curls, a thin nose, a high forehead, and full lips, which strikes me as odd. I thought lips withered with age. They also have a similar jut to the jaw and sharpness to the cheekbones.

There are, however, differences.

Honoree's skin is a spotty canvas of light

164

and dark flesh. Maggie's skin is smooth and pale brown, and her voice is soft, breathy, and poetic. Honoree's voice is rough, dismissive, and crude. Luckily for Maggie, she doesn't have large pointy ears that stick out from both sides of her head like an elf in a graphic novel.

"Is that you, Sawyer? Why are you hiding in the corner?"

I drop my backpack and step forward. "Miss Honoree. How are you today?"

"Where you been? You didn't come back."

"My apologies, but I'm back and anxious to talk to you."

She raises her left hand briefly before hiding the arm beneath the sheet. Her wrist is a twisted, swollen joint the size of a golf ball. It must be an arthritic condition, but there is also a long puckered scar, a scorching burn from the middle of her forearm to her shoulder.

"What are you gaping at?" One eyelid closes as the other eye glares. "Stop staring at my disfigurement. Happened a hundred years ago in a fire when I was a child — kerosene spilled from a lamp and lit up my arm. It stopped hurting a long while back." She frowns. "What are you doing here?"

I tear my gaze away from her burned arm. "I hoped we could start fresh."

"I don't trust you to stick around."

I inch forward. "Give me a chance. I'll prove I'm trustworthy."

"How? As soon as you get what you need, you'll be on your way back home."

"I promise I'll return the next day and the next day, and the day after that. I won't duck out on you as I did before. My project is already a year late, but I am committed to finishing it in the next two weeks." I capture her gaze. "That can only happen with your help."

"I'm not so sure about that," she says, sizing me up. "What made it late? Your project. What happened that you couldn't finish it a year ago?"

Her directness doesn't surprise me too much. "What made my project late? Let's call it life — and death." I add the latter for the sake of accuracy.

Honoree turns and rests her cheek against the pillow as she looks up at me. "There's a chair in the corner. Pull it over here, close to the bed."

I glance around the small room, still firing my claustrophobia on all cylinders. The narrow beam of light from the hall window is a godsend. I plant the chair close to the bed and sit.

Honoree lets me settle before she begins.

166

"Yes, that is better."

I remove my iPad from my backpack. "Whaddaya say we watch a video. I have footage from a 1925 motion picture. I think you'll recognize one of the chorus girls." I adjust the over-the-bed tray table and place the tablet in the center, so Honoree has a good view.

"What the hell is that?"

"An electronic tablet, an iPad."

"Looks like a tiny TV." She points at the television on the wall. "That's a bigger one up there. What do I need this for?"

"When it's on, you'll see just fine." I open the app and tap Play. "Do you know any of them —" I nod at the screen. "The girls dancing?"

"Too blurry." She points at the tablet. "I might recognize her. The one in the middle. You think it's me, don't you?" She smiles at the figure on the monitor. "What a pretty little chorus girl. One of the best in the city."

She stares ahead with dull eyes as if traveling back in time.

"I'll have a better film clip in a week or so. Do you recognize any of the dancers? Or one of the men standing off to the side of the frame? One of them might be Oscar Micheaux."

"I told you. Too blurry." She wraps gnarled

fingers around the railing. "Where's Lula? I need my pillows fixed. I wanna sit up."

"You are sitting up."

"I want to sit up straighter."

"Let me help." I move to adjust her pillows. "Is that better?"

"Uh-huh. Just fine."

I think she saw something in the clip. I start to ask her what — but she waves her arm, the one without the scars.

"What was I sayin' about Micheaux . . . ? That's okay, I remember." She places a hand on her throat. "How that man liked to showboat. Let me tell you — he'd walk into a party and take over. I swear. Like he was in charge of everything, and everyone in the room were actors in his motion picture. He would tell people why his movies were the only movies people of the Race should see." She shook her head. "Some of us enjoy watching Charlie Chaplin. I even liked the Keystone Cops and Fatty Arbuckle before he hurt that girl. I heard tell he was the worst kind of man when it came to women. But there were a lot of men, colored men, too, who got worse around women."

There is a radiance about her now. Alertness kindles her eyes but also tightens her skin, and her cheekbones lift. I put away my iPad and remove my camcorder from the backpack. "I want to record you. Do you mind?"

"Go ahead." She waits for me to set up.

"All right, then. You were talking about Oscar Micheaux."

"He was a handsome man. Had a perfectly round head — like a black ball. He was tall, too — not as tall as some men I knew."

She talks about Micheaux for the next hour without prompting, although I start to believe she's pretending. Especially when she reminisces about an afternoon in the spring of 1926, dining on caviar and champagne — with Oscar — at the Green Door Tavern. That one made me smile.

Still, I'm just fine with her fanciful tales. Somewhere in her jumbled memories is the truth.

"Good morning, Sawyer." It's later the same day and Honoree is confused, but I let it pass. She is sitting upright in her bed, a pair of reading glasses on her nose, a Bible in her hand. I'm surprised. It never occurred to me she could see well enough to read. Then again, why wear glasses unless, unlike my grandmother Maggie, she hasn't memorized the good book.

"I'm glad you feel well enough to talk to me twice in one day, Miss Honoree." I move to her bedside.

"You didn't bother me as much as I thought you might."

I chuckle, enjoying her wit, or is it just the way she talks? Her age makes polite chatter pointless, since it consumes time she doesn't have. Either way, I haven't known her long enough to decide. I take a scrunchie from my pocket and fasten my dreads into a ponytail. I am ready for battle.

"Hello, Miss Honoree." Lula nods a greeting as she enters the room and crosses to Honoree's bedside.

I nod in reply and hide my agitation at being interrupted before I can begin.

Patiently — okay, not too patiently — I shift from one foot to the other and watch Lula check Honoree's pulse and fluff her pillows.

Suddenly, Honoree is coughing, a scary gagging cough that keeps coming.

"Are you okay?" Lula places a hand on her shoulder, supporting her as the spasm plays Ping-Pong with her body. She calmly pats Honoree on the back and doesn't appear alarmed, but I am. It rattles my chest. The cough is so powerful and loud, as if her rib cage will break into pieces.

After a few endless moments, Honoree's coughing jag subsides.

"Are you feeling better?" Lula massages Honoree's upper back. "Did Sawyer upset you?" she asks with a small teasing smile in my direction. Or at least I think she's teasing. "Anytime you want him to leave — just let me know." Or perhaps not.

"I have not done anything," I say in my defense. "We barely talked before she started —"

"Oh, he can stay," Honoree whispers, but then clears her throat and speaks with authority. "We've been talking just fine." Her face is flushed, but her voice has that zip again. "What were we talking about?"

I give Lula a quick *Told you so* glance before I return to Honoree's bedside. "We can start now if that works for Miss Lula."

She twists her mouth and sighs heavily. "As long as Miss Honoree is comfortable, you can proceed. But let's keep it short for today. I'll check back in a few minutes to see how the two of you are doing." She smiles at Honoree, gives me a death glare (not actually, but I love hyperbole), and then she's gone.

I remove my camcorder and tabletop tripod from my backpack. "I'd like to record this session," I say to Honoree, moving closer to the bed. I adjust the tray-top table and set up my devices. "Just some basic questions to start. Are you ready?"

"Are you?" Miss Honoree looks suspiciously at the camera facing her.

I smile. "Yes, everything is ready to go. Now, what's your birthday?"

"December thirty-first, but I can't recall the year. When were you born?"

"New Year's Eve, huh?" I chuckle. "And we're still playing this game?"

"You bet your ass. You made a deal."

"Okay. May 1, 1990. And by the way, records show you were born in 1905."

"I don't feel that old. I mean, one hundred and ten is ancient. I feel younger — one hundred and five or one hundred and six."

"You are one hundred and nine and five months, which is splitting hairs, I know. I like to round things up. Not a lot of difference once you get over one hundred." I shrug. "By then, it's gravy."

"You try getting this old and then ask me about the difference."

I concede her point and move on. "Where were you born?"

"Baton Rouge, Louisiana, or thereabouts. What else do I know — my mama's name was Cleo. I can't recall my father's name." She pauses. "What's your father's name, Sawyer?"

"His name is Marvin, but you mentioned

Baton Rouge. I have a photo of Maggie, my grandmother, outside an old house in Baton Rouge." I rifle through my backpack. "I believe it was taken just before she sold it." I remove a photo from the stack and flip it over. "Around 1990, I think."

Honoree's body stiffens, and her nose wrinkles in an attractive sneer. "What house? Maggie White never owned a house in Baton Rouge."

I am caught off guard by her harsh tone. "Um. Well, she didn't own it when you knew her. The family that raised her left her the house, I imagine, and she sold it in 1990."

"Maggie never owned a house in Baton Rouge!" Honoree's voice is brittle, loud, and persistent. I hit a nerve.

"I have the bill of sale," I say, hoping to calm her. "It was in a box in the attic."

"Maggie never owned a goddamned house in Baton Rouge!"

That didn't work. "I'm sorry, Miss Honoree. It's not a big deal. Let's forget about it. We can talk about something else."

"I'm done talking." Honoree shuts her eyes. "I'm tired."

Lula returns as if summoned by magic. "Would you like Sawyer to leave?" She marches by me.

"Come on, Miss Honoree." I look at Lula, at a loss. "I have no clue what got her so mad."

"She's just tired. Let's take a break, and you can come back after dinner or maybe tomorrow."

I gather my things from the table and shove them into my backpack. "Crazy," I mutter, walking out of the room. "All I said was Baton Rouge, and you would've thought I had called the hounds of hell."

CHAPTER 15
HONOREE

Saturday, October 24, 1925

Honoree awoke to a shout and a bang. A door had slammed shut, and an angry mother's tongue crackled like gunfire. It was her neighbor, Laura Lee, fussing at one of her five children. Something about leaving the door open and letting the cold in. Poor child's ears had to ache from the flurry of damnations Laura Lee hurled.

Honoree's eardrums certainly did. All she wanted was to sleep for a few more minutes without dreaming. She tossed aside her mother's quilt and rose from the cot, but her knees wobbled, and she sat back down.

Gunfire. Blood. Ezekiel had begged her to leave town. It wasn't her fault the barkeep was dead.

Christ. The envelope was hidden in the heart-shaped basket. She had looked inside, but only after she'd returned home from the Dreamland. Even if she had opened the

175

envelope before, it wouldn't have mattered. The only thing that mattered was that she'd been hired to be in the chorus at the Dreamland Cafe.

She walked over to the sink and turned on the faucet and cupped her hands beneath the running water. Her sudden gasp of delight took her back a step. She had expected a sobering cold splash, not hot water!

Honoree could count on one hand the number of times the water was warmer than an iceberg. She grabbed the washcloth, some broken pieces of Ivory soap, and started scrubbing: her face, throat, armpits, and legs.

"Honoree!"

This voice on the other side of the door didn't startle her; it belonged to her neighbor, Kenny.

"Honoree! You are in there. I can hear the water."

She gripped the edge of the sink. "Stop banging on the door, Kenny. I'm not dressed. Come back later."

"I got something for you."

"And I have hot water for the first time in God knows when. I intend to wash up before the water goes back to ice."

"You had a telephone call at Mr. Turner's

Grocery Store, and they left a message."

No one in the building owned a telephone — no one in the building could afford the phone lines, anyway. She used Mr. Turner's number in case someone had to reach her in a hurry.

"Honoree, come on now."

"Slip the note under the door."

"Come on. I ran all the way here to hand-deliver this message. Least you could do is let me in."

"You're such a brat." She turned off the faucet. "Hold on, hold on. Let me find my sweater."

"Hurry up. It's cold out here."

She put on the sweater and unbolted the door.

Long and lean, Kenny tripped into the kitchenette, his big boots covered with mud, his thin limbs swinging loose and free.

"Good morning, doll." He shucked out of his peacoat and flung it over the back of a chair. "When did you start getting phone calls from the Dreamland Cafe?"

"Why wouldn't I get a call from the Dreamland Cafe?" She kept her voice rough, but a hummingbird was flapping its wings inside her rib cage. "It is my new place of employment, after all."

"Gosh almighty, Honoree. You got hired

at the Dreamland Cafe. I didn't believe it possible. Congratulations!"

She smiled. "I told you about climbing the ladder to success."

"That was three years ago, and back then, doll, I took your proclamations with a grain of salt." Kenny smoothed the whiskers on his chin. "Better be careful, though. Reaching too high too fast can cause a tumble."

"Don't you worry, Kenny. I'll avoid your mistakes."

His face crumbled, and Honoree could've kicked herself for bringing up his failures. A former student at the School of the Art Institute of Chicago, Kenny was one of two coloreds to graduate in 1918. *A talented Negro painter,* his instructors had called him, but Kenny smoked reefer cigarettes and drank hooch by the gallon and ran around with handsome men who didn't care about him. He got hurt, made mistakes, and in between lost sight of his dreams.

"I don't appreciate you bringing up my past," he said quietly. "I thought I was offering advice. I forgot you take care of yourself."

"I do, and I'm sorry, but I believe life happens when you make it happen." Despite Honoree's bold talk, the wings inside her chest hadn't stopped flapping. The message

178

from the Dreamland Cafe wouldn't be good news. "Don't you have something to give me. A message?"

Kenny melted into the chair and stretched his long legs beneath the table. "There was a ruckus this morning at the Dreamland. Did you hear about it?"

"How could I when I just woke up?"

Kenny pulled out a slip of paper from his pocket. "A bartender was gunned down, killed right inside the joint."

Sweet Jesus. News spread like wildfire in Bronzeville. Unless Kenny had overheard her and Ezekiel that morning, but Kenny would've mentioned that. "I told you I ain't got nothing about what happened at the cafe." She nodded at Kenny's hand. "Give me my message."

He pushed the paper to the middle of the kitchen table. "They want you at the cafe by one o'clock. A woman named Zelda left word with Mr. Turner. She also said you better be on time. See, written right here. 'Be. On. Time.' "

Honoree snatched up the piece of paper. "Thanks, Kenny. What time is it now?"

"Almost noon." He reclined against the chair and placed his arms behind his head like he would remain in the same spot all day. "Get dressed."

"You need to leave."

"Why? You always let me stay." Hastily, he removed a sketchbook and pencil from his peacoat pocket. "I'll draw a picture of you — getting ready to work at the Dreamland Cafe."

"No, Kenny." Usually, she didn't mind him drawing sketches or taking pictures with his Kodak Brownie, but not today. "Go on now. I'm serious. Time for you to leave."

"Damn, Honoree. You have a new job, and you forget how to be polite." He jammed the sketch pad into his coat pocket.

"I was not that polite before." She smiled to soften the truth of her words. "Now go on. I need to dress — and the message says I can't be late."

There were so many things that could've caused Zelda to call and leave that message. The meeting could be about something other than Houdini with all the happenings on the Stroll.

A block from the cafe, however, Honoree could barely walk. Dread stuck to her Mary Janes like a thousand chips of stone. *Stop fooling yourself. The meeting is about Houdini.* Anything else wouldn't be her kind of luck.

It was a little before one o'clock when she walked through the kitchen's back door. A crowd had already assembled. Dancers from the audition, a few musicians from the band, and a couple of cooks busying themselves at a counter with flour, butter, and eggs. Everyone looked uneasy, shifting from foot to foot, waiting for the finger of blame to point in their direction.

The old waiter with the shoe-polish black hair was on the other side of the kitchen. With a firm grip on her box purse, Honoree headed toward him.

"Chester Maximilian," she called after him, but he darted into a corner next to a smooth-top stove. "Chester, or is it Maximilian?" She couldn't recall which name was first. "Would you stop running, please."

"I ain't running."

"Then why are you acting like an army of ants crawled into your pants?"

"I'm tired. I fidget when I'm tired."

"I'm tired, too." No time to waste, she asked the question plainly on almost everybody's mind. "Why are we here? Do you know?"

"No, ma'am. I don't."

"Come on. I can tell when someone is hiding something. You're watching those doors as if Saint Peter himself is about to stroll into this kitchen."

He bounced on his heels, his twitchy gaze

looking for an exit, but Honoree blocked the small man's path.

"We were here late — you, me, and your girlfriends," he said in a whisper. "Mr. Buttons don't like waiters hanging around after work. So, y'all need to keep quiet about last night and what happened — especially about the gin and all."

Honoree's shoulders relaxed. "Don't worry. I have no intention of mentioning last night to anyone. I just wanted to make sure we were of the same mind."

"Yes, ma'am. My mind is the same as yours. If Mr. Buttons finds out I messed with his liquor, he'll toss my ass out in the street. I don't want to lose a job over a couple of bottles of hooch."

"Makes sense. So if anyone asks what time we left, you'll say three o'clock this morning, and none of us went anywhere near the main dining hall."

He nodded vigorously and turned to go, but Honoree placed a hand on his shoulder.

"Come on, tell me. Do you have any idea why we're here?"

The old waiter smoothed his whiskers into place. "The cops want to talk to those of us who worked late."

She feared she might upchuck, the way her insides twisted. Questions from Zelda or Mr. Buttons, she could handle. Talking to coppers made her ill.

"Will those other two girls keep quiet, too?"

"Don't worry about them. You keep your mouth shut. I'll handle those two."

"My lips are sealed, Miss Honoree. You never need to worry about me."

"Thanks, Chester."

"Excuse me, ma'am. Maximilian. Maximilian Chester. That's my Christian name."

As Maximilian tottered away, Honoree scanned the room, searching for Colethea and Hazel. She had to make sure they understood how to keep their mouths shut.

It didn't take long to find them. Huddled in front of a cabinet of pots and pans, they were smoking cigarettes, wearing ratty fur coats, bright red lipstick, and an extra layer of dark eyeliner.

"Did you hear what happened?" Hazel said as Honoree approached.

"About the barkeep?" Honoree replied.

"It's all over the Stroll," Colethea chimed in.

"The minister at the chapel on Twenty-Second Street knew, too."

Colethea frowned. "You go to church?"

"Hush up," Hazel replied. "I do any number of things that are none of your beeswax."

Colethea tugged on Honoree's sleeve. "I hope nobody saw us last night."

"That's what I wanted to talk to y'all about. Maximilian, the old waiter, had said the same thing." Honoree pulled Hazel in close. "We shouldn't mention our trip to the dressing room, and we left the cafe at three o'clock — if anyone asks."

"Of course someone is gonna ask!" Colethea exclaimed. "A man's dead. There will be questions."

Hazel waved her cigarette. "Wait one minute. I understand about the stolen gin, but why lie about visiting the dressing room?" She flicked cigarette ashes on the floor. "We were long gone by the time the barkeep was shot."

They were long gone, but not Honoree, she thought. She hunted in her purse for a pack of cigs. She was there when he died. "None of us were anywhere near the Dreamland when he was killed, but why risk getting caught up explaining things to the cops?"

"I ain't afraid of no coppers," Hazel declared. "What we did was no big deal." Hazel had put out her cigarette and removed a pack of gum from her pocket. "Did you steal those bobbles? Is that why you want us to lie about the dressing room? You're a thief?"

Honoree blew cigarette smoke at Hazel. "I'm not a thief. Cops twist things up — you say one thing —" She shrugs. "We don't want Maximilian to get in trouble for getting us drunk."

Hazel laughed. "We shouldn't be working at a speakeasy during Prohibition if having a few snorts is a problem."

"I don't like coppers, neither," Colethea said. "All this talk about what we drank and when we left makes it seem like we don't care about a man's death. The whole bloody mess is giving me palpitations." She swallowed. "I still say we do like Honoree wants."

Hazel sighed. "Fine. I won't say nothin'."

Honoree took Colethea's hand. "Long as we stick together, everything will be fine."

Hazel waved her pack of Wrigley's Spearmint. "Y'all want a piece of gum?"

"I do," said Colethea.

"First, I want both of you to swear." Honoree looked from girl to girl. "We've gotta tell the same story."

Hazel passed a stick of gum to Colethea. "All right. All right. I swear."

Unwrapping her gum, Colethea nodded. "Me, too."

"Thank you. Thank you very much," Honoree said. "I'll take some of that gum now."

CHAPTER 16
HONOREE

No sooner than Honoree had confirmed Polka Dots and Finger Waves would tell the same story, four people walked through the swinging doors into the kitchen.

A dark-skinned man in a double-breasted suit led the way, along with two police officers and Zelda, who didn't look as stately in her green taffeta as the night before in red.

"I'm William Buttons, the owner of the Dreamland Cafe," said the man in the suit. "We had a terrible thing happen this morning. George 'Houdini' Mills, one of our barkeeps for the past four years, was shot to death in the dance hall."

A loud gasp shot through the room, the expected reaction to the words *shot to death.* Even if, like Honoree, they knew about the killing.

"Let's bow our heads for a brief prayer for the dearly departed, Houdini. A jovial young man who loved to share his passion for whiskey and good food." Mr. Buttons smiled. "His Sunday cookouts made us family, and his gumbo will be remembered for many years to come."

That got a chuckle from the crowd, but Zelda waved a firm hand, and the room silenced. "May the Lord bless and keep George in his loving arms," she said.

Heads bowed. A chorus of *amen*s rang through the kitchen. Mr. Buttons's benediction was the loudest and the last. "These two police officers of the Race are investigating the murder and need our help," he said, without showing the slightest concern about cops in a hooch-serving nightclub like the Dreamland. "This is Officer Joseph MacDonald and Officer Carter Weatherspoon from the Second Ward Precinct."

Officer MacDonald stepped forward. "We're here to ask you questions about the shooting this morning." The shorter of the two coppers had a dimpled chin, giving him the appearance of a kinder man, even when he frowned. "We'll begin interviews right off."

Honoree removed her cigarettes from her purse. A puff or two would loosen the knot in her chest.

"Most of you didn't leave the cafe until late, according to Mr. Buttons and Mrs.

Hunter," said Officer MacDonald. "You may have seen or heard something — you might not even realize its importance, but it could help our investigation."

Then his tone changed. "Until further notice, while we investigate Mr. Mills's murder, the Dreamland Cafe has been closed by the commissioner of police. I trust you all will be forthcoming. The longer it takes to find Houdini's killer, the longer the Dreamland will remain closed."

Shut down. Closed. Honoree took hold of Colethea's arm to keep her balance. If not for the room full of people, she would've dropped to her knees and wept.

The officer continued. "Understand that everything said during these interviews will be held in confidence until the court date." He pointed around the room. "I assure you. No one will learn about what you say to us today. Retaliation will not be a concern. You will be safe."

Colethea nudged Honoree and whispered, "If not a concern, why mention it?"

Honoree agreed. "Colored people don't retaliate. They take care of business right on the spot."

"I can't believe they closed the Dreamland Cafe," Colethea said.

Hazel patted her on the back. "A man was

just killed in Mr. Buttons's establishment. He can't go back to selling hooch and having half-naked chorus girls prancing about. Wouldn't be respectful. Just wait and see. The cafe will open back up in a few days."

"It better." Colethea sighed. "I have a baby to feed and a man to keep from gambling away the rent money."

"You girls hush up. We ain't finished." Zelda shot hard eyes in their direction.

Mr. Buttons thanked the officers and gave instructions to those gathered. He and the taller officer would lead the musicians and waiters to the dining hall.

Honoree followed Colethea and Hazel.

Seconds later, they lined up behind Zelda and Officer MacDonald in front of Zelda's office.

"Y'all will meet with the copper in my office, one at a time," Zelda said. "The rest of you will wait in the hallway until I call you."

MacDonald opened the office door and gestured for Zelda to lead the way. Then he closed the door behind him.

A dozen girls lined the hall outside Zelda's office. Honoree, Colethea, and Hazel stayed near the top of the staircase.

"I thought the cop wanted to get started in a hurry." Colethea held Honoree's hand. "What are they doing in there?"

"Hold your horses." Hazel leaned into her hip. "Can't rush a copper. Learned that from one of my sugar daddies."

Colethea poked her in the shoulder. "Why you make a joke out of everything? The barkeep was shot a few minutes after we left. We were awful close to getting killed ourselves."

"Hush your mouth," Honoree said in a hard whisper, looking around. "Remember, we were long gone by the time Houdini was killed. Don't forget. Long gone."

Zelda opened the door and stepped into the hall. "Officer MacDonald is ready to begin."

More than two hours passed before it was Honoree's turn. Even Colethea and Hazel talked to the officer before her. Each girl had sworn to keep their promise, which Honoree had no choice but to believe as she entered Zelda's office.

The sweet, floral smell struck her immediately. Zelda had to keep a jug of rosewater somewhere. Its scent filled the room.

MacDonald stopped scribbling on the sheet of paper in front of him but didn't look up. "Have a seat."

Honoree sat in the chair and folded her hands in her lap.

"You were one of the three girls from the audition who stayed late to sign contracts."

"Yes, sir."

"What time did you leave?"

"Before three o'clock."

"Who was with you?"

"Colethea and Hazel."

"Colethea Johnson and Hazel Reeves."

"Um, I guess, yes. I — I don't recall their surnames."

"The three of you left together after you finished in Mrs. Hunter's office?"

"Mrs. Hunter, sir?"

He jabbed the paper with his pencil but didn't break the point. "This office. Zelda's office."

"Yes, sir," she said through dry lips. "We changed into our street clothes and left right after."

He looked up, and Honoree swallowed a gasp. His eyes were the color of dark honey. They were lovely eyes that didn't fit with his weathered face. "Where did you change?"

"In the rehearsal room, a few doors from where the audition took place."

He wrote something down. Short questions, short answers. If this continued, she might be able to get through it, except her mouth felt like it was full of Miss Hattie's

192

sawdust.

"How about Ezekiel Bailey? Can you tell me the last time you ran into him?"

Her body went rigid; every bone, muscle, and drop of blood froze in its place. Lord. Lord. Lord. What had Ezekiel gone and done?

"Miss Dalcour? Do you know Ezekiel Bailey?"

She sucked in a big gulp of air and exhaled slowly, hoping to loosen the suddenly cramped muscles in her throat. She didn't care if the copper noticed. She had to keep from choking on her fear. "My family used to work for his family." The smartest way to tell a lie was to include a piece of the truth. "That was a few years back."

"When was the last time you saw him?"

"Friday night at Miss Hattie's Garden Cafe."

"Last night?"

"Yes, sir."

"How long was he at Miss Hattie's?"

"When I left, he was still there."

"And you haven't seen him since?"

She crossed her legs. "No, sir. Not since I left just before midnight. When I headed across town to the Dreamland for the audition."

She rubbed her palms on the skirt of her

shift. "Why are you asking about Mr. Bailey?"

"You aren't the one asking questions today, young lady," Officer MacDonald said without rancor.

"Just wondering, sir. Hate to think the son of my family's former employer had something to do with a shooting."

Officer MacDonald placed the tip of his pencil between his teeth, watching her for a long, uneasy moment before he spoke. "How well did you know Mr. Mills?"

Honoree's foot started shaking, and she uncrossed her legs. "I had never met the man. That's why I don't understand why you're asking me these questions —"

"You have no idea why someone might want to kill him?"

She took a deep breath. "Nope. Last night was my first time inside the Dreamland Cafe, and after the audition, I left with my new friends. Sorry, but I can't help you."

The officer studied her face with honey-colored eyes. "Are you sure?"

"Yes, sir. I mean no, sir. I can't help you. I'm positive."

He dropped his pencil. "We're done, then. You can leave."

"Thank you." She stood and backed away, nodding goodbye, and then turned and fled

Zelda's office. The faster and farther away she got from Officer MacDonald, the better.

It didn't take long for Honoree to return to the neighborhood and head to Mr. Turner's Grocery Store. She stood in the canned goods aisle with a sweaty brow and damp armpits, staring at a shelf of Campbell's pork and beans. Thing was, she couldn't rightly recall if she had one or two cans of beans in her cupboard. Guess she had a good reason for her memory being all foggy.

She'd seen a man gunned down, had lied to coppers, and the Dreamland Cafe had shuttered its doors. That constituted enough rough times for a lifetime. She deserved a night off.

She dug into her purse, found a penny, and walked over to the cash register. The idea of returning to Miss Hattie's and having to deal with Archie made her want to wretch.

"Good afternoon, Mr. Turner," she greeted him.

"Honoree." He was a portly man who wore thick glasses but always had a friendly smile.

She handed him a penny. "Could you dial up Miss Hattie's Garden Cafe?"

"You've been busy lately," he said, dialing.

Then he passed her the receiver.

"What is it, Honoree?" Miss Dolly snapped, already irritated.

Honoree coughed and sniffled, selling the act. "I can't work tonight. I have a stomach illness and been upchucking all day."

"Still feel poorly from last night, huh?" Miss Dolly's tone was surprisingly sympathetic. "You might have the Spanish flu."

"I don't have a fever."

"Uh-huh." Miss Dolly's breathing changed to take a drag from a cigarette. "A bartender got shot and killed at the Dreamland Cafe. Gunned down like a common hoodlum."

Miss Dolly paused again, inhaling her cig. "Between Al Capone's Outfit and Hymie Weiss's North Side gang, working at a jazz joint during Prohibition, even one in Bronzeville, is risky business."

Miss Dolly went silent, not smoking, only quiet. "I hope you don't have the flu, but you best be back at work tomorrow if you want your job."

She hung up.

"You didn't seem that sickly when you walked in," Mr. Turner said, narrow eyes judging her.

Honoree lowered her head, a touch of shame putting a flutter in her stomach. "A

196

lot is going on in my life, Mr. Turner." She felt obligated to explain. "I couldn't go to work tonight."

"Known you since you were a baby in your mother's arms."

"I don't remember my mother carrying me."

"Don't get snippy," he said with a smile. "I'm only saying that whatever is going on, you shouldn't be telling fibs. A lie will catch up with you."

"Not if I get good at it," she said with a small smile.

Mr. Turner pushed his glasses up on his nose. "I thought you were a better girl than that, Honoree. Your papa wouldn't be pleased."

"Don't worry about me. I'll be back on the job tomorrow. You have a proper evening."

As she left the store, a newsboy stood on the corner. "Wanna buy a paper, ma'am?"

"Yes, I do." She handed him a nickel and, standing in the middle of the sidewalk, rifled through the pages, searching for the posting of the winning policy numbers.

Hot damn! She found the numbers on the sports page. Eighty-seven betting slips — all of them winners! She could be wealthy if she cashed them in — something she couldn't do.

She hurried home to the kitchenette and went to her mother's Singer sewing machine. There was the tall stack of wicker baskets — all shapes and sizes, filled with rhinestones and tassels. Near the bottom was the heart-shaped wicker basket with the envelope.

Honoree placed a hand over her heart as another round of nerves sped through her body. A herd of wild beasts stampeded across her chest. She couldn't catch her breath.

Sewing calmed her nerves; sewing, and stitching, and cutting out patterns. A new dress with tassels and beads and a plunging neckline could go a long way in healing her mind, body, and soul.

She searched through the stack and found a few yards of gold lamé and a yard or two of gold lace. Not the expensive material sold at Marshall Field's, but that didn't matter. She could make artificial silk look like diamonds and pearls with her eyes closed.

Sitting cross-legged on the floor, she cut the pattern using old newspapers. Occasionally she uncrossed her legs and stretched them out in front of her. The aches and pains from sewing were a decent kind of tired. Just like wearing a new dress would help her feel better, or not as bad, about returning to Miss Hattie's Garden Cafe.

CHAPTER 17
SAWYER

Sunday, June 21, 2015

The next day, I'm at the vending machine, banging my fist lightly on the side of the snack-filled metal box. I have a decision to make — Reese's Peanut Butter Cups, Three Musketeers, or Snickers.

"I'm sorry about this morning, Sawyer, but she's still tired and doesn't want to see anyone now. But maybe she'll feel better later today and change her mind." Lula stands beside me, where she's been for a few minutes, explaining why I will not be admitted to Honoree's room.

I don't bother to threaten her with the mighty Mrs. Hendrickson. Lula is resolute, and I'm gun-shy about my Maggie deception. Still, I'm not happy.

"She'll be in a better frame of mind tomorrow," Lula says unconvincingly. "I'm sure."

"Didn't you say that yesterday?" Feeling a

surge of panic, I admit the obvious. "I won't be able to finish my project if I keep tripping over land mines with her." I push a dollar bill into the slot. "I did what she asked. I told her something about myself, and all was good — until I mentioned the house in Baton Rouge."

Lula leans against the vending machine. "That did rile her up. She was still talking about it when I brought her dinner last night."

"Do you know why?" I ask.

"I'm clueless," she replies. "Why don't you ask your grandmother?"

Perfect timing for me to hem and haw since Maggie has no idea about my trip to Chicago. "Maggie's eighty-nine years old and not spry like Honoree. I would rather not bother her, if possible."

"Maggie?" Lula looks shocked.

"Yeah. I call my grandmother by her first name." I don't linger on this subject. "Do you remember anyone else asking Miss Honoree about Baton Rouge?"

"Does she live alone? Is there someone you can call to ask her?"

I hesitate to tell her the reason I can't call my grandmother. "Maggie and I don't talk."

"How's that?"

"Not on the telephone and rarely in

person. Remember, I said she's not as lively as Honoree. She has a nurse who takes care of her. A nurse who was kind enough to let me into the house so I could help pack up her things, and I'm the only family member who keeps in touch with her."

Lula nods. "So you lied about her giving you permission to come here and talk to Miss Honoree?"

Damn. She had nailed me. "I exaggerated. She probably wouldn't have minded if I'd asked, but she can't answer the Baton Rouge question, even if I had cleared things with her first."

I wave my hand dramatically. "Maybe someone else knows what happened in Baton Rouge."

Lula sighs. "She's been in Chicago so long I thought she'd been here all her life. I think everyone did."

I tear the wrapper off the Reese's. "Not staff, then, how about her visitors? One of them may have some information about Baton Rouge."

"In the three years I've worked here, Miss Honoree has had only one visitor. That was more than a year ago."

"Who was it? Do you have a name?"

"I wasn't here that day. I remember because it was the talk of the floor for a week.

He was African American, middle-aged."
She grinned. "They said he was memorable.
Tall and handsome." She bit her lower lip.
"If someone visited her before I started here
— we should check the records, which
aren't that good and would only go back a
few years — I could ask my aunt Deidre."

"Why your aunt?"

"She's a registered nurse, among her other
degrees, and worked here for several years
before me. And before her, my mother,
brother, and grandmother worked here, but
she worked with Miss Honoree."

Lula is staring at my Reese's Peanut Butter Cup. "You want one?" I ask.

"Sure."

I give her a cup and feel a connection over
our shared passion for chocolate and peanut
butter. "If you don't mind me asking, what's
the deal with you and your family working
here?"

She takes a bite and holds up a finger. I
nod with an understanding smile and wait
for her to swallow.

"Members of my family have worked here
for decades, since Miss Honoree arrived in
1985." Lula smiles. "I like to think of the
Kents as Honoree's adopted family."

"Pretty remarkable your family's dedica-
tion to senior care." I put another dollar in

the machine. "Maybe I can interview some of them for my thesis."

"I'm not sure Honoree would like any of us telling you what we may or may not know about her. I think you've noticed she prefers to strike deals first and talk later."

"Honoree's story may be hers to tell," I begin, "but I don't think she would mind if you and your family helped her tell it — do you?"

She sighs heavily. "Honestly, I think she would."

"Now, tell me who died."

It's later the same afternoon and only three minutes into my conversation with Honoree, and I'm ready to walk. Christ. Who died? She wants me to recount the deaths in my family. Why? For entertainment? I respect that she's elderly. I do, but damn. She's not crazy. She's not senile. Her question is morbid and cruel, and again, I want to ask, *Why?*

"Did you hear me?"

I scrub my hands over my face. I need a damn shave, and I also think she's still pissed about the Baton Rouge thingy.

"Sawyer? You heard me. Who died?"

"Yes, ma'am." Relentless is her middle name. I exhale my free will into thin air and decide just to answer the damn question. "My mother passed when I was twelve."

Closing her eyes, Honoree presses lips together as a trace of sadness etches through her features.

"Are you okay?" I ask.

"What?" Her eyes open. " 'Course I am. So, your mother died. What killed her? Cancer? An accident?"

"This is morbid," I say. "But it was cancer."

She nods. "Vile disease. Had it twice in my long life."

I dig into my backpack, praying that we're done with this line of questioning.

"Your father isn't dead, but how about anyone else?"

Christ. The word *relentless* cannot be underused with her. "Since you won't let this topic go," I say with as little emotion as humanly possible, "my sister, Azizi, died in March 2014 in a car crash."

I glare at her, but pity deepens the lines in her face. "I'm sorry for your loss."

"I am, too." I say this matter-of-factly, but the accuracy of my words could split the San Andreas.

"I thought the law made people wear seat belts these days."

"Yeah," I say slowly, unsure of where she's

going with this even if coincidentally, she's right. "Azizi had unbuckled her seat belt."

In the corner of my eye, the glimmer that is Azizi turns.

"I was driving," I blurt. "We'd been talking, and she reached in the back seat and —"

"You got hit then. After she took off her seat belt."

"Yes, and what in the hell is your fixation on seat belts?" I rub my fingers over my eyes, careful not to push too hard out of frustration. "Do you mind if we change the subject? Can we go back to Oscar Micheaux?"

"I met him a few times, at parties, mostly. He was mighty loud. Always trying to get people to be in his films. That picture was taken by a neighbor outside the Dreamland Cafe."

My ears are buzzing. Azizi is standing next to the bed with her feet in fourth position, torso erect, arms set, plié, and go — pirouette after pirouette, and the nightmare returns.

Hands on the wheel. Hands over my hands. Azizi lies on the side of the road, legs crushed, arms broken.

I can't. I just can't. I try, but my calves are cramping, and I nearly hit the floor.

"What's wrong?" Honoree asks.

"Nothing, keep talking."

"You're acting strange," she says, stating what I consider the obvious. "You keep staring at me, above me, around me, like you are lookin' for something I should be saying, but you can't find it or —" She pauses dramatically. "Is there someone in the room you want to talk to?"

A chill runs up my legs, caterpillars on the backs of dragons. How does she know? My vision tunnels, the room closes in, and I'm pulling barbed wire through my lungs instead of oxygen. Christ, I'm going to lose it. "Miss Honoree, can we talk about Micheaux tomorrow? I need to leave."

"Where do you have to go? I thought you came here to see me."

"I'm sorry. I wish I could explain." I grab my backpack.

"I'm not surprised you can't keep a promise."

I am halfway down the hall. I arrive at the elevator bank and punch the button. Okay. Okay. O-fucking-kay.

I am not losing it, and I won't let them — Honoree or Azizi — defeat me.

The elevator doors open, and I step inside. My brain is humming, repeating my new mantra.

Honoree is the story. Honoree is the key. I grip the railing.

Ghost or no ghost. Honoree's questions or not. The only thing that matters is the thesis. The only thing that matters is finishing the film — but Honoree is the key.

I look up at the roof of the elevator, expecting to see Azizi floating above me, and I want to scream at her for reminding me what I didn't do and what I can't get past. Christ. Give me a freaking break. As if I could forget.

CHAPTER 18
HONOREE

Monday, October 26, 1925

Honoree swept into Miss Hattie's an hour before showtime, hips swinging, hair freshly pressed and curled, makeup just right. She looked like she didn't have a care in the world. She was young and pretty and dressed in her new gold lamé shift, slit to the middle of her thigh, and everything was jake, except everything wasn't jake at all.

It was a typical Monday night. King Johnny and his band were wailing, and the cafe was full of railroad workers and hoofers, dancing hard and kicking up so much sawdust, Honoree couldn't wipe the grit from her eyes fast enough.

"Hey, Pete," she said, putting on a happy face as she eased into an open spot at the bar. "How you feelin'?"

"You okay, Honoree? You don't look so good."

"I'm fine. Just here to do my job."

"Strange things happening at Miss Hattie's these days." His voice was heavy. He knew more bad news than good. "You better watch yourself. I got a feelin', Honoree. Things ain't right around here."

"As if they ever have been, Pete."

A pogo stick that looked like Bessie was jumping and waving from the other end of the bar. "I love your dress," she shouted as she drew closer.

"I should've expected you to be the first girl I saw tonight. Why are you here so early?"

Bessie squeezed in next to Honoree. "Miss Dolly gave me an extra job. I have to clean up the cafe every day." Suddenly, Bessie hugged Honoree around the shoulders. "I'm so glad you're here. I thought for sure I'd never see you again. I figured you would be dancing at the Dreamland Cafe."

Honoree scanned the nearby faces, but no one seemed to have overheard. "Don't say anything to anybody about the Dreamland Cafe," she whispered.

Bessie looked at her with hurt feelings. "I'm sorry, but I wouldn't mention it to anyone else, I swear — but did you get the job?"

Honoree bit her tongue to keep from cursing. "Oh my God. I just said don't talk —"

210

"I won't, but that don't mean I can't talk to you about it, does it?"

Shaking her head, Honoree pulled a cigarette from her purse. Then she signaled Pete. "Gin, with all the fixings and make that twice as much gin."

"Guess what? I talked to Virginia," Bessie said, tugging on one of her coarse curls. "She's gonna fix my hair Wednesday night."

"Isn't that nice of her." She wished Bessie would hush. Being back at Miss Hattie's had put Honoree in the vilest mood that not even a new dress could fix.

Pete placed a large glass of gin in front of her.

"Thank you."

"I took your advice," Bessie said.

"What advice?"

"I quit that man who was hitting me."

Honoree chugged half her gin in one gulp, burning her throat as if she'd swallowed kerosene. She blinked back tears. "Good for you," she said, though she didn't mean it. What did she care about Bessie's troubles when she had so many of her own?

Bessie was standing next to her, swinging her hips, with a genuinely happy smile on her face. So bright, Honoree smiled back despite herself.

"The only problem," Bessie began, "is he

kicked me out — but with Miss Dolly having me clean up the cafe every day, I have to be here early, so I just don't leave."

Suddenly Bessie gasped in delight. A hand covered her mouth, while the other one grabbed Honoree. "Look! Look at Trudy! Is she wearing a mink coat? And that dress. A mighty fine dress. And so short — I can see her knees."

Honoree glanced and promptly glanced away, not wanting to catch Trudy's eye. But there she was all right, flopping into the cafe in a beaver coat, not mink, and a department-store dress.

"I don't give a never mind about her," she said, removing Bessie's hand from her arm. "You spent the night at Miss Hattie's without getting caught?"

Bessie faced her. "All night long. In the basement, but nobody saw me sneak in." She smiled at Trudy. "Her dress is almost as pretty as yours."

"It must be later than I thought," Honoree said abruptly. "We should get going." She gulped down the rest of her drink.

Bessie pouted. "We still got a little time before the show."

"I said, let's go, Bessie, or stay. I don't care. I'm leaving."

■ ■ ■ ■

Honoree didn't leave right away. Trudy had
marched into the storage room behind the
bar, the only entrance to the stairwell leading to the basement dressing room, and
Honoree didn't want to run into her. Not
just yet.

Ezekiel may have done as he'd promised
and set Trudy straight about the envelope,
but Honoree didn't want to learn otherwise
in a back room filled with bottles, glasses,
and plates.

"Why are we waiting?" Bessie asked. "I
thought you were in a hurry."

"I'm thinking." Honoree was stalling.
Then after a few minutes, when it was safe,
she headed downstairs with Bessie on her
heels.

They reached the dressing room, but
Honoree stopped Bessie from opening the
door.

"Why aren't we going inside?"

"I'm eavesdropping." Honoree could
swear Miss Dolly had mentioned Houdini's
name. "Miss Dolly is yapping about the
Dreamland Cafe, talking like she was there
and watched him die."

"Watched who die?"

"Hush. It doesn't matter." Honoree shoved the door open. "Evening, ladies."

"Look at you in your fancy dress." Edna Mae scooted around on her crate, eyeballing Honoree from head to toe. "If that slit were any higher, you'd have to shave your bush."

"Why are you so rude?" Bessie circled by Honoree, hopping down the steps.

"Hush your mouths," Miss Dolly said. "And don't interrupt me again. I'm telling the story about that killing Saturday morning." She took a drag from her cigarette. "As I was saying, the barkeep was shot in the face. And it took him an hour to die."

"How do you know how long it took?" Trudy stood in the doorway, lighting a cigarette. Where had she been?

Miss Dolly gave Trudy the side-eye. "If another one of y'all interrupts me again, I swear to God."

"Tell me, how long did it take for him to die? Were you there?" Trudy stomped down the steps, her eyes blazing, or were they merely red-rimmed? Had she been crying?

Trudy stopped a foot away from Miss Dolly with her lips trembling. "A man shot like him doesn't take an hour to die. They don't lay there cockeyed like in a cinema. Their body flails like a fish with a hook in

214

its mouth."

Trudy was right, Honoree thought. That was the kind of jerking and shaking she saw her father do when he was struck by the automobile. He twisted and turned, fighting against death until his life seeped into the dirt like warm honey. But it surely didn't take an hour for him to die.

"The newspaper said there were not any witnesses," Edna Mae said.

"I don't care about no newspaper. Word on the street is enough for me," Miss Dolly said, smearing on eyeliner. "People lie to cops and reporters all the time."

Virginia wiggled her fingers, causing heads to turn her way. "I hearsay Mr. Buttons didn't leave the cafe until after four o'clock. He might've seen who shot the barkeep."

"What I heard, too," Miss Dolly continued. "Mr. Buttons was there late enough to hear the gunfire."

"That barkeep was a big man," Virginia said. "Probably took a couple of men to kill him."

"I wish to heaven y'all would shut the hell up." Trudy's voice crackled with rage.

"What's wrong with you?" Edna Mae said. "There's no need to yell at us."

"Y'all are like a pack of hungry bobcats chasing a squirrel, talking any ol' way about

215

a dead man. Let him rest in peace."

Miss Dolly flicked two fingers at Trudy. "A man got gunned down at a nightclub, and we work at a nightclub. It seems worth our time to chat about it. Maybe we can help stop trouble from coming here."

Trudy glared at Miss Dolly with an expression of total disbelief. "You don't give a damn about the barkeep or trouble at Miss Hattie's. You just enjoy flapping your gums about somebody else's misery."

Trudy lit a cigarette, her trembles gone. "Did any of you ever meet George 'Houdini' Mills? That was his name, you know. Did you ever dance with him on a Sunday at the Dusty Bottom? Did he ever cook you a pot of his mother's recipe for chicken stew? He was a man, a kind man, a good man who treated people like human beings and knew what it meant to be a friend."

The room was dead quiet. Honoree had never heard Trudy speak so earnestly about anything or anybody.

"I am so sorry," Virginia said, sympathy in every syllable. "We didn't know you knew him."

"He was a brother to me," Trudy said hoarsely.

Miss Dolly snorted. "I thought you only liked white men with names like Hymie.

Never knew a fat Negro boy to turn away from trouble."

There was a flurry of movement, but luckily, Edna Mae was close enough to grab Trudy before she reached Miss Dolly. "How dare you! You have no right to say things like that. No right!"

Trudy squirmed out of Edna Mae's grasp. "Leave me be. I ain't gonna hurt her. Not right now." She opened her hands and shook them, releasing her rage into the air. "Got bigger chickens to fry than to get into a bitch brawl with a has-been who never was."

"Who you talking about?" Miss Dolly leaped to her feet, her chair tumbling to the floor behind her. "I will slap you into next Monday."

Trudy stood still with a hand of defiance fisted on her hip. "Miss Dolly ain't nobody to be afraid of. She's just another one of Archie's castoffs. He found someone new to run his cafe."

A spattering of voices droning *Lord have mercy* swept the room. Even Honoree moved her crate a few inches, out of harm's way, expecting a scratching, hair-pulling fight to commence.

But nothing happened. Trudy's words of truth about Archie, which Honoree suspected referred to Ezekiel, had taken the fire out of Miss Dolly. She righted her chair and sat, and, without speaking, began polishing her makeup for the show.

Trudy had not moved. She just stood there, chest heaving for a long moment, until she turned and headed toward Honoree.

"What is it?" Honoree asked.

Trudy stood over her, doing nothing except lighting a cigarette and blowing smoke.

"What do you want?" Honoree repeated.

"Why'd you do it?" Trudy whispered.

"Why'd I do what?"

"Don't lie to me." Trudy crouched down on one knee next to her so that nobody could overhear. "Why didn't you give Houdini the envelope?"

"I did give him the envelope."

"No, you didn't. He got shot because he didn't have what he was supposed to have."

"You asked me to deliver it, and I did as you asked."

Trudy dug a fingernail into Honoree's thigh. "You're a liar."

"And if you don't get your hands off me —"

"Stop jawing, you two." Miss Dolly had gotten up from her seat. "It's showtime."

"You heard her." Honoree stood and moved away from Trudy. "We've got a show to do."

"You heard her." Honoree stood and
moved away from Trudy. "We've got a show
to do.

CHAPTER 19
HONOREE

The Rock Island railroad boys kept the
chorus girls busy until well past the last
show, demanding rotgut by the pint and
passing out dollar bills by the fistful to sit in
their laps.

Honoree avoided Trudy the rest of the
evening, and as soon as she found the right
moment, she slipped downstairs and dressed
in a hurry.

Crossing in front of the bar, heading
home, and leaving Trudy Lewis and her
troubles behind her, Honoree was heading
home until Crazy Pete called after her.

"Archie wants to see you in his office."

"What for?" she asked, stopping in her
tracks.

"Your girl done ratted on you."

No doubt he meant Trudy. "What did she
tell him?"

Pete was wiping down the bar, cleaning
up spilled hooch. He gripped the rag in his

fist and braced himself against the bar. "I believe it had to do with you not being sick the other night. Said you went to an audition at the Dreamland Cafe."

A thousand pins pricked her flesh. "And that is what Trudy told Archie?"

Her body stiffened. "Is Archie mad?"

"Archie? Mad?" Pete gave her the side-eye. "I warned you, Honoree, you know how Archie can be."

"Lord Jesus." That she did. That she did indeed.

Archie's office was in the back of the cafe, near the kitchen, in a small room with a desk, a couple of chairs, a moldy Persian rug, and two of Kenny's paintings nailed to the wall. Holding a stinky cigar and a glass of whiskey, he sat behind an oak desk, looking like a large black bear in a cloud of smoke.

"Have a seat," he grumbled.

Obediently, Honoree lowered herself into the armchair on the opposite side of his desk. But she twisted her torso at an angle, placing an elbow on the chair's bridge to show off the mound of her breast. Then she crossed her leg, revealing as much of her upper thigh as the skirt's slit allowed. "Pete said you wanted to see me."

221

Archie took in every inch of her poise. His bulbous eyes ogled her, but not like she was meat. There was something else on his mind. "How are you? Feeling better?"

"Feeling just fine."

He watched her over the rim of his glass, a dangerous glint in his eye. He might not be yelling, just yet, but it had to be on its way. Why else ask to see her?

"You wanna snort? Good whiskey."

Common sense advised her not to refuse. "Sure, I'll have a drink."

A square crystal decanter and matching glasses rested on a tarnished silver platter. Archie filled a glass and passed it to her, but her nerves were fragile, and she blurted, "I know what Trudy told you."

Archie rolled a cigar between his thumb and forefinger. "Trudy mentioned that the other night you took off for an audition."

Honoree uncrossed her legs and adjusted the slit to hide her thighs. "What happened the other night doesn't matter. I'm here now. You don't need to be mad. When I got the invitation, I decided to go to the audition, so there'd be no bad blood between you and Mr. Buttons."

He laughed. "So, as a kindness to me, you convinced Trudy to take your place, lied about being sick, and went to an audition to help me avoid trouble with William Buttons. How thoughtful, Honoree."

"You're welcome, Archie."

The swivel chair creaked as he pitched forward. "Friday night, I saw you on the dance floor. You and my policy wheel operator. You two know each other well, don't you?"

"Are you talking about Ezekiel?"

"Who else have I seen you dancing with, other than a line of chorus girls?"

"You got it wrong, Archie. Didn't Ezekiel explain?"

"I didn't ask him. I'm asking you."

This was not the conversation Honoree had expected. Archie acted like he was stuck on her. "My parents worked for his parents, and we met each other when we were children. The only thing between us is the past. Years ago."

"Liar." He picked up his burning cigar from the ashtray. But his fingers twitched, and uncertainty staggered his speech. What was going on with him? He blew a cloud of smoke. "Telling lies is in your blood."

"I don't lie."

Archie lowered his head, collecting himself it seemed. Was he speaking the truth? Did Archie care about her?

When he looked up, his eyes were bloodshot and unquestionably sad. "You were necking on the dance floor, but you say there's nothing between you and Ezekiel." He chugged his drink and poured another. "That boy wants to fuck you. And almost did in front of my customers and me —"

"Don't use that kind of language. I hate that word. And you're wrong. He was drunk, and — and I told him to keep his hands off me, and he did."

A vein in Archie's forehead became as thick as a piece of rope. "You do me a disservice, Honoree. Always have. Been stuck on you since I found you in the trunk of my automobile. All the things I've done for you, I did because of how I feel about you."

Honoree sank into her seat. "You don't care about me, not that way. You care about making money and policy gambling. You and I laid together three times two years ago — and haven't talked about it since. Christ, Archie, you trust me to fix the math in your accounting books and to dance on your stage six nights a week, but that's all there is between us."

"Look at you. Got me all figured out. We started in a bad way. I know that, but things have changed."

"Damn it, Archie. You hit me. Slapped me across the face when I told you I no longer needed your help with my rent. I made enough money dancing to pay my bills." She gripped the arms of the chair. "That got you mad enough to slam the spit out of my mouth."

"Sure. I lost my temper, but I could've fired you." He walked around the desk and stood in front of her. "The way you two were hugged up, brought back memories. Memories of me being the one you used to wrap your arms around." He sat on the edge of the desk. "I ain't got no control over my memories."

He sipped his drink. "I didn't need Trudy telling me one goddamn thing about that audition. I knew."

"What do you mean you knew about the audition?"

"The news reached Miss Hattie's from the Stroll that afternoon. When you left Friday night, I called Will Buttons and made a deal upfront."

"What kind of deal?" Honoree said weakly.

"A simple deal. Buttons agreed to a loan. If they hired you, he'd introduce me to the right people in exchange for you dancing at the Dreamland for a while." He chuckled. "And don't give me those large sad eyes, sugar. You should've known getting away from me wouldn't be that easy."

The emptiness inside her belly, her chest, was a valley of dead leaves. Up and down. Every time she had a shot at the good, the bad was on its heels. And now, Archie was telling her the unbelievable.

A sudden laugh spewed from his lips.

"What's so funny?" She rose from her chair, needing to feel solid ground under both of her feet. "What the hell is so funny?"

"I'm not telling you shit until you sit down."

"No." She stepped toward the desk.

"Sit down, or I'll break your leg."

Trembling, she lowered herself into the chair. And this was how he showed his love. "Thank you."

Choking down his laugh, he cocked his head at her. "For what?"

"For showing me the Archie I know."

Archie crossed the distance between them and seized her by the shoulders. "I do care for you."

"Let go. You're hurting me."

He released her, and she fell limply against the bridge of the chair. "You belong to me. I decide what happens to you."

He turned his back and walked around his desk, leaving her shaking.

"Don't you worry," Archie said. "The Dreamland will reopen soon. You'll get your chance on the big stage. Then you'll be back at Miss Hattie's by Valentine's Day." He smiled, the sadness returning to his eyes. "You're too much of a crowd-pleaser, Honoree. Too much of a showgirl. I could never give you up for too long."

He wiped his Chaplin mustache with a finger. "Go on, now, girlie. Skedaddle. I'll see you tomorrow."

CHAPTER 20
SAWYER

Monday, June 22, 2015

Five o'clock in the morning, I lie in bed, blinking at the laser-bright light coming from the nightstand and the stream of pings coming from my phone. Without looking, I know the text messages blowing up my cell are from my father. It's midday in Paris, but the man is oblivious to time zones.

He's lost any polite concern over waking me. Although, I have not slept in over a year — and likely neither has he, but still.

Another ping.

Should I give the old man a break and reply to his text? If I don't respond, he'll be on the next flight from Paris to Chicago — or flapping his arms and proving, once and for all, that man can fly.

Sitting upright, I switch on the lamp on the nightstand, pick up my cell, and read the messages.

Dad: You awake? How was your flight?

How's California?

Me: I'm not in California. I'm in Chicago for a few days, doing some research for the film.

Dad: I know several curators at the Chicago History Museum who could help you.

Me: I'm cross-referencing some facts on Micheaux and Armstrong in the 1920s. Final-pass stuff. I don't need help.

Should I tell him about Honoree? Or the crate in Maggie's attic? He might already know about it, but he and Maggie were never close, not even when my mother was alive.

Me: I am interviewing a 110-year-old-woman who knew Micheaux. Can you believe it?

I wait for the dots — but see nothing.

Me: She's the last of a kind. No one else is around who remembers the 1920s — at least no one I know. And she's lucid — has all her wits about her.

The dots. Then finally . . .

Dad: Can you trust what she's telling you? Doesn't sound like someone I'd want to stake my thesis on.

"Not your thesis, Dad," I say aloud, but I don't type those words.

Dad: I hope she doesn't disappoint you. I would hate for you to spend the summer being led down a primrose path.

What in the hell is a primrose path?

229

Me: I know what I'm doing.
Dots.
Dad: Have you been in touch with your adviser? If the elderly woman doesn't pan out, let me know, and I'll put you in touch with some professional researchers.

Dig. Dig. Dig. Why can't he ease up? What's his deal? Drilling me about this, that, or the other. Back off.

"You back off," I say, staring at the screen of my cell.

Me: I've done my research. I'm not a screwup, Dad. I'm not unreliable. Last year, I had a reason for not finishing the project, if you remember.

Dots.
Dad: I don't think of you as unreliable.

Shit. The dots. The damn dots.

Here it comes. Here it comes. My dear dad is about to throw his grief for his dead daughter and disappointment in his pill-popping son in my face.

Dad: Sawyer, it's hard for me, too. I'm sorry about what happened in Paris. You did good work, and I should've said so to your face.

Dad: You still there?

I let him watch the dots for a minute longer.

Me: No problem. I'm good. But I need to go. I want to get in a run before Chicago turns into an oven.

Dad: I'll text you later. We should touch base regularly. I want to keep abreast of your progress. OK?

Fuck. Stop worrying! I wasn't trying to kill myself. You don't need to watch over me.

Me: Yeah, sure. Every day.

I don't bother to wait for any more dots. I put down the phone on the nightstand, crawl back into bed, and look at the dresser.

Nearby, Azizi leans against the wall; her legs crossed at the ankles, her head tilted to the side, exposing her long neck. She told me once about the esthetic of a long throat and sinewy arms, and how they enhance the beauty of a ballerina's line, especially in arabesque.

My reaction to that information was to administer an eye roll that could be seen two towns away. But I understood what she meant — just too much of a big brother to admit it.

I pull the sheet over my head. Too early to run. I'll sleep a few more hours and then prepare for another day with Honoree and Lula Kent. I close my eyes. Sleep finds me quickly, as does the nightmare.

It starts with hands on a steering wheel, not just my hands, but Azizi's hands, too.

She's pissed and intoxicated and grabs the steering wheel. I scream at her to let go. I beg her to let go.

Then we are all there — my mother, my dad, my grandmother Maggie — all of us helping me steer the car, but they can't help. The car careens off the road toward the biggest fucking tree in Southern California as an SUV smashes into the driver's side. My side. The impact spins us 360 degrees. Screeching tires. A scream. The noise paralyzes me. The pain steals my breath.

Silence descends like an unwanted guest, taking up every inch of space, sharing nothing, offering no reprieve, other than the deadly stillness.

A dream-instant later, hands lie on my chest, coaxing me to breathe.

I wake up, and my head hurts. The pain splits my skull, and I pat the nightstand, searching for my prescription. Damn. I swallowed my last tramadol six months ago, the night I tried to forget Azizi's face, her cries, her pleas.

Let me die. I want to die. I can't live like this. (Who's talking? Me or her?)

Silly girl. You were perfect. The best of us . . . but you never saw past that tree.

PART 3

CHAPTER 21
HONOREE

Tuesday, October 27, 1925

Honoree left Archie's office at two o'clock in the morning, searching for a place to hide. A quiet corner where she wouldn't run into Miss Dolly or Archie's brother, Dewey, or anybody — a small, dark space where she could scream, collapse, and weep.

She barreled toward the back door. The crisp, late-night air would calm her, but just as she reached the kitchen, she heard voices and disappeared into a corner.

Standing next to the stove, Ezekiel was using his teeth to rip open a loaf of Wonder Bread. In work boots, brown trousers, shirt sleeves rolled up to the elbow, and suspenders, he looked more like the boy she remembered than the man in the fancy suit with back-alley manners she had tangled with a few nights before.

He lifted fried meat from the skillet and folded a slice of bread into a fist-sandwich.

After a big, sloppy bite, he wiped his mouth with the back of his hand, and Honoree smiled.

The other man, a cook, judging from his apron, held a large butcher knife, slicing a slab of meat on the cutting board. On Tuesday nights, Archie sold pork sandwiches and fried potatoes sprinkled with plenty of salt in a brown paper bag for twenty-five cents.

Honoree had never seen this cook before, but Archie went through cooks like water down a drain.

"Mr. Booker T. Washington had it right, Mr. Bailey. Colored people need no help pulling ourselves up by our bootstraps. We do best when we keep the white man out of our lives, out of our business."

"Have you read Du Bois's *The Souls of Black Folk*?"

"I don't read nothing by that man," said the cook. "He talked ill of Booker T. Washington — may he rest in peace — and that don't sit well with me."

"Du Bois didn't speak ill of Washington — they disagreed. Debate between intelligent men of the Race should be encouraged."

The cook glared. "The Race should do what we know. Leave the white man be. We don't need to live where they live. You make good money, running a policy wheel in the colored part of town. Making just as much cabbage as them rich white folk uptown make. You don't need a white man's help to make money."

Even from where she stood, Honoree could tell Ezekiel was uncomfortable with the cook's reference to his illegal profession. "Yes, I believe in supporting our neighborhoods, but what if one day, all the Black people leave Bronzeville? Want to see some other part of Chicago? Some other parts of the world?"

Ezekiel added a friendly smile, but his gaze slid toward the archway where Honoree was hiding, which wasn't the best place to hide. Spotting her had been easy. With a sigh, she walked into the kitchen, stopping a few feet from the cook and Ezekiel. "How you two boys doing?"

The cook nodded shyly, but Ezekiel scarcely glanced at her. He just kept talking.

"Mr. Du Bois has written that the Negro should be accorded the same equal rights that the world gives the white man. So no matter where we live or want to live, we should have the right to choose, and have the right to be whoever we want to be with whomever we choose to be with — it's our right as citizens of these United States."

The cook cleared his throat. "I don't want nothin' to do with a white man's world. I do just fine, living in Bronzeville with folk I can trust."

"That is also your right, sir."

The cook reached into a pocket and pulled out a handful of coins. "I'm feeling lucky. I need to place a bet today. What's your birthday, Mr. Bailey? I'll bet on you."

Ezekiel frowned, not amenable to sharing the information. "Not sure that is such a good idea."

"July 1, 1903," Honoree said, stepping farther in the room. "Use three, nine, and seventy-one."

The cook's eyes glowed. "You that chorus girl who figures out the lucky numbers for Archie's policy dream books."

"Correct."

The cook grinned. "I best bet on these numbers before the day gets away from me." He wove toward the front of the cafe. "Be right back."

Honoree walked over to the worktable across from Ezekiel. "I was heading outside for some fresh air and didn't want to interrupt."

"You okay? You look —"

"Everything's copacetic." She craned her neck to the side, tempted to blurt out everything about her conversation with Archie. But it wasn't the time. A cloud of smoke rose behind Ezekiel's head. Quickly, she circled him. "The pork is burning." She turned off the stove and moved the pan from the burner. Shaking her finger as if scolding a child, she said, "Remember, I saved your life."

"Thank you."

"How come you didn't keep your promise?" she asked.

"What are you talking about?"

"Trudy took a swing at me — not an actual punch, but she went off on me in front of a bunch of people about Houdini. In the dressing room. In the basement. In front of everyone. Trudy blamed me for the barkeep's murder. Told me that Houdini got killed because he didn't have the" — she paused to make sure they were still alone — "that damn envelope."

"I'll talk to Trudy again."

"I thought you said she would do what you told her."

Ezekiel glanced at the short hallway where the cook had exited. "Let's take this conversation outdoors."

"I don't wanna go outside."

"Neither one of us wants to be overheard discussing Houdini's murder."

She looked through the small window next to the door. "It's raining. I don't have an umbrella."

"It's drizzling. Hardly a raindrop falling from the sky."

The look on her face must've convinced him she and any kind of rain didn't mix. He lifted a peacoat from the back of a chair. "Put this on."

She set her mouth to object, but Ezekiel, straightening to his full height, held the coat beneath her nose.

She snatched it from his outstretched arms.

Raindrops danced in the moonlight, and a slight breeze pushed across the sky. Cold and beautiful, the drizzle fell like crystal beads, landing silently on the hood of Dewey's pickup truck and turning the dirt into mud.

Honoree glanced from one end of the dead-end patch of alley to the other. It was barely wide enough for Dewey's pickup, let alone Archie's Model T, let alone her and Ezekiel.

He walked onto the landing, and Honoree hugged the peacoat around her shoulders.

She wiped the rainwater from her cheeks with the back of her hand.

Ezekiel walked by her, down the steps, kicking puddles of water like a kid and not inclined to talk until he was farther away from Miss Hattie's.

She followed him.

He planted himself next to the hood of Dewey's truck and shoved his hands into his pockets. "I had nothing to do with Houdini's death. A friend got in touch with me and told me what had happened and that you might be in danger, and I don't want to see you hurt."

"I don't believe you, but what I want to ask you has little to do with the barkeep's death. What do you know about the deal Archie made with Mr. Buttons?"

Ezekiel searched her face in that way he used to when he could see inside her soul. But they were children then, and now his examination made her uneasy.

"What deal, Honoree?"

"Archie bargained me off to Mr. Buttons."

He stepped toward her but kept his hands in his pockets. "What are you talking about?"

" 'To have come near to sing the perfect song.' " She began the poem by Paul Laurence Dunbar with a bitter sting to her tone.

241

" 'And only by half-tone lost the key.' "

Ezekiel cocked his head and continued the stanza from the poem he used to read to her. " 'There is a potent sorrow, there the grief, the pale, sad staring of life's tragedy.' " He looked at her with mournful eyes. "What happened with Archie, Honoree?"

"How come good things go hand in hand with the bad?" she asked, wondering if Ezekiel could answer and solve her problems. "I auditioned for a job at the Dreamland Cafe and got the job, and then saw a barkeep shot. The night we make love, you leave town the next morning. See what I mean? Bad and good. Good and bad."

His lips moved. He wanted to speak but had trouble forming the words.

"Don't talk. I shouldn't have said that last part. This is about Archie and Mr. Buttons."

He narrowed his eyes. "Tell me what happened with Archie."

"He arranged my audition at the Dreamland Cafe — and also arranged me getting the job, but only until Valentine's Day. Then I'm back at Miss Hattie's like I'm on loan, which is not a deal I can live with."

"And you want me to fix this?"

"Never seen Archie do something someone else told him to do, except for the other night when you told him to take his hands off me."

Ezekiel nodded. "We have a history, but are you sure Archie is telling the truth about this deal with Mr. Buttons?"

"Why would he lie?"

"Archie lies about a lot of things."

"Good point," she admitted.

"Making sure you keep your job at the Dreamland, if and when it reopens, might risk my partnership with Archie."

She bristled. "You don't have to make it sound ridiculous or impossible. You owe me."

He pressed his lips together to hide a small smile.

"What's so funny? You better not be laughing at me. You don't have the right."

"I was not laughing at you." The whisper of a smile disappeared. "I do owe you, and I'll do what I can. It might take some time. With all the ruckus over the barkeep's death, I can't promise to get it done right away. But I will do what I can."

Should she tell him his time may be short? If the coppers put him away for killing Houdini. "The cops think you had something to do with Houdini's death," she blurted.

"What do you mean?"

243

"The other day, the cops asked me questions about Houdini's murder. They also asked if I knew you were back in town."

Ezekiel took his hands out of his pockets and folded his arms across his chest. "I knew Houdini, but knowing a dead man is not a crime. Don't worry about the cops." He smiled with one side of his mouth. "And don't worry about me. I can take care of myself."

"I'm not worried. February is a long ways off, and I wouldn't want —"

"Me to end up in the hoosegow before I fix this trouble you're having with Archie and Mr. Buttons?" He chuckled. "I understand, Honoree."

"And you'll square things with Trudy, too?"

He moved in closer, his breath warm on her face smelling of cigarettes and Wonder Bread. "Don't you believe me?"

The scent of his soap, clean and fresh, mixed with his sweat was intoxicating. She shivered and looked into his eyes. The glint of humor helped get rid of the chill, but there was also something else, something dark and unexpected, and she didn't like how it made her feel. She shoved him in the chest. "How dare you!"

Of his own volition, he took a step back.

Honoree couldn't have moved him otherwise. The smile on his lips, however, was still not right, and the suddenness of his desire caught her unprepared. What was going on with him?

She shoved him again. "I can't believe you."

"You thought I wanted to hurt you."

"You were going to kiss me!" She pointed a finger. "I do not exchange favors, Ezekiel. This is about repaying a debt. You. Owe. Me."

"Jesus Christ." He grabbed her shoulders, holding her firmly so that she couldn't run. Not that she planned on running. She intended to stand her ground.

"Yes, Honoree. I wanted to kiss you. Being around you is more challenging than I thought it would be."

"Let go. We made a deal. The new you and the new me. A deal. Can we stick to that?"

"Get your hands off her! Right now. Or I swear!"

Honoree turned. The loud girlish voice had come from the kitchen door, and Bessie was rushing toward them, waving a long stick. Her eyes were wild and trained on Ezekiel.

"Hold on, little girl." He released Honoree's shoulders and retreated, his hands up, palms out.

Honoree edged in between him and Bessie, searching the girl's face for a sign of common sense. "He wasn't hurting me. We were talking. Only talking."

Bessie stopped her charge, but the wild look in her eyes kept Honoree rooted in front of Ezekiel.

"Bessie, listen. I'm fine. Ezekiel didn't want to hurt me."

Honoree clapped her hands in front of Bessie's face, making sure the girl's rage hadn't made her deaf and blind. "Do you hear me?"

The fury slowly left Bessie's eyes. She lowered the stick but still cast an untrusting glance at Ezekiel. "You sure, Honoree?"

"I'm positive," she said, taking short breaths to exhale her nerves. "And what are you doing out here, dressed like that? You'll freeze to death." Bessie was still wearing her costume, a pair of brightly colored bloomers, and a midriff top.

"Miss Dolly sent me to fetch you. The cook said you were out here — with him." Bessie gave Ezekiel another dark look. "Those railroad workers want another show."

"It's three o'clock in the morning."

"Don't matter to Miss Dolly or Archie what time it is."

Honoree took off Ezekiel's peacoat and handed it to him. "I'd better go."

"I'll be in touch."

"When?"

He had lowered his hands but remained behind her. "I'll find you when I know something."

Honoree nodded at Ezekiel and smiled, a weary, apologetic smile. Then she grabbed Bessie's hand and dragged her back inside Miss Hattie's Garden Cafe.

"Are you crazy, coming after Ezekiel like that?" Honoree dragged Bessie by the arm through the kitchen. "What was on your mind, girl?"

"I was afraid for you," Bessie squealed. "Ezekiel could've hurt you with a snap of his fingers. He's twice your size."

"Ezekiel is twice everyone's size but would never hurt me. Not that way."

They rushed by the railroad workers and slammed the storage room door behind them, but Honoree didn't move toward the stairwell. She had to collect her thoughts.

The room had a clean odor, sweet and sharp — fresh lemon and honey drowned the stench of beer and whiskey. A drink would calm Honoree's nerves, but that was unlikely now. She released Bessie's hand.

"What's wrong?" Bessie touched her arm.

"Why you always pawing at me?"

"Why you getting mad? I didn't hit Ezekiel. Didn't touch him."

Bessie eyed her with suspicion. "You carry a torch for Ezekiel? I mean, are you in love with him?"

"Why would you say something like that?"

" 'Cause you ain't mad at him," she said. "When I saw you through that window — he was looking at you with a fire in his eyes, and I picked up a stick." She considered her words. "If you missed that look, you must love him something awful."

"What do you know about love?"

"Nothin'. I never loved nobody. Too much trouble to love a man. You told me that."

Honoree laughed. "I told you something like that. I said I would never let a man hurt me more than once, but you might be right about love. It is too much trouble."

"If I were gonna love somebody, it'd be you."

"I never loved a woman that way and would rather lie with a man than a woman, anyhow."

"I didn't mean in bed together. More like sisters —"

Honoree started down the stairwell, not sure how she felt about Bessie's admission. But her words had touched Honoree. Though she wouldn't admit it out loud. "Sorry for snapping; been dining on upset and woe for a week."

Bessie smiled. "I'm learning the things I worry about only matter when I worry about them. So I don't worry about them."

Honoree figured on that for a moment. "Like letting a man beat you?"

"I don't let him beat me anymore. I listened to you and told him to keep his hands off me."

"I'm glad something I said made a difference."

They had reached the bottom of the stairwell.

" 'Course, he put me out after I told him," Bessie said. "But I don't care."

"He did what?"

"Kicked me out, which is why I've been sleeping in the dressing room."

"You can't stay down here forever. What if Archie or Dewey find out, or heaven forbid, Miss Dolly? I told you the first night — she don't tolerate squatters."

"Don't worry — already found someplace to stay. Or, I should say, Virginia found me a room at the brothel around the corner."

249

Honoree stopped and stared at Bessie wide-eyed. "I swear to God. Virginia has a mean streak as wide as Miss Dolly's behind. You can't stay there."

"She said I'd be fine. Nobody gonna beat me up or nothin'."

"The men who visit those establishments will surely grab your ass and won't be polite about giving you more than a pat on the backside."

Reaching the dressing room door, Honoree shoved it open. "You need someplace to stay, but it ain't in no whorehouse."

"What took you two so long?" Miss Dolly had her skirt hiked up, hiding her flask in a pocket sewn on the underside of her garment.

"Why you always putting your foot in my beeswax?" Honoree stomped down the steps, still fuming about Virginia's vile idea for Bessie. "Not every conversation has to do with you, Miss Dolly."

"Shut up and get dressed," Miss Dolly snapped. "Trudy and Edna Mae need your help. They can't keep those railroad boys entertained by themselves all night long."

Virginia was in her sights now, and Honoree went after her with venom in her veins. "And you? Lord have mercy. You got nothing but nerve. A room in a whorehouse?

Shame on you."

The chorus girl threw her cigarette butt on the sawdust. "What's your beef? Where else is she gonna stay? She's dumb as dirt and dances like a broke-legged duck. She would be lucky to survive on a street corner. I got her a good room."

The desire to smack Virginia in the mouth overwhelmed Honoree. It took all of her strength to tame her temper. "Bessie will stay with me. I'll make room for her — until she finds someplace to live that's not a whorehouse."

Bessie moved into Honoree's kitchenette that night, with a satchel full of old clothes, knit jerseys, cardigans, and a serge skirt. It appeared her things had not been washed or mended since she arrived in Chicago.

"I can't believe you are doing this for me, Miss Honoree. You sincerely don't mind me moving in with you?" Bessie stood in the doorway, wide-eyed like a doe in the moonlight. The rest of her glowed like Honoree had handed her the keys to the Taj Mahal.

"I have rules," Honoree said. "You can stay until you get a place of your own or find someone else to live with."

Bessie looked down at the floor. "I'll behave. I promise. You won't have no trouble from me."

Honoree sighed. There was no turning back. "My kitchenette is small, but I sleep on the cot. You sleep on the floor. There are blankets over next to the Singer sewing machine," she said.

A wide grin stretched from one side of Bessie's plain face to the other. "I'll sleep anywhere you say."

CHAPTER 22
SAWYER

Monday, June 22, 2015

Despite the nightmare and my text-athon with Dad, I finally get my ass in gear. I make it to the Bronzeville Senior Care Facility midafternoon, coffee in hand, but my thoughts are out of order. My mind is still in the car — then on the side of the road, and later in the hospital, accepting, questioning, knowing: I had survived. Azizi was the one who was dead.

I pull my chair up alongside Honoree's bed.

"Do you have a middle name?"

My spirit is shredding, and I don't grumble about this out-of-nowhere question. "I have a middle name that I don't tell people."

"You better tell me. We made a deal."

I chuckle. She has a way of making her rudeness feel charming — and, of course, she hasn't forgotten our challenge.

"If you insist. It's Langston. My grandmother persuaded my parents to name me after the poet Langston Hughes."

"Maggie did that?"

"Yes," I say, but then I add, "Did you ever meet him in the 1920s?"

The corners of her mouth sag. "Probably. Can't recall." She wraps a clawlike finger around the bed's side railing. "Why did she insist? What does she know of Langston Hughes?"

"She knew quite a bit about him." I lean forward, oddly eager to talk about Maggie's fifteen minutes, or more like years, of fame. "She met him in 1960 at the NAACP awards. He was accepting an award, and a mutual friend introduced them. She was a poet and had published several books of poetry. Won some awards, too. And was on the governor's shortlist for California Poet Laureate a few decades ago, until she got sick."

There is something in Honoree's eyes — surprise? Sadness? Grief.

"Is she dead?"

"No. No. She's not dead. I didn't mean for it to sound like —"

"Fine. Fine."

The sharp change in her manner shocks me into momentary silence.

"What do you want me to see today?" she asks.

"Well," I say, regathering my senses as I set up the camcorder, tripod, and spin the tray-top table in front of her. "First, however, I want to share a photo. There are three women in the picture: Lil Hardin Armstrong, Louis's second wife; Alberta Hunter, the blues singer and composer; and Honoree."

"I recognize Lil. She played the piano. But who's the one over there?"

"Her name is Alberta Hunter. A popular blues singer and songwriter in the 1920s and the 1930s. She also made a comeback in the early 1980s and sang at a club in Greenwich Village called the Cookery."

"How come you know so much about her?"

"I've done my research," I say rather proudly, but then I admit to having help. "Her name, Alberta Hunter, is printed on the back of the photo, along with your name and Lil Hardin's." I turn over the picture and perform a little show-and-tell. "So I looked her up."

"Why are you so sure that's me? Other than my name printed on the back of the photo?"

"They say the eyes don't change with age."

"I heard that, too." She winks, smiling. "I just wanted you to say it." She points at the photo, except she's staring at the back with the names. "Whose handwriting is that?"

I flip it over. "Maggie's."

"You sure?"

I studied every photo in the long-ago box, taking for granted Maggie had written all the names and dates. "Why? Why are you asking?"

"This one with Alberta Hunter. The handwriting lines up perfectly. Someone used a ruler to write it."

I pick up the photo and examine it. Then I remove the other two dozen pictures from my backpack, and like a dog smelling a fox, search for the block-style handwriting. There are only two photos with it. "You have sharp eyes, Miss Honoree."

I stare at the writing, but my brain isn't accepting what I'm seeing. "It looks like my sister's writing or my mother's. They had similar signatures." A muscle in my neck throbs as I reel from the possibility Azizi had found Maggie's long-ago box before me.

"What is it, Sawyer? Why are you so quiet? Did I say something to upset you? I'm sorry if I did."

Was she sorry? The urge to confess seizes

me. "I blame myself for my sister's death, and so does she."

Honoree lifts her chin. "Why would you say something like that? You can't read the minds of the dead."

I lower my voice. "Her ghost haunts me." I smile, hoping to diminish the absurdity of my words. "She's standing next to your bed." I keep a flicker of humor in my eyes. I don't want to frighten Honoree with the manifestations of my guilt.

"Ghosts, huh?" She shrugs, causing me to think my admission is the most boring thing she's ever been told.

"You're mighty young to be bothered by ghosts," she continues. "Live as long as me, and you get used to 'em. Some folk call 'em memories, but what are memories but the ghosts of people lost and left behind?" Her sigh is long and thoughtful. "Tell me more about your ghost, and I'll tell you about mine."

This is uncomfortable. It is one thing to see a ghost, another thing to tell someone you see a ghost, and another ball game altogether when the person you share your crazy with comes right back at you with crazy of their own.

"How about if we drop the subject."

"The thing about death" — Honoree taps

her chest as if warding off a demon — "we don't have the slightest idea of when it will happen, and unless you're old or sick or the doctors have told you to write your will, you don't expect it. Your sister was young when she died, and I'm sure she had no plans to die. So, you seeing her ghost could be your way of keeping her memory with you."

I sink into the chair. My legs uncross, my arms dangle at my sides. I drop my head back and sigh, releasing a year's worth of pain and guilt, but on the next inhale, I swallow it all back, gather myself, and begin. "I didn't start seeing her until last winter. My grief barometer is out of whack. I never go through shit in the right order."

"Watch your mouth." Honoree's reprimand is gentle. "I know what you mean about ghosts. Mine is with me all the time. One ghost, in particular, is a constant bother," she says, her words tinged with weariness. "I wonder why she haunts you, though? What happened to her?"

The question is one I ask myself a thousand times a day, and not once have I gotten an answer I will accept. "I was driving, and she was talking about her move to New York City and leaving home, leaving Dad. She made me promise to tell him everything about why she was leaving, but not until after she was gone. When it came to hurting my dad's feelings, she was a coward. They were inseparable after my mom died. But as usual, she put the burden on me of telling him the bad news."

Honoree chuckles. "It's never what you did, but what you didn't do."

I rise and go to her; my hands grip the railing, and I search her watery-eyed gaze. "Christ. I never told him that she planned to move to New York."

"Is that why she's riled up?"

Azizi sits on the edge of Honoree's bed, looking serene and mildly impressed.

"Could be," I say to Honoree. "Seems such a small thing, though. Kind of a bullshit reason to haunt me."

She cuts me a look.

"Sorry," I say with a sheepish grin.

With an eyebrow lifted, she says, "Are you sure she's mad at you? Or is there something else bothering you about that night?"

I wipe something from my eye. "Well, I was driving the car, and I didn't die. There's that."

CHAPTER 23
HONOREE

Wednesday, October 28, 1925

Honoree had given up all hope the Dreamland Cafe would ever reopen. What had Miss Dolly said? She'd be dancing at Miss Hattie's until the day she died. Vicious chatter from a venomous tongue, but her words still stung like the crack of a whip.

Sitting in Miss Hattie's dressing room, Honoree mended a hole in her pantaloons, something the chorus girls did once a week. They came in early to sew up the rips and holes in their costumes.

"Ouch!" Honoree had stabbed her thumb.

"What's wrong with you?" Edna Mae sat on the crate next to her.

Honoree waved her finger in the chorus girl's face.

"I don't mean that. You awful quiet tonight."

"I'm usually quiet."

"Not when Miss Dolly and Archie are out

of town. No one around to bother us tonight."

"Around or not," Virginia quipped as she darned a pair of stockings, "I do what I want to no matter who's watching."

Edna Mae ran a stitch and yanked the needle and thread into the air. "I was talking to Honoree. Besides, got a mind to —"

"To what?" Virginia asked sharply. "You got no business asking Honoree why she ain't talking. She doesn't need you giving her a talking to."

"Both of you stop jabbering." Honoree couldn't handle either one of their opinions. "You're giving me a headache. And I'm going home early to get away from all this noise."

"Oh, no, you don't." Virginia jerked to her feet. "If anyone gets to leave, it should be me."

"Neither one of you is leaving. If you do, I'll — I'll tell on you," Edna Mae said weakly.

Honoree shoved the rest of her things into her shopping bag. "I'll see you ladies tomorrow."

She marched up the steps, but Bessie ran into her.

"What's wrong with you, girl?" Honoree asked, holding her shoulders to keep her

261

still. She looked a mess, hair sticking out in all directions, her eyes the size of cake pans. "Catch your breath and tell me what's going on?"

Gasping for breath, she nodded and blinked. "Ezekiel and Dewey." She sputtered and coughed. "You gotta stop 'em. Stop 'em before one of 'em gets killed."

Edna Mae sighed wearily. "How is Honoree gonna stop two grown men from killing each other? Let 'em kill each other. Two less fools for us to deal with."

"Hush, Edna Mae," said Virginia from the bottom step. "Go on, Bessie. Talk to us, child. Is Crazy Pete around? Should we call the cops?"

"Oh Lord, no cops." Honoree immediately thought of Officer MacDonald and his questions about Ezekiel. "Let's find out what's going on first before we call the cops. Calm down, Bessie. Men are always arguing about something."

"It ain't that." Trembling, Bessie seized hold of Honoree's shoulders. "Dewey has a .38 Colt revolver behind the bar, and Mr. Bailey ain't got no weapon I can see. Except for his fists."

"I never knew Dewey kept anything other than a baseball bat behind the bar," Edna Mae said.

"Are you sure?" Honoree asked.

"Yes, ma'am."

"All right. All right," Honoree said. "I don't know what I can do or say, but —"

"Somebody gotta do something." Bessie's hands dropped to her side, but her face was twisted with fear. "And that something better happen in a hurry or one of 'em is gonna be dead."

Honoree ran up the stairwell into the storage room with Bessie on her heels but stopped when she reached the door, cracking it open to take a peek.

It was the middle of the afternoon, and there were no customers, no musicians, no cooks in the cafe — just Dewey and Ezekiel, and a room full of crates to be unloaded.

Ezekiel was at the end of the bar, square-shouldered with his body puffed up like a barrel made of muscle and rage. On the other side, Dewey's hand hovered over the Colt revolver resting below bar level, meaning Ezekiel had no idea Dewey had a weapon within reach.

She turned to Bessie, cowering behind her. "You stay right here and don't come out no matter what. You hear me?"

Bessie nodded, but her eyes were saucers. Honoree understood her fear and thought about walking away, but what if she could do something to stop Ezekiel and Dewey from fighting or killing each other?

"Listen, Bessie. You keep still. I mean it. Open your mouth and promise me that you'll keep quiet and not move."

Bessie moistened her lips. "Yes, ma'am. I mean, I promise, Honoree. I ain't moving an inch."

"Good." Honoree walked out of the storage room toward Ezekiel, greeting Dewey with a smile and a nod. "How's it going?"

Both men gave her a hasty glance but immediately resumed glaring at each other.

"This is not your business, Honoree," Ezekiel said, without taking his eyes off Dewey.

She stepped in next to Ezekiel, speaking loud enough for Dewey to hear. "If you two fight, the police will have to break it up, and then the coppers will close this place down. And if either one of you happens to have some betting slips in your hip pocket, no matter how many coppers Archie has paid off this week, you'll still end up in jail."

"Stop running your mouth, Honoree," Dewey's voice blasted. "This ain't about you. This is men's business."

The muscles in his arm flexed as he leaned forward. He must be thinking about pointing that gun at Ezekiel.

"Nothing but a surefire stint in the hoosegow for ninety days," she exclaimed, wanting to keep his attention. "Unless someone bails you out."

"Pipe down, Honoree," Dewey barked.

"Don't talk to her like that." Ezekiel grew even taller as he pressed against the bar. "You talk to me."

"I already told you what I had to say to you," Dewey growled.

"You're a cheap hood pretending to be a big man, and you haven't said anything that would make me think any different."

If only Ezekiel would keep his mouth shut and stop taunting Dewey. "I need to talk to you, Ezekiel, about Mr. Buttons."

"Not now, Honoree. Not until I finish this conversation."

"We can end this conversation fast," Dewey said, one of his hands moving out of sight.

Honoree pushed Ezekiel in the shoulder. "Both of you hush."

"I warned you," Ezekiel said between gritted teeth. "If your brother learns about your bootlegging concern, he'll kill you before Capone has a chance to do it."

Dewey surged forward. "You can't tell me what to do."

"Mark my word, Dewey. If you don't stop, Archie will beat you half to death." Then Ezekiel laughed. "But you're such a fool, you'll just keep spouting off to anyone who will listen about how you're saving your brother's ass."

"Why are you acting all high and mighty? You just showed up here, and, all of a sudden, you're in charge." Dewey's arm moved, and Honoree angled her body between Ezekiel and Dewey and the Colt.

"Ezekiel, we are leaving now."

There was a confused expression on his face when he looked down at her. Something dire had formed without warning, landing in his path without reason. He wrapped a large hand around her forearm, attempting to move her out of his way, but she shoved him in the chest. "Ezekiel, you've got to come with me. Right now. Please."

The muscles in his face tightened into sharp edges and deep hollows, and he might explode if she said another word, but that would be better than seeing him get shot.

She lowered her voice. "We can go wherever you want to go, but we need to leave."

"Oh, so you gonna hide behind a girl's skirt, huh?" Dewey spat on the floor.

"If you go near my brother with your

bullshit again, I will kill you, Dewey."

Ezekiel's voice chilled her soul. But, dear Lord, this had something to do with one of Ezekiel's brothers. Tempers could go haywire at any moment. She grabbed Ezekiel's arm again. "Let's go."

The street was busy, full of laborers hauling milk and ice and laundry, paperboys heralding the evening news, and automobiles bumping over concrete and cobblestones. Gamblers, musicians, and flappers strolled alongside stockyard workers, depot janitors, and house servants, all rushing toward whatever backbreaking chore defined them.

Honoree and Ezekiel walked in silence.

With his hands shoved into his pockets and his eyes black with rage, he couldn't be trusted. If she loosened her grip, Ezekiel would bolt back to Miss Hattie's to dismember Dewey with his bare hands. Pistol or no pistol.

Honoree hooked her arm around his forearm, tightening her grip while smiling friendly-like as they passed people on the street. A sweet-looking couple on a Wednesday afternoon — that's how they appeared to those who noticed, she imagined.

Ten blocks into the walk, thunder clapped over Lake Michigan. They turned the corner near Mount Olive Baptist Church, and within a block, Mother Nature had dumped a cold mix of rain and sleet on top of their heads.

"We've got to get out of this." Honoree let go of his arm and covered her hair as best she could. She scampered beneath an awning in front of a storefront with a CLOSED sign in the window. Ezekiel moved with her, raising the collar of his peacoat to protect himself from the rain.

Honoree blinked water from her lashes, while Ezekiel remained silent. "I'm sure you'd rather not talk about what happened at Miss Hattie's, but what is there between you and Dewey? There were signs of trouble that first night I saw you."

A sharp inhale of breath, but he didn't speak.

"Did you know Dewey keeps a Colt .38 revolver behind the bar? He practically waved it in your face — and you just stood there — behaving like a very foolish man."

"Sometimes I am foolish," he said, finally opening his mouth. "But the Graves brothers, Archie and Dewey, aren't reasonable men."

"I have worked at Miss Hattie's for three years. I know how those boys can be."

"If you know, then why have you worked

there for so long?"

She twisted her neck and, for her trouble, got a close-up view of the jaw muscle twitching beneath Ezekiel's thin beard. "I had no choice. Why do you work for him?"

"I could go on and on answering that question."

"I'm sure you could, but you won't."

He folded his arms. "Me? What about how you behaved that first night? I thought you and Dewey were an item. Then I learned it was mostly Archie who lapped behind you like a rabid dog."

"Is that why you don't like him — because of me?"

"You do have them wrapped around your finger."

She had Ezekiel wrapped around her finger once upon a time. The memories of how they used to be together kept rolling back, trampling over her like mice in a cornfield.

Travelers scurried over the sidewalk seeking shelter from the storm. Another clap of thunder drove Honoree into the folds of Ezekiel's overcoat, quivering.

"You always hated bad weather, Honoree."

Self-conscious, she jerked away from him but not too far as to abandon the protection of the awning or his solid frame. "It doesn't bother me no more. I grew out of that childishness."

The next blast of thunder pressed her against the wall, the meager protection of the awning forgotten.

"Hey, I'm fine," Ezekiel said. "You can go home. I'll hail you a cab." He jutted his head from beneath the covering, but the storm intensified, drawing him back.

"There won't be any cabs," Honoree said. "Not in weather like this."

He blinked water from his eyelashes and wiped the moisture from his face. "We'll wait here until the rain stops, or you'll be soaked to the skin."

The water bounced off the ground. Honoree edged back, away from the street until her spine touched the door. Ezekiel stood in front of her, blocking the wind and the cold.

"Why did you come upstairs?" he asked. "To save me?"

"It was Bessie. She's fickle. One day she wants to knock you in the head with a stick, the next she wants to keep you alive." She paused. "She told me Dewey had a gun and all you had were your fists."

"I had hopes you came running because you care about me."

"You didn't give me any word on Mr. Buttons, and I wanted to know what you had

270

learned before Dewey shot you. That was the basis of my concern about your well-being," she lied.

He moved from beneath the awning. "The weather seems to be letting up."

Another bolt of lightning blasted across the sky. A stiff breeze rode with it.

"Still raining cats and dogs."

"If we can't get you a cab," Ezekiel said, "I know where we can go."

"Why didn't you mention that earlier?"

"Are you ready to make a run for it?"

Honoree nodded. "Lead the way."

"We'll be indoors and out of this weather in another block," Ezekiel shouted over his shoulder. "Hang on!"

He grabbed her hand and took off at a run, with her at his side. She tried to keep up, but his long legs hopped quickly over pools of water and mud while her short strides struggled to keep from falling in.

Inpatient or frustrated by her slow pace, he lifted her off the ground with an arm around her waist. Her legs barely touched the ground until they reached the doorstep of another storefront.

"Come inside." Keys in hand, he unlocked the door, entered, and pushed the light button on the wall. "Come on. It's dry as a bone here. I promise."

271

She took his hand, and he led her inside. "Where are we?"

"The Bailey Brothers Auto Body Shop," he said proudly. "Wait a moment. I'll get some towels." He took off toward the rear of the shop.

Motor oil, rubber tires, and gasoline hung heavily in the air. A series of shelves, a wall of cabinets, a double door led to what had to be a garage.

Cold water dripped from her hair. She wiped her cheek, but her clothing, her skin, were soaked.

"This place looks familiar," she said out loud.

Ezekiel reappeared with an armload of towels, handed her one, and kept the other two for himself. "Your father used to come here back when he took care of my father's automobiles."

"I remember." She looked down at her ruined coat. Her silk blouse clung to her curves, and her cotton chemise was see-through. "I need to change."

He tilted his head toward the rear of the shop. "Jeremiah keeps a set of overalls and some extra shirts in the back."

"Jeremiah?" He was the middle brother, close to her age, while Ezekiel's youngest brother, Marcus, was just shy of fourteen years old. At that moment, there were questions about family and such she hadn't asked, but neither had he. "How are your brothers — and your mother?"

Ezekiel spoke solemnly. "My brothers are alive. Jeremiah is here in Chicago with me. Marcus is in New York City with my mother."

"I'm sorry about your father." Mr. Bailey had died right after the family had left home, according to a newspaper article a year later.

"I'm sorry to hear about your mother."

"She's not dead. She just left me. That's all." She started to ask him how he knew, but he was already explaining.

"That's what I mean. I'm sorry she left." He whirled toward the rear of the store. A moment later, he returned with a pair of overalls and two button-down cotton shirts.

She held the trousers up by the waistband. "Oh my Lord. These are taller than I am."

Ezekiel shook his head, the smile on his lips growing wide. "Sorry. Marcus's clothes would've worked better. He's much smaller. Not a giant like his big brothers."

Still, holding up the trousers in front of her, she looked from the pants to him. "I can roll up the cuffs."

"Too much fabric to roll up. I'll find a pair

of Marcus's coveralls." He looked uneasy, holding the extra clothing in his hands.

"While you're doing that, where's the java? You have any? I can make us a pot."

"Sure do." He set off down the short hall. "The kitchen — and the java — are back here."

Honoree followed Ezekiel to the rear of the shop, passing by several rooms and peeking inside as she did. One had a printing press for Ezekiel's policy betting slips, she wagered, and another was a storage room filled with crates and a large chifforobe. The last one held two narrow beds with a stack of blankets and pillows lying on top of unmade mattresses.

"Where would you like to change?" Ezekiel asked. "The Palmer house or the Ritz?"

She smiled at his joke and recalled the many times at the Bailey house when he'd tell tall tales and make everyone laugh with his lovely sense of humor.

She squeezed water from a handful of her bobbed hair. "You didn't answer me before — what is it with you and Dewey?"

"He tried to get Jeremiah involved in his fucking bootleg business."

"Last time I saw Jeremiah he was almost as tall as you."

"I know he can take care of himself. But Dewey is bad for business. He makes stupid mistakes neither my brother nor I can afford."

"Oh, so Archie asked you to keep an eye on him?"

He laughed. "Yes. You know the Brothers Grimm well."

She cocked her head. "Grimm. Their surname is Graves, though grim works better."

"Let me get you some of Marcus's things." He walked into the room with two beds, went to a dresser, and opened a drawer. "Here you go."

He excused himself, leaving her alone to change out of her wet clothes. She heard him in another part of the store, making noise with pots and pans, hoping that meant he was making coffee. The bumps rising on her skin were the size of blueberries. She slipped on the shirt and pulled on a pair of overalls. The clothes were miles of fabric too large, but they were dry, and in a few minutes, she started to feel less frozen.

Ezekiel returned, wearing dry clothes and holding two cups of steaming java. He passed her both cups. "Hold these, please." He pulled a folding table from a corner along with two chairs and set them up quickly before inviting her to have a seat. "Not quite the Ritz but not bad, don't you think?"

She sat and sipped the hot brew, sighing with delight as the warmth coated her lungs. "Maxwell House?"

"Nothing but the best for my guest."

He was charming — the real McCoy when behaved.

"Why'd you leave town?"

His gaze did not waver when he replied. "I left because of my father. That night three years ago, after being with you, I learned he'd been involved in an insurance scam and hurt a lot of people. Black people. He also angered some dangerous men. White men. After his scam fell apart, he lost their investment, their money. He tried to fix things, but he failed, and we had to leave town."

Ezekiel took a sip of his coffee and wiped his mouth. "I had to protect my brothers and my mother. So we closed the house and vanished," he said, as if reading from a book.

It unnerved Honoree. "I don't understand why you didn't tell me this that first night."

"I didn't want you to feel sorry for me. You were never one to hide your feelings, and if you pitied me —" He reached for her then, but she leaned away from his touch.

"I should go." She stood. "Where did you put my clothes?"

"It hasn't stopped raining."

"I'll catch a cab."

He stood, too. "You've been asking me to tell you why I left since we saw each other at Miss Hattie's." He circled the table. "What more do you want me to say?"

There was gravel in his voice and pain. Still, she longed for him to admit how much he had hated leaving her behind, how he knew she'd be upset, how his feelings for her hadn't changed. But he didn't have anything more to say. He stared straight ahead, mouth shut.

Thunder boomed. She jumped, and he wrapped an arm around her waist and pulled her to him; a hand lifted her chin, forcing her to consider his eyes. But all she saw was his mouth descending upon her.

Lips touched, and her emotions tightened in her chest, as her fingertips pulled at his shirt.

The kiss was not the sweet childish thing they'd shared three years ago. Now his mouth was rough, and she kissed him back, matching his desire with an open mouth.

She hugged him around the waist and held him as fiercely as he held her. It was as if she had fallen into a bottomless well, drowning in his fire, and his fury, and his passion.

Then, suddenly, the kiss ended — but Ezekiel's mouth lingered over hers, his hard breaths a desperate contrast to her soft sighs. He held her shoulders and brushed his lips against her cheek. "I want you to stay and be with me."

There were so many things Honoree desired from her life, but three years ago, desire had only one name — Ezekiel.

And what had she accomplished sharing her body with him? The pleasure of his touch, his heart beating against hers, his scent filling her nostrils and her soul?

And what did he leave her?

Nothing but heartache. Nothing but loneliness. Nothing but the strength to say what she had to say, even if her lips wanted to say something other than "I'm sorry, Ezekiel. I can't. I've got to go."

CHAPTER 24
SAWYER

Friday, June 26, 2015

I am in my favorite chair at the senior living facility, but this is my first visit to Honoree's room in several days. After confessing about my sister's ghost, I took a few days off. I used the time to write, edit, walk, eat three squares, and not speak to another human other than to say, "Excuse me," or "Make that a grande cappuccino with extra foam." I also avoided Mitch's calls about his money, and refreshed my email every ten minutes, hoping for an update from the restoration company. That was day one. Day two was my solo version of Netflix and chill.

Now it is Friday morning. I'm ready for the next round with Honoree, except before either one of us can open our mouths, Lula pushes a cart into the room, and I smell eggs.

"Mealtime already?" Honoree isn't pleased with the interruption.

"Yes, ma'am." Lula adjusts the tray-top table, puts down a plate, and removes the cover. I clear my throat to avoid laughing out loud, but I can't stop myself and let loose.

"What's your problem?" Lula asks.

I point at the tray, shoulders shaking, and wipe a tear from my eye. "It's a plate of green eggs and ham."

She grimaces at the scrambled egg, cubed ham, and spinach dish, but then a smile dimples her cheeks.

"What are you two giggling about?" Honoree barks.

Lula holds a fork of food. "Sawyer's reminiscing about his youth and Dr. Seuss."

"You two children and your silliness." Honoree ignores the food. "Is she still here, Sawyer? Is she still with us?"

Lula looks at Honoree curiously and then at me as I choke to death.

"Yes, I'm still here," Lula says emphatically to Honoree while eyeballing me. "What's wrong with you?"

"We ain't talking about you, Lula. Sawyer knows who I'm talking about." Honoree scans the room.

She is about to spill my ghost story all over the floor. I am not amused and raise a finger in protest. "Hush, Miss Honoree.

That conversation was between the two of us."

"We are keeping it between us. Lula don't have any idea what we're talking about. Do you, child?"

"I certainly don't." Lula still holds the fork of food in front of Honoree. "I'm sure I don't want to."

"We're just talking gibberish, Lula — which is as much as you need to know. Isn't that right, Sawyer?"

"Yes, ma'am."

Lula ignores us, hums a tune, and focuses on feeding Honoree, but the feisty old gal refuses to be spoon-fed. But she can't hold a fork with her gnarled fingers.

After a while, I notice Lula is singing under her breath.

"You have a nice voice."

"She sure does." Honoree pushes aside the fork Lula holds. "She sings the blues every Wednesday through Saturday night at some joint on Lincoln Avenue."

"Thanks for the plug," Lula says with a smile. "Are you done?"

Honoree nods. Lula returns the tray to the cart and prepares to exit. "You've had your fill, I see. I'll leave you two to your conversation."

With a sharp turn of her head — but I

still catch the remnants of a smile — she struts out of the room.

"Do you remember anything about your trip from Louisiana to Chicago?" I turn on my camcorder.

"Jesus, boy. I was a child, three or four years old when we traveled up north. The most I remember was walking for long spells and boarding a train." Her eyes light up. "Lots of colored folk died that summer."

"Which summer?"

"The summer the Negro boy wanted to swim on the beach and the whites wouldn't let him. I was there, but I didn't get hurt. Lots of houses burned to the ground, and colored folks killed. But I ran. That was 1918. No. 1919, late summer. Awful hot."

"Called the Red Summer. I read about it, but I think you were older. More like thirteen that summer."

"Maybe, I don't recall." Honoree coughs and stares at the ceiling. "Your grand-mother's husband, his name was Norman. I never liked him. Reminded me of my mother — a cold fish, but Maggie thought he was the bee's knees because he played baseball."

I nearly fall off the chair. "You knew my grandmother's first husband? I thought she left Baton Rouge when she was a child?"

"She was a child when she married Norman White. He was much older than her. Maggie was fifteen when they met, and he was staring thirty dead between the eyes."

"She still talks about him. She loved him a lot, and he's been dead since —"

"Killed during the Korean War — Norman Francis White. I never thought she loved him that much. What Maggie loved was baseball, and Norman played baseball." She squints at me. "I like football. Men hit each other and growl like dogs. That game makes much more sense to me."

Honoree pats her chest with her good hand. "Norman helped organize the Los Angeles White Sox, one of the first teams in the Negro baseball league."

"Yes, Maggie loved baseball, too." It was a passion she and Azizi had shared. Two women, separated by two generations, watching grown men hit a ball with a stick. I am not a fan, which must rile Azizi.

Torturing me, she stands on the other side of Honoree's bed, mimicking a batter at home plate, swinging a pretend bat, spitting fake chewing tobacco, and deliberately making me smile.

"I can't stand the game."

"Neither could —" Honoree starts blinking rapid-fire as if something has landed in her eye. "I mean, I prefer boxers and fisti-cuffs. Football is the sport to watch."

Suddenly, her body jerks from the fury of a wretched coughing spasm. A muscle squeezes in my chest. I search her face. This happened to Maggie once — a memory slip, a bad cough, and the very next thing she was having a stroke.

"Smile for me."

Confusion clouds Honoree's eyes. "I don't have a thing to smile about."

"Do you recognize me?" The strain in my voice scares me, but Honoree is clearing her throat once — twice — three times.

"Honoree, say something. Please."

"I know who you are and stop hovering."

Thrilled by the sound of her voice, I exhale, but I'm still worried. What are the other signs of a stroke? I hunt for a dangling arm, a drooping left or right side of the face, slurred speech — but she just spoke, so her voice is fine — but I don't wish to take any chances. "I'm going to ring the nurses' sta-tion." I move toward the landline on the nightstand next to her bed.

"You touch that phone, and you won't see me for a week. I swear to God. I'm fine. Just tired."

I step away from the nightstand. "Okay. Calm down. I won't call. Relax."

I turn toward the wall clock and slip my cell phone out of my pocket. Without looking at the keypad, I text Lula. Some high school skills are forever useful.

"Hey, I need to hit the men's room." I backpedal toward the door. "You'll excuse me." I don't want her to think I'm as worried as I am, but when I reach the front desk, I am sweating, and my voice is an octave shy of shouting.

A female attendant with thick braids crowning her head like a turban winces when I speak.

"Something is wrong with Honoree Dalcour. I think she's having a stroke."

"I'll check on her now." She rushes off toward Honoree's room.

An instant later, Lula passes by, giving me a sharp nod as she heads for Honoree's room, too.

My legs are stiff, and my headache is fire, but I don't move from the reception desk. I am in the same spot as when they left when Lula returns.

"How is she? Is it a stroke?" There is a hitch in my voice. "Is she dead?"

Lula shakes her head. "She needs to rest. Why don't you take another day off?"

"Thank God, it wasn't a stroke. Maggie had a stroke once, while I stood by dumb as dirt, watching it happen. I was eight or nine, but I should have known something was up."

"You were right to worry, but for now, she's doing well."

I rub my palm across my brow. "I'll check in with you tomorrow." I start to move by Lula, but she's in my way, not defiantly, just enough of a roadblock that I can't run. My distress is palpable.

"I received a text from my aunt Deidre. She searched her cloud. The man who visited Miss Honoree a year ago also came to visit her in 2002."

"You're shitting me."

Lula pulls her cell phone out of her pant pocket, swipes, and reads. "He also has the same last name as you."

Amazing how bullshit happens in threes. I take two days off, Honoree is too tired to talk today and tomorrow, and the microphone drops. "Let me guess. His name is Marvin Alexander Hayes."

Lula's surprised expression confirms my not-so-wild guess. "You're right. You know him."

"Of course I do," I say with an uneasy chuckle. "He's my father."

CHAPTER 25
HONOREE

Early November 1925
(The first few days)

The sky was bright blue, and the sun golden yellow, and the temperature warmer than any single November day Honoree could recall. Although it was only the first day of the month and the weather in Chicago changed on a dime.

After waking up at noon, she grabbed a late breakfast, a boiled egg and a cup of java, and asked Bessie if she wanted to join her for a walk through the neighborhood. Bessie agreed, but their stroll took them farther than Honoree had planned. They ended up in the heart of the Loop near her favorite department stores.

Carson Pirie Scott, Marshall Field's, and Mandel Brothers — the fashion, the fabrics, and the wealth — Honoree loved everything in those stores but never made a purchase. Dancing at Miss Hattie's, a girl didn't make uptown-department-store money. Honoree window-shopped. She studied the latest dress patterns and examined the reams of silk, linen, cotton, wool, and rayon in brilliant greens, yellows, reds, and vibrant blues.

Rich white folks lived on the Gold Coast, which was somewhat close to the Loop, but farther north. Honoree slipped into that neighborhood occasionally to rummage through garbage bins and unguarded crates of excess clothing. When her luck was riding high, she'd find some beautiful fabrics, lace, twine, needles and thread, and discarded fancy dresses. It wasn't thievery, exactly, but her forays were far less expensive than shopping at department stores like Marshall Field's.

By early evening, she and Bessie were back in the neighborhood at Mr. Turner's Grocery Store, and Honoree was apologizing for missing Sunday service.

"I'll try to make it next week." She smiled. Mr. Turner always asked.

"Sure you will," he said, squinting over his spectacles with the look of a man who expected the same excuse from her the next Sunday.

"I'll take two bottles of Coca-Cola and two Baby Ruth candy bars." A minute later, she was standing next to Bessie, who was waiting, head back, eyes shut, facing the sun.

"This is like one of those days in Jacksonville." Bessie opened her eyes and took the bottle of Coca-Cola from Honoree's hand.

"When were you ever in Jacksonville?"

"I was born on a farm outside Jacksonville. My pops grew corn and raised pigs and chickens. My mother planted beans, tomatoes, and strawberries, and my brother and I shucked corn and string beans." She took a swig of her soda. "I skinned two rabbits before I was six."

"For some reason, I thought you worked the Chitlin' Circuit."

"I did — but that was after my brother was killed and we had to leave the farm in the middle of the night."

"What did he do to get killed?"

"I don't rightly recall what he did, but they hung him for it, or as my father said, he got lynched. I was a kid when it happened. He was quite a bit older than me. Sixteen, almost a man when he died."

"Your parents went from farming and burying a child to performing on the circuit?"

"Oh, no. They died a few weeks after we left Jacksonville, caught the Spanish flu. Most of the people we met in the circuit died of the Spanish flu," Bessie said, sounding accustomed to bad times.

A newsboy walked toward them, making a ruckus, shouting something. Honoree wasn't paying attention to his noise or the honking car horns, or the people walking by. Bessie's story had touched her heart. Not only because of the tragedy of her tale, but how casually she'd told it, without a tear shed, or any other emotions.

"Honoree, did you hear that?"

"I heard you, Bessie. I'm sorry your life has been hard, but —"

"Hush!" Bessie raised a quick finger. "Not me, but the paperboy. Did you understand what he said?"

The paperboy was shouting, "Dreamland Cafe to reopen Saturday night!"

Bessie squealed. "Open Saturday! Does it mean you can go back to work?"

"Yes. I think so. Yes. They must've found Houdini's killer. Thank the Lord!" Honoree had to stop herself from breaking into a jig.

She ran to the newsboy, who stepped back, his eyes big and mouth wide open. She'd scared him.

"Wanna newspaper, ma'am?" he asked, shaking.

She handed him a nickel and took a copy. The *Whip* was another Chicago weekly newspaper for Negroes. The front-page article described the Dreamland Cafe as the grandest of the grand. Hand-painted shades hung from the domed ceiling with red, white, and blue incandescent electric lights, and a new Brussels carpet. It was the most beautiful dance hall in the world.

The article went on to talk about Mr. Buttons and the rumors about him and the murder of George "Houdini" Mills. The newspaper emphasized they were only rumors and that Mr. Buttons was an up-standing man of the Race.

Bessie leaned over her shoulder. "Can't believe you're going back to work. I'm so happy for you."

Honoree tucked the paper under her arm. "You wait here," she said. "I finally get to make this phone call."

Honoree hurried back inside the grocery store and handed Mr. Turner a coin.

"I'm gonna make a fortune off you, Ms. Dalcour."

"No. I don't think so. This will be the next-to-last call I make for a while."

"Who do I need to dial up first?"

"The Dreamland Cafe."

Honoree took the receiver from Mr. Turner's hand and recognized Zelda's voice immediately.

"Is it true?" She listened intently, smiling from ear to ear. "Yes . . . yes. I'll be there. See you then . . . thank you . . . thank you!"

Honoree passed the receiver to Mr. Turner. "One more call, to Miss Hattie's Garden Cafe."

"I got your Miss Dolly on the line." Mr. Turner handed her the phone.

"Hello." Honoree waited for a reply, but there was only silence. "This is Honoree. I won't be coming back to Miss Hattie's — I got a new job."

Miss Dolly finally spouted a few nasty words about Honoree's constitution, followed by a warning about Archie's uncontrollable temper once he heard the news.

"I wager he already knows and won't be mad."

Honoree finished the call and thanked Mr. Turner. Once outside in front of the store, she hugged Bessie. "I'll never have to dance across that crappy stage again. Hallelujah."

Bessie wiggled free of the embrace, not as cheerful as before.

"Why are you looking so solemn?" Honoree asked.

"We won't be dancing together anymore."

"We live together and can dance together at home." Honoree sighed. "It'll be better for us not to spend so much time together, anyway. We'll have more to talk about in the evenings."

Bessie blinked back tears and put a grim smile on her face. "I'll keep you up-to-date on all the news at Miss Hattie's."

Honoree didn't give a hoot about the news from Miss Hattie's, but she didn't say that. "Come on, Bessie. Let's celebrate. The Dreamland Cafe is opening back up, and I feel like making a new dress with sparkles, and I'll make you one, too."

Honoree returned to the Dreamland Cafe Tuesday afternoon for her first official rehearsal, just like Zelda had instructed on the telephone — and it was a doozy of a rehearsal, too. "I thought we practiced in the same room where we auditioned?"

"Not today," Hazel said.

Honoree rushed by Colethea and Hazel into the main dance hall. Most of the chorus girls had already piled onto the stage. The dance master strolled in next, looking dapper in his suspenders, red shirt, and black breeches, and pointing his cane at the piano player, directing him to the balcony. Both men appeared the same as the night she first saw them. Superior, self-contained, and in charge.

"This Saturday, on opening night, I expect

perfection," the dance master said. Then he proceeded to lead the girls through three straight hours practicing routine after routine. Until finally, he said, "Take a break."

The chorus girls collapsed where they stood, gulping air, dripping sweat, massaging sore limps, and begging for glasses of water.

Colethea tapped Honoree's shoulder. "Do you see who's watching us?" She pointed toward the bar.

Squinting, Honoree tried to make out the figure on the other side of the room. A woman stood in a beam of light, wearing a floor-length mink coat and a rhinestone-studded cloche hat. Petit but statuesque, she had an air of self-confidence that made everything that wasn't her seem flustered and flabbergasted. Honoree yelped like a puppy. "Lil Hardin Armstrong. The Queen of the Stroll. The Wizard of the Keys. The ritziest twenty-seven-year-old woman in Chicago jazz music and married to New Orleans trumpet player Louis Armstrong — oh my God."

Colethea grinned. "Child, calm yourself."

Lil sat on one of the barstools and opened her ravishing mink coat.

"Is she wearing the new Chanel tweed

suit?" Honoree muttered. "The one with the sequins?"

"I have no idea what the suit's called other than swell."

Honoree thought about how the dance master had worked the chorus, and every ache in her body seemed suddenly wholly worthwhile. "She's why he rehearsed us so hard."

"You're right," Colethea said. "She and her husband's band are opening here next week."

"I heard, but I never expected her to show up at a rehearsal."

"He's being billed as the greatest trumpet player in the world."

"Of course he is."

"Everyone likes how Louis blows."

"Girls!" The dance master signaled the piano player in the balcony. "Let's go through the number again. From the top."

A groan went through the room. Honoree sprang to her feet and strutted to the center of the stage. She shook her hands and shoulders and tapped her feet, performing full out every step of every movement the dance master showed them. After two more run-throughs, the piano player finally stopped playing for the night. The dancers bent at the waist, sucking wind. Honoree scanned the bar for Lil Hardin Armstrong, praying she was still there, watching.

And she was, sipping a drink from a tall glass.

Honoree wiped her brow. It had been perfect; her first rehearsal at the Dreamland Cafe had been ab-so-lute-ly perfect.

The next day, Honoree was on her way to another rehearsal, but the weather, being Chicago weather, had changed seemingly overnight from sunny and splendid to cloudy, rainy, and dreadful.

It made her late, and she raced into the alley behind the cafe, blinded by the rainstorm's thick downpour. Which partly explained why she ended up lying on her backside in a puddle of soupy mud.

"Damn!" Honoree lay on her rump. Legs stretched out before her. "Damn." She rolled onto her hands and knees, rose to her feet, and noticed a ripped seam in her dress. Because of her fall, she'd not only be late for rehearsal but arrive looking a filthy mess.

"Damn!"

The curse had not come from Honoree's mouth. There was another body in the mud mumbling a string of profanities. How had Honoree missed her and the beautiful, full-length mink coat she wore. She also had on a gorgeous pair of Mary Jane shoes with rose-colored ribbons, or they'd been rose-colored before they were ruined.

"Oh my, are you all right? Are you hurt?" Honoree reached for her hand, but the woman was searching for something and eventually lifted a mud-streaked box purse from the mire.

"Thank goodness. I thought I'd lost it."

"I'm sorry. My apologies. I didn't see you with the rain coming down so hard and all."

The woman raised a finger. "Stop babbling. I'm not hurt, but I could use some help getting out of this mud."

Honoree took her outstretched gloved hand and helped her to her feet. Once erect, each woman gave the other a head-to-toe exam. Honoree recognized her, lost her breath, and suddenly wanted to die. "Oh my God. Lil Hardin Armstrong. I can't believe I knocked the Queen of the Stroll into the mud. I am so very sorry."

"Please, stop apologizing." Ms. Hardin adjusted the cloche hat on her head. "Let's get inside before we drown in mud." She hurried up the steps and into the kitchen.

Honoree followed, struggling with the desire to keep apologizing. "I'm not clumsy," she said, as they walked briskly through the kitchen. "Anything ripped or torn, I can fix. I'm an excellent seamstress."

"I saw you rehearsing yesterday, didn't I? You were working on a new production number. It looked like the cat's pajamas."

Honoree's heartbeat was a thousand-drum serenade. "Oh my! Did you think so? We saw you watching us — and you noticed me. Goodness!"

Ms. Hardin smiled. "What's your name?"

"Honoree. Honoree Dalcour." She had spoken so fast that she bit her tongue, but not even pain could lessen the width of her grin.

"Such a fancy name. You aren't French, are you?"

"My papa was Creole, and I was born in Baton Rouge, but I've been in Chicago since 1909. So, most of my life."

"You know Louis was born in New Orleans."

"Yes, ma'am."

"Don't *ma'am* me. Call me Lil." She smiled warmly, then started down a hallway with Honoree at her side. "Where'd you work before you started here?"

"A colored-only speakeasy near the stockyards. The Dreamland is my first job at a black-and-tan." Honoree shrugged out of her mud-covered coat as they walked.

Lil arched a brow. "A lovely gown. An

original?"

Honoree smiled proudly. "I made it my-self."

Lil tilted her head. "What was your name again?"

"Honoree."

"You could give our costume mistress a few lessons." Lil touched the stitching on the waistline. "Nicely done."

"Thank you, Ms. Hardin. I mean, Mrs. Armstrong."

"Now, what did I say?"

"Sorry, I meant Lil."

"Do you make clothes for people other than yourself?"

"Are you asking if I take dress orders?" Honoree said. "Other than gowns for my roommate and me, I've made some costumes for the chorus girls at Miss Hattie's."

"I could use some new gowns. Wouldn't be the Queen of the Stroll without some one-of-a-kind dresses in my wardrobe."

"I can do that — make you some original gowns. It would be my honor."

Ms. Hardin smiled. "I'd pay you, of course." She removed her gloves, tugging one elegant finger at a time. "Come to my dressing room tomorrow night. You can take my measurements, and we can talk about fabric and colors."

"Yes, ma'am," Honoree said, adding a nervous chuckle. Was she talking to Lil Hardin? Was it a dream? Hopefully, she wouldn't spoil it by having a conniption. "I use a sketchbook, too, and can show you some of my dress design ideas."

"Swell. I think our meeting was meant to be. I look forward to seeing you tomorrow."

Honoree took Ms. Hardin's hand and started shaking it until the woman winced. "I'm sorry." She released her, grinning. "This is wonderful, ma'am. Just wonderful."

"Now, what did I say about calling me ma'am?" Ms. Hardin said flatly.

"Sorry, I meant see you tomorrow night — Lil."

After rehearsal, Honoree practically floated home and bounded into the kitchenette, her excitement uncontainable. "Guess who I ran into, I mean ran over, this afternoon?"

Bessie sat at the table, shoulders shaking, hands over her eyes, fat tears dripping from her chin.

"What in damnation is wrong with you?" Honoree asked.

The tears continued with no words coming from her lips, only blubbering.

"I can't help unless you tell me what's wrong."

Bessie kept whimpering. Honoree dropped her bags and sat at the table across from her. "Let me take a look at you." She moved her hands. The girl had a bruise on her jaw the size of a strawberry, and one of her eyes was swollen halfway shut.

Honoree leaped to her feet, hurried to the door, and bolted it. "Who did this to you? Did you go back to the man who beat you? Did he beat you again?"

"I had to go back. I had to talk to him."

Honoree moved her chair next to Bessie's. "Talk to him about what? You don't need him for nothing."

"I'm sorry."

"Nonsense. You don't need to be sorry. This guy is the goof." Honoree touched Bessie's hand. "What's his name? Who is he?"

"No. You don't need his name."

"Is it Archie? Is that why he gave you the job?"

"You don't need to know," she said, gulping sobs.

Looking at Bessie's swollen face, listening to her crying, Honoree felt sick to her stomach.

She rose and went over to the sink, wet a

washcloth, and returned to Bessie. Taking hold of her chin, she wiped her nose, her tears, and her bruises.

"Stop bawling. I guess I understand needing the company, but after being on my own for so long, I always feel lonely now and then."

"I'm not lonely. That's not what's got me upset." Bessie looked at Honoree with swollen, tear-filled eyes. "I think I'm gonna have a baby." The sobbing escalated, giving Honoree a moment for the shock to settle in.

"Are you sure? Do you even understand how pregnant feels?" Honoree had no clue herself about how it felt, but there was something she did know. "Did you have your monthly?"

She shook her head between sniffles. "Not in two months. Since before I met you at Miss Hattie's."

Honoree grabbed her hand and squeezed. "Did you tell the man who got you pregnant? Is he the one who hit you? What do you want to do?"

Another rush of tears fell over Bessie's cheeks. "I wish he were dead. I wish I never met him. I'm a dancer now. I can't have a baby. I don't want a baby."

Bessie neared hysteria. Honoree could do

nothing but listen.

"I didn't do the things a smart girl does," Bessie said. "I forgot about the vinegar and the sponge. And he — he was always in a hurry. Never gave me time to get ready."

Honoree closed her eyes. The bad and the good again. It never seemed to fail. Only a couple of days since they had heard about the reopening of the Dreamland Cafe and just a few hours since she had met Lil — and this happens. "So the father is the same man who hit you?"

"Only bedded one man since I been in Chicago. It means he has to be the baby's daddy, right?"

Honoree rubbed Bessie's fingers, making little circles over her knuckles, hoping to soothe her. "Do you want to keep the baby?"

Bessie blinked up at her. "I don't know. I don't know what to do. I ain't got no money for a baby. I won't be able to dance, and the baby's father, he don't want me any-more, and I don't want him anymore, either. I told him what you said about him not hit-ting me. I told him my friend knows better than him about how people should be treated. He didn't like hearing it."

"Do you want me to ask Ezekiel for help? He is a pretty important man around town, since he runs the policy gambling wheel for

Archie. He could talk to this man and make him give you some money, but you have to tell me his name."

"That would be awfully kind of you and Ezekiel." Bessie rested her head on Honoree's shoulder. "I don't want you to find out his name. I don't want to think about him again." The weeping returned, louder and wetter than before. "What will I do with a baby?"

"We can't talk about it until you calm down." Honoree rose. "I'll make you a cup of tea." She pulled her mother's quilt from the cot and wrapped it around Bessie's shoulders. "Why don't you lie down."

"On the cot?"

"Yes. And all alone. I'll sleep on the floor."

It took an hour for Bessie to doze off. Honoree sat at the kitchen table, trying to remember every moment of her meeting with Lil Hardin Armstrong. But all she could think about was the good and the bad.

Like a field of dead dandelions popping up to ruin the view, the good and the bad, the back-and-forth kept slouching her way.

CHAPTER 26
SAWYER

Saturday, June 27, 2015

This is bull. My father had met Honoree, visited her the year my mother died, and again after Azizi died — but hadn't mentioned these visits when I told him I was in Chicago, interviewing a 110-year-old-woman for my film project. Here, he'd met her two goddamned times, a decade apart — each time when death had knocked at our family's door — but somehow forgot to tell me?

There has to be an explanation — something that will make sense and answer the question: *Why?*

In my room at the hostel, I'm staring at nothing and seeing everything. I have to call him and ask him, no, demand the truth about his visits to Honoree. But I don't want to hear his voice telling me lies. I open the app on my cell and text him.

Me: We need to talk.

Dad: What happened? Are you okay? What did you do?

Wow. Right off the freaking bat, he jumps to conclusions.

Me: No, I haven't harmed myself, or done some other wrong thing.

Why can't a son reach out to his father about something other than a car crash? Or to apologize — sorry, I swallowed too many pills?

Dad: What's going on?

Me: Tell me about Honoree Dalcour and why you visited her. Two times. Once when Mom died and again after Azizi.

Dad: Let me call you.

Me: I don't want to talk now. Text.

The dots play across the cell phone's screen.

Dad: I should've said something.

You damn Skippy.

Me: Like what?

Dot. Dot. Dot.

Dad: Before she got sick, your mother and I were helping curate a museum project on the Jazz Age. One afternoon she wanted to check the box in your grandmother's attic. There were some things we could use inside that box, she said.

Lorraine didn't want to ask Maggie straight out. They didn't get along, either. So, she "bor-

rowed" what she wanted. Lol.

That gave me a chuckle, too. Mom and I had used the same technique with Maggie.

Dad: We had intended to return the papers during our next visit, but then your mother was diagnosed.

A few months after she passed, I decided to finish the last project we started together. I couldn't locate the papers Lorraine had borrowed. Still, I remembered the name Honoree Dalcour and the Bronzeville facility, and while on a trip to Chicago, I called the facility and ended up on the phone with Honoree.

I couldn't believe she was still alive. I told her about Maggie's documents and Lorraine, and she insisted I stop by and visit her.

She told me Maggie had stolen those things from her when she put Honoree in the facility in 1985.

Then she gave me some bullshit about a curse.

Until this last text, I am starting to believe Dad had a heart-driven reason for visiting Honoree, at least the first time. Then he talks about a curse, and I've had enough.

I switch screens, key in his number, and he picks up before the first ring ends.

"Sawyer. Yeah. I'm sorry, I should've said something when you called."

"A fucking curse?"

A pause. Perhaps he's alarmed by my language, but damn, what does he expect?

"Dad!"

A sigh. "She said the women in our family were cursed." His voice is audible but steady. "They came from a line of bad women, starting with Maggie. Cursed to suffer pain-filled lives, dark and tragic, because of their roots."

He pauses again. The silence goes uninterrupted. I want him to keep talking while I process this insanity.

"I thought she was just an old woman struggling with her decline," he says. "Then she began ranting. Half of what she said, I took as the ravings of a lunatic and walked out. Your mother was dead, and I didn't need an elderly woman to tell me her ridiculous fantasies about my wife. I had wanted to finish this last project for Lorraine, but Honoree's nonsense about curses did something to me, and I couldn't."

His voice hitches, and I almost stop him. Tell him I don't want to force him to relive the pain of Mom's death, but I can't. I don't. I need to hear it all.

"Twelve years later," he begins again. "Azizi died. I couldn't get Honoree's words out of my head. I had to see her again and make sure. She was not some hoodoo priestess, not a soothsayer. But that time was worse. She kept shouting, 'I told you. The women are cursed.' She's not senile. Just cruel."

"It's not a hoodoo anything. She is capable of cruelty and hate when it comes to Maggie."

"But why? Maggie's money has helped her live a reasonable existence for more years than anyone has any right to hope for."

"It has something to do with a house in Baton Rouge."

"Oh my. Baton Rouge. One of the documents your mother took from Maggie was about Baton Rouge. I can't recall specifics, though."

Come on, Dad. Use that big brain of yours and remember.

"Something to do with a house?"

Another long pause. "Yes, a deed to a house."

"Maggie sold the house in Baton Rouge in 1990, but Miss Honoree claims she never owned it to sell."

"Around 1990, but your mother had a 1938 deed that named another owner."

"Who? Do you remember who owned the house in Baton Rouge?"

"Yes. Yes. I remember. It was a woman named Bessie Palmer."

CHAPTER 27
HONOREE

Early November 1925

On Saturday night, the Dreamland Cafe reopened. But Honoree missed the whole whangdoodle. She was on the third floor rehearsing the new vaudeville act with Colethea and Hazel. After three hours of hard practice, the dance master ended the rehearsal. As soon as he said they could go, there was a flurry of arms, legs, and lace-trimmed, sleeveless dresses, as Honoree and her friends changed lickety-split and raced into the dance hall for the midnight show.

The cafe was packed, and they made it no farther than the edge of the room. Rising onto her tiptoes, Honoree tilted her head back to see the band in the balcony — and get a peek at Louis Armstrong.

"Have you ever heard anyone play the trumpet the way he does?" Colethea yelled into her ear.

She slid sideways and stepped in front of

Colethea. She didn't want to miss a second of what was happening in the balcony. It was a celebration. The first time in her life she'd heard Louis Armstrong play his trumpet and she was watching him with her own eyes. The musicians in the band would mumble or shout from the rafters about Armstrong's talent. Most jazz musicians from Miss Hattie's had to trust what they'd heard about him from other musicians. Some had heard him on a phonograph. He'd had a record out in 1922. But nothing compared to being in the same room, listening to him play.

She couldn't stop bouncing. The music had every bone in her body jumping and jiggling. It was the same with the customers around her. Feet stomped, hands clapped, fellas and flappers were arm-in-arm, swinging and jerking. The sound of Louis Armstrong's horn and Lil's piano were like witchcraft, black magic, and no one could keep still. Maybe that's why old settlers and church people called jazz the Devil's music. It just had too much rhythm and too much swing to come from anywhere else.

Honoree tried to push her way onto the dance floor, but she ended up rooted to the same spot until Louis Armstrong blew his last note.

"Amazing," Hazel said, sounding hoarse. She had stayed next to Honoree until the set ended, shouting and bellowing like most patrons.

"I wonder what they're doing after the show." Hazel stared wistfully at the balcony.

"Celebrating, of course."

"Do you think we can get an invitation? I'd love to be at that party. Think of the men who will be there. Rich. Handsome." Hazel laughed. "If not handsome, talented."

Honoree had a similar thought. "We haven't had our debut performance yet. They don't know us. But once they do, we'll get invited."

She had kept her encounter with Lil Hardin to herself — so she wasn't exactly telling a fib.

"Maybe we'll get a chance to hang out with them socially," Colethea said.

"Maybe one day."

It was all Honoree could say since she and Lil were on their way to becoming fast friends if Honoree had anything to say about it. And it was time she was right about something.

The next Sunday evening, Honoree scurried through the kitchenette, searching for her gloves.

"It's a party for Louis Armstrong's friend Cab Calloway. He's a singer who got hired in the touring revue *Plantation Days* —" She raised the pair of lambskin gauntlet gloves in triumph. "I found them!"

Bessie sat at the kitchen table, mending one of King Johnny's shirts. It was her new gig, laundering and mending shirts for the boys in the Creole Jazz Band. It allowed her to chip in more cash for rent, and Honoree didn't argue. A baby was on the way, after all.

"Damn," Honoree cursed. "Where did I put it?"

"Now what are you looking for?"

"My purse. The pink-and-black beaded clutch with the metal handle."

"With the fancy design and the push-pull closure?" Bessie put down her sewing and turned in her seat, nodding toward the Singer sewing machine. "There, Honoree, on the windowsill."

"The fanciest thing I own." She waved the purse at Bessie. "Well, other than my dresses."

"Heard plenty about your dresses being the most beautiful in Chicago. More than a dozen times." She stabbed her needle into a buttonhole.

"Yes, you have. But I don't exaggerate

about my creations," Honoree said in a friendly tone despite Bessie's blatant dig. But Honoree forgave her since her morning had begun with upchucking. A show of temper was justifiable. "Lil likes fancy things, too, and throwing parties."

"I thought you were dropping off the dresses you sewed for her."

"I am."

"Then, even though you didn't get an invitation" — Bessie held up the shirt, examining it for more holes — "you should stay."

"Good Lord. I've been running around here like a chicken with my head cut off, putting on my best rags and carrying my new handbag. Of course I plan to stay for the party — whether I can wrangle an invite or not, I'm gonna try."

"You'll get invited." Bessie sighed. "You always get what you want."

Honoree paused. Bessie had sounded exhausted and unhappy. Stuck in the kitchenette, vomiting half the day away, she had a good reason to be sad, even sharptongued. "You should join me."

Bessie looked at her like she had two heads. "Stop teasing. I don't need to come."

"Put on a dress and do it quick. 'Cause I'm running late." Honoree looked her in the eye to make sure she understood. "It'll be fun. And I want you to come. But don't be mad if Lil doesn't ask us to stay."

Bessie pushed away from the table and moved around the kitchenette faster than fire. "Will there be cake?"

"Maybe. Maybe not, but it's not a birthday celebration. Calloway's birthday isn't until Christmas. He'll be on the road before then. More of a bon voyage."

"A bon, what?"

"French for leaving town."

Honoree looked at the parcel of dresses, fancy dresses, too, that had taken every free hour she wasn't dancing. "I should've thought of this earlier. I do need help carrying Lil's dresses."

Bessie washed up at the sink and, minutes later, put on Honoree's silver lamé.

"You look lovely, Bessie," Honoree said, moving toward the door. "Now, let's blouse."

Lil Hardin and Louis Armstrong lived in a ritzy part of town, on Forty-Forth Street a few blocks west of South Parkway. Their home was one of those lovely stone bungalows with a triangle roof and a tall chimney, a sunporch, and lots of big windows. So many windows, Honoree wondered if the house had room for walls.

"Come right on in, Miss Honoree. And who's this little girl?" Maximilian Chester greeted them.

"I am not a little girl," said Bessie, miffed. "I'm almost eighteen."

"You're sixteen," Honoree corrected her. "But you don't have to put on airs for Maximilian. He's a waiter at the Dreamland — and by the way, what are you doing here?"

"Moonlighting for Miss Lil."

Impatient to enter the house, Honoree peeked over Maximilian's shoulder. The interior of Lil's home was as glamorous as the outside, and there were plenty of walls. The dining room and living room, she glimpsed, were colorfully decorated with modern furniture, silk drapes, and lampshades. Honoree loved lampshades.

Maximilian was speaking. "This way, ladies. The party is in the center of the house, living room, dining room, and parlor."

Honoree glanced at Bessie and then Maximilian. "We aren't here for the party. I'm dropping off some dresses I made for Mrs. Armstrong, I mean Lil."

Bessie raised her arms, showing off the bundle.

He nodded and led them through the

small parlor into a hallway connected to the dining room — and Honoree stopped to stare.

Sun-bright yellow and green floral end chairs, a forest-green silk mohair upholstered sofa, porcelain table lamps with hand-painted bases, and silk bell shades — it was a page from *Motion Picture* magazine, except better. The only furnishings that didn't fit were two large paintings hanging above the fireplace. They seemed too stoic, too stiff, not quite right for the Queen of the Stroll. They were more like the French paintings Kenny talked about at the Art Institute of Chicago.

"I should introduce Lil to Kenny," she said to Bessie. "His paintings of chorus girls and jazz bands, or even his photographs of flappers and Bronzeville, would better suit the furniture."

Bessie's response was a soundless, mouth-open expression of awe. She had never seen anything as marvelous as Lil's home in her life.

"Mrs. Armstrong will be right out. Wait here," Maximilian said. "And don't worry about the shouting. Those two like to talk loud." He was referring to the screaming match on the other side of the door. Honoree started to object about being abandoned, but he'd already walked away.

"Should I wait on the porch?" Bessie asked.

Honoree took the bundle from her arms. "No, not on the porch, maybe in the dining room. This will only take me a moment."

The party hadn't started, but the house was set up for entertaining. The phonograph was in the dining room, and the tables and chairs had been moved against the windows, leaving plenty of room for dancing. Bessie wouldn't be in the way.

"I'll be right there as soon as I'm done."

With no other choice but to eavesdrop until someone opened the door, Honoree settled in for a listen. The Armstrongs were discussing a lanky bug-eyed Betty — Lil's words — who had tried to cash in on Louis's New Orleans charm. Lil wasn't having it. Louis swore he never messed with any woman in Chicago, other than Lil. A few choice words later, the door opened.

"Hello," Honoree said, feeling she'd been caught stealing the silverware.

The couple stood on opposite sides of a bedroom. Two single beds, a set of dressers, some lamps, and end tables were all Honoree dared to glimpse. She wanted to keep her eyes on Lil, difficult to do since she couldn't help being a nosy busybody.

Dark-skinned with a thin layer of processed hair on his head, Mr. Armstrong dabbed sweat from his brow. When he spotted Honoree, he smiled. The man wasn't Joe Brooks, but he had a devastating smile.

"And who's this?" His voice drawled with a tangy mix of swamp water and hot peppers. Honoree's father, also from New Orleans, had the same twang. Louis glanced at his wife.

"She's one of the girls from the chorus and a seamstress, too. See the bundle in her arms?"

"What's your name?" Louis opened a drawer.

"Honoree, Honoree Dalcour."

The drawer opened, he removed a white handkerchief and strolled over to Lil. "Nice to meet you, Honoree." He walked by her into the hallway. "Don't take too long, honey bunny. We're gonna have a mess of people show up here tonight." He blew Lil a kiss and left.

"Let me see those dresses." Lil ushered her into the bedroom.

A small-boned woman with a well-rounded figure, Lil made creating fashions for her effortless. She and Honoree had similar shapes, although Honoree was taller. "I brought you three dresses to try on. I

319

hope you'll like at least one of them. But I can always make adjustments if the size is off."

Twenty minutes later, Lil had tried on all the dresses. "I love them," she said. "I'm going to wear the navy-blue silk tonight." It had a pale pink sheet panel and rhinestones and pearls sewn on the seams.

"It looks great on you."

Lil dipped a hand into her purse and removed a stack of dollar bills. "Twenty bucks? The rest of what I owe you, right?"

"Yes, ma'am."

A few seconds later, Lil was twirling in front of her floor-length vanity mirror. "This is perfect. They are all perfect. Next, I love a floor-length dress."

"I can do that."

"Excellent."

Honoree folded up the burlap and wandered back toward the door, uncertain of which way to go or what to do next.

Lil stood in front of the mirror. "You should stay for the party."

"That would be great," Honoree said but then remembered. "My roommate — I mean my sewing partner, she came with me. I wouldn't want us to impose."

"No problem. Y'all are both welcome."

A giggly feeling flashed through Honoree.

"Thank you. Thank you, ma'am. I mean, Lil."

Lil laughed a rich, spicy laugh, like someone who ate filet mignon every meal. "Then come with me. Let's see who showed up for my shindig."

CHAPTER 28
HONOREE

"Look who's here!" Lil squeezed Honoree's elbow as they entered the dining room. "I can't believe my eyes. Alberta Hunter! I thought she was in Harlem." Lil touched Honoree's shoulder. "Got some gossiping to do with that girl. You go on now. Enjoy yourself. I'll catch up with you in a few."

Abandoned. Just like that, and Honoree was on her own. Not even Bessie had stayed where she was supposed to.

Not usually shy about mingling, Honoree had learned her version of etiquette on the other side of town. The people at Lil's party were the entertainment industry's New Negroes. Musicians, actors, actresses, and blues singers who demanded fair wages, regular hours, and days off. They also cursed less and were better looking than the hard-drinking, hard-living people who patronized or worked at Miss Hattie's.

Feeling more than mildly out of place,

Honoree crept into a corner near the buffet to watch Lil and learn before she embarrassed herself.

Lil was a fireball. Elegant and confident, she commanded whatever type of attention she desired. People listened to her when she told them nothing at all.

When Honoree met people, she swung her hips and bounced her bubs to hold their attention. But Lil and her gal friends, well, they were appreciated for what was on their minds, not the snugness of their shifts.

"Honoree, where have you been?" Lil called, waving from across the room. "Come on over here. I want you to meet some people."

She wandered over slowly, but Lil didn't seem to notice her awkwardness and introduced her with flair to Alberta, Fats, and someone named Earl.

Honoree smiled and nodded and hoped she didn't look foolish. Then a tall man with a striking way about him joined the group, and everyone's faces lit up, including Lil's.

"Oscar, I'm so pleased you were able to come tonight." Lil kissed him on one cheek and then on the other, gushing over him like he was a prize bull. "I'm so happy you made it."

"I told you I'd be here." He planted his

lips on Lil's hand. "Is this the girl I wanted to meet?"

Smiling, Lil tilted her head at Honoree. "Yes, sir. That's the one."

Oscar sized her up with glowing eyes. "She's such a pretty child."

Lil made a sweeping gesture with her hand. "May I introduce Honoree Dalcour, and this is Oscar Micheaux, writer, director, producer, filmmaker." Then she giggled next to Honoree's ear. "And he's been dying to meet you."

Both Lil and Micheaux laughed, holding their bellies, sharing a friendly joke.

Honoree smoothed her skirt over her hips. "Hello, Mr. Micheaux."

A jovial man with kind eyes, he bowed, a Rudolph Valentino kind of bow. "You are lovely." He extended his hand.

Honoree reached out to shake his hand, but he surprised her and kissed her knuckles.

"It's a pleasure to meet you, sir," Honoree said, hiding her astonishment with a grin.

"She does have a look." Oscar still held her hand. "You are a lovely dancer, too."

"That she is," added Lil.

"You're too kind. And thank you for the compliment, Mr. Micheaux."

"It's Oscar, sugar."

"Oscar." His flattery had tongue-tied her, but ambition was always top of mind. "I would love to be in a motion picture."

"She's not shy." Lil smiled. "She's in Mr. Buttons's new vaudeville production."

"When does this new act debut? When's your opening night?" Oscar pinched her cheek. "I'll make sure to be there."

Honoree swallowed a shriek. Instead, she smiled daintily as the conversation continued. Out of the corner of her eye, she spotted Bessie near the phonograph standing next to a couple of young men as Louis Armstrong's Hot Five recording with OKeh Records played.

There was a man seated next to her, his features hidden from Honoree's view, who was holding Bessie's attention. Honoree sensed something familiar about the man she could barely see in the tilt of his head and the breadth of his shoulders.

Then he stood, and Honoree reared back on her heels.

Ezekiel had Bessie giggling like a schoolgirl, only a few weeks after she tried to bash him in his head with a stick.

"Excuse me, I'm sorry," she said to Lil and Oscar Micheaux. "I see an old friend."

Honoree had not set eyes on him since the auto body shop. Walking toward him, she felt the nerves in her stomach tingle. "What are you doing here?" she said when she reached Ezekiel.

"Chatting with your housemate. She's been catching me up on the happenings at Miss Hattie's."

"You've been away? I had no idea you'd left town — again."

"Only for a few days," Bessie said with a silly grin on her lips. "He went to Detroit to visit friends."

"And how do you know his travel schedule?" Honoree asked, swallowing the unexpected gulp of jealousy in her throat.

"He just told me," Bessie offered.

"Do you mind — I need to chat with Ezekiel."

"Oh." Bessie looked unsure of where to go. "I guess I could eat some more food from the buffet."

As Bessie wandered off, Honoree turned to Ezekiel, only to discover disapproval in his arched brow.

"What did I do?" she asked.

"What's your beef with Bessie? She's a sweet girl who adores you."

"So you forgave her for trying to clobber you with a stick?"

"She misunderstood what was happening between us."

"And the next time she misunderstands, should I let her have a crack at you?" She took a breath. This was not a reason to walk across the room. "Let's forget about Bessie for a moment. Have you talked to Mr. Buttons?"

"Yes, and you're square with him."

"Just like that? Are you sure? And with Archie?"

He nodded, and she exhaled, relieved.

"Thank you, Ezekiel." She stepped in close to him. "Is that why you're here? To give me the good news? You could've left me a message at Mr. Turner's."

"I'm here because it's a party, and I like parties." He beamed at her in a way she hated to like but did. "What are you doing here, Honoree?"

She was about to give Ezekiel an elaborate reply, but Oscar Micheaux was slapping him on the back and greeting him like a long-lost friend.

"Ezekiel! Where have you been?"

"Around. What are you doing here? I thought you were in Harlem."

Then Lil arrived, and Ezekiel was kissing her on the cheek. "You look lovely, dear."

"And what do you think Oscar is doing?" Lil said. "Trying to talk these lovely ladies into making a motion picture?"

Ezekiel placed a hand over his vest pocket, protecting his wallet. "And raising funds for your next film, I'm sure."

Micheaux laughed. "Doesn't everyone want to be in the movies?" Oscar put an arm around Honoree's shoulders and squeezed. "Especially this beautiful young girl."

"Now, don't you get too attached to my friend," Ezekiel said with a slightly jealous tone. "She and I are old acquaintances who've only gotten reacquainted recently — and I would hate to lose her to showbiz fame. But her talent is worthy of the big screen." He turned and, in the most gentlemanly way possible, took Honoree's hand and stared romantically into her eyes. "I should tell you the story of how we met. It would make for a great love story in one of your motion pictures."

Honoree gasped — a love story. "He's teasing, of course."

Seeing her dismay, he laughed out loud. "Never."

Oscar's arm fell quickly from her shoulders as if caught messing with another man's wife. He cleared his throat. "Tell it. I love a good love story."

Ezekiel scratched his forehead, apparently

figuring out what kind of story he should tell.

Honoree's nervous laughter filled the lull. "Our story would make a lousy motion picture."

Ezekiel muttered a passionate disagreement. "I'm not so sure about that, Honoree." The arched eyebrow was meant for her. "We were children, and her mother and father —"

"These good people do not want to be bored with that old story." Honoree's voice was light and playful, but that had nothing to do with her jumbled insides. Lil and her friends didn't need to know her family had worked as servants in the Bailey home.

"Excuse me. I need another minute of your time, Ezekiel." She smiled at Oscar and Lil. "A friend of the family asked me to deliver a message if I ran into him, and I've run into him. If you would excuse us."

Honoree led Ezekiel toward the buffet table, thanking the Lord he hadn't resisted, but then that changed.

"Don't manhandle me, Honoree. I'm not that kind of fella," he said, smirking.

"I couldn't have you embarrassing me. I don't want Lil to know my parents worked for you. Or that I used to wash and iron your clothes."

"Honoree, I only intended to tell them we were friends and played together when we were children. Why do you have such little faith in me?"

"My days of putting my faith in you are gone." She said this without the usual sting in her heart. "I'm trying to make friends with these people. They can help me with my career. Unless you mess it up."

"Sweetheart, I'm not here to mess up anything for you." He lowered his voice. "The fact is these people are my customers."

"You came to Lil's party to take bets?"

"No, Honoree." The dimple in his cheek deepened. "I don't run numbers. I operate a policy wheel, but I also own an auto body shop. You were there, remember?" The teasing grin on his lips was annoying. "And since I can't be trusted, I'll also tell you that my brother and I worked on one of Louis's new automobiles, which I dropped off a few minutes ago."

"Oh." It was all she could think of to say. She snapped open her purse, removed a cigarette from her pack of Marlboros, and waved it in his face. "Can you light this, please?"

He fought a smile as he pulled a box of

matches from his pocket and lit her cigarette and then his own. A smoke ring rose between them, and for a moment that didn't feel too awkward, they stared into each other's eyes. She saw humor and affection in his gaze, but she wondered what he saw. Should she ask, or let the moment pass?

She inhaled the cigarette smoke deep into her lungs. "I think we should get back to the party," she finally said.

"No, I think *you* should. You've got Lil and Oscar under your spell; why don't I leave you to work your magic?"

Honoree tugged on his sleeve. "You're right. She's the bee's knees." She snuffed out her cigarette in an ashtray on the buffet and led the way back to Lil and her friends.

"Would you like a drink?"

Honoree whirled toward the voice behind her. Oscar Micheaux was holding a coupe of champagne. "Hope I'm not interrupting."

"Not at all, Oscar," Ezekiel said. "Sorry to monopolize this young lady's time. Old friends and all, you understand —"

"No worries. I was keeping an eye on you, wanted to make sure you didn't sneak off," Oscar said.

Honoree sipped her champagne as Lil swept over to the group.

"Have you met our guest of honor, Cab Calloway?"

Honoree shrugged, attempting to mask the excitement bubbling inside her.

"Would you like to meet him?"

"Love to, but can Oscar join us?" she said with a flirtatious lilt. "I want to learn more about your next movie. I've seen *Body and Soul* — it is glorious."

Ezekiel whispered in her ear, "I think I'll leave you now. You have this party well in hand." Then he raised his voice. "I hope you all won't mind if I excuse myself. I have some policy work to do this evening. No rest for the wicked —"

"Ahem, so you're a numbers man?" Oscar said, sounding critical.

"I know you aren't a fan of racketeering. But a Black man in America does what he can to contribute to the economy in Bronzeville."

"The auto body business doesn't pay you enough?" Oscar said.

"Ezekiel is a man with any number of skills," Lil said. "Auto repair, gambler, brawler, entrepreneur. In his short time back in Chicago, he's proven himself an invaluable man to know."

"Thank you, Lil." He bowed and kissed her hand.

She giggled. "And he's a charmer."

"Maybe you should be in one of my movies, then," Oscar chimed in.

Honoree grinned, but she was suspicious of Ezekiel's easy laugh and how he chatted effortlessly with Micheaux, Cab Calloway, and Lil. And they wouldn't let him leave. He kept talking, moving smoothly from topic to topic like any of the New Negroes. Race politics, the unionization of the Pullman porters, and whether a white boy in St. Louis named Bix could hold his own against Louis. But to Honoree, the real wonder was Lil; she was the real McCoy. "How are you enjoying our new record?" Lil asked the group.

There was a pause as everyone keyed in on the record playing on the phonograph. "Is that the one you recorded with the Hot Five, 'Gut Bucket Blues'?" Ezekiel said. "Surefire hit."

"Yes." Lil seemed impressed. "We only finished recording it the other day at OKeh."

"I know. I have eyes and ears in all parts of Chicago," he said, bowing. "And speaking of which, now I must excuse myself. I have another appointment."

There was a general sigh of disappointment; even Honoree had enjoyed his entertaining sidebars.

He took her hand and gallantly kissed her palm. "It was a pleasure having the chance to catch up, Honoree."

Honoree touched his sleeve as he turned to leave. "Let's make sure we find time to get together soon," she said, but realized with a slight panic that some might misunderstand her invitation. "In case there are more details on that business we discussed."

Amusement darkened Ezekiel's eyes. "I'm at your disposal."

Then he was off to wherever it was he had to be. Honoree watched him walk away, the handsome man with his Joe Brooks style and thick, wavy black hair, and when his eyes weren't black with rage, the specks of blue shone like the rhinestones in her best dress.

She and Ezekiel had fit well together when they were young, and from the eyebrow wagging of Lil and her friends, they fit well together still. Their kiss at the auto body shop had given her a jolt, admittedly. Was she falling back under Ezekiel's spell?

Honoree was not a fool, but Ezekiel was like a rod of the best silk fabric. She couldn't afford to own it, but pure silk was always something to be admired.

Turning, she gave Oscar Micheaux a flirty smile and said, "I can't believe you're already working on another film. What's its name? And is there a role for me?" She laughed, the way a carefree girl laughed with nary a worry in her head, and when Oscar laughed along with her, she tried to contain her excitement.

CHAPTER 29
SAWYER

Sunday, June 28, 2015

Sunlight slips through an opening in the hostel's blackout drapes. I had clicked off my cell hours ago — after I finished with my father. Now, I lie in bed, wrapped in sweat, drowning in the aftermath of another dream. But not the hands-on-the-steering-wheel dream.

In this one, Azizi is dancing, dressed in her ballerina outfit, pink and satin; her round face glows, but her collarbone is as thin as the blade of a knife. She looks beautiful and broken. I ask her if she's happy, and she smiles and says, *Not yet. Not right now. But soon, Sawyer. You wait and see.*

This dream bothers me. It should be a pleasant memory, but it hurts my heart.

Perhaps we are the same, my dad and I, seeking answers to life's tragedies in old documents, old women, old dreams, and

336

ghosts because we can't let go.

We wallow in grief and thrive on our broken hearts. But I want to change. I need to change. And the first mile on the road is to do whatever it takes to finish the thesis.

I think Maggie is more than the owner of a box filled with memories.

I will talk to her. Demand she tell me the truth, but first, I want to hear Honoree's story about Baton Rouge and Bessie Palmer and why she told my father "our women" were cursed.

Sitting on the edge of the tin desk in jeans and a loose-fitting plaid shirt (her other favorite outfit), Azizi nods and smiles. I believe she agrees.

Later that same day, I enter Honoree's room. We've got a lot to discuss, but for the first time since we met, none of it has to do with Oscar Micheaux, Louis Armstrong, or Chicago in 1925.

She is holding her Bible but places it on her stomach when she sees me. "What are we talking about today?"

Leaving the chair in the corner, I sit. "I talked to my father, and he told me he'd visited you twice. Once after my mother died, and then again, after my sister died. Do you remember?"

"Had lots of visitors over the years."

According to Lula, she has had only two visitors in more than a decade. But I don't call her on her exaggeration. Not when the fault could be a shaky memory or a wish for what might've been.

"What is your father's name?"

"Marvin Hayes."

"I remember him." She glances up at the ceiling. "I told your daddy the women in your family were cursed."

"Why would you say something like that? It stuck with my dad. It hurt him. It hurts me; after losing my mother and my sister, I'm still hurting. What you said was cruel and unforgiving. What did my dad do for you to say something so horrible to him?"

"Not your father. I don't care about him. I know what's what when it comes to curses, and I don't have to explain nothin' to you about why I said it." She is adamant, hostile. I don't know who she is right now.

"Come on, Honoree. This is important. Did it have something to do with Baton Rouge? Or Bessie Palmer?"

Her expression changes. The years sink into every wrinkle in her face and throat, and a sadness I can't imagine hollows her eyes. "I don't want to talk about Bessie Palmer. And Maggie never owned a house in Baton Rouge." Honoree wraps a withered hand around the railing. "Maggie should've never left Baton Rouge with that man. She should've kept her behind where she was."

"What is upsetting to you?" I am on my feet. "Why does a house in Baton Rouge and who or who doesn't own it bother you?"

There's a growl in the back of her throat. "You're like her — never telling the truth."

"Like who, Honoree? Tell me what's going on. I won't judge you. I just want answers."

"Your precious Maggie lied; don't you understand? Everything about her is a lie." There are tears in her eyes, but I don't believe she's crying. "Everybody lies, boy. You don't know Maggie the way I do. She can't help but lie. It's in her blood." Her laugh is too loud. Too sharp.

"Maggie cares about you. Why else has she taken care of you all these years?"

"Didn't she tell you? Didn't she tell you who I am?"

"You are her next-door neighbor. Her friend."

"A decent daughter would've told her child, told my great-grandchildren, I existed. Told you, my great-grandson, I was alive."

"Who are you talking about? Who told you that?"

"Maggie is my daughter. My only child. My flesh and blood, and she abandoned me. Left me in Baton Rouge alone for no god-damned good reason at all."

I jerk forward. "Damn it, Honoree, that's not true. Maggie never knew her mother."

"Don't you curse at me. Maggie is a liar. She didn't want nobody to know about me." Her eyes are red-rimmed, and her skin darkens.

I pace and can't stop shaking my head.

"She was an orphan. You two were neighbors. She would've told me."

"Told you what? That she had a mother who was alive, who she only bothered to see, or talk to, or write to once in thirty years? What kind of child doesn't want to see her mother? What kind of woman is Maggie White?"

"I should go so you can calm down."

"You remind me of Maggie," she said. "When the going gets tough, she makes hay in the other direction. Runs at the slightest heartache. A coward."

Damn. "I'm not a coward," I say calmly.

"And I told you not to curse at me."

What the hell? "I didn't say anything."

"I can read your mind."

"Jesus Christ."

"See. There you go, cursing again." Her

340

eyes close and lights out. Clear the auditorium. Beyoncé has left the building.

"Honoree. Don't pretend you're sleeping. I know you're awake."

"Sawyer, I could hear you halfway down the hall." Lula stands in the archway of Honoree's room, not looking pleased. "What's going on? This isn't good for her." She gives me a crippling glare. "This kind of bickering isn't good for either one of you. Come on. Get out of here." She steps aside to let me pass and follows me. "I can't believe you raised your voice to Miss Honoree."

I close my eyes briefly. Lula didn't witness the last time Honoree and I got into it. But I can't explain. "Sorry."

"Have you forgotten she's an older woman?"

I am pacing in the hall outside her room. "Of course I know how old she is. But did you hear what she said?"

"No, Sawyer. All I heard was shouting." Lula touches my forearm, an effort to stop me from pacing, which works.

"I have the day off tomorrow," she says. "How about if you meet me at the Harold Washington Library. My aunt Deidre works there. She can help fill in some of the gaps about Micheaux in Chicago in the 1920s. I think you — and Miss Honoree — could use another break from each other. Sawyer? What do you say? Library. Aunt Deidre?"

In light of what has just been told, a trip to the library could prove or disprove Honoree's latest tall tale.

"Yes. Yes. I don't need any more research on Micheaux, though. Will your aunt help me find everything there is to know about Miss Honoree?"

"Miss Honoree?"

"Her family, her friends, where she was born, where she lived, everything and anything that can be documented. Can she do that?"

Her expression of concern is replaced by curiosity, and she says, "I'll ask her. I'm not sure what she'll find, but I'm sure she'll try."

It's more than I can expect. "Excellent."

CHAPTER 30
HONOREE

Late November 1925

For the next week, before and after the show, Honoree (and sometimes Bessie) was invited to the Armstrong house for parties, lunches, and noodle juice — and the consumption of finger sandwiches with names such as *tutti frutti, devildine,* or *beef jelly.* All eaten while drinking the brown-colored lukewarm water called tea. None of which were the bee's knees Honoree had imagined.

Lil's china tea set was very pretty, though. The lips of the cups were gold-trimmed, and the paint didn't rub off when Honoree scratched the rim with her fingernail. Decorated with hand-painted pink flowers, they reminded her of a hydrangea garden.

She may not have enjoyed the food or the tea, but Honoree loved her new friends, especially Lil. Talking about the latest fashions, flipping through motion picture magazines, and shooting the bull, the Sunday afternoons and late-night gatherings had made the last couple of weeks the best weeks of Honoree's life. How could she not want every day to be like the day before?

"I'm buying a house," she announced to Bessie Sunday morning between bites of fried eggs and toast. "A bungalow like the one Lil and Louis Armstrong own — and on the same block. All I need is some money for a down payment."

Honoree lifted a fork to her lips, watching for Bessie's reaction. Not that her opinion had a ghost's chance of changing Honoree's mind, but somehow, if she agreed or disagreed, it would matter.

"Why don't we throw a rent party?" Bessie blurted.

"Throw a party in the kitchenette and charge people to come over to eat and drink?" Honoree grinned. "What a wonderful idea!"

The Sunday morning after Thanksgiving, Honoree and Bessie prepared for the rent party. Racing through the kitchenette, Honoree felt like a chicken without a head. She'd told every musician, dancer, waiter, chorus girl, singer, and neighbor she knew. And most of them swore they planned to attend.

"Rosie from the Diamond Diner is bringing macaroni and cheese." Standing over the kitchen table, Bessie shoveled down a spoonful of oatmeal. "She's also making pork and beans, your favorite, and fried potatoes and fried chicken." She swallowed the last of the oatmeal and gulped down a cup of coffee. "We can pay her after the rent party."

"One pan of baked pork and beans and some chicken should go into Laura Lee's flat. King Johnny will bring a couple of musicians. Kenny is loaning us his phonograph and a stack of new recordings. The band can play outside on the porch." She stopped. What had she been searching for? "Now, Ezekiel promised to bring a case or two of whiskey. Maximilian said he'd borrow a jug of Mr. Buttons's best beer."

Honoree checked off items from the list in her head.

"I hate the smell of beer." Bessie pouted. "You sure I can't lie down for half an hour before they come?"

Sweet Lord. "Stop whining. You sleep eighteen hours a day, and a few hours less sleep won't kill you." Honoree untied one end of the clothesline. "You're less than four months pregnant but behave as if you been pregnant for a year. You ain't even show-

345

ing." She glanced at Bessie's midsection. "Well, not much. Besides, Jeremiah will be here with the tables soon. You can show him where they go."

"Who's Jeremiah?"

"Ezekiel's younger brother. He's around my age. I think. Can't recall exactly." Honoree gathered a pile of clothes from the clothesline. When she finished folding them, she'd find a place to stow them. "I can't wait to live in a house with a closet and a dresser drawer."

"And an icebox and a stove with two burners."

"You're right." Honoree gave up the search and placed the undergarments and other items on the kitchen table.

"Once you get dressed, take these clothes and the sewing baskets, except for the heart-shaped baskets, over to Laura Lee's. She has an empty bin we can use."

"What are you going to do with those?"

"Don't worry about 'em. I'll put them away."

Bessie poured herself another cup of coffee. "How long have you lived here?"

"What made you ask me that?"

"I don't know. You got so much old stuff here, like the Singer sewing machine, and the baskets — and the quilt your mama made. It reminds me of something I saw in a house down south. The quilt had been passed down, from grandma to daughter, mother to child."

"I have no idea how old the quilt is, or who owned it before my mama. It doesn't matter. I'll take it with me when I leave." Bessie's questions bothered Honoree. Stirred up sentimental silliness she preferred to keep buried with all the old stuff that filled the kitchenette. "Since you have so many feelings about this old place, you can stay here when I move out."

Bessie gasped. "Oh, no. I didn't mean I didn't want to come with you to the new house. I was only wondering if you were ready to go." She twisted her lips to the side. "I'll keep my mouth shut if you're gonna fuss."

"Sounds like a good plan. Now, go on and get dressed."

Honoree had lived in the one-room flat since she was four years old and had a story for every corner, every piece of furniture, everything in the kitchenette. It all belonged to her. Even Bessie had become part of the furnishings. Still, it didn't mean she wouldn't move out as soon as she had the cash. It was time to let go of the past. "Is there any oatmeal left?"

"No," Bessie said. "The macaroni and cheese will be here soon. We'll have plenty of food."

An hour later, they had washed and dressed when Jeremiah knocked on the door.

"Have you met my roommate, Bessie Palmer?"

A handsome young man, Jeremiah was of similar height and width as his older brother, Ezekiel. But his eyes most often sought the ground. "Ma'am."

The one word was a greeting meant for both of them.

"Follow me," Bessie said with a striking giddiness. "I'm gonna show you where to put the tables."

Honoree stared in disbelief. Was she flirting with Jeremiah? Goodness. Lately, she darted from teary-eyed and belligerent to chatty and playful in a heartbeat. Jeremiah was very different from Ezekiel. He kept silent in the company of others, unlike his big brother.

There were three sturdy tables loaded into the cargo bed of his pickup truck. One table he carried into the alley and deposited near the foot of the stairs. Another, he lugged up two flights and pushed against the railing on the platform in front of Honoree's door.

Then, after moving a rocking chair into Kenny's flat, he dragged the last table into the kitchenette.

"We still need more room," Honoree said in a mild panic.

Jeremiah looked from Honoree to Bessie. "Ma'am. The cot?"

"What about it?" The two girls spoke in unison.

He lifted the cot and stood it on its end, careful not to hit the ceiling. Then he placed it in the corner next to the sewing machine.

Honoree squeezed Bessie's hand. "Excellent, Jeremiah."

"Ma'am." Another one-word response, which Honoree took as *You're welcome.*

"Thank you, Jeremiah." Bessie grinned.

Jeremiah hooked his thumbs on his suspenders. "Ma'am."

Honoree winced. One more *ma'am* and she'd smack him upside his head. But then, she might have to tussle with Bessie from the adoring look in her eyes.

"What do you think, Bessie? How does the place look? Didn't Jeremiah do a great job?"

"He sure did. A perfect job." Bessie's smile was as smooth as melted butter. "Looks mighty spiffy. I'd say Jeremiah is a swell egg."

■ ■ ■ ■

Partygoers arrived around nine o'clock, dropping their nickels into the bucket Honoree placed outside her front door. People she could trust, like Bessie and Kenny, collected the money. Every few minutes, they emptied the bucket and brought Honoree the loot. In between, Bessie traipsed behind Jeremiah wherever he went while Kenny wandered through the party, taking photos with his Kodak.

The weight of the coins pulled down Honoree's coat pocket, making her happy but also sad. Was she going to move? Leave the only home she remembered and the memories of the family she'd once had?

Distracted and melancholy, she stayed in the alley, enjoying the comfort of the bonfire Jeremiah had built — as the temperature hovered near freezing.

Bessie joined her. "I think we made enough money for the down payment and a new stove and an icebox."

Honoree's chest closed. "Maybe. Maybe not."

"We could be in a new house by January."

"More likely not until spring, but —" She eyed Bessie's belly briefly. "No worries, we'll move long before your baby is born."

Bessie smiled. "I can't believe this is happening."

"Neither can I." Honoree paused. "How's the bar in my place? Has Ezekiel run out of booze yet?"

"He's gone through three crates. I helped Jeremiah toss the empties into the bonfire."

Between the bonfire, some food, and dancing, she should thank Ezekiel for helping out. "I'll go see how he's doing."

As Honoree entered the kitchenette, Ezekiel stood behind one of the sturdy tables Jeremiah had carried up the stairs. A crowd surrounded him, and they oohed and aahed like watching a boxing match. Rising onto her tiptoes, she saw him hunched forward, his head down, looking at the tabletop. Still, she couldn't see.

She eased by a couple of large-boned fellas and a scantily dressed flapper until she stood across from Ezekiel. That's when she got a clear view of what he was doing — a whopping surprise.

Ezekiel was performing a card trick — three-card monte and with flourish and flair. No wonder the crowd had gathered. His sleight of hand was flawless. A smile brightened his face, and his eyes sparkled, his enthusiasm visible from where she stood. He ended the trick and bowed to an enthusiastic round of applause.

"Thank you. Thank you," he said, addressing those gathered. "Sadly, though, my liquor crates are empty, and my skill with cards has reached its limit. There should be some beer next door, in the photographer's flat."

A few groans of disappointment, but more cheers praised Ezekiel and his card skills. The crowd filtered away as Honoree approached. "I see you ran out of hooch."

Ezekiel winced a grin. "Sorry. I thought I'd brought more than enough. Didn't expect all of Bronzeville to be here."

"I never imagined you knew three-card monte."

"Even an old dog has new tricks." His chest puffed up. "I have great hands, Honoree."

"A doctor's hands."

A flash of pain in his eyes and a grimace in the lines around his mouth — damn. Why did she say that? She hadn't meant to remind him of the man he'd promised to be.

Ezekiel shoved the deck of cards into his pocket. "You have to do something clever to keep the mob calm when the booze runs out at a rent party."

She moved to the other side of the table. "I didn't mean anything," she said.

"It doesn't matter."

"It does matter." It had to, since he couldn't look her in the eye. "Thank you for the booze, for tending bar, for the tables, and for fixing things with Mr. Buttons."

"You thanked me, and we shouldn't talk about it here." He lowered his voice. "Remember, many of the folks here are my customers. I don't want them to think I do favors for some people and not for others."

"Some people, or just me?"

"Only for you, Honoree."

She believed him, and the realization gave her a hard shiver.

"Are you cold?" He raised a hand. "Do you want my coat?"

Before she could reply, a frantic male voice hollered, "Ezekiel!"

They both pivoted toward the door. Jeremiah was running toward them, the expression on his face thoroughly unsettled.

"Dewey Graves is here. Showed up down at the bonfire."

Ezekiel turned to Honoree. "Did you invite him?"

"No. Never. You know Dewey. He'll show up for no good reason other than to cause trouble."

Ezekiel scowled. "He needs to leave."

"Honoree!" Now it was Bessie yelling and running at them. She shoved Jeremiah's sizable frame aside and grabbed Honoree's arm. "There are a bunch of white boys outside."

"What white boys?" Ezekiel asked.

"In the alley behind the building." Bessie panted. "It's one of them athletic clubs."

Honoree knew all about the "athletic clubs," groups of white boys who hurt Negroes who had moved into a white neighborhood and crossed the athletic club's race line. They firebombed houses, burned them to the ground — and the coppers let 'em.

Jeremiah placed a hand on his brother's shoulder. "They're here for Dewey."

"It's not an athletic club. They don't come this far south," Ezekiel said. "You two stay here." He headed off with Jeremiah at his side.

Partiers milled around, whispering. Others headed toward the window, which overlooked the alley. They peered down, searching for the white faces as the embers of the bonfire gave some dim light.

Honoree wasn't keen on taking orders from Ezekiel but waited a beat before following him with Bessie tagging along behind her. A group of white men, six of 'em, had

354

gathered at the bottom of the stairs.

Ezekiel and Jeremiah stopped at the end of the first flight. Honoree watched from behind a narrow strip of wood, but they blocked her view of the white men. It didn't, however, prevent her from seeing the crowd surrounding them, her rent party guests. Quiet as mice, they seemed to be waiting for a cue to run, she imagined. The way Ezekiel and Jeremiah behaved told everyone these men were dangerous. The two brothers were also outnumbered and on their own.

"Ezekiel?" Honoree had breathed his name. He turned, but his eyes held so much violence, she shrunk a step away.

"Go to Kenny's and take Bessie with you."

"Go on," Honoree said to Bessie, removing the girl's small hands from at her waist. "Do as Ezekiel says."

"Honoree, I was talking to both of you!"

"Don't yell at me," she said, but the deadly look in his eyes screamed this was not the time for her stubbornness.

"Fine." She snatched hold of Bessie's hand and climbed a few stairs until she reached her idea of a safe distance. Then she turned back to watch.

Dressed in long tweed coats, the white men hid their eyes beneath the brims of their fedoras. Only one of the men held his head up, his focus on Ezekiel. Stubs of black hair covered his face and neck, and an ugly gash crossed his chin. The same man limped forward. "Where is he?"

"Not here," Ezekiel replied. The scarred man limped up the stairs, meeting Ezekiel halfway.

"Don't lie." The man sniffed the air. "His stink is filling my nostrils, or this part of town has enough colored stink here already. I can't separate his stench from the rest of y'all. What do you think, Ezekiel?"

Honoree's heart pounded wildly in her rib cage. Bessie now clung to her waist, her small fingernails digging into her flesh.

"Go on now. Go on over to Kenny's," Honoree said.

Bessie nodded feebly but didn't budge. Honoree sighed and went back to watching Ezekiel.

With steady hands, Ezekiel pulled a pack of cigarettes from his vest pocket and brought a cig to his lips. He didn't gesture for a light, but Jeremiah, with a flaming match in hand, a move that seemed practiced, lit his brother's cigarette. Inhaling deeply, he drew the Chesterfield into his lungs. Ezekiel stepped down, one step, but still towered over the gimp.

The white man said something Honoree couldn't understand, but the next part was a fire engine's bell clanging in her ears.

"Tell Dewey, Capone ain't gonna give him another warning. He's still selling bootleg hooch, already enough to get him killed."

"I'm not his keeper," Ezekiel said.

"The only reason he's alive is his brother. So tell Archie to take care of it." He tipped his hat. Then he and his gang trekked back through the alley and into the dark.

Honoree slid from her hiding place but almost retreated as Ezekiel raised his voice.

"Fuck!" He faced his brother. "I'll kill him."

The murderous rage in Ezekiel's voice might be unfamiliar, but his rigid frame made him appear capable of anything, of everything. God.

"Who were those men?" she asked, moving as close as she dared. "Why did Dewey come here?"

"Looking for my brother to save him, I wager." Jeremiah's gaze never left Ezekiel's face.

"They followed him here."

Ezekiel took off quickly with Jeremiah at his heels. Honoree wouldn't get any answers standing on the stairwell. If Ezekiel found Dewey, it would be a disaster.

She had to stop him, make him talk, make him think before he killed a man. Pushing through the stunned crowd, she called his name, but Ezekiel and Jeremiah had disappeared into the night.

■ ■ ■ ■

PART 4

■ ■ ■ ■

PART 4

CHAPTER 31
SAWYER

Monday, June 29, 2015

The next morning, I arrive at Harold Washington Library at ten o'clock with six everything bagels, cream cheese, napkins, plastic knives, and a coffee thermos in the bottom of my backpack. I'm hoping security won't take my breakfast gift for the two ladies helping me with my latest drama.

I reach the other side of the checkpoint, breakfast still in the bag, and Lula is waiting. "Hello."

"Good morning, Sawyer." She hooks her thumbs on the belt loops of her pants.

This is my first time seeing her in something other than blue scrubs. She looks just as lovely in a sleeveless pale yellow blouse and khakis as in her uniform. She signals me to follow her to the elevator bank.

"Remind me what we're looking for again."

"We are on a hunting expedition. In

search of Honoree Dalcour, who claims my grandmother Maggie White Hendrickson is her daughter, making Miss Honoree my great-grandmother."

The elevator doors open, but we don't step forward. We stand in the small hallway, alone. Lula is staring at me with a slack jaw and a gray pallor that tempts me to check her pulse.

"It is what we were shouting about yesterday," I explain. "I don't believe she's lying."

"Oh my God, Sawyer. Is that even possible? Are you okay?" She sounds appropriately shocked. Her concern for my well-being is a bonus. "I don't understand. Why would she make up such a crazy story?"

"I don't believe she made it up," I repeat.

The elevator door opens again, and we step inside but do not speak. I want to give her a few minutes to wrap her head around this news. I spent the entire night mulling it over.

We disembark on the sixth floor, and I follow Lula to an open space, the size of a small cafeteria, except without food, only desks and partitions and computers and rolling metal carts.

Lula's aunt Deidre is a librarian and archivist, and her office is in one of those open environments that remind me of a maze of desks, ergonomic chairs, twentysomething-inch computers, laptops, and printers.

"Deidre, this is Sawyer Hayes. He's the filmmaker I told you about who's interviewing Miss Honoree for a documentary for his doctorate thesis."

"A pleasure to meet you." She gestures for us to sit. I remove my bag of goodies from my backpack. The ladies smile appreciatively, as I do my best not to stare. Deidre is not what you might expect. Two or three decades older than Lula and me, but clearly she's hipper than either one of us.

Her generous Afro is freestyle and dyed a shade of red you might call crimson, which she adorns with different-colored hairpins and bows. A long, loose dress flows as she moves, but her boldest statement is her eye gear — oversize, round-rimmed glasses with red bedazzled frames. I learned about bedazzling from my sister, so I have a fondness for Deidre.

"Thank you for your help with Honoree's mystery visitor," I say, still taking in her workspace.

"I understand he's your father."

"Yes. A long story I would rather not go into." I say this with a smile and without a hint of rage. "That's a lot of books." I nod at her desktop.

"Yes, it's a mess." Deidre settles into the chair behind her desk, and a pile of books and papers. "I have a method to the madness, I assure you."

"I believe you and am all ears," I say.

"We are in luck. I found several documents I believe you'll find interesting." Deidre pushes a stack of papers aside. "Take notes, but I will give you photocopies of most of this."

I remove my iPad, thumbs poised. "Ready."

"Honoree Dalcour was listed in the 1910 census in Baton Rouge with her parents, Cleo and Rufus Norman. She was five. In 1920, she and her mother were in the census in Chicago. After that, Honoree didn't appear again until 1970. She lived in an apartment on Sixty-Seventh Street and South Shore Drive."

"Is that unusual, the census gap?"

"Yes and no. It happened in the poorer neighborhoods," Deidre says.

"She lived by herself?" Lula asks.

"No. She lived with a woman named Gertrude Morgan, a grocery store owner who passed away in 1982," Deidre adds, fishing for something in her desk drawer. "Is that name familiar?"

"No." I glance at Lula. "So this was three years before Honoree moved into the facility. Maybe this woman was her caregiver."

"Or her friend. We don't know. Remember, Miss Honoree didn't move in on her own," Deidre said. "Your grandmother arranged Honoree's move into the senior-care facility. I was working there then, and the same age as Lula."

The two women smile at each other with the familiarity relatives share so easily. "The Dalcour name is Creole."

"Seems right," I reply to Deidre.

She hands us some small paper plates and coffee cups and nods toward my thermos.

Deidre passes us a sheet of paper. "I found a contract Honoree Dalcour signed for Dreamland Cafe in October 1925."

Lula and I share a grin.

"Cool as hell." I rub my hand over my mouth. "I don't know if Lula mentioned, I have video footage of Honoree dancing at a nightclub in the twenties."

"Also cool, but I have more." Deidre removes a folder from one of the piles on her desk. "I understand you have photos of Honoree with some historical figures. We found a collection of photography from a man named Kenny Miller. He was a student

365

at the Art Institute of Chicago, a painter and a photographer." She hands me photocopies of the photos. "He knew Honoree and Oscar Micheaux. Several of the photos include captions that name the dancer, Honoree Dalcour, and Micheaux while working on a film project. See the camera setup."

"Amazing. This is close to being the proof I need that Honoree was in a Micheaux film," I say to Lula eagerly. "And if that film is a lost Micheaux?"

Lula smiles, throwing some significant pride in my direction. "I'm thrilled for you. No way you won't finish it and pass with flying colors."

"Yep." I make a fist and tap Deidre's desk. "I think so."

"Not done yet, guys. I have more. One of Kenny Miller's photos is of a guy named Jeremiah Bailey and Honoree. It looks like a bunch of photos taken at a party."

"Wait, wait, wait. How'd you get this done so fast?" I ask.

"Summer interns, darling. Summer interns." She grins. "We checked the African American newspaper database and found two news stories about Jeremiah Bailey. One in the *Defender.* He was questioned about a shooting at a speakeasy in 1926. Then his obituary was in the *Baton Rouge Post,* a Black newspaper. He died in 1928 and was survived by two brothers, a younger brother, Marcus, and an older brother, Ezekiel, and Jeremiah's fiancée — Bessie Palmer."

"Jackpot," I say. "The same name my father told me was on the deed for the house in Baton Rouge. The one my grandmother sold. I have a copy of the bill of sale. I mentioned the Baton Rouge house to Miss Honoree. She was not happy."

"Not happy? She became unhinged," Lula says bluntly. "I could hear them yelling from the other end of the hall."

Deidre looks bewildered. "I didn't find anything about a house in Baton Rouge owned by Margaret Hendrickson or Honoree Dalcour."

"Just Jeremiah and Bessie Palmer?"

"Jeremiah must've left her the house in his will before he died. I didn't find a will, though." Deidre chews the inside of her cheek, watching me with something on her mind. "Can't you ask your grandmother how she came to own the house? Did she buy it from Bessie Palmer, or did this Palmer woman give her the house?"

"Yes, it would make things easier if I talked to Maggie."

My laugh is short and troubled because

now I feel like a bad grandson. "I don't know. She's always been Mrs. Margaret Hendrickson, or Maggie White, widow to Robert Hendrickson, who died of Alzheimer's, and Norman White, who died during the Korean War. I didn't know she had any connection to Baton Rouge until I discovered Maggie was paying the bills for an Honoree Dalcour, who lived in a senior facility in Chicago."

"That's not all of it." Lula's glare pointedly says *speak up.* I oblige.

"Honoree told me yesterday she's my great-grandmother. Maggie's birth mother — something I never heard before."

Deidre blinks. "Is it true?"

"I believe so."

"You're not sure? I heard some hesitancy in your voice."

I shrug, averting my eyes because she's not wrong.

Deidre pulls her glasses down on her nose and says, "Sounds like you should ask your grandmother some questions, Sawyer."

CHAPTER 32
HONOREE

Monday, November 30, 1925

The day after the rent party, Honoree woke up early and worried. The night before, Ezekiel had taken off after Dewey with murder in his eyes. If he had found him, one of them was dead. And the thought of Ezekiel dead frightened her more than she wanted to admit in that emotional place where she still cared, and cared so much she couldn't imagine a world without him.

He was in her blood, in her bones, and that morning, she wouldn't accept anything less than seeing him with her own eyes, alive and breathing, and in one piece.

She left Bessie with a dollar for breakfast and instructions to pick up some fabric and a rod of ribbon at the five-and-dime. A visit to the store would give Bessie an errand, and the fresh air might help her stomach.

Honoree arrived at the auto body shop shortly before eight o'clock. The sign on the door read, SHOP CLOSED.

She peered through the stained-glass window. He was standing behind the counter, arms straight, palms pressed into the countertop, wearing a filthy T-shirt and overalls.

"Ezekiel!" She banged on the door. "Ezekiel!"

The door opened, and she launched at him. "Why do you have a 'closed' sign on the shop door? It's a workday, and you should be working. You —"

A gasp lodged in her throat. His face, his handsome face, had been pummeled. "Oh my God. What happened? Christ. You found Dewey, didn't you? Christ. Thank God you aren't dead."

For all appearances, he looked an inch from the grave. A swollen eye, bruises on his jaw and forehead, clothing caked with mud, and bloodstains. "You didn't kill him, did you? Tell me. Did you kill him?"

Ezekiel rubbed a hand over his head, turning his smooth black hair into a pigeon's nest of curls. The same hand then scrubbed at his chin, and a grimace closed his eyes. "I was in a ruckus, but you'll be pleased to learn that Dewey lives, or he was still breathing the last time I saw him."

"Which was when?"

Ezekiel lifted his shirt, and a groan escaped his bruised lips. There was a large patch of dried blood from a gash in his side. Still, the blood concerned her less than his breath. "Are you drunk?" Honoree asked. "My Lord, Ezekiel."

Slowly, he wheeled away from her and staggered toward the rear of the shop. He kept stumbling, striking his shoulder against the wall in a failed attempt to walk a straight line.

She followed him. "For a man who used to hate booze — you smell like you bathed in a barrel of gin."

He turned. A long purple bruise rode down the side of his neck to the edge of his jaw.

"Jesus Christ." A wince narrowed his red-rimmed eyes. "Can you speak without shouting? My head will come off if you don't quiet down."

"Is your brother here?" She marched by him. "Jeremiah!"

"Honoree. I beg you — please stop shouting." Ezekiel pressed his hands to either side of his head and leaned against the wall. "Jeremiah is not here."

"I need to look at the wound on your neck."

He pushed away from the wall, but his

371

knees gave way, and he started to fall. She darted for him, catching him by the arm, but he was too big and fell to his knees. "If you hit the floor completely, I won't be able to lift you back up."

His eyes rolled, and he grabbed his stomach.

"I warn you. Do not upchuck on me. I will punch you in the neck."

A small smile interrupted the pain on his face. "I promise I won't vomit."

He held a finger to his lips as if the gesture alone would prevent him from emptying the contents of his stomach.

Honoree was relieved he hadn't killed anyone and wasn't dead himself. On the other hand, finding him drunk kept her ill mood pounding hard and fast through her veins.

She led him into one of the rooms in the back of the shop where he and his brother slept.

He pointed at the washroom but slumped into a chair. "I can go no further at the moment."

"I can see that. Is there a basin in the washroom? I'll wash off some grime and blood before you climb into bed. Take off your shirt."

He lifted his shirttail from his waistband

but gave up on the buttons and yanked the shirt over his head.

Honoree gave into a giggle. "You look like Buster Keaton, stumbling, staggering, falling. Just stay down until I come back."

She went to the washroom, pulled a towel from the rack, grabbed a bar of soap, and filled a bucket with water. A moment later, she knelt in front of him.

"I'm checking for any other open wounds," she explained, not wanting to startle him with her touch. "So Dewey's not dead, but you two fought."

"I caught up with him in the home of an uptown Negro family and persuaded him to engage in fisticuffs."

"You what?"

Still on the stool, he suddenly pitched toward the floor, until his hand slammed against the wall, stopping his fall.

"I box for a fee," he said in a rough voice. "Last night, I won the fight and received a few rounds of bonded bourbon for my trouble."

"You boxed Dewey?"

"It was a gentleman's battle."

"Such a foolish thing to say."

"No. Never foolish. Pissed, drunk, but never foolish." His hand on the wall, he pushed himself to his feet, unbuckled his belt, and pulled down his trousers.

"Ezekiel!" She covered her eyes.

"I have on briefs, Honoree. Too damn cold to run around outside without an extra layer between my pants and my bare legs. A pair of long underwear would've been better."

She uncovered her eyes and took in his muscular frame. Three years ago, their lovemaking had been a tangle of arms, legs, and lips, but it was mostly clothed. She'd never seen his nude torso, and he didn't have the muscles he had now back then.

"I remember being with you," he said, his voice suddenly somber.

"I remember, too." She swallowed.

"There were several layers of slips and skirts."

"And shirts." She wrung the water from a sudsy cloth and wiped his shoulders and upper arms. He rested the back of his head against the wall, but he watched her from beneath hooded eyelids.

"Honoree," he said, his voice deep. "There's almost nothing I wouldn't do for you."

"*Almost* is the word that echoes, Ezekiel."

"I can't complete my business with Dewey and Archie if you're involved."

"I'm already involved because of that damn shooting." She dropped the cloth in the basin. "I don't want to talk about this right now. You're too full of gin."

He slumped forward. "Yes, I am, but why are you here? Were you worried about me?"

"That scene last night was scary."

"Should never have been brought to your doorstep. That was Dewey's fault."

"Houdini and the envelope? That was Trudy's fault."

"No. That was my fault."

She started to ask him to explain further, but his eyelids fluttered shut, and the liquor reeked from his pores. "I'm gonna finish washing you up. After that, put on a nightshirt and go straight to bed. Get some sleep. We can talk later."

It took a few more minutes to persuade him to do what she needed him to do without whining. His big body was difficult to handle, especially when his muscles were mush and his bones useless. Finally, she had him cleaned up. The next hardest part was getting him into the bed. He kept grabbing her in the most inappropriate places. But she gave him a one-time pass due to his drunkenness.

He sat on the edge of the bed, struggling with the nightshirt she'd handed him.

Bloodshot eyes met hers. "You'll be here when I wake up?"

"Go to sleep. You'll feel better when you're sober."

Honoree helped him into his nightshirt and watched him curl up beneath the covers and fall asleep. She was tempted to stay, Lord knows. Each time she ran into him, there were signs — signs of the boy she used to know, the boy she still might love. Just not enough to add up to a full deck of cards.

Once she was sure he'd fallen into a peaceful sleep, she tiptoed from the room.

Almost a week later, on the first Sunday in December, Honoree grabbed a few dollars from her stash and told Bessie to put on her best shift, a dress Honoree had made her. They were going out on the town — lunch at a diner and a trip to the cinema. Risky business considering the rent party hadn't made as much dough as Honoree had hoped. The white thugs had put a damper on the hoopla, ending the party prematurely, but the day was too wonderful to stay inside.

The grumpy Bessie responded with an enthusiastic *yes,* which surprised Honoree. Bessie was struggling. Her morning sickness lasted half the day, and her swollen ankles took the rest of the day to shrink back to normal. Still, Bessie was more than ready to leave.

On the way to the L station, Honoree called Ezekiel at the auto body shop, inviting him to join them if he had time. It was fine if he showed up, and no worries if he didn't. They'd been seeing more of each other at the Dreamland Cafe and at Miss Hattie's when Honoree would walk Bessie to work. Always friendly and proper since the rent party.

She and Bessie boarded the L train to South Parkway and the Majestic Theater. Honoree loved the L train, a big circle of tracks that carried folks from one side of the city to the other in minutes. The Stroll was Honoree's heart, but even if she danced in Paris, France, or on Broadway, Chicago was home.

Huddled up in their warmest layers, Bessie nudged her in the arm. "What are you daydreaming about?"

"The last time I went to the cinema," Honoree began, "I saw a Charlie Chaplin motion picture, but I can't recall the title."

"Isn't that the actor Archie likes?"

Honoree nodded. "Probably why I don't remember the movie —"

"You don't mind seeing the same Oscar Micheaux movie again?" Bessie asked. Honoree had explained that she didn't mind. Watching *Body and Soul* would be different after meeting Oscar.

"I think it's one of his best movies." Bessie pointed. "The Diamond Diner is on the next block."

With an after-church crowd filling the booths, Honoree and Bessie sat at the counter while looking up at the chalkboard and the daily specials.

"I'll get a cup of coffee and a cinnamon roll," Honoree practically mumbled, shy about overindulgence, although everything looked delicious.

"I want ham and eggs, and biscuits, hot biscuits, and a sweet roll, too."

"That is breakfast food, not lunch."

"And the cinnamon roll and coffee is what?"

"Cheap," Honoree said.

They were approached by a slender woman with deep dimples and a smile so wide her cheeks had to ache. "Bessie, how are you?" She leaned over the counter, cupped Bessie's chin and kissed her on the cheek. "Been thinking about you. How did the party go?"

"Just fine, ma'am," Bessie responded. "Everything was copacetic."

She tilted her head at Honoree. "Is this your roommate, the chorus girl?"

"Yes, ma'am. Honoree Dalcour, originally from Baton Rouge, Louisiana."

Honoree side-eyed Bessie. Had she mentioned Louisiana to Bessie? She was a Chicago girl. "Hello."

"I'm Rochelle Diamond. Everyone calls me Rosie." She peeked at Bessie. "She's my cousin, twice removed."

"We ain't related," Bessie said, shaking her head. "She worked side by side on the Chitlin' Circuit, a few years back."

"You were a baby, child. On your own and doing just fine. But for me and mine, we worked that circuit for thirty years. Probably since right after the Emancipation."

"Rosie was the one who gave us a pan of macaroni and cheese for the rent party."

Honoree warmed. "Thank you. The food was delicious."

"I'm surprised you two aren't busy sewing things for Christmas."

Bessie patted Honoree's hand. "We're out on the town. Going to a motion picture after we have lunch."

Rosie frowned. "Without an escort? Just you two girls, alone?" She tugged the tie around her apron, pulling it snug. "You modern girls don't have a care in the world."

"Oh, no. We aren't going alone. Honoree's man is meeting us at the movie."

"He's not my man, and this is way too much chatter. I'm sure Rosie has other things to do besides listening to us go on and on." She nudged Bessie. "What do you want to eat? My treat."

Rosie gestured toward the chalkboard. "Take a look at the Sunday special — roast pork, rice, kidney beans, green beans, peach cobbler."

Honoree patted her tummy. "I gotta keep my stomach flat. My costumes are skimpy," she said with a laugh.

"You already a thin girl. With all that dancing you do, you should eat. How about the beef casserole?"

The beef casserole dinner was $1.00. With the price of the cinema and the streetcar, the Sunday outing was adding up. She still had to save for the down payment for the house near Lil.

Bessie groaned. "She's worried about spending too much money."

"And you aren't?"

"I'm not as worried about money as you."

Rosie placed a cup of coffee in front of Honoree and brought a glass of milk for Bessie.

"You'll never enjoy life if all you think about is cabbage, and I ain't talking vegetables." Rosie slammed her hand down on the

380

bar, chuckling at the joke. "I got a shop full of customers. You two are having the Sunday special, and you'll both eat every bite of dessert, too."

Less than an hour later, the girls had eaten heartily, cleaning their dinner plates and splitting an extra dessert when they couldn't pick between the apple pie, vanilla custard, and peach cobbler.

They left the diner, and Honoree wasn't sure she could walk to the corner without rolling over. "I ate too much."

Bessie marched silently ahead.

"How are you?" Honoree called after her.

"A bit queasy. Rosie and I were never as close as she thinks. I saw her once in a blue moon. She wanted to be my friend."

"She seemed friendly enough."

"Everyone is friendly in the beginning."

They arrived at the Majestic Theater and took their seats, ten rows back from the screen.

"Where's Ezekiel?" Bessie asked.

"If he doesn't make it, I'm sure we'll see him later," Honoree said, but quickly added, "I'm too excited to worry about him, anyway."

The lights dimmed, and the patrons quieted. The picture had to do with an escaped prisoner pretending to be a minister, hiding out in a small town. He falls in love, steals money, watches his love die, and kills a man. But then there was a twist. One of the characters was dreaming and it turned out the escaped prisoner might never have existed. Paul Robeson mesmerized Honoree.

"That was incredible," she whispered to Bessie as they headed for the exit. "I'm sorry Ezekiel missed it."

They walked out of the theater into a dark, snowy evening, and Bessie hooked her arm through Honoree's arm.

"I love the cinema," she said. "If I were prettier, I could be an actress. I pretend things all the time, and I'm good at it. I could star in a movie. But Oscar only wanted you."

"He was all talk. I haven't heard from him since that first party."

"He'll come back around. They always do for you." Her voice dropped low; Honoree could barely understand what she was saying.

"Why are you behaving so odd?" she asked Bessie. "Sometimes I think you're mad at me. Or is it the baby that has you in a foul mood?"

"What happened to Isabelle in that movie could happen to me, except it wouldn't be a dream. I'll end up with a no-good man who hurts people and die stupid from grief."

"What are you talking about? You're not some girl in a motion picture. Don't take what you see on the screen to heart. The film ain't about real life."

Honoree pulled Bessie around so she could see her face. Snowflakes had landed on her cheeks and eyelashes. Honoree gently brushed them away. "Now, tell me what's wrong."

"A colored girl don't matter." Her lips quivered. "And never will."

"What?"

"You trust Ezekiel. Why? He shows up, and you chase me out of the kitchenette or run off with him, then you don't see him for days. You wanna know why? 'Cause we don't matter. He too busy racketeering and running with women like Trudy who don't require much thought."

"He doesn't run with Trudy, and I don't know why you are so riled up. Ezekiel is my business and none of yours." Honoree stomped off.

"I hate them!" Bessie screamed behind her.

Honoree turned to see what all the fuss was about. But perhaps her eyes deceived her.

Bessie was stomping and shouting, "I hate them. The bastards keep hurting you and hurting you!"

She rushed toward her. "Stop screeching. Lord Jesus. You're making a scene."

"And then they hurt you again. I hate them!"

Honoree wanted to shake some sense into her, but she didn't get the chance.

"Don't touch me!" Bessie raised her hands and balled them into fists, with fat tears streaming down her cheeks.

"Calm yourself." Honoree looked around, hoping no one would call the cops on them. "Have you gone mad — huffing through your nose like a boar in the woods, clawing at snow like a wild beast? What has gotten into you?"

People made a full circle, avoiding the freak show, as they walked by.

"Please relax, Bessie. You're hysterical."

"I ain't hysterical. I'm just mad. Mad. Mad. Mad." Bessie sobbed, rib-cracking sobs.

Honoree wished she could disappear as passersby paused to stare at the commotion Bessie was making. "I don't know what's going on with you, but I'm not gonna let you act like an idiot on a Sunday afternoon, not after we've had such a pleasant afternoon. If you want to behave like a fool, at least let's go back to our neighborhood."

The watery anguish in Bessie's eyes dripped over her cheeks and chin, soaking her lips as she opened her mouth to speak.

"What?" Honoree's temper shortened. "What do you want to say? Spit it out!"

Another gulp, then finally, she spoke. "I don't want this baby. I swear to God! I wish it would die in my belly!"

CHAPTER 33
HONOREE

Sunday, December 6, 1925

Bessie cried so hard; the girl could hardly stay on her feet. Block after block, Honoree pleaded with her to stop wailing but only convinced her to take a step or two before the sobs overcame her.

After several false starts, they eventually reached the tenement building. Honoree had an arm wrapped around Bessie's waist, hauling her up one stair at a time. She didn't see Ezekiel until he spoke.

"What's wrong with her?" He moved to her side, helping her keep Bessie upright.

"She's pregnant and sixteen years old, and the man who got her this way isn't the kind of man she wants to be around."

Ezekiel glanced at Bessie's stomach.

"What do you expect to see?" Honoree said. "She's only a few months pregnant from what we've figured out. So too soon for her belly to show much, especially since she's wearing a coat."

Ezekiel opened his mouth, another question in his eyes, but Honoree raised her hand, stopping him. "I want to make her a cup of coffee and put her in the bed."

"I'm okay," Bessie said, sniffling. "You can go off with Ezekiel if you like. I'm fine staying home alone."

"Well, I'm not fine with you being alone." Honoree fired an exhausted look at Ezekiel. "You were supposed to meet us at the cinema." Honoree fished in her box purse for her keys and unlocked the door.

Ezekiel remained in the doorway. "I'll talk to you tomorrow," he said, turning toward the staircase.

"I said," Bessie raised her voice, "I wanna be by myself."

"We weren't going anyplace in particular, were we, Ezekiel?"

"No place in particular." He held his fedora, rubbing the felt brim.

Bessie clucked her tongue. "He's not telling the truth. Where were you taking her?"

Ezekiel shook his head.

"Tell her."

"The Dusty Bottom."

Honoree felt a twinge of disappointment. The after-hours spot was an all-night dance hall she had wanted to go to for ages.

Performers from the Stroll favored the place, and on Sunday nights, chorus girls, musicians, and waiters, having a collective night off, partied until dawn on spirits, jazz, and wild hoofing.

"I can't tell you to leave," Bessie declared. "This is your flat, but all I want to do is sleep."

Honoree looked from Bessie to Ezekiel. "Are you sure?"

Bessie nodded.

Honoree stepped outside the kitchenette. "Bolt the door behind me."

The bolt slid into place, but Honoree wasn't relieved. "I don't know, Ezekiel."

"You heard her. She wants to be alone." He took her hand and guided her down the staircase. "I parked the car in the back of the building,"

They turned the corner, and Honoree's feet stopped moving. "That's not your automobile. It belongs to Archie."

"Jeremiah is working on my car, and Archie insisted I borrow his." Ezekiel seized hold of her hand. "What's wrong, Honoree?"

She staggered backward, the cold ignored as heat rushed through her body. "Did you tell him where you were coming tonight?"

"No, why would I?"

"Did you know I met Archie in this car?"

Ezekiel held on to her arm, but she jerked free of his grip. "No, I didn't. What happened?"

She pressed a hand against her chest, kneading a sudden sharp pain. "After you and my mother left, I was broke, hungry, and alone. One night, my only choice seemed simple — work at a whorehouse or die. I didn't make it to the whorehouse, though. I wandered into an alley with a Model T and an unlocked door. I curled up in the rumble seat, beneath a pile of blankets, to get warm. The alley was behind Miss Hattie's, and the Model T belonged to Archie."

"Honoree?"

"Let me finish. Archie found me in the trunk and took me in, and since I would end up a whore anyway, why not start with the man who brought me in from the cold?"

"Honoree, please. I don't need to hear this."

"Yes, you do. Not because I'm punishing you, or trying to make you feel guilty. I need to explain why I can't step inside that car." She couldn't seem to help herself. Every word, no matter how much pain it caused her, let alone Ezekiel, couldn't compare to what ate at her insides. "Archie is the father of Bessie's baby. She won't admit it, but why else would he hire her the way he did unless it was some kind of payment for beating her and taking advantage of her? She's a child. Younger than I was when he —"

"Oh God, Honoree."

"Don't give me your rage. Archie never raped me. He slapped me around, but the first night I lay with him, I needed to be someplace other than the car's rumble seat. It took a few months, but soon our relationship changed. I am resourceful, you see." Her lips curled uncomfortably at the memories, and the knife of regret stabbed her in the gut, but bitterness followed. "We became business partners. You're familiar with the idea. Just like the two of you are business partners."

He turned and brushed a hand over her cheek, wiping her tears away.

"Not now, Ezekiel. I just can't."

"It's okay. I understand. And you're right. You shouldn't leave Bessie." Ezekiel walked her back to the kitchenette, but before he turned to leave, he asked her, "May I kiss you on the cheek?"

She shrugged without passion, without feeling, but with certainty. "Maybe tomorrow."

Honoree tossed logic aside. Not a smart decision. Perhaps her worse decision of 1925. But Archie should pay for what he'd done to Bessie — and her.

Vengeance is mine . . . saith the Lord.

Her mother would quote the Bible when she was angry, and her favorite verse had lodged itself in Honoree's mind. Except Honoree wanted things squared away with Archie Graves sooner than later.

He was Bessie's baby's father. She was convinced. Archie had beaten her, taken advantage of her, and deserved to have something terrible happen to him.

By Sunday night, her body trembled with rage, and her thoughts were a tune on repeat. Rising from the cot and putting aside a book she couldn't recall reading, she put on a sleeveless black silk number with crystal beads and gold fringe dangling from the hem, and a neckline that plunged to her belly button. She told Bessie she was meeting Ezekiel and made her promise to stay put.

Honoree arrived at Miss Hattie's, checked in on the barkeep working — Dewey, whose mood, as usual, was vile. In his office,

Archie sat working on his books, as expected.

Honoree knocked and opened the door on a *Who's there?* She entered his office and greeted him with a hesitating smile. "Hello, Archie."

"What brings you here on a Sunday?" he said coolly. "Come to help me with my math?"

His broad nose and silly mustache annoyed her, but she swallowed her contempt. "You don't need me. I'm sure Ezekiel takes care of that for you now. His math is better than mine." She sat in the chair on the other side of his desk. "Rumor on the Stroll is you are the up-and-coming big cheese in policy gambling."

She crossed her legs, keeping a close eye on Archie's movements. Pretty soon, he would be pissed, and she had to gauge her distance. "You could be the next policy king. Mr. Buttons introduced you to some of his friends in high places, important people like the owner of the *Defender,* Mr. Abbott; the mayor; and the superintendent of the police department. To name a few."

"What is it, Honoree? I don't believe you're here to pass the bull—" His voice dropped. "Not dressed in a slick number like that."

She uncrossed her legs and broadened her shoulders. The next words from her mouth demanded her body be erect with an unbreakable spine to match her gumption. "Give me some money for Bessie."

"Whatever the hell for?"

" 'Cause she's gonna have a baby, your baby, and you raped her, and she's around fourteen years old — and the newspapers would love to get the story." Brave and bold as she may sound, she still might faint if he came at her. "You have to do something for her, or —"

He hunched forward and growled. "Shut your trap. You better have some proof before you start spreading lies, missy. That kind of lie can get you badly hurt — you and your whore of a roommate."

"Bessie didn't tell me. I figured it out for myself, and it's not a lie."

"You wouldn't recognize the truth if it were painted on the insides of your eyelids." He opened the desk drawer and removed a cigar. "Whatever is in her belly ain't my bastard."

"Why did you hire her without her knowing how to dance?"

"That's my damn business." He rose and circled the desk, faster than a mad cow could fall over.

Honoree shot to her feet and backed toward the door. "I don't believe you, but it doesn't matter. You are making lots of dough these days." The more she talked, the more courage she found. "I-I'll just spread a rumor about you liking to mess around with children. I met Mr. Buttons. He's a decent man and might change his mind about partnering with a man like you."

Sweat beaded on his forehead, and he simmered, like a pot of overcooked stew. He slumped against the edge of his desk. "Sure, William Buttons is a good man, and Ezekiel worked on his good nature and convinced him to cancel our deal, but I won't let you put me in another predicament with Buttons." He took a puff from the cigar. "Ezekiel may have intervened for you this time, but next time, he won't. We've got too much on the line."

"What do you mean? What's on the line?"

He laughed. "After Ezekiel leaves town, and he will leave, you'll be on your knees begging for your old job back. Whatever promises Ezekiel has made or will make — will go poof, and I'll be waiting. Because no rumors you spread about some child I might have fathered or might not have will matter. The next time Ezekiel leaves, he won't be coming back. He won't be here to save your ass."

Honoree stepped toward him, only stopping when she couldn't find anything within arm's reach to hurl at him. "This is about what you did to Bessie, not Ezekiel. He's not going anywhere. He wouldn't have come back only to turn around and run off again."

Archie laughed. "You're foolin' yourself if you believe that."

"What makes you think he's going to leave?"

" 'Cause I know him better than you."

Honoree took a cab to the Bailey Brothers Auto Body Shop. She didn't telephone Ezekiel to warn him about her visit. It was late, and he hadn't been at Miss Hattie's. So where else would he be but at his shop?

When she opened the door, a bell rang overhead, and Jeremiah, who was behind the counter, turned to look at her (frankly, he stared). Ezekiel stood next to him. A sharply raised eyebrow was the sign of his disapproval. "Such a fancy dress to wear on a Sunday." He didn't mask his judgmental tone either. "Where've you been?"

Honoree had almost forgotten about the dress she'd worn to Miss Hattie's. "With Archie," she said, trusting brevity would lessen the weight of it all.

Ezekiel circled the counter and strode toward the back of the shop, his broad shoulders hardening against her. "What's going on that you had to spend time with Archie? You two make up?"

"That's an unkind thing to say. I hate Archie."

"Then why go see him?"

"Archie hurt Bessie and got her pregnant. I wanted him to do something to help her. Make him give her some money. Give her something besides grief."

He stopped in the middle of the hall, his back still to her. "Archie isn't the kind of man to step up and take on responsibility."

"Why aren't you looking at me? Turn around," she ordered.

He spun toward her. The anger in his eyes chilled her blood. "I didn't realize you cared so much about Bessie or how much you wanted Archie to admit what he did to her."

"It matters. But Bessie wasn't all we talked about." She fastened her fists on either hip. "He claimed you wouldn't be around to help Bessie or me if we needed it."

Ezekiel moved toward her, his large frame imposing in the narrow hallway. "I don't have any idea why Archie would make such a claim. Haven't I done enough to prove how much —" His jaw tightened, and he pressed his lips together. "Look. I made a deal with the cops and answered some questions about my dealings with a man named Tony Gallo. The next thing I knew, the cops reopened the Dreamland Cafe."

"Who's Tony Gallo? Does he have anything to do with Houdini's murder?"

Ezekiel rubbed his chin. "Gallo is nobody you need to worry about. He works for Capone. And anything that has to do with Capone is of interest to coppers."

She sank against the wall. "Is that why you weren't arrested? Because you have something on Capone, or maybe this man Gallo, in your pocket?"

"No. I just helped some people who needed help."

"Would this help hold water if you were dead?" She paused. "Or if you left town and never returned?"

"What's got you going, Honoree? Why did you meet with Archie dressed like that?"

She wet her lips. "Archie told me you'd be leaving town soon. Why would he say that? Does he know something I don't?"

"I have no plans to leave town."

"Strange. Then why would Archie say he knows you better than me?" She stepped into him, close enough to put a hand on his chest, but she didn't touch him. "Maybe he does know you better. You came back to town for him, not for me."

"The easy answer is you're right, but you're wrong." He placed his hands on her upper arms, lightly, gently. "Trust me. I will explain, but I need more time. I need to finish what I started."

She backed away from him.

"Honoree, don't run away from me. Please. I beg you. Can't you put the past three years behind us for a little while?" He reached for her. "I care about you and never meant to hurt you. It was the last thing I wanted, but I can't say anything more. Not yet."

CHAPTER 34
SAWYER

Tuesday, June 30, 2015

I am in Grant Park, near Buckingham Fountain, with my cell phone to my ear, waiting for Maggie to pick up. The nurse has told her I'm on the line and promised her nothing's wrong.

My calls are notoriously few and far between because, historically, they've been drenched in drama. I sometimes wonder if Maggie fears the sound of my voice — or anything having to do with me on the other end of a phone line.

Hello. I killed my sister in a car crash.

Hello. My father told me he wished I had died instead of his precious, darling little girl.

Hello. I overdosed on pain pills.

You know — those calls.

On the other hand, she's eighty-nine years old, and I do not wish to cause her grief. But this is huge — is Honoree Dalcour telling me the truth? Is she Maggie's mother,

399

my great-grandmother?

There is a gulp on the other end of the line, but I reassure her — everything is fine. My limbs are intact. My head is on straight.

We exchange a few pleasantries, greetings, *How are you? Hope you are fine,* et cetera, et cetera, et cetera. Then, I let her have her say because she's angry at me about taking some things (a lot of things) from her long-ago box.

"I'm angry with you, Sawyer." Her voice is gravel and sand and concern, giving my guilt a new check mark.

"I'm sorry about that," I say sincerely. "I had to do something big, or I was afraid nothing would change for me. I had to finish the thesis, but I needed help, and you told me about the box."

"When did I do that?"

There was silence, but Maggie knew what I meant. She'd watched my decline. I had lived with her since my release from the hospital. Maggie had been the sole witness to the sad state of my grief, guilt, and shame, which was a monumentally long, lousy stretch.

"I need to talk to you about something, and I hope you won't be upset."

"The longer you take to tell me, the more likely I'll take whatever you say poorly."

"I'm in Chicago."

"I assumed as much."

"I've been recording Honoree Dalcour's oral history for my documentary. I got the idea from the papers and photos in your long-ago box."

"The long-ago box belonged to her. She gave it to me when I moved her into the Bronzeville Senior Care Facility."

"She claims she's your mother."

Silence, but surprise travels on the heels of the expected. "The old woman told you she is my mother?" Maggie's voice peeled through the phone with a curious calm.

"You told us you were an orphan, which I told her, but I couldn't give her answers to questions about your family's surname or who raised you. Or how you came to own the house in Baton Rouge." The pauses in between feel chaotic and calm at once.

"Did she give birth to me? Yes."

I am speechless. My lips quiver as I attempt to form words. "But she's never been a mother to me."

Maggie is so matter-of-fact I'm stunned. "You admit it. Just like that. Nothing to add?"

Silence.

"You paid her bills for thirty years because she's your mother. Except you don't speak

401

to her. Or tell anyone in the family she exists. I don't get it."

"Guilt demands its pound of flesh."

"You kept this from Dad, Azizi, and me, and — did Mom know?"

"I don't think she did. I thought she figured it out once, but then she got sick, and everything having to do with the old woman was forgotten."

"Not everything. My father visited her twice. After Mom passed and then again after Azizi died." I wiped my mouth. "What happened with you two that made you so angry, so bitter, so unforgiving?"

Suddenly, she's talking about Norman White, her first husband. I can hear it in her voice, how she still grieves for the man. Her mother hated him, but Maggie didn't marry him to please her.

"Doesn't explain what happened between you and Honoree," I interrupt. "Doesn't explain why you waited until Mr. Hendrickson died to take care of her."

"Your grandfather was a good man but a white man. He never knew what it meant to be Black in a world ruled by white men. So I kept things from him. Some things he didn't need to know." A weary sigh. "I found her in a broken-down slum apartment." Her voice loses steam. "The same flat where I found the box."

"When you moved Honoree into the Bronzeville Senior Care Facility in 1985."

"Yes, Sawyer. You're right."

"When was the last time you saw her?"

"In 1985."

"How about the last time you talked to her?"

"Also 1985," she says. "I do not need to speak with her — I needed a clear conscience."

"Maggie, who was Bessie Palmer?"

Silence.

"Maggie. You know that name, don't you?"

"I'm not answering any more questions, Sawyer."

"Come on, Maggie. Why should any of this be such a secret? It happened decades ago."

"It happened a hundred years ago, ninety years ago, yesterday. I don't know my father's name." She huffs. "Ask the old woman what happened to Bessie Palmer or any of those people she once knew. Anything more you need, you'll have to hear from her lips."

CHAPTER 35
HONOREE

Thursday, December 10, 1925

On top of the dressing room counter at the Dreamland Cafe, where Honoree kept her makeup and hairpins, was a long white box tied with a lush red ribbon.

After only a month, and six parties, six new dresses, and more than a dozen private rehearsals, Honoree had impressed the dance master and won Mr. Buttons's confidence. Tonight would be her first solo performance — and the white box was a gift of congratulations.

She untied the ribbon and tossed the lid on the floor, revealing a dozen long-stem red roses. There was also a note, in a small white envelope. The signature, written in a bold, cursive hand, belonged to the renowned Oscar Micheaux.

Honoree covered her mouth but felt her cheeks flush. She never expected him to show, not after just one night of flirting,

flirting and promises. Micheaux was Lil's friend, and Honoree, just another bimbo at a house party.

"Stop gushing over those flowers," Colethea said. "Let's go see who else is in the audience other than your admirers."

Honoree pulled back her hand. "Why should I stop? These are the first flowers I ever received in my entire life. It's a moment to enjoy." She glanced from Colethea to Hazel, who had strolled up beside them.

"The moment's up," Hazel said with her usual effortless charm. "We can also find where your admirer is sitting and where to toss that extra shimmy."

Each girl grabbed an arm and pulled her through the hallway to the edge of the stage. The three dancers peeked around a black curtain, spying on the VIP tables. Honoree rose onto her tiptoes, but her view was still blocked.

"Some of Chicago's wealthiest and most influential people are here tonight, but I can't see a thing." Honoree craned her neck. "There are way too many couples on the dance floor and too many tall cigarette girls with leather trays strapped around their throats."

"I can't neither." Colethea leaned into

Honoree's shoulder. "Where are the VIP tables?"

"How would I know?" Honoree exclaimed.

"Let me look." Hazel pushed Honoree and Colethea aside.

"Point out the most famous people," Honoree said. "I don't recognize anyone by sight. Oh. Oh. There's Oscar Micheaux!"

"I see him." Hazel lifted her chin. "Over there. Sitting at the table in the second row, across from Micheaux, is mob boss Papa Johnny of the Chicago Outfit. Capone's crew."

Colethea butted between Honoree and Hazel. "That ain't Papa Johnny. I heard he's on the lam in Italy," she said.

"He resembles Papa Johnny." Hazel nodded toward another table. "There's Alderman Louis B. Anderson."

"He's the second Negro man in Chicago to hold an elected office," Colethea chimed.

Hazel shrugged. "I think he's with his friend Mr. Abbott."

"He runs the *Defender*," Honoree said.

"Oh, my! The Black Valentino."

"Lorenzo Tucker!" Honoree and Colethea said in unison, followed by a round of giggles.

Hazel hushed them. "He's the most handsome Negro man in the world."

"Even Ezekiel might take a back seat to Lorenzo." Honoree still held a hand lightly over her mouth. "Who's with Alberta Hunter? She's sure having a helluva time."

"That's Charlie Chaplin."

Honoree squinted. "That's not him. Where's his mustache?"

"He doesn't always wear that toothbrush mustache. It's a costume for the movies."

"I had no idea."

"Norma Shearer," Hazel whispered, pointing. "She's talking to Paul Robeson and his wife."

Colethea raised a brow like it would help her hear better. "I bet they're talking Race politics."

Hazel nodded in earnest agreement.

So many different people coupled up, sitting together at the same round table with colored waiters filling glasses and serving food. Dark skin, light skin, white boy, white girl stitched together in a quilt called the Dreamland Cafe. All listening to the same jazz music played by the greatest trumpet player in the world.

And Honoree Dalcour, she smiled giddily, the best dancer in the world, the next Queen of Sheba, and her next stop, Broadway's bright lights — if she worked hard enough, had enough good luck, and not too much more bad luck.

The band started up, and the jazz rhythms made Honoree's heart race faster, matching the quick feet of the hoofers on the dance floor.

This was Honoree's throne. Here, she was Josephine Baker and Florence Mills in one small, vibrant package, showing off her talent and dazzling the audience watching her.

She shimmied and high-kicked across the stage, the beads of her Egyptian costume sparkled, her jeweled scepter majestic, and her gold headdress perched elegantly atop her head.

The number ended, and she galloped across the stage to a fanfare of trumpets and cymbals and castanets.

Taking her bow, Honoree lingered near the lip of the platform, enjoying the applause and the cheers. She waltzed to the dressing room, her thoughts in the clouds, her Mary Jane pumps barely touching the hardwood floors.

"What a crowd!" Honoree said.

"Did you see all the handsome men?" asked another girl.

Between cigarettes and the next routine, the girls hastily stripped off their costumes and changed into robes amid a flurry of chatter, sweat, and talc powder.

Honoree sat in her chair, shaking, her spirits soaring with excitement. Her first solo performance at the Dreamland Cafe was a swell time. Better than in her dreams. Hot damn!

"Miss Honoree." A waiter called her from the doorway. "Honoree Dalcour!"

"I'm over here."

Walking toward her, he carried a long white box, twice the size as the one from Oscar.

In the other white-gloved hand, he held a note card. A showgirl received one of those notes when a VIP was inviting her to join their table. It was an honor and meant a healthy tip, hobnobbing with the wealthiest, most influential patrons in Chicago.

"Give me that." She seized hold of the note card and the flowers before the waiter had a chance to hand them to her.

A warm tingle stirred in her stomach with only a touch of apprehension. She recognized the handwriting: Ezekiel. He wanted her to join him and his guests at his VIP table. Well, wasn't he a hoity-toity man about town?

"Tell him I'll be right out," she said to the waiter.

Shimmying out of her costume, she changed into a jade chiffon gown with a sheer lace bodice and low back decorated with a rhinestone clasp at her waist. A jeweled silver headband adorned her new boy-cut hairstyle, and she double-looped a long strand of white pearls around her neck, allowing the length to touch the middle of her back with a loose strand at her bosom.

She glanced in the mirror. "Now. What am I missing?"

She dug into her shopping bag and removed her orchestra-length cigarette holder.

"No. Not the cigarette holder." Colethea pointed. "The peacock feather hand fan. Now that's elegance."

Honoree considered the chorus girl's idea. The fan was gorgeous. "I'll do both," she said, with the cigarette holder in one fist, propped on her hip. On the other hand, she fluttered the peacock fan over her breasts. One last glance in the mirror, and she tilted her head and smiled.

"Stop preening." Hazel laughed from her chair. "You are a looker and can make a dead man's heart go thump-thump. No need to add the extras."

"Fortunately, the man I'm looking to dazzle is very much alive," Honoree said with a wink and thought maybe being a special friend of the man Ezekiel was now might not be that bad after all.

She strolled into the dining hall, elbow bent, her orchestra-length cigarette holder held just so, and blew smoke rings to halo her head. Her long pearls, knotted beneath her bosom, swung over the sheer fabric of her jade dress to the rhythm of the bass picker's chords and the sway of her hips.

Envious and lustful eyes, male and female, followed her as she passed by, but she scarcely noticed. She was fixed on Ezekiel.

"Hello, everyone." She smiled her brightest as she reached the VIP table.

"Thank you for accepting my invitation." Ezekiel stood, looking like Joe Brooks, with a broad grin, deep dimples, and kind dark eyes.

His beauty and his size blocked her view of everyone but him. He pulled out a chair and gently touched her shoulder as he guided her into the seat.

"Ezekiel, what a surprise."

The other people at the table were invisible until she sat next to Archie and suppressed a groan. She greeted him quickly, with more of a snarl than a smile. She turned to nod at the white man at her other shoulder — but then her heart stopped.

How could this happen?

The flash of gunfire, bright-red blood, a mumbled cry, and the memories trampled across her back and crushed her bones. Pain and fear lanced through her, slice after slice, cutting into her soul.

How could this happen?

The white man who gunned down George "Houdini" Mills stood with his hand extended to greet her.

"Please meet Mr. Tony Gallo," Archie was saying. "Tony. This is the beautiful, extraordinary Honoree Dalcour."

Pretend. Pretend to be shy. Pretend to be overcome by humility, not by fear and confusion. She kept her head down. In case the truth showed on her face. It was clear she had seen him, had watched him murder a man.

Panic had locked her up in a hard shell. It hurt to breathe — the smile on her lips was a frozen gash filled with broken glass.

"Mr. Gallo," she said, her lungs burning as her stomach twisted into knots.

"A pleasure to meet you. You're a fine dancer and pretty as a button, too." Tony Gallo touched her arm. "Have we met before?"

Now she might scream. "I don't believe so, sir."

"You don't know this girl, Mr. Gallo." Archie pinched her on the cheek. "I'm not sure I know her, acting all sweet and quiet. Usually she can't stop yammering. You must make her nervous."

Ezekiel filled a coupe with champagne. "Are you thirsty?" There was a coolness about him. Honoree sensed he didn't like Archie's familiarity, or the attention Gallo was giving her. With these two men at his table, why in Christ's name had he invited her to join them?

She gulped down the drink, the bubbles stinging her nose.

"What do you think, Mr. Gallo?" Archie grinned like a rabid dog. "Is she spiffy enough for your party?"

Ezekiel placed his elbows on the table, propping his chin on his knuckles. "What party?" The glare he dealt Archie was deadly.

"Mr. Gallo is throwing a party at the Plantation Cafe on New Year's Eve and looking for some extra girls to perform." Archie grabbed the champagne bottle and filled Gallo's glass. "That's why we wanted her to join us. So that we could extend an invitation."

Gallo laughed. "Coming from Capone, this is more than an invite. Think of it as a command performance." He winked at her. "By a marquee star." Gallo eased back in the chair. "For a New Year's Eve party for my boss, Al Capone. You're a real doll, sugar — prettiest colored girl I seen in ages. Archie said you were an up-and-comer and would be flattered to entertain Mr. Capone."

Honoree stopped staring at her coupe of champagne and looked at Ezekiel. Archie had no right to offer her up like prime rib.

She gulped her drink, and Ezekiel refilled her glass.

"A party for Mr. Capone sounds swell." It hurt to breathe, to swallow, to think. "Sorry, guys, but I have another show."

She went to stand, but her knees were water. She touched the edge of the table, using it as a pulley to help her from falling, but she didn't hit the ground. Ezekiel held her chair out and, in a gentlemanly flourish, had taken her forearm. No one realized she was coming undone.

"You haven't said thank you to Mr. Gallo," Archie said. "Where's your manners, Honoree?"

"Of course, Mr. Gallo. It would be the cat's meow to dance for Mr. Capone." She gave them a closed-mouth grin. "I am sorry to rush off. I have quite the costume to wiggle into before the next show."

"We'll be right here," Archie said. "Waiting."

She smiled a broad, sweeping smile without making eye contact with any of the men.

A pivot and a strut across the dining hall, and without glancing over her shoulder, she sensed every pair of eyes at Ezekiel's table watching her. She spun on her heel, waved a light, cheery showgirl wave and disappeared behind the curtain.

Honoree rested the back of her head against the wall. Her hands and feet were numb, her eyeballs ached. If she stayed still for a minute, just one minute, she could make it to the dressing room, crawl under the makeup table, and stop breathing.

She stood, trying not to be afraid, and opened her eyes.

"Honoree, what just happened?"

Ezekiel's face was a mask of worry she wanted to trust. If only she could rest her head against his chest, feel his arms wrap around her, push aside the fear, the panic, and the numbness. But what if he was the cause of the danger that surrounded her?

"Excuse me. Get out of my way." She headed for the staircase, but she couldn't walk away without asking. She whirled around. "Why did you invite me to that table with that man sitting right there?" Her voice had risen, but the screeching startled her. She placed a hand on her chest to slow down the gunfire going off behind her rib cage. "Did you know, damn it."

His blue-black eyes softened with concern. "Did I know what?"

"Gallo is the man who shot Houdini."

His brown skin faded to ash. "What?"

"Gallo killed Houdini." A sob worked its way into her throat, and she covered her mouth with her hands to keep from screaming.

Ezekiel scrubbed his fingers through his hair. "Jesus Christ."

"I don't understand." Her voice was shaking. "Why did you bring him here tonight?"

Ezekiel rubbed his head, turning his processed waves into messy curls. "He's our banker for the policy business. Archie insisted he join us, Honoree." His words drifted into the air. He seemed as stunned by what had happened as she. "I suspected Gallo was involved in Houdini's death. I knew it, but I never thought he'd do the deed himself."

The missing pieces of Ezekiel's story started to turn from Jell-O into a solid form. "You were in business with Gallo before

Houdini was killed. The envelope was why Houdini died. You and Gallo are in cahoots. Did you come to me that night for the envelope or to kill me?"

"Goddamn it, Honoree. I would never hurt you. I was trying to protect you."

"Don't you dare. Don't you dare yell at me!"

He grabbed her shoulders. "You lost your mind? God. Keep quiet. Someone could overhear you. That envelope is still missing. Houdini didn't have it. Gallo still wants it, and I still want to keep you away from this entire mess."

The strength left him like a balloon had popped in his chest. His arms dropped limply to his sides. "You blame me — but I swear I didn't know."

She checked around. Had anyone joined them in the hallway? "I'm afraid to believe you."

He shut his eyes for a second. "My business with Archie and Gallo goes way back, Honoree. Back to the night I had to leave town. The contents of that envelope were going to help me get back some of what I lost that night."

"The envelope, Houdini, and Gallo." All connected. The sinking feeling would bury her. "I didn't want to believe it, but it's true.

It was my fault Houdini died."

"Don't talk crazy. If anyone got him killed, Honoree, it was me."

Her throat closed, and she pressed her lips together. The world needed to shut its mouth.

"Give me a few days. You said Gallo never saw you that night. He doesn't remember you. So you'll be okay." His hand reached for her chin but paused as the distrust entered her eyes. "All I need is a few days. I promise, Honoree, and I'll set things right."

CHAPTER 36
HONOREE

Friday, December 11, 1925

The police station was on Twenty-Sixth Street in the Second Ward. Honoree stood at the front desk, clutching the handle of her box purse and avoiding anyone who walked too close.

Christ, she hoped no one had followed her. If only the patrolman behind the counter would stop shouting into the receiver and ask her what she needed. She could say her peace and be on her way. Until then, she remained rooted to the spot, despite her body trembling.

"The mayor's office is fighting a war," the man shouted into the receiver. "The commission cares only about taking down Capone and his Outfit. Every other crime in the city can wait."

The bull-size man, his scarred bald head glistening with sweat, sorted through a stack of paper as he talked on and on. "What do

419

you want, girlie?"

Finally, he looked at her, and every bone in her body wanted to take a step back. The same hideous gashes and raised mounds that scarred his head covered his face. The aftermath of a long-ago battle with small-pox.

"Is Officer MacDonald here?"

Contempt covered his face as he eyed her dress and bobbed hair. Anytime she left her neighborhood, or ventured too far away from the Stroll, this judgment was what she got.

"Someone else can help you."

"Is he here?"

"He'll be here for his shift. You can wait over there and stay out of the way, under-stand?"

"Yes, sir, but may I ask what time his shift begins?"

"Ten o'clock."

"Ten o'clock this morning?"

The man sucked his teeth. "He'll be here straightaway. Now do what I said and sit."

A wooden bench with no cushions was pushed against the wall. Honoree sat with her knees pressed together, holding her hands in her lap, striving for prim and proper and wishing she'd worn plain clothes.

A steady stream of folks, men mostly, paused to glare at her before they reported a theft, a man who beat his wife, a bartender who brandished a rifle, or a minister whose collection box was missing.

Honoree sat stiffly, tolerating the scrutiny for an hour before Officer MacDonald strolled in and sat next to her.

"Hello, Honoree."

"You remember me?"

"Of course I do. We've met a few times before." He removed his hat, like a gentleman talking to a lady. "You were a child with long braids the first time we met. You asked Officer Murray and me to find the man who drove the car that killed your father."

"I don't recall meeting you before the Dreamland Cafe," she said with a gulp in her throat. "I do remember Officer Murray. He would drop to one knee whenever he talked to me so that we chatted eye to eye."

MacDonald grimaced for no apparent reason. "The second time we met was three years ago on the corner of State and Twenty-Sixth Street."

"You were with Officer Murray, and I asked him about the Bailey family. They were missing." She steadied her nerves with a deep breath. "Then you knew I lied when we talked at the Dreamland Cafe. Why didn't you mention this then?"

"I was looking for a killer. Not a lovesick little girl. Besides, you didn't remember me, and now I understand why."

"Where is Officer Murray?"

MacDonald lowered his head. "He died. Killed in the line of duty. One of three hundred and twenty-nine murders in Chicago in three hundred and fifteen days, according to the *Tribune*." He tapped his hat against his knee. "I had a feeling that afternoon at the Dreamland you wanted to talk. Is that why you're here, to talk about George Mills, or Houdini, as he was called?"

She blew out a breath. "What if I told you a colored girl witnessed a white man — someone who worked for Capone, but wasn't Capone — kill a colored man? What would you tell her to do?"

MacDonald scratched his brow. "To put one of Capone's men behind bars, a judge needs hard proof. You give the cops that, and nothing other than a bullet in my back will keep me from doing my job."

"Even if he's a white man?"

"Decent cops want the killing to stop. Too many dead bodies in the streets because of bootlegging and racketeers."

"What if the bullet ends up in my friend's back?"

"Trust me. I can help your friend."

"She's not a trusting girl," Honoree said with a short laugh.

He nodded. "I understand, but when you and I talked at the Dreamland, I asked you about Ezekiel Bailey."

"You did."

He smoothed the brim of his hat. "He's been running with some of Capone's boys. Him and Archie Graves. Maybe he could help you and me."

Honoree stared at her hands. "You think Ezekiel knows who killed Houdini? Or do you think —" A knot twisted in her chest. "He didn't kill him."

"Maybe not, but he's in league with Capone's boys and what they're doing in Bronzeville" — he paused — "that information might be helpful."

"She'll think on it. My friend, that is." She started to rise, but MacDonald touched her arm.

"When you make up your mind, come see me," he said. "You never struck me as a gal who didn't think for herself."

Honoree now stood firmly on both feet, her purse held tightly in her hand, her coat buttoned at the throat.

MacDonald placed his cap on his head. "I trust I'll see you soon, Ms. Dalcour."

Honoree telephoned the auto body shop from a nearby diner. Jeremiah picked up the line. Ezekiel had gone to Miss Hattie's, something he didn't usually do in the middle of the day, but he'd received a message and left. Twenty minutes later, Honoree walked into Miss Hattie's.

The speakeasy was empty except for Ezekiel — and Dewey, shelving bottles of hooch behind the bar. Ezekiel sat on the other end of the room at a table near the stage, smoking a cigarette and stacking silver coins.

"Do you have another cig?" she asked when she reached him, although there was a pack in her purse.

He held up his hand. "I got this one from Dewey."

"You two kiss and make up?"

"I don't give a flying leap about Dewey Graves." Ezekiel glanced across the room at the bar and then extended the cigarette to Honoree. "He can't hear us. You wanna drag or not?"

She took the cig and inhaled. A pleasant burn filled her lungs and spread across her chest. "Thanks." She reached over the table to give him back what was left of the smoke. "Keep it. You look like you need it more than me."

"How would you know?"

"I was there last night."

"I was there, too, and what happened — happened to me. And I don't look that bad."

He chuckled. "Sorry, you look lovely." His focus returned to the coins on the table. "I don't believe Gallo recognized you, but a friend is helping me find out."

The sound of Gallo's name brought back the fear from the night before, and she dug the toe of her shoe into the sawdust. "This friend who called you — you trust him?"

"I trust him, and you should, too." Ezekiel arranged the coins into a new stack. "The same man told me you were at the Dreamland Cafe the night Houdini was killed."

Honoree sat erect in her chair. "Tell me his name."

"Maximilian."

"Maximilian Chester?" She should've guessed. Each time she came across him, his kindness, whether that first night at the Dreamland Cafe or Lil's parties, should've been a giveaway. "Does he play the piano?"

"He does play, and he's a longtime friend of my mother's family." Ezekiel fingered the coins. "He met you once when you were six or seven and said it would be tough to forget your eyes or your name. He always called you the prettiest girl."

"Did he also see the man who killed Houdini?"

Ezekiel's shoulders sagged on a long, heavy sigh. The bluntness of her question chilled the air between them.

"No. He left the balcony after finishing a smoke and was in the hallway when he heard the gunfire. He rushed downstairs and saw you hightailing toward the exit. He got out of there fast, too, but then telephoned me."

"He's been watching over me." She wished her stomach didn't feel so queasy, but she had to tell Ezekiel about the copper. "I went to the police station to tell them who killed Houdini." She waited for an outburst, but there was no surprise, no flash of temper, no shouting, no slamming his fist. Ezekiel shoved a coin aside with a fingertip.

"I wish you hadn't done that," he said. "I asked you to give me a few days, but you still can't bring yourself to trust me. Why?" Ezekiel splayed his fingers, the skin over his knuckles pulled tight. "Don't bother. I know the answer." Ezekiel searched his pockets. "You sure you don't have any cigarettes? Rather not ask Dewey for another."

She reached into her purse and passed him her pack. He lit two and handed one to her.

"I didn't tell him Gallo's name. I simply mentioned a white man who worked for Capone."

"What's the officer's name?"

"MacDonald."

"What did he say?"

"Not much." Her lips felt as dry as sand.

He took a long drag from his cigarette, pulling so much smoke into his lungs he could launch a steamer.

"I pretended I was asking for a friend, a friend who witnessed the shooting of a Negro man by a white man."

Ezekiel's hand jerked, and a coin slid toward her, but he quickly scooped it up.

She settled in the chair, her bones melding into the wooden seat and her spine curving against the chair's bridge. What should she tell him about MacDonald? "The cop knew you worked with Archie and that Archie was in business with one of Capone's men, doing something more than selling whiskey in Bronzeville."

"Which is against the rules of racketeering." Ezekiel sighed. "Capone doesn't try to muzzle our lucrative policy gambling business as long as we colored folk buy our bootleg from him at whatever price he sets." Ezekiel picked up a coin and moved it from knuckle to knuckle on one hand.

"Is that why you and Archie were with Gallo? You're working with him on something to do with policy gambling?"

"I think, somehow, MacDonald is aware I had a run-in with Gallo the night I left town," Ezekiel said, ignoring her question.

"You met Gallo three years ago?"

"I didn't know him. Met him once the same night I met Archie. That's when I learned he and Gallo had worked on a failed insurance scam with my father. My father, the great Titus Bailey, owed Gallo a lot of money."

The bleakness in his voice, the strain around his eyes, Ezekiel's pain flowed like a river into the sea. Honoree hated to see him suffer.

"I'm sorry. That must've been difficult. But your father's choices had nothing to do with you."

Ezekiel looked up from the coins. "I killed him."

"Who?" she asked, not following what he meant. "Who did you kill? Your father?" A nervous laugh escaped her lips. "No, you didn't."

He smiled ruefully. "Thank you for thinking such a thing is unimaginable, but I promise you, I did."

"You killed him?" Disbelief twisted through her body, as her hopes and dreams dropped next to Ezekiel's coins.

He couldn't kill. No matter how much had changed, he couldn't kill. She lifted her head.

"How did it happen, Ezekiel?"

He swept the coins off the table into his fist. "My father went insane, attacked my mother and offered my brothers to Gallo as if they were slaves on a slaver's block.

"Father was desperate to salvage his reputation. His sons were his collateral. They could run numbers, sell bootleg whiskey, do whatever was necessary to repay Gallo." Ezekiel's laugh echoed with a heartless throb. "My mother said no, and he hit her. My baby brother, Marcus, reached him first, but Titus threw him across the room. I had no choice. I had to stop him."

Honoree couldn't believe her ears. Mr. Bailey, not as tall as Ezekiel, was a massively built man three years ago, and stronger than his sons.

The three boys and their mother had to be terrified.

"My father's body was lying on the floor in the parlor when Gallo showed up. He told us not to worry. No questions asked. He would keep my secret in return, but I owed him a favor." Ezekiel chuckled. "The last surprise of the night, Gallo made a telephone call, and Archie Graves arrived to dump my father's body in the Chicago River."

Honoree heard every word, but her thoughts reeled between disbelief and wishing nothing had happened. She touched his cheek. "I am so sorry, Ezekiel. So very sorry."

"Did you honestly think I'd leave town, leave you, without a goddamned good reason?" He placed his hand over her hand and pressed her palm to his cheek.

"I didn't know."

"Of course you didn't know. How could you? I killed my father, and that will be with me for the rest of my life." He inhaled with a small tremor. "I won't spend the rest of my life in debt to Gallo. I can't live like that, and I won't have my brothers, or my mother, live with that weight, either."

"How? What can you do to Gallo? What power do you have over him?"

He squeezed his eyes shut. "He's Archie's banker. For the policy operation. Something that's strictly against Capone's deal with the policy kings. My plan is simple — I'm going to make sure Capone finds out what Gallo has been up to."

He abruptly stood and stepped away from the table. "Would you like a drink? I could use a drink."

The crack in his voice broke her heart.

CHAPTER 37
SAWYER

Wednesday, July 1, 2015

I shower, put on a clean pair of jeans and my classic Spike Lee *Do the Right Thing* T-shirt. I think about ordering a 2XL and mailing it special delivery to my dad, but he wouldn't get the joke. I'm not feeling that funny any damn way.

I reach the Sage Fool's Pub close to midnight. Standing room only, I fight my way to the middle of the bar, passing by a large room, stanchioned off, with small round tables and short, squat stools. It is where live music plays. A stage is positioned in front of a wall-length picture window, a drum kit, and a few small klieg lights finish off the ensemble.

The joint is at capacity. I move into an open spot and wave at one of the bartenders. "Do you know where I can find Lula Kent?" I shout above the noise.

A blond man with a Viking beard and a

massive amount of muscle doesn't glance away from his blender. He replies loudly over his shoulder, "What about her?"

This isn't casual bartender-speak, but I ignore the attitude. "Is Lula working tonight?"

The Viking turns, and his blue eyes hold the same bad attitude as his tone. "Why do you want her?"

None of your fucking business is what I start to say. But the dude is taller than me, broader than me, and could beat my comparatively skinny ass with a martini shaker. "Ease up, man. I only want to say hi. She and I — well, we work together."

He points at the wall behind him. "Look up, man."

The leaderboard is three feet tall, and scrawled in white chalk in huge letters is Lula's name — and the start time of her next set.

"My bad," I say to the Viking. "A double shot of Patrón. Neat."

He makes my drink. I pay him, turn, and angle through the crowd to the music room.

The band — a bass guitarist, a drummer spinning his sticks, and a tenor saxophone player — walk from the audience onto the stage. A redheaded woman in a black sleeveless shirt already sits at the keyboards.

When the lights dim, my imagination takes me back to a 1920s speakeasy. Cigarette smoke and whiskey and perspiration float into the room. A jazz quartet plays in a balcony, and a tough-voiced songstress belts the blues.

It isn't 1925, but time surrounds me. The past is a perfect blues song, and I imagine Honoree strutting across the stage, and the hairs on the back of my neck rise.

Someone bumps into me, and I am back in the present. An empty table is against the wall. I swallow my tequila and take a seat.

Lula strolls onto the stage in a strapless black sundress with red flowers and steps into a spotlight, illuminating her face. The lighting adores her cheekbones, her full lips, and the roundness of her head and the length of her throat — even her natural short black hair sparkles. Everything about her glows — especially her smooth black skin.

I tilt my head back and hold my breath. Damn, she looks different out of her blue scrubs, but the same. Regal. In command. Beautiful.

She taps the microphone and moistens her lips, a slight show of nerves. "Good evening, my name is Lula Kent." She introduces the band, makes a joke about the weather, and begins to sing.

Her voice, a rough, raw alto with a soul-stirring vibrato, is sex in middle C.

I stop thinking, stop worrying, and stare at her, hypnotized by her voice and the shape of her mouth.

A woman's mouth tells a story: a twitch in the corner, an upturn, a downturn, the seductiveness of a smile. A woman's mouth conveys truth without making a sound. I wrote those lines in a screenplay.

Now, Lula can sing her ass off. Her next song is a tune by Nina Simone, "Sinner-man." The song is not an easy cover, but she nails it. As the set ends, the applause takes a few minutes to wind down. The room empties slowly. I don't move from my seat.

The lights come up, not too bright, and Lula steps from the stage.

Standing with slick palms and a throat as dry as sand, I tug on the collar of my T-shirt.

Ready. Set. Go.

I approach Lula, who still smiles but not at me. A couple had paused to praise her. After a few minutes, the last admiring patrons depart. The room is empty, except for the musicians and me and Lula. I keep my distance, a few feet from her; the musicians huddle.

"You don't have to stand over there, Sawyer."

"I probably should've called, right? Sent an email or text or something."

"Are you okay? What's up?"

"Lula." We're interrupted by one of the musicians. "Great set, girl." The other band members stroll by, each extending accolades with just as much enthusiasm. Lula introduces me, and after a brief chat, the drummer ropes off the room with a stanchion.

"Do you have a moment to talk?" I ask her as soon as we're alone.

She glances at a nearby table. "Let's sit. I have another set in thirty minutes, but we can chat for a few." She rests her elbows on the table, and I'm floored again by her beauty and how adorable she is. "Sawyer, I'm getting antsy. I'm glad you're here, but this doesn't feel like a social visit."

"No. No. No. I wanted to listen to you sing." It is an innocent statement, but it didn't help that my voice cracked.

She tilts her head, studying my face. "What's going on with you?"

"I'm waiting on the link to the film. The one I had restored. Still don't have proof if it's a lost Micheaux."

"Okay." She's waiting for me to get to the point.

I plant my elbows on the small round table, wishing I hadn't given up cigarettes after the crash. I could use one or ten, or even a hit. "I talked to Maggie White. Miss Honoree is my great-grandmother. Unless the two old gals formed some sort of conspiracy — for no rational reason. I don't know, but it's messing with my head."

Lula looks grim. "We can't do anything about this tonight, Sawyer. Whatever this is. Can you hang out until my set is done?"

"I can't explain why I'm dropping this on you — not your trouble."

She touches my hand and squeezes hard. "No trouble. I understand family and secrets. The stuff that remains unspoken. You're lucky. The key players in your mystery are alive and kicking. Knock on wood. You can still get answers."

She's right, but my melancholy shifts into place. "I should return to the hostel. Do some writing. Edit some recorded interviews. You know, do some work."

She reaches over the small table and takes my hands in hers. "I said wait for me."

I smile, nod, and settle back in my seat, but first, I stop a waitress and order another tequila.

CHAPTER 38
HONOREE

Thursday, December 24, 1925

It was late on Christmas Eve. Honoree had taken a couple of nights off and was curled up on the cot, legs crossed, shoulders slumped, threading a needle. She had two things on her mind: Ezekiel and dancing at Capone's bash on New Year's Eve.

In a battle between what caused her the most worry, Ezekiel won. He'd taken his father's life, and she understood why, but what had it done to his soul? *How do you forgive yourself for killing your father?*

"Damn."

"What's wrong?" Bessie sat at the opposite end of the cot, mending a hole in a musician's shirt.

"Nothing." Honoree brought the thread to her lips to moisten the tip. Her grip had slipped, and she had to thread the needle again. "Nothin's wrong."

Honoree walked over to the Singer and

438

dropped her sewing kit into a basket. Outside the window, the snow was falling
sideways, and the wind howled like wolves
in the woods. She guessed about the wolf,
having not left Chicago since she was five
years old. "There'll be two feet of snow
outside by morning."

Bessie huffed. "You've been acting odd
since you saw Ezekiel. Talking about the
weather, missing work at the Dreamland,
moping around here — that's not like you."

"Why I missed work is my business,"
Honoree said, unwilling to admit Bessie had
guessed right. "I won't be fired. I have
friends in the right places, like Lil and Mr.
Buttons."

"You're crazy not to go to work, no matter what happened with Ezekiel."

Honoree squinted at her. "I should be the
one asking how you're doing."

"I hate being pregnant. Other than that,
I'm the cat's meow."

"Too late to do anything about being pregnant."

"Never too late."

There was such vinegar in her tone,
Honoree shivered. She strolled over to the
sink. "Are you serious about getting rid of
the baby? You know that's dangerous."

Bessie didn't look away from her stitching. "I'm just talking. There ain't much I can do. I'm in, I guess."

Honoree turned on the faucet, cupped her hands beneath the water, and splashed her face. "We should go out on the town. Both of us."

"Eleven o'clock on Christmas Eve, and you just said it was snowing cats and dogs."

"Sounds like a great night to hear some music and do some dancing."

Bessie stomped across the kitchenette, a complaint in every step. "You want to go out, go ahead. I don't want to."

"Yes, you do. You have the blues. The only way to rid the body of the blues is to go out dancing."

Bessie stared at the floorboards. "Where are we going?"

"The Plantation Cafe."

Bessie put down her sewing. "That place is a watering hole for mobsters, whores, pimps, and bootleggers — the most dangerous nightclub on the Stroll."

"Every speakeasy in Chicago is dangerous," Honoree shot back, ignoring the bite of guilt she felt in her stomach. "I know — but I need you with me."

Bessie groaned. "You do? At least we'll be a few blocks from the Dreamland Cafe." She walked over to the sink. "Lessens the chance of someone running into you."

"Everybody we know will be at the Dreamland enjoying the music of Louis Armstrong, Lil, and the Syncopators." Honoree grabbed the silver lamé with the fringe skirt from the hanger bar. "Put this one on — and don't look at me like that. Your belly is big, but you'll be a looker in this number."

"Silver is not my color," she said, washing her armpits.

"You were fine with it when we went to Lil's."

"I want to wear the pink one."

"No." Honoree removed the green shift from the wall hook, thinking Bessie might be right, but her belly would show in anything else. "The green has a white chiffon overlay. It'll be gorgeous on you."

Bessie pouted but took the green dress. "What will you wear?"

"The red sheath with the sequins and floral bead panels. Red is a showstopper."

"Humph. The neckline touches your belly button."

Honoree folded her arms over her stomach and smiled. "My intention is to be noticed."

"I was right. This does have to do with Ezekiel," Bessie said sharply.

"It has nothing to do with him."

It had to do with Tony Gallo, but that was none of Bessie's concern. Gallo was a co-owner of the Plantation Cafe, along with Capone himself. With any luck, one of them or both men might be at the Plantation Cafe tonight, celebrating the holiday.

Honoree was frightened out of her mind at the thought of seeing Gallo again. Still, maybe she could help Ezekiel and herself, by giving Gallo something he might find useful — the envelope with eighty-seven betting slips. It might not be the brightest idea she'd ever had, but like Ezekiel, Honoree hated being indebted to a man, especially a killer like Gallo. And whether it was debt or something else, she intended to break free of him, and Archie.

It was her first trip to the Plantation Cafe and Honoree hated the place the instant she entered. A three-story building, like the Dreamland Cafe, a black-and-tan nightclub with the same crystal chandeliers, bow-tied waiters, and elaborate floor show, but the Dreamland had a friendlier atmosphere.

Coloreds who patronized the Plantation Cafe were herded behind a velvet rope, segregating them from the club's white patrons. A few colored girls ventured on the white side, but they were light-skinned and on the arm of white men in tweed suits or tuxedos and tails.

"Can I help you, ladies?" The maître d' was clean-shaven with skin so smooth it shined. He bowed, greeting them politely, but his pleasant smile didn't keep him from pointing them to the colored section. "This way, please."

"Thank you." Honoree sneered after the man as he walked away, but then she examined her surroundings. "I won't get anyone's attention back here."

Bessie adjusted the seam of her shift. "I don't like this place."

"Neither do I. But there's a man I want to see, and I hope he's here."

"Who is it?"

"No one in particular — just a guy I met." Rising to her tiptoes, Honoree scanned the room, looking for Tony Gallo. "He'll remember me."

"Who you talking about? Who will remember you?" Bessie seemed miffed. "Of course whoever it is could never forget you. What did you say? A man who don't remember a girl who looks like you ain't got the sense he was born with." She sighed.

"Not sure I said that exactly, but it sounds like something I might say."

"Why did I have to come here with you?"

" 'Cause a woman alone gets pegged as a whore. I couldn't risk not getting in — or getting in for the wrong reason."

"I don't like being around white folks. They keep staring at us."

"Stop staring at 'em. They'll tire of lookin' after a while." Honoree smacked her lips. "I've got to find a way on the other side of this darn rope."

A few light-skinned colored girls in the corner shook their rumps to attract the maître d's eye. He strolled over, and one of the girls pressed a wad of cabbage into his palm. Quick as that, he lifted the rope.

"Oh, is that how this works?" Honoree said quietly.

"How what works?" Bessie asked.

Honoree pointed at the three girls moving into the main dining hall. "They are greasing pockets to get on the other side of the rope." She frowned. "Anything goes wrong, you hightail it to the Dreamland Cafe. Colethea is working tonight. She'll help get you home." She pulled Bessie to her side. "Don't forget. You leave here, and Colethea will take care of you."

"What kind of trouble? Why would I need to leave? I can help." She patted her stomach.

"I don't want you wrapped up in my mess."

"I'm not leaving, Honoree."

"Fine. Stay here. The man I came to see is over there — and I'm about to move to the other side."

Honoree slipped off her fur-collared coat and handed it to Bessie. With a shimmy, the dress fell into place.

"Just in case," Honoree warned. "Don't forget Colethea."

Hands on her hips, she sauntered over to the maître d'. "Hello, cutie."

"Hello, cutie," he said.

"I wonder if you could help me." She wet her lips and batted her eyelids. "I am a friend of Tony Gallo's, and he left his yellow-gold cigarette case, the one by Fabergé, in my boudoir. I wanted to return it, personally."

His gaze froze on her chest.

"I don't trust anyone to give it to him but me."

His hairless face contorted, but his voice was steady. "I ain't no fool, ma'am." He looked into her eyes. "You ain't showing me nothing I ain't seen before, but I do admire your style. Mr. Gallo got plenty of colored girls. You're lovely, for sure, prettier than most of the women here on any given night."

"If I'm so pretty, escort me over to his table. He'll be glad to see me."

"Show me the cigarette case."

She fingered the latch on her purse and whispered, "I have two ten-dollar bills here. One is yours now. The other, when I get over to Mr. Gallo's VIP table."

"Humph." He reached for the open purse.

She stepped back, snapping it shut, but not before removing a ten-spot. "We got a deal?"

The maître d' earned another ten when he escorted Honoree to Tony Gallo's table.

Ten people sat at the round, mostly men. The women languished in laps or hung on to a man's shoulders, with their bosoms and buttocks within reach. At least no one else wore red. The only colored girl with any flair, other than Honoree, was the blonde sitting in Gallo's lap.

Well, ain't that the cat's pajamas!

The blonde on Gallo's lap was Trudy Lewis. What was she doing at a club owned by Capone? Hymie Weiss and the North Side gang were her cups of tea.

Trudy hadn't spotted her yet, but this

didn't change Honoree's loosely devised plan.

"Craziest story I ever heard." Trudy blithely adjusted her body in the man's lap, snaring Gallo's attention and that of every other man and woman at the table. "I bet that's true."

Standing behind a group of women, Honoree didn't listen to Trudy's story. She observed Gallo. He had the build of a hunting dog, and the features she'd never forget: the large beak nose, small cold eyes, and white man's skin.

"Capone loves jazz so." Trudy jiggled on his lap. "Isn't that true, Tony?"

Gallo laughed, then pushed Trudy from his lap, not gently. "He also loves a sexy colored showgirl." He wiped his nose. "Where's my goddamned drink? Nigga waiter was supposed to bring me a drink an hour ago."

Trudy swept blond curls from her face. "I'll get that drink, sugar."

He pinched her on the rump. "You're a doll."

Trudy flashed a grin, but a shadow crept into her eyes as she walked by Honoree. "What do you think you're doing here?"

"None of your beeswax."

Trudy's lips drew back. "We'll see about

that." She strolled off, going after the waiter and Gallo's drink, Honoree presumed. She hoped she wouldn't return too soon.

Honoree slid into the spotlight; the plunging neckline of her shift, exposing the glistening mounds of her bubs.

"The beauty from the Dreamland Cafe," Mr. Gallo said, a drink in one hand, the other reaching toward her ass. "What's your name again, sugar?"

"Honoree, Mr. Gallo."

"The colored girl with the French name."

Patrons scooted chairs and leaned torsos, opening a path. "You invited me to dance at Mr. Capone's party."

"When did I do that?" His gaze traveled from her hips to her breastbone to the hollow of her throat. The smile on his face spread into a broad, ugly grin. "Perhaps I did invite you."

Christ. Had he changed his mind? Or he was soused to the eyeballs and couldn't remember anything about that night.

He waved at one of the other girls at the table. "Get her some champagne, and I'll have another bourbon."

Gallo angled his chair, trapping her knees between his short, sturdy legs and sandwiching her between his thighs. He inched forward, and his broad face blocked her view, the thick odor of whiskey rolling off him like smoke. "What you playing at, girl?"

"I ain't playing at nothin'. I saw you over here and wanted to thank you. A colored girl like me isn't invited to dance for Mr. Capone every day."

"You ain't as good a liar as you think, but I am. I saw you. That night, thinking I couldn't see you. Now, pick your kisser up off the floor. I ain't gonna hurt you. If I'd wanted to hurt you, you'd been hurt two months ago. Them boys of yours, Archie and Ezekiel, are my business partners, and they wouldn't let you double-cross me."

The trip to the Plantation Club was supposed to square things with Gallo — get her and Ezekiel out of debt, but the envelope with the betting slips was still inside her box purse.

Gallo had seen her the night he murdered Houdini and seemingly had no fear of retribution for murdering a Negro. Houdini's life didn't matter to Gallo. Honoree wouldn't matter, either.

Gallo rubbed his calloused fingers over her arm and, pausing at her waist, tugged on the fabric of her dress. "You a stupid little girl, but the prettiest chocolate child I've ever seen."

"Let her go," said Ezekiel's dangerously

deep voice.

Breathing was a thing Honoree could do later. Where had he come from?

"She's my girl, Gallo. Let her go."

"Who do you think you're talking to, boy?" Gallo glanced around the table, smiling as if nothing unusual had happened or was about to happen.

He then shoved Honoree off his lap, but Ezekiel caught her before she hit the floor. Then he moved her shaking body aside, putting some space between her and Gallo.

"I could kill you here and now," Gallo said with a grim smile.

"It's one thing to kill a Black man at an empty bar. Another to kill a man, even a colored man, in a room full of people."

"You are a brazen boy, Ezekiel Bailey."

"Maybe, but I'll walk out of here with my girl. And we won't talk about tonight ever again."

"Are you threatening me?" Gallo asked in the tone of a man who'd never heard something so outrageous.

Suddenly, Ezekiel was on one knee next to Gallo's chair. Honoree could barely hear what he was saying, but she heard enough.

"Capone made a deal with the policy kings in Bronzeville," Ezekiel said. "Buy his bootleg whiskey, and he'll keep his hands out of policy gambling in the Black Belt."

"So what? You, me, and Archie made a different deal."

"A deal Capone knows nothing about."

Gallo chuckled, but his eyes were small, angry marbles. "You bet on a dark horse, boy — a mighty dark horse. You gonna double-cross me? I don't think so. Don't forget. I know how your daddy died."

Ezekiel rose from his knees. He backed away from Gallo and took Honoree's hand. "Time for us to leave, Honoree."

He nodded at Gallo, and when they reached the other side of the rope, he spoke low and hard. "What were you thinking? Did you want to get killed?"

"How did you know I was here? Did Bessie call you?"

"No. She didn't call me."

"I don't see her. I don't see her anywhere." Honoree jerked her hand free and went over to the colored maître d'. "Did you see my friend? The girl in the green number who came in here with me?"

The man squinted. "She left a while ago."

Ezekiel took her by the arm. "We can't stay here, Honoree. We've got to go."

"Was she alone?"

Ezekiel squeezed her arm. "We've got to go."

Panic swelled in Honoree's throat. "Who did she leave with?"

"Calm down, Honoree." Ezekiel led her toward the door. "Why couldn't you just wait?"

"I don't wait. I take care of me. Now, where's Bessie?"

"She's with Trudy."

"What do you mean, she's with Trudy? Why?"

"Wait until we are outside. I'll tell you then."

On the sidewalk outside the Plantation Cafe, Honoree snatched back her arm and marched across the street, heading for the Dreamland Cafe.

"Where are you going?"

"Bessie wouldn't have left without telling me."

"Trudy drove her home."

"What?"

"Trudy called me. I was at Miss Hattie's. She told me you were here up to your eyebrows in shit. I told her to take Bessie home."

Honoree grabbed his coat sleeve. "What do you mean Trudy called you?"

"You jealous? No need to be. Never a need to be, but Trudy isn't as bad a girl as you think."

"I guess you know her better than me."

"Yes, I know she had a beef with Gallo, long before he killed Houdini."

Honoree shivered; snowflakes melted on her bare shoulders and covered her throat and most of her chest. "I think I left my coat inside."

"Bessie has it."

"So everything has been handled. I should thank you," she said, her tone loaded with sarcasm.

"I don't care about you being angry. This wasn't smart, Honoree."

"Gallo had his thumb on you and me, and I hate these men with the power to tell me what I do, when I do it, and where."

Ezekiel draped his suit jacket over her shoulders and led her to the corner. "I'll hail a cab."

"You knew, didn't you? You knew Gallo killed Houdini. You knew he knew about me being there. Is that why you came to my door that night — and lied?"

Ezekiel raised his head, glancing up at the stars. "I honestly didn't know. I just wanted time to figure a way out from under this." He stepped into the street, waving at a slow-moving Checker cab. "Hold up, chief!" he yelled.

The cab pulled over to the curb. Ezekiel

opened the door and helped her inside. When she was seated, he gave her address to the driver.

"We've got to do something, Ezekiel. I can't live with that man hovering over me like I'm dead meat. I'm not dead meat, Ezekiel."

CHAPTER 39
SAWYER

Thursday, July 2, 2015

"Sawyer, you awake?" Lula appears from the back of the apartment wearing a short silk robe, furry slippers, and horn-rimmed glasses.

When did we get so casual with each other?

"You look like somebody stole your puppy." She moves around the bed, hugging the wall. Is she scared of me? What did I do?

I make my eyesight work better and notice the apartment is a one-room studio. There's a window and a door, which I assume leads to the bathroom.

I recall stumbling through the streets of the city, staggering at Lula's side, but I don't remember how I ended up in her bed. "Damn. How many shots of tequila did I have?"

"More than one too many."

I roll over and realize I'm wearing nothing but boxers. God, I hope I didn't embarrass myself. I push the sheet away and place my feet on the floor. "I don't mean to mess up your morning routine."

I want to rise and put on my T-shirt, sneakers, and jeans, neatly arranged over the back of her desk chair. I go to stand, but the room spins, and I flop back down.

"You didn't mess up anything," Lula is saying. "You shouldn't be so hard on yourself."

"You are being polite. I can still smell the tequila on my breath."

She sits close to the headboard, her legs tucked beneath her, leaving plenty of space between us. "I admit you were trashed."

"Was I rude? I'm usually a happy drunk. A little sloppy, but a laugh riot." I wait for her to let me off the hook, but no luck.

"You weren't the least bit funny." Lula massages her foot as she doesn't look at me.

"Was I disrespectful?" Then I thought about the Viking. "I didn't fight with the bartender or anything?"

"No. No. In your state, the only person you hurt was yourself."

"Then what did I do?"

Lula stretches her arms above her head, yawning. "You told me how worried you were about Miss Honoree not being Miss Honoree. How she lied to you, but not just you, but your mother and your father, and your grandmother Maggie."

"Seems like I told you everything."

"Pretty much, I guess."

I want to slip back under the covers. "I'm taking it too hard, but the lies, one lie on top of another lie, are exhausting."

She moves in a bit closer and nudges me lightly on the leg. "Why don't you chill? You carry tension around like designer luggage. Something you're afraid to lose. But I don't mind having you around, now that you're sober."

"Are you sure?"

"Sure, I'm sure." Lula unfolds her legs, stands, and hugs her robe around her extra snug. She looks down at me and smiles. "Before we leave, do me a favor."

"Sure, anything."

"For the love of God, take a shower."

I jokingly sniff my armpits, cringe, and give her a mock salute. "Yes, ma'am." She laughs and tosses me a towel.

CHAPTER 40
HONOREE

Friday, December 25, 1925

The day after Honoree visited the Plantation Cafe was Christmas, and her biggest concern was not whether she had a gift to give anyone, or her rash decision to visit the Plantation Cafe. Her worry was whether she and Bessie would freeze to death.

The city was an iceberg buried in two feet of snow. Everything, everywhere, and everybody was cold. The only way to warm up in Bronzeville was to light a match and burn anything that might give off some heat. Fires were set in alleys, on stoops, in tin basins, and inside kitchenettes. People burned furniture, old clothes, newspapers; they set fire to whatever could fuel a blaze.

One hundred fires, according to Kenny, when he'd stopped by earlier with the late edition of the *Tribune*.

Honoree and Bessie were curled up under her mother's quilt, with a pile of winter coats, a fur shawl, and odd pieces of fabric, on top of the quilt.

"Merry Christmas," Bessie muttered between a shiver and a sniffle.

"Merry Christmas," Honoree said dully. How merry could this day be? The pipes beneath the kitchen sink were frozen. No water to make a cup of coffee or a pot of tea or to boil an egg.

"The *Tribune* said the temperature would be zero degrees today." Bessie sneezed. "Excuse me. And — and a hundred fires burned last night."

Honoree poked her under the pile of covers. "Exactly what I just read."

"I'm cold." Bessie groaned. "We should go to the Dreamland Cafe or Miss Hattie's. I bet they have heat."

Honoree didn't want to risk a run-in with Gallo, or Archie, or even Ezekiel. She was staying in. "I don't want to do that. They might be on fire, too."

"Kenny would've told us."

"If you're too cold to stay here, Bessie, you can go to Miss Hattie's by yourself."

"I could, but I have other places I could be."

"What other places? Oh, let me guess." She rolled her eyes upward like the answer was on the ceiling. "Virginia's whorehouse or maybe someplace with Trudy?"

Bessie had gone on and on about her drive home from the Plantation Cafe with Trudy. Made it sound as if the Queen of Sheba had given her a ride.

"Trudy's gonna dye my hair this weekend," Bessie declared. "She said I'll look swell as a blonde."

"You gonna color your hair the same shade as Trudy?"

"She was awful kind to drive me home. We should be friends with her. She ain't as bad as some people make her out to be."

"Did she ask you to say that?" Honoree was suddenly too warm and kicked her legs from beneath the pile of clothes and her mother's quilt. "Let's stop talking about Trudy. I don't need the aggravation."

Bessie wrinkled her nose. "You smell something?"

Honoree leaned forward. "I hear something." It was Laura Lee — shouting from the other side of the wall.

"Fire!"

"Oh my God," Bessie wailed.

"Hush!" Honoree's body shook. She was a runaway train, bumping over the tracks too fast and furiously. "Smoke. It could be nothing. A few flames coming from a pot on Laura Lee's stove."

Laura Lee's voice screamed: "Fire! Fire!"

Honoree pounded her fist against the wall but then drew back. "Ouch! It's hot as Hades." She pointed Bessie toward the window. "You see any smoke?"

Bessie raced to the windowsill. "Yes! Coming from the second floor."

A knock at the front door. More yelling. "The building's on fire!" She recognized the voice of Laura Lee's eldest boy. "Get out before you burn!"

Honoree pivoted. "The fire is on the front porch."

Heat rose through the floorboards, burning the soles of her feet.

"Coming fast."

"Too fast!"

Bessie closed the distance from the windowsill to Honoree in a breath. Her arms wrapped around Honoree's waist, but Honoree unhinged herself and grabbed Bessie's shoulders. "We gotta leave now."

Free of Bessie, she whirled around, picking and choosing what to take and what to leave behind. She scooped up an armload of sewing baskets, including the heart-shaped one, and then fabric and dresses. "Grab what you can and throw it out the window," she instructed Bessie.

They needed to hurry. Two flights up. The

461

steps weren't too steep, but the kitchenette was already filled with smoke.

"Bessie!"

"I'm right here." She climbed back through the window. "We can make it down the stairs, but we've got to hurry. Fire is coming through the windows on every floor!"

Honoree's lungs burned. Smoke seemed to be everywhere. She couldn't breathe, but she couldn't leave, not without saving more of her things, more of her memories.

"Whatever you are looking for," Bessie shouted, "you best find it quickly. We need to leave."

"Go on! I'm right behind you."

Her mother's quilt. Where was it?

Dropping to her knees, she crawled toward the cot. A loud crash and a burst of heat widened a crack in the wall, splitting the plaster into shreds.

"Come on!" Bessie screamed from the window.

Honoree found a piece of cloth. It had to be the quilt, but she couldn't see — too much smoke.

She moved toward the window and grabbed what she hoped was the quilt. But just before she reached the windowsill, she picked up one of the heart-shaped sewing baskets. She vaulted through the window onto the rear porch.

Together, she and Bessie stumbled down the staircase, passing by the flames shooting from the windows. Her heart pounded. Too many memories, too much of the family that had died or abandoned her, memories she couldn't watch burn.

Honoree moved toward the stairwell with Bessie grabbing at her. "Let go!" She pushed her aside and limped toward the stairs. The first step crumbled beneath her, and she lay in a pile of splintered wood.

A sharp blow to her hip and a searing pain exploded in her leg. The sob started deep inside her chest; the grief trapped in her throat by the trembling hand she held over her mouth.

The only home she knew was gone. The kitchenette where her father, mother, and baby sister — had lived, and died, and argued, and left — burned to the ground. Gone. The flat where she and Ezekiel had made love. The Singer sewing machine. Her dresses. Her lovely dresses. Those memories. Gone. Nothing left but bags of needles and thread, pieces of fabric, and lost dreams.

She lay on the ground, her legs useless, her heart broken, hugging her mother's quilt to her breast. And she cried — the dull echo of her sobs eclipsed by the fire truck's clanging bell. They had finally arrived to pour water on the ashes.

"Honoree!"

She wiped her eyes and tried to sit up.

Bessie lumbered toward her, a heavy weight in her arms, her face covered in soot and dirt. "I have it!"

Honoree choked on the words. "What do you have?"

"Your mother's sewing machine. The Singer."

"Honoree." *Ezekiel.*

He was kneeling in the snow next to her. Where had he come from? Or was she dreaming?

"All gone." The cold numbed her lips. "I don't know what to do."

"You are all right, Honoree."

"What are you doing here?"

"I told you I'd come today."

"Oh yes, Gallo." She spoke the name without care, as a mountain of orange and red flames, painted on a midnight canvas, rose behind Ezekiel's head.

On the sidewalk, in the snow, shivering with cold, blackened with soot, her neighbors sat motionless, exhausted by fear, fire, and loss. People Honoree had known for the past decade, tears streaming, mouths flopped open, eyes blankly staring, as their lives burned to the ground. Laura Lee and her five children huddled in silence on a steamer trunk. Kenny sat on the curb rifling through a camera case, a box of photos, and rolled-up canvases.

"Come home with me." Ezekiel loomed next to her like a giant bird.

"You don't have room at the auto body shop for Bessie and me."

"Not there, the house on Champlain Street."

The Bailey house? Not once in her life had she spent a single night at Ezekiel's parents' home. "You won't mind Bessie and me staying there?"

"It's my house. I own it. So, no. I won't mind."

She wanted to sleep. To close her eyes and rest for a long, long while and then wake up from this nightmare. "Okay. Yes, I will."

Ezekiel picked her up and carried her across the street toward the truck. He called over Jeremiah, and he loaded the items she and Bessie had saved. The four of them squeezed into the front seat. Honoree sat in Ezekiel's lap with Jeremiah behind the wheel. Bessie latched on to Honoree's side and curled herself into a small ball to fit in the space next to Honoree.

As the truck drove away, Honoree didn't turn around to see the flames and ashes. She sat stiffly, looking straight ahead.

"Honoree, how's your leg?" Ezekiel asked.

What was wrong with her leg? "It hurts." She nuzzled into his side with eyelids as heavy as her heart. The next instant, she awoke, and the truck was parked in the driveway of the house on Champlain Street. The last time Honoree had seen the Bailey house was the summer the Baileys disappeared, and she'd sat on the stoop, weeping and waiting for hours.

Ezekiel, the man who had broken her heart, now carried her into the foyer and toward the staircase, passing by the parlor and the den. With each step, Honoree's chest tightened.

From room to room, wall to wall, nothing had changed. The walnut dining table was still polished to a glossy shine. The oil lamp painted with honey blossoms and blue hummingbirds swayed from the ceiling. Rose-colored glasses and dogwood bowls lined the shelves of the china cabinet. The staggering scent of kerosene, the damp wool of the Oriental rugs, and the burn of the Black Cat stove polish still thickened the air.

There had never been enough air in the

Bailey house. Never room to breathe. Ezekiel reached the top of the staircase, and Honoree closed her eyes. When she opened them, she was sitting on the bed, and Ezekiel had turned down the sheets. Too exhausted to speak, she watched him as he carefully removed her shoes, her sweater, and her shift, leaving her in her cotton chemise. She burrowed beneath the covers, and he placed a thick wool blanket over her.

"Where's my mother's quilt?"

"I'm not sure, but Bessie will find it, and when she does, I'll bring it to you. For now, I want you to rest. I'll be back in a few minutes to check on your leg and your ankle."

"How's Bessie?"

"She has a nasty burn on her arm."

"The same arm where she was burned before?"

"I think so. But I'll take care of her. She'll be fine, Honoree. Close your eyes and sleep."

PART 5

PART 5

CHAPTER 41
HONOREE

Saturday, December 26, 1925

Daylight from the bedroom's bay windows heated Honoree's face and throat and scared her nearly to death. She scrambled upright in the bed, grimaced, and exhaled slowly, calming herself before tucking the sheet across her lap. There were no flames in Ezekiel's bedroom, only the lingering odor of smoke and memories. Also, something was wrong with her leg.

"How are you?"

She jerked sideways, startled by Ezekiel, sitting in the rocking chair next to the bed. "Morning," she said softly. "How long did I sleep?"

"A few hours."

"Have you been here all night? Watching me?"

"Yes." The twitchy smile on his lips mirrored the concern in his eyes. She chewed the inside of her cheek. "What's wrong with my leg?"

"How does it feel?" He had a hand on the sheet next to her feet. "Do you mind?"

She shook her head.

He pulled the sheet to her knees, exposing the bandage on her calf and another around her ankle.

"When did you do that?"

"Last night." He examined his handiwork somewhat awkwardly. "You didn't budge when I bandaged you up. You were too tired. It was the smoke. You swallowed quite a bit." He handed her a glass of water. "See if you can keep some of this down."

She took a sip, but her lungs seized, and the coughing spasm rifled inside her rib cage.

Ezekiel removed the glass from her hand before she dropped it and patted her upper back. "You'll be fine."

"You sure? Everything hurts," she said. "I should get up."

"And do what? No, rest your leg."

"I am tired."

"Would you like something to eat? I can bring you a tray."

Feeling her eyelids droop, she scooted down in the bed. "I think I'll sleep a little longer."

"I'll come back later with some food." He

paused at the door. "I'm so sorry." Ezekiel rubbed a rough hand through his hair.

"Careful. You'll pull out all those pretty waves."

He looked away, but not before his eyes darkened. What else was on his mind?

"This is my fault," he said quietly.

"What? The fire? Fires were burning all day everywhere." She coughed.

He reached for the pitcher of water, but she shook her head. Anything might cause another coughing spasm.

"It wasn't your fault, Ezekiel. You didn't set the fires and didn't break my ankle."

"Not broken."

"I was scared." She snuggled beneath the sheet. "There was never any heat in that old building."

He stood next to the bed. "I'm so sorry, Honoree."

"Stop saying that. People were freezing and wanted to be warm."

"The fire in your building might've been caused by Gallo's men. Those boys knew where you lived." His words made goose-flesh rise on her skin. "That's why I'm saying, my fault."

"Come here." She shifted to the middle of the bed, pulling up her mother's quilt and smiling. "Bessie had it?"

He nodded.

"Come lie with me."

Ezekiel wiped a hand over his eyes. "I'm wearing my work shoes and overalls."

"You know how to wash clothes. My mother taught you." Something in her heart turned, and her throat closed on a sob. "I want you to hold me. I need to be held." She placed her hand over her heart. "I think you could use some holding, too."

"Yes, ma'am." He unlaced his shoes, kicked them off quickly, pulled down his suspenders, and crawled into the bed next to her, fully clothed.

"Go to sleep now." He hugged her to his chest. "I missed you so much." He planted a kiss on her forehead. "My sweet, sweet Honoree."

Other than the bathroom, Honoree had remained in the second-floor bedroom since the night of the fire. It had to be Tuesday but smelled like Sunday. The aroma of breakfast — bacon, eggs, grits, and bread — wafted through the house. Her lungs still felt full of smoke, but she couldn't stay upstairs forever, not with her stomach growling with hunger.

Honoree washed, put on her undergarments and the matronly green dress Ezekiel had placed on a chair next to the bed. She limped down the staircase to the kitchen, pausing at the entrance.

Jeremiah had three pans on the stove, frying bacon and ham, and scrambling eggs, and boiling grits. Bessie stood nearby, rocking back and forth, holding a needle and thread and a shirt, sewing on a button. Ezekiel sat at the head of the rectangular kitchen table, drinking from a steaming cup, and searching the pages of a newspaper.

It was a beautiful, happy scene of a family in a motion picture or magazine on a typical Sunday morning. All that was missing was her mama at the stove, fixing breakfast, and her father instructing the Bailey boys to finish their chores before eating.

She fluffed her matted hair and limped forward, navigating each step purposefully. "Hello."

Ezekiel snapped to his feet and rushed to her side. "Honoree, you're up. You sure it's a good idea?"

"I'm not going to fall over." She took his hand and allowed him to help her to a chair at the table. "I'm much better. Thank you very much."

Bessie sat next to her. "I was worried about you."

"I'm fine. How are you doing? Let me

see." Her gaze landed on the girl's belly. "How's the baby?"

"The bee's knees, I guess. It doesn't do much but jump and hiccup."

It was the kindest thing Bessie had said about her baby. Honoree figured Jeremiah standing within earshot was the reason. "I'm glad."

Jeremiah put a plate of food in front of her that looked like a holiday feast. "Bless your heart."

For a few long moments, the only sound in the kitchen was the clang of Honoree's fork against her plate and the noises she made, gulping down her breakfast.

Ezekiel chuckled. "Don't eat too fast. You'll upset your stomach." He folded his newspaper. "We put your things — the things you and Bessie, and Jeremiah, saved — in the shed. We hope to get rid of some smoke." He sipped his coffee. "I should tell you your building burned to the ground. You won't be able to return."

Honoree placed her fork on the side of her plate. Her home for most her life was nothing but a pile of ash and destruction. "Did anyone die?"

Bessie shook her head. "Jeremiah drove by yesterday, and folks were scrounging for what they could find in the rumble. They said no one perished."

That news lightened Honoree's heart. She may not be neighborly, but her neighbors were family. After living in the kitchenette for most of her life, she felt the pain wouldn't vanish in a day. "How about my sewing baskets?"

"I got most of them out." Bessie grinned. "Including a couple of dresses and the basket with the money."

Honoree closed her eyes briefly. "Thank God. We aren't destitute."

She lifted a fork of food to her lips, but the room was suddenly quiet, and everyone was watching her. "Isn't anyone else eating?" she asked. Jeremiah moved from the stove with two plates.

"Ready," he said, serving Bessie and Ezekiel before sitting across from her with his meal. However, three pairs of eyes were still on her.

"What's been happening?"

Ezekiel dropped his fork with a clang. "Nothing. Nothing at all," he said in a rush as if a train car had fallen off the tracks.

"Tell her, Ezekiel." Jeremiah didn't look at his brother or eat his meal. "No reason not to. She's staying here now."

Ezekiel pushed his plate a few inches away and placed his arms on top of his head. The gesture lasted only a few seconds before he splayed his fingers on either side of his untouched meal.

"What is it?" Honoree asked tensely. "What happened?"

"Dewey's a boob," Jeremiah mumbled.

Honoree was confused. "Why would any of us care about Dewey Graves?"

"Dewey didn't stop bootlegging when he was told to, and now he's causing Archie —"

"And Ezekiel and me," Jeremiah added roughly.

"Some trouble," Ezekiel finished his sentence.

Meanwhile, Bessie was muttering curse words under her breath. Frustrated, Honoree put down her fork. "Please explain."

Ezekiel sagged back in the chair. "Archie wants to meet at Miss Hattie's tonight. Gallo wants Dewey handled."

"Gallo wants him dead," Jeremiah corrected him.

"And wants Archie to get it done." Ezekiel pressed his lips together, his eyebrow climbing to a point.

"What does that have to do with you?" Honoree eyed him and then Jeremiah.

"We'll have more details when we meet with Archie," Ezekiel replied. "Which is all I know now."

"Other than Gallo's mighty pissed at us, too." Jeremiah picked up his fork but held it midair. "We can't leave them here, alone."

"Why not?" Bessie spoke up, squirming in her seat. "I don't want to go to Miss Hattie's." She glanced at Honoree. "We don't care nothin' about Dewey's or Archie's problems."

"Archie knows you're here. That means so does Gallo, and with this mess with Dewey putting Gallo in Capone's crosshairs, I don't trust him not to latch out blindly at Archie or —"

"At us." Jeremiah didn't hesitate to show his displeasure.

"We just want to keep a close eye on you two until we learn what Archie and Gallo are planning," Ezekiel said.

"How do they know we're here?" Honoree raised her hands, palms up.

"Perhaps one of your neighbors saw us put Bessie and you into the pickup truck."

"Probably Kenny," Bessie said.

"She's right," Honoree remarked. "He sold a few of his paintings to Archie. Jeremiah, you remember him. You met him at the rent party. He likely went to Archie to sell whatever he saved in the fire." She gulped the last of her coffee. "Does Gallo still want me to dance at the party? After what happened at the Plantation Cafe?"

"You're not dancing at the party, Honoree. You're not dancing anywhere until your leg heals."

"How long will that take?" Honoree drummed her fingernails on the tabletop, but Ezekiel offered no answer. "When my leg heals, I will return to the Dreamland Cafe, and find a place to live."

"Your leg will take a few weeks, Honoree."

"It will heal." Nothing else could happen to her. Nothing else could go wrong. Her leg would heal, and just like that, she'd be back to dancing at the Dreamland Cafe.

Please, Lord. Let the fire be the last of the bad. Let there be nothing but good times ahead. Hear my prayer, Lord. Thank you. Amen.

CHAPTER 42
SAWYER

Monday, July 6, 2015

I hold on to the railing at the foot of the bed, staring at Honoree, who snores lightly and appears content. I turn to leave, but rustling sheets and her voice stop me.

"Just nodded off."

"Or were you resting your eyes?" I say. "I'll come back after you've gotten some rest."

"Yes, I'm tired, but you don't have to leave. Stay. I'm always tired. Can't be this old and not feel time passing in your bones, in your skin, behind your eyes. I close 'em so often 'cause they've been watching life a long, long time."

I came for the truth, but perhaps, the only truth that matters is that this old woman is still breathing, talking, thinking. Seeing.

She sighs. "You haven't talked about your sister lately."

"What do you mean, Miss Honoree?"

481

"I've been thinking about asking you about her for two days."

"Why?"

"You're not as mad at her for dying as you used to be."

I circle to her bedside, wondering how Honoree stepped inside my mind. "How can you tell?"

"Your eyes — they aren't as sad as when we first met."

"That was a month ago."

"I lost someone I loved very much, too. Since you told me about Azizi, I'll tell you a story."

"Okay, Miss Honoree."

"It happened on a Sunday morning in April; the weather was warm and sticky, different from most spring days in Chicago. Papa and I were on our way to the five-and-dime. We'd bought several cans of pork and beans and corn and a bag of flour from the corner grocery. Mama also needed a package of needles and a new spool of black thread. So you could say we were on our way to the five-and-dime because of Mama."

Honoree pauses to cough and struggles to sit up higher but waves away my helping hands. "We passed a newsstand. I pulled my hand free from Papa's to look at fashion magazines. I loved fashion. Papa went to grab my hand back, but he never stopped moving his feet, and he stepped off the curb, and the automobile hit him — ripping him from my fingertips forever." Tears well in her eyes. "Later, Mama said he'd died because of me. Mama cried all the time after Papa died, her heart broken because he was gone, but I believed her for years. Thought it was my fault Papa died." Honoree looks at me. "But my mama was wrong. An accident took him. Nothing more. Just God's will."

"Right. God's will." I press my shoulders against the bridge of the chair. "Doesn't that bother you? What God does from what he doesn't do? It's so arbitrary."

"What do you mean? What's that word?"

"Arbitrary?" I shrug. "Random. No rhyme or reason. Your father's death wasn't your fault. But we can't control life or death if we're decent humans. We live our lives and try as hard as we can to do the right thing." I reach for my backpack, but her grim expression touches me.

A dark longing fills her eyes. "I've done some things I regret — lied about a lot of hurtful things, too. I had a reason, most of the time." She yawns, a body-shaking yawn. "Would you lie for a good reason?"

483

"A good reason to some might be the equivalent of unplugging a dam to someone else." I wait to hear what Honoree will say, but I see — and hear — her snoring. She's dozed off and doesn't appear to be faking.

As I watch her sleep, in the corner of my mind, I am waiting for Azizi to appear on the bed. But I haven't seen Azizi's ghost in what feels like quite some time.

Only a few days have passed, I know, but perhaps, those were the last days.

The URL drops into my in-box around nine o'clock Chicago time. Before I open the email, I say a little prayer. Then, WTH, I open it.

Hot damn. Hot damn! Confirmed. Authenticated. It is Micheaux's work — an original. Twenty minutes of film history. The thrill is like reaching a mountaintop, swimming a channel, or breaking the record for the hundred-yard dash.

I open the new file of the footage, not the blurry film clip I showed Honoree that she could barely see. This one will be clear, sharp, visible. I am excited, thrilled to see my great-grandmother, Honoree Dalcour, when she was a girl of nineteen. The girl Maggie hated and would continue to hate until the end of time.

That's a long time. I don't see myself capable of disliking someone forever, not even my father. Eventually, I'll forget we don't get along. Family isn't perfect and not always lovable. If you doubt me, let's check with my mysteriously secretive grandmother, Maggie White.

I stop my musings and hit play. Hallelujah. The images are infinitely better than the pieces of footage I originally salvaged.

I fast-forward to the scene at the Plantation Cafe.

I find it, and I rewind and watch again. That's when the hammer falls from the sky. Thor's hammer, too, at least when it comes to family history, and the tall tales people tell.

The young woman in Maggie's photographs with the name Honoree wears a sleeveless costume; her arm has no scars. No sign of an encounter with a kerosene lamp in her youth. But there is another girl, shorter, rounder, with a darker complexion — her arm is puckered with scars.

I don't know her — the woman dancing in the film with Honoree Dalcour.

Someone is not the woman I believed her to be.

I slip into the Bronzeville Senior Care Facil-

485

ity late at night. I'm not sure how to say what I have come to say, or whether it matters.

"Who's there?" Honoree's hoarse voice pierces the darkness. "Lula?"

"No, ma'am, it's Sawyer."

"What are you doing here? What time is it?"

"Around midnight."

"They catch you in here, you'll be in trouble. Not even my Lula can save you."

I turn on the table lamp and sit in my chair, noticing the veins and the soft, paper-thin brown skin of Honoree's hands. "Do you remember when Ezekiel died?"

She looks fragile, less in charge than she did two days ago. "I lost track of him sixty years ago," Honoree says gruffly.

"We can't find a record of his death. Do you recall when or where he passed? That might help."

"Rest assured, he's dead. What difference does it make when?"

I move to the other side of the bed.

"I don't mind talking about Jeremiah. He was the nicer of the two Bailey brothers I met." She narrows her eyes. "I spent a lot of time with Jeremiah. He liked me the most in the beginning."

This late at night, her room has a different aura, and yes, I use that word on occasion. Mystical — no. Magical — not. Mysterious — could be. The corners of the room seem alive. "I heard from the restoration company today. The reel of film I found in Maggie's long-ago box — it's been authenticated as a lost Micheaux."

"Been what?"

"They proved the reel was from one of Micheaux's films, a motion picture made in the 1920s. That included you in a nightclub scene, filmed in 1925."

"Are you sure it was me?"

"That's an intriguing question," I say, smoothing the stubble on my chin. "The answer is complicated. Yes, I'm sure it's you. But you aren't the woman you say you are."

"I'm your great-grandmother."

"Yes. Maggie confirmed you are her mother and my great-grandmother." I press my lips together. You see, part of me has reached my limit. "You and Maggie love secrets."

"I could give less than a good goddam about secrets or love. Although I've enjoyed keeping secrets from you, one of which, I'll keep until the day I die."

"Your real name?"

She cackles, that crazy, breathy laugh-grunt people make when they are too full of vinegar, as Maggie would say.

"I don't care about that," she blurts. "But since you're asking, I wager you already know."

"What is it?"

"I used to be Bessie Palmer. Bessie Louise Palmer was my birth name if I recall." Her lips tremble. "You should've figured that out a week ago. Once your father told you about the deed. Maggie never owned a house in Baton Rouge. I told you so. You should've listened. You should've taken my word."

CHAPTER 43
HONOREE

Wednesday, December 30, 1925

It was early afternoon when the Bailey household — Honoree, Ezekiel, Jeremiah, and Bessie — entered Archie's office. Honoree figured if Ezekiel and Jeremiah had to keep an eye on Bessie and Honoree, they would keep an eye on the Bailey brothers, too.

An unusually dark, dank day, a cast-iron table lamp provided some light for the filth on the floor and the scratches on the desktop where Archie trimmed his cigars. Honoree was bothered by the smell. Sweat and spilled hooch filled her nostrils along with cigar smoke, and whomever Archie had diddled the night before.

"My brother is a goddamned screwup!" Archie slammed his fist on the desktop. "A fool who shouldn't be allowed to wash his own ass." He spoke without regard for Dewey, who leaned against the wall with an

489

open jug of beer, swilling it down in gulps.

Honoree stood behind Ezekiel, wishing to be out of sight and hopefully out of mind. Archie's temper was on fire, and she didn't want to be singed by flames meant for Dewey.

"I — I was helping," Dewey said in between swigs.

"Dry up, you stupid fool." Archie raised his fist, glanced at the desktop, but apparently changed his mind about another strike. Instead, he pulled a cigar from his desk drawer and chopped off the end with a small sharp knife.

Honoree feared Archie's anger because it spun in so many directions at once. It was difficult to escape his wrath. Dewey wouldn't be the only target. He was simply the first.

"The man wants you dead, Dewey," Archie grumbled. "Shit, I want you dead. But, I ain't ready to kill my brother, even if he's a goddamned fool. But I sure ain't ready to have someone else do it for me."

Dewey's bloodshot eyes dulled. For the first time since Archie had started in on him, he looked worried. He loosened the collar of his shirt and leaned against the wall. Sweat dripped from his brow down his cheek. "What you gonna do, then, brother?"

Archie shrugged. "You're leaving town. I'm shipping you off to Alabama. And Ezekiel is going to tell Gallo he shot you dead."

Honoree glared at Ezekiel. This was something she didn't know about and couldn't believe her ears. "What kind of half-baked plan is this? Mostly sounds like Ezekiel signing his own death certificate." She stomped her foot. "And what if Gallo wants to see Dewey's dead body? I know I would."

Archie coiled like a Louisiana cottonmouth preparing to strike. Even his bulging throat resembled the venomous snake. "You listen here, girl. Your boyfriend knows what he's doing. He wants this deal to work as much as me. Maybe more. Don't you, Ezekiel?"

A look passed between the two men that Honoree didn't like. "Well, aren't you going to tell us what's going on? Or at least tell us why I need to be here to watch you call your brother names?"

Dewey stepped into the middle of the room. "I don't need Ezekiel telling Gallo he killed me. Ain't nobody who knows me will believe that shit no way."

"I can make him believe," Honoree said, ignoring Ezekiel's piercing glare. "Gallo wants me to dance at Capone's New Year's

Eve party, right? How about if I bring Trudy? She's an acquaintance of Gallo's, too. Between the two of us, we can convince him that we saw Dewey's dead body."

"Besides not liking that idea, what about your leg?" Ezekiel said. "What if Trudy says no? What if Gallo says yes, but Capone and his boys want more than to see some colored girls dancing on a stage?"

Archie stopped chewing his cigar and lit it. "Gallo wants you to dance in a motion picture, too. I told him you'd do it. He likes you, Honoree." Then with a sly glance at Ezekiel, he added, "As we all do."

Ezekiel spoke up, then, his voice rough, his words harsh. "Gallo is making deals with his cock."

Archie circled his desk, and his large, bruising body moved quickly as a cat. "What the hell, boy?" He stopped in front of Ezekiel. "I want to do right by my baby brother. Keep him alive, even if I never see him again. You have two brothers. And your girl is willing to help out. I don't see a problem here." He whirled at Dewey. "Do you?"

Neither Ezekiel nor Dewey responded. They were too caught up in their hatred.

"I don't see a problem," Honoree said. "No problem at all."

"Thank you, missy. I knew you were a sweet gal. Always a sweet, old, dependable gal."

A cold wind ripped through Miss Hattie's. Someone had come in the front door as someone walked out the back. Honoree looked from the archway to the bar, and the door to Archie's office was shut. He needed to talk to Ezekiel about some policy business, a private conversation that didn't require anyone's presence other than the two of them. She left them to their dealings and sought out Crazy Pete.

He was stocking the bar, getting ready for another night at Miss Hattie's, but he was dragging as if the night had already come and gone. But when she walked up, his bright smile, dentures in place, warmed her heart.

"Why you limping, Honoree?"

"I hurt my leg when my building burned down. How you been?"

"I'm sorry you got caught up in those Christmas fires. Quite a few tenement buildings burned to the ground that day."

"Mine was one of 'em," she said quietly. "Could I have a drink? I'm waiting on Ezekiel to finish up with Archie."

"Your usual, sweetheart?"

She smiled. "Sounds divine."

He sorted through the bottles on the back shelf, pulling out his best bottle of gin, the one he kept hidden just for her. But when he turned, a pained expression creased his brow. "I don't have any fixings up here yet. Can you handle the hooch straight?"

"I can handle it, but I don't want to." She pushed away from the bar. "It's in the back, right?"

"No, I left the honey in the basement. I don't have any lemons, I don't think, but I can't remember if we ordered any. I should probably go to the store."

"Don't worry, I'll bring up a couple of jugs of honey. That will get you started."

Before she made a move toward the basement, Ezekiel and Archie were at the front door, and Ezekiel didn't look pleased. "Archie and I are making a trip to the Plantation Cafe. Stay here until I return," he said to Honoree.

She rolled her eyes. "I can get home."

"Your leg isn't what it's supposed to be. Just wait an hour."

"I'll keep an eye on her," Crazy Pete said.

"Call my brother Jeremiah at the auto body shop."

"What you say?" Pete cupped his ear.

Ezekiel repeated. "Tell him to come over

here and take her home."

Crazy Pete scowled at Ezekiel. "I said I could watch out for her."

"All right. All right. I'll be back in a few minutes," Ezekiel said, and left the cafe following behind Archie.

Pete turned and gave her a wink and a smile. "When did you and Ezekiel start up?"

"I ain't even sure we started up," she replied. "We just ain't yelling at each other as loud as before." She laughed. "I'm going downstairs to find that honey."

A few minutes later, she was strolling by the furnace, trying to remember the corner where the jugs of honey were stored. Then she remembered the day Bessie had appeared from the shadows, smelling of dirt and bruises. She pushed the button on the electrical box on the wall and trotted down the dressing room stairs. There she found a jug of honey and some lemons. Pete must've ordered them and forgot.

A sudden loud noise startled her and the lemons fell from her hands. Dewey was in the doorway, a swaying, red-eyed mess, completely zozzled.

"You surprised me. I was getting some honey. Pete's going to make me one of his concoctions."

Fumbling with his belt buckle, Dewey

staggered down the three steps into the dressing room. He looked horrible, clearly soused, and he smelled worse. In the short time since leaving Archie's office, he must've stumbled, headfirst, into a jug of rotgut.

"I'm sorry Archie lit into you like that." She had to say something. The boy seemed beat down like a boxer after a few thousand rounds with the heavyweight champ.

He took a shaky step toward her, and she fought the urge to hold her nose. He reeked of whiskey and marijuana cigarettes.

"What are you looking for over there?" His lips pulled back, showing bright pink gums against black lips.

"Would you do me a favor?" she asked pleasantly, fearing his temper. She hoped he wouldn't notice the jar she held. "I need to head upstairs. If you find a jug of honey, could you bring it up for Pete? Y'all gonna need it behind the bar tonight."

"I ain't gonna need shit behind the bar tonight." He talked as if alone in the basement, muttering to himself. He looked at her. "I got to leave town, remember. You were there when my brother told me to get out."

Now her hands shook, her fingers going numb. The other lemon fell to the floor.

"He's trying to keep you from getting killed."

Dewey seemed more unlike himself than usual — and Dewey's tempter frightened Honoree more than ever.

"Excuse me." She went to move by him.

"Why are you with Ezekiel?"

"I need to get upstairs; do you mind?"

"I asked you: why are you with him?"

"If you find the honey, just bring it on up to Pete."

She went to circle by him again, but once more, he blocked her path. Drunk or not, he was quick. Maybe if she answered his question . . .

"I ain't with Ezekiel. We're just friends."

Dewey's features tightened, and a scary hollowness darkened his eyes.

She took an awkward step back, her ankle gave, and she stumbled, falling hard into the sawdust.

Dewey's big, rough hands gripped her shoulders, lifting her, holding her like a rag doll in the air. Unable to twist out of his grasp, she raised a hand to slap him in the face, but his lips curled into a hideous grin, and he flung her into the wall.

Her head struck the hard surface, blurring her vision. She slid down, nearly to the floor, but struggled to keep some of her balance. The last thing she wanted was to be on the ground with him standing over her. Honoree forced herself back up, working through the pain.

"You drunk bastard! Have you lost your mind? Don't you dare manhandle me!" The blow caught her on the cheek, crushing her face into the wall.

"Shut up!"

Pain crawled across her jaw like fire. Dewey grabbed her wrist. She punched him in the chest, his arms, his chin, but he took each blow and wouldn't let go.

One large hand took hold of her left arm, bending it a way it shouldn't be bent. His other hand reached under her dress and pulled at her bloomers.

Honoree screamed, or she had intended to scream, but Dewey slugged her again, closed-fisted. Tiny stars filled the room. Sweat fell from his face onto hers.

"Shut up." His voice vibrated with violence. Now he had a hand around her throat.

Gagging, coughing, unable to breathe, Honoree clawed at his forearms with her free hand. He needed to loosen his grip on her neck. She needed to do something to stop him from killing her.

The corner of his eye dripped blood. If

she'd hurt him once, she could do it again. But how? Then she rammed her knee upward, striking him between his legs. His face twisted in agony, but he wouldn't let go of her throat. And still, she couldn't scream.

"Bitch. You fucking, loathsome bitch. You and your fancy man. If Ezekiel hadn't come back, my brother would've gone along with my plan, listened to my ideas. Archie wouldn't be treating me like shit, forcing me out of Chicago, if it weren't for Ezekiel Bailey."

He threw her to the floor, and she crawled away from him, heading toward the door and the hallway, but her leg and ankle, swollen like her throat, wouldn't let her move as fast as she needed to. If she could make it to the stairwell, beat Dewey up the stairs, she could reach the storage room behind the bar. If she yelled, Crazy Pete would hear her.

Dewey grabbed her waist and shoved her to the floor. Rolling her onto her back, he pinned her to the sawdust. Straddling her, he put all his weight on her sore leg, and she cried out.

"Stop!" she croaked, unable to yell with a swollen throat.

"Why are you with him?" He was tearing at her garter and her panties. "You know what he is? Your boyfriend. The wannabe doctor. He ain't nothin'. Ain't nobody. Just another nigga just like me. Nothing special. Nothing special."

Dewey wrapped a large palm and fat fingers around her neck and pawed her body with his other hand, his touch blinding her with disgust. She gagged, trying again to scream but with no sound coming out.

God, why couldn't she make a sound, other than a grunt or a groan? Why take her voice? Pete was a flight of stairs away, but he didn't know what was happening to her; otherwise he and his cane would knock Dewey to the ground.

"You fuck Ezekiel, don't you? I can see it in your eyes. You like it, too. Don't lie. I know you do."

His hand closed into a fist, and the blow blinded her, the pain anchored inside her head. His body covered hers, his weight holding her in place as she drowned in the sweat dripping from his face and his whiskey-soiled breath.

Oh God. He was trying to get inside her. She kicked her legs, frantic, thrashing, hitting him with her feet in his legs, stomach, wherever she could hurt him.

Tears soaked her cheeks. She lay sprawled

on her back, her dress pulled up around her waist. The taste of blood and the pain in her legs didn't matter. She couldn't struggle; she could only wait for him to kill her.

Then the world shifted.

A loud crash and Dewey rolled off her, holding the side of his head, groaning in pain. Another blow hit him on the other side of his head, and he slumped forward.

Honoree tried to see what was going on — what or who had stopped Dewey? She crawled toward the nearest wall and pressed her back against the cold, hard surface.

"Who's there?" She blinked twice, squeezing tears from her eyes, bringing the world into focus.

There was a shadow, a brown-skinned girl holding a long stick, a broken broom handle. Honoree blinked again. Bessie was standing over Dewey's hunched body.

"Oh, thank God." Honoree tried to stand, but her limbs twisted with pain. Nothing worked — her arms, her ankles, or her head. "Help me, Bessie. Please, God, help me get away from him."

Holding the broken broom handle in her fist, Bessie seemed to be in a trance. A noise rustled next to Honoree, and she turned. Dewey's leg had twitched. With his hand flat on the sawdust, he pushed up onto his side and rose to his knees, shaking his head. "I'm gonna kill both you bitches."

Dewey reached for Honoree with a bloody hand. Bessie stood behind him, holding the stick.

"I never liked fucking you," Dewey said to Bessie. "Such an ugly cow of a girl." He turned toward Honoree, who scooted away from him.

"Come back here. I ain't finished with you yet." Dewey held her ankle and wrenched it until she screamed.

Bessie raised the stick above her head and plunged the broken broom handle into Dewey's back. He grabbed at his chest, expecting to see what had struck him, poking through his sternum, but then he tumbled forward, collapsing onto his chest, head twisted sideways, eyes wide open, mouth gurgling.

Honoree had seen plenty of blood lately, but Dewey's blood was everywhere.

CHAPTER 44
HONOREE

Wednesday, December 30, 1925

"We gotta call somebody, Honoree! We gotta call somebody right away." Bessie pointed at Dewey's body. "We can't move him. He's too big."

Honoree's ribs ached; jabbing pain circled her waist and crawled up her spine and across her shoulder blades. She grabbed the front of her drop-waist dress, pulling the fabric away from her skin, making room for the sob clawing at her throat — she opened her mouth, and a deep, hollow wail filled the room.

Once she dreamed of Broadway. Of Paris, France. Of the Dreamland Cafe. Dreams. "The blood. There's so much blood." And some of it was hers.

"You're right," said Bessie. "We need to clean up the blood."

"Yes, we need to —" Honoree tucked her legs beneath her and tried to rise to her feet,

503

but she only made it as far as her knees and then only while using the wall as a crutch.

"That's okay, Honoree. I'll go upstairs and call Jeremiah. He should be at the auto body shop. We need to hurry, though. Before Pete gets back."

"Where'd Pete go?"

"He went to buy some lemons. Told me to come down here and tell you. That's when I saw Dewey and killed him."

God help her. "There was nobody upstairs?" Honoree asked. "There were lemons down here. He must've forgotten. Where were you, Bessie?"

"I was in the kitchen, making a sandwich." Bessie was staring down at Dewey's body. "Pete came, ate half of it, and asked me to watch the bar while he went to the store. He didn't know where Dewey had run off to." Suddenly, she kicked him in the leg and waited with her foot lifted off the floor, ready to jam her heel into his head if he moved.

His eyes were wide open. "He's dead, Bessie. He won't be waking up." There was no flailing like a fish out of water, the way her father had died, or even Houdini. Death had sneaked up on Dewey.

Honoree's heart pounded wildly in her chest, a drum line marching against her rib cage. Bessie's breathing was steady. Honoree looked from her to Dewey's body and clamped a hand over her mouth to push back the vomit rising into her throat.

"It'll take Jeremiah a few minutes to get here," Bessie said. "While I'm gone, you find a bucket and some rags. We need to clean up the blood."

"Why aren't you scared?"

"I'll be right back."

Bessie bounded up the stairs, and every muscle in Honoree's body recalled every blow, every slap, every pain Dewey had inflicted upon her.

She leaned heavily against the wall, her legs soft like wet sponges, and her knees, warm taffy. "Oh Jesus." Honoree slid to the floor, lowered her head into her hands, and the room went black.

"Honoree. Honoree! Wake up, Honoree!" Bessie was at her side, her hands under her armpits, helping her to her knees. "You must've fainted."

Honoree struggled to her feet. "I'm all right. I can help."

"You don't look good."

Footsteps. Stomping down the staircase. Honoree held her breath. Bessie held her hand. "Don't worry. It's Ezekiel and Jeremiah."

"How do you know?"

"Honoree." Ezekiel dropped to his knees beside her. "Oh, Honoree." His eyes darkened with concern.

"I'm sorry," she said, sobbing. "I'm so sorry."

"What are you talking about, Honoree?" He wrapped strong arms around her, and she collapsed into him. "What are you sorry for?"

"I should've left Chicago that night Houdini died. I should've left." The tears flowed down her face, salty tears on her lips, and water running over her chin. "Why am I so goddamn stubborn, Ezekiel? Why?"

"You didn't do anything wrong." He touched her cheek. "Jeremiah will take you and Bessie to the house. I'll clean up this mess."

"Oh, God, what will Archie do when he finds out? What are you going to do with Dewey's body?"

Ezekiel lifted Honoree's chin, forcing her to look him in the eyes. "Do not worry about that. You go home. Jeremiah will take you. Bessie, you stay with her. Jeremiah, get back here as soon as you can."

Once inside the Bailey house, Honoree hobbled up the stairs. The need to bathe consumed her. She had to wash away Dewey's touch, his sweat, the mix of their blood on her skin.

She grabbed at her clothing, stripping off her torn shift, her shoes, garters, and stockings.

"You'll need to burn these," she said to Bessie, who watched over her from the bathroom doorway.

"I'll take care of it." Bessie scurried into the bathroom, shoved the clothes into a corner, and started to prepare the bath.

Honoree stood naked, arms hanging at her sides, unable to help or decide what to do. She could still feel Dewey's hands touching her, grabbing her, hurting her, and see the hate in his eyes, the pain he wanted to inflict upon her. It would be impossible to forget how he'd looked when he died — or Bessie's eyes when she killed him.

Bessie turned the knob on the faucet and pushed the rubber stopper into the drain. "There are towels in the bin and several different bars of soap. I'll get everything. You get in the tub."

"I'll wash in lye soap to get Dewey's blood off me," said Honoree, but Bessie was holding a bar of Lux soap. "Never taken a bath in a tub before. In a bucket, a stream, or a lake, but that was when I was only a kid."

She lowered herself into the steaming water, drew her knees into her chest, and wrapped her arms around her legs.

"I should call the police and tell them I killed Dewey Graves," Bessie said. "That way, I'll be in jail and safe from Archie's vengeance." Bessie dipped her finger in the water. "It sure is hot."

"You can't go to jail. You're pregnant. Think of your baby. What would the coppers do with a woman with a child?"

"I don't care about the baby. They can put it in a home, an orphanage. I don't want it."

"You don't mean that."

"Yes, I do. I care nothin' about it. Just like I don't care nothin' about killing Dewey. The way he had you pinned on the floor, his pants open in the front. I knew what he was about to do, and I had to stop him." She wrung out the wet towel and lathered it up. "When he woke up, and went after you again, I had to be sure he was dead. So, I put that stick in his back."

She washed Honoree's shoulders. "I thought about hitting him in the head one more time. But I preferred him dead. What was happening to you reminded me of what happened the first time he came at me." Bessie moved a curl aside from Honoree's forehead. "If you duck your head in the water, I'll wash your hair."

Honoree gasped. All this time she — "What do you mean the first time he came at you?"

"Dewey was the one who was beating me when I first came to Miss Hattie's. Took me down into that basement and forced me to do things with him. Made me promises, too. That's how I got the job working at Miss Hattie's. Not because of Archie but because of Dewey."

"Lord, Bessie." Honoree hung her head. "I'm so sorry."

"Don't you worry about it now, Honoree. That job didn't make it right for him to hit me. Or make me do things I didn't want to."

"You should've told me it was him." Here she had it wrong all this time. It was never Archie.

"When you came into the dressing room that night, I thought it was Dewey coming back for me, and I hid in the corner." She paused. "I've been with a man before, more than one. I used to work the Chitlin' Circuit. But Dewey, he was mean. I couldn't — I wasn't — you see, I'm the dumbest Dora in town. Ain't pretty. Ain't smart. But you were nice to me. And when things got worse with

Dewey, you invited me to move in with you."

Honoree stared at the bathwater that had turned red with blood. "Help me out. I need to get out." She reached for Bessie, who took her wrists and helped her from the tub. "Pass me a towel." She removed the stopper.

Bessie emptied the tub and wiped it clean, refilling it with fresh, hot water. Honoree sat on the toilet seat and watched, shivering slightly, but feeling her body come back to her. "You need to wash, too."

Bessie stripped out of her clothes. They climbed into the tub and washed each other's hair.

"Is Dewey your baby's father?"

Bessie bowed her head. "He's the only man I've been with since I arrived in Chicago. So, yes, the baby's his."

"Lord have mercy," Honoree whispered.

Bessie tilted her head and sighed. "I ain't worried about Archie, neither. There are quite a few people that could be blamed for his brother's death before me — or you."

"But one of those people might be Ezekiel."

Honoree rubbed her hand over her soapy head. "Fill that pitcher with some water so we can rinse our hair." They washed and rinsed and when they finished, they got out of the tub. However, Honoree still felt dirty. "Fill it again."

Bessie did. "You'll feel better soon."

"I'll never feel all the way better." Honoree hugged her shoulders and, after a while, climbed from the tub. Then she asked Bessie to fill it one last time. "I'm worried about Ezekiel."

"Ezekiel is a smart man, Honoree. He'll leave Dewey's body someplace where Archie won't find it — at least not too fast. We'll have plenty of time to figure out what to do."

Bessie rose and stepped out of the tub. Honoree did as well.

"We should go to New York City," Bessie said, wrapping a towel around her waist. "Never been to New York City."

"Neither have I." Honoree turned on the faucet and rinsed the tub before putting the rubber stopper back in the drain. "Let's take another bath. I'm not clean."

CHAPTER 45
SAWYER

Friday, July 10, 2015

The sun rises over Little Italy, Taylor Street, and the buildings east of Cook County Hospital (not the actual name, but it's the name Honoree uses and I bow to her wishes). I arrive early Friday morning. The doctors give Honoree a room with a view that faces Lake Michigan — per her request. The hospital is not anywhere near the lakeshore, but Honoree longs to see the sunrise.

"It's a matter of a few days, maybe hours," Lula tells me, wanting to make sure I'm prepared.

Different from the caretakers at the senior-living facility, the nurses at Cook County focus on the bags of medicine hanging upside down on the long poles next to Honoree's bed. They are preoccupied with checking her pulse rate, her blood pressure, and how much of her urine is in a plastic bag.

"I came across our neighbor Kenny after the fire, just before we left for Louisiana. He was on a corner, selling boxes of his photographs and paintings, and some motion picture reels he'd stolen." Honoree's face wrinkles into a frown. "I had Jeremiah buy me one of those boxes."

She fists the fabric of her nightgown to the left of her heart. She will tell me this story, even if it kills. And I'll listen, although I don't want to go into the quicksand with her.

After a moment, she raises her hand. "Did I ever tell you how much you remind me of Jeremiah? I know I thought Ezekiel at first but considering you ain't related to either one of them, sometimes you remind me of the one and then the other. You don't look a thing like 'em, but the way you listen, the way you're careful when you speak, watching your words because you understand their power — that's where you remind me of Jeremiah."

"I wish I could've met them."

"Ezekiel spoke his mind but didn't always have the patience to figure out the damage that can be done with a word."

"Never bothered to get to know too many people other than family." I laugh. "My family was broken. Now the only chance I have left is with my dad." I think of Azizi, but without the pain, only the sorrow of missing her. I think of Maggie, but she will never admit to anything wrong, so much like her mother she'd never believed.

"The other one," Honoree begins. "My friend Honoree, she never backed away from a problem, a challenge. She surely never gave in to the men who tried to hurt her or love her."

"You saved her life, you know."

"What? I killed a man I wanted dead." Honoree squeezes my hand and smiles, a naughty girlish smile. "Black folks disappeared back then. No one cared if a colored man up and vanished. Ezekiel and his entire family up and left for three years, and nobody noticed."

Her hand covers my hand, and she pulls me closer, although I'm already too close. "My child found out. I hated her because Jeremiah left a letter lying around. I lost my temper and struck her down." Her tongue flicks from between her teeth.

"Yes, sir," she says in a gentle tone. "Every time I looked at my daughter, I thought about that goddamned Dewey Graves — and I hated him and hated her, too. I tried to let that hate go, but I never could. Still hate them both to this day, and that's God's truth."

CHAPTER 46
HONOREE

Thursday, December 31, 1925

It was Honoree's birthday and New Year's Eve and she was busy packing. She had decided to leave town, and Bessie had agreed to join her.

In the kitchen with Bessie, she prepared a food basket for their journey, which meant leaving early on New Year's Day (Capone's party be damned). It was a journey Honoree had no choice but to take. There was nothing left for her in Chicago, not with men like Archie and Gallo believing she owed them something or that she was their property. Starting fresh in Harlem wouldn't be too bad as long as her leg healed.

"The train ride to New York City takes two days," Bessie said. "How much should we bring?"

Cans of pork and beans, a basket of fried chicken and cooked potatoes, and a container of boiled eggs were assembled on the kitchen table. There was also a can of Maxwell House coffee.

"If we find some way to boil water on the train without spending money," Honoree began, "fresh coffee will tide us over."

The front doorbell chimed.

"I haven't heard that sound in a long time."

"What is it?" Bessie asked.

"Someone's at the front door, you silly."

Bessie glanced anxiously toward the front of the house. "It's not Ezekiel or Jeremiah. They wouldn't use a doorbell."

"Then we'll just have to see who rang the doorbell, won't we?" Her words carried courage, but her insides knotted.

"Is it Archie?" Bessie's voice trembled as she trailed behind Honoree into the foyer.

"No, it's not him," Honoree said with confidence. "Archie wouldn't ring the bell. He and his goons would break down the door."

When Honoree opened the front door, the last person she expected stood with her blond hair freshly curled and dark red stain on her lips.

"Hello, Trudy."

"Honoree? What a surprise to see you here." Trudy strutted by her, peeling off elbow-length lambskin gloves. She wore a fur coat, a mink, which she didn't take off.

"What do you want?" Honoree asked.

"I've never been inside Ezekiel's house," Trudy said, peeking around corners. "Though, it appears to be what I expected of the Baileys. Living mighty high on the hog."

"I asked you a question," Honoree repeated.

Trudy strolled toward the parlor. "I'm looking for Ezekiel."

"He's not here."

Trudy peered over Honoree's shoulder. "I see your friend, the ragamuffin, is here, too. Hi, Bessie. Sorry we missed the chance to do something with your hair. Pesky fires made a mess of our weekend plans."

Bessie peeked around the corner. "Hi, Trudy."

"Apologies for calling you a ragamuffin. But you told me your good friend, Honoree, called you that the first time you met. And I want to be your friend, too."

"Is that why you're here, to make friends with Bessie? I thought you wanted to see Ezekiel, who ain't here, which means you can turn around and leave."

"Why you so mad at me? Ain't nothing between Ezekiel and me but business matters."

Honoree had to bite her tongue to stop from cursing Trudy into next week. "What the hell are you talking about? Have you forgotten about the envelope and Houdini? You put me in the middle of a mess that changed my life. Hell. Now you waltz in here and act as if nothing happened."

Trudy ventured into the parlor, seemingly having lost the ability to hear Honoree. "If I owned a house like this, you would never be left here alone. Especially the way things are these days. Between the white man's rules, and colored people wasting their pennies on policy gambling and getting scammed by their own race — it's a hard life for those of us with ambition."

Honoree stood between the hall and the archway. Not taken in by Trudy's little speech, she blocked her path. "Spit out what you came to say. I'll give the message to Ezekiel."

The expression on Trudy's face hardened. "I guess I can trust you since you care about him." She slapped her lambskin gloves into the palm of her hand. "Tell him that Archie is looking for him. For some reason, he's decided Ezekiel killed Dewey."

"Ezekiel didn't do anything to Dewey," Bessie said.

"Shut up, girl," Honoree spat. "Someone

519

had to tell Archie that lie. Was it you, Trudy?"

"Stop being a fool. Why lie on Ezekiel? Gallo is the one that put this mess in Archie's head. He's the one who wants Ezekiel dead."

"Gallo is lying."

"And when did a white man choose not to lie on a colored man when he wants something from him?"

"How'd you find out about this?" Honoree asked Trudy.

"I was in the room when Gallo was bragging to his friends about it."

"Oh, and he didn't bother to keep this bit of business from you?"

"Gallo don't consider colored girls anything more than a romp in the hay. We don't think. We can't hear and can't hurt him. So, sure, he'd say most anything in front of me."

Honoree rubbed her palms together. The truth of Trudy's words were proven the other night when Honoree had foolishly gone to the Plantation Cafe. "Would you like a cup of java? Why don't you join me in the parlor, Trudy."

The blonde stiffened, suspicion printed across her face. "I wouldn't mind a cup."

Honoree nodded at Bessie. "Can you bring us a couple of cups of coffee?" she said, as if she were the lady of the house.

Honoree led Trudy into the parlor and slipped off her mink. They sat on the Danish chairs with the mahogany frames and soft cotton cushions.

Trudy kept a wary eye on Honoree until Bessie returned with the coffee and Dole pineapple slices, fresh from the can. Trudy cracked a smile. "What's with the hospitality?"

"I'm gonna come clean with you. Gallo killed Houdini, and I saw him do it, and if I can't get out from under Gallo's thumb, he'll either kill me or take away my freedom, turn me into someone — who can only do his bidding."

Trudy sipped her coffee. "When I saw you at the Plantation Cafe, I figured he had a beef with you. So that means he has Ezekiel in his sights, too."

"Thank you for helping Bessie that night. It would've been bad news for us without you stepping in."

Trudy forked a pineapple slice and wiped her mouth with a napkin. "Not wanting to be tapped for Houdini's murder is why Gallo put Archie on Ezekiel." She smacked her lips. "Go on."

"Right," Honoree said with a sigh. "What can we do to stop Archie from gunning down Ezekiel? Is there a way to stop Gallo?"

Trudy's hand trembled and coffee splashed on her muslin dress. "Best bet would be for Ezekiel to leave town, but he won't do that until he's ready."

Honoree leaned forward. "What if we could get Gallo and Archie in trouble with Hymie Weiss?"

Trudy puckered her lips. "Sure, we'll just tell him to do whatever we have in mind for him to do." The sarcasm in her tone filled the parlor.

"I'm not talking for the sake of running my mouth. Wait a moment." Honoree hurried upstairs and retrieved the envelope from the heart-shaped sewing basket. She returned to the den and handed the envelope to Trudy. "It's the same package you gave me the night Houdini died."

Trudy's hand closed around it. "You had it all this time."

"What if you give the envelope to Hymie Weiss? Or Capone himself? Gallo killed to get his hands on those betting slips. They must be important — and we know a white man in the policy gambling racket in Bronzeville isn't allowed."

"These were important to Gallo two months ago, Honoree."

"Come on, Trudy. You love messing up a

white man's plans. That's what you do. I'm sure you can find some way. If you want to help Ezekiel."

Trudy twisted her mouth to one side. "I see where you headed." She wiped a finger over her upper lip, careful not to smear her lipstick. "There is one time when a white man will listen to a colored girl and believe everything she has to say." Trudy stuffed the envelope in her box purse. "I don't know if I can get this done, but I'd love to see Gallo dead in the street. My family lost a bunch of money to him and Ezekiel's daddy when they ran that insurance scam. A lot of people in Bronzeville did, and that includes Houdini."

"I know about what happened with Ezekiel and his father. Or some of it."

"Ezekiel isn't his father's son and has been trying to make up for his daddy since he got back in town."

"I realize that now," Honoree said. "But why do you care so much about Ezekiel?"

"He is family, not by blood — but by what we've survived. There ain't nothing between us but a mutual hatred of Tony Gallo and men like Archie Graves." Trudy gulped her coffee and took another bite of pineapple. "Tell Ezekiel I stopped by, won't you?"

"I will."

Trudy slipped her mink back on, pulled on her gloves, and walked toward the front door. "Nice seeing you, too, Bessie. Sorry we didn't get to bleach your hair. Maybe next time."

It was midnight. Everyone was sitting at the kitchen table eating the supper Jeremiah had prepared, and Ezekiel was telling them about the telegram from his mother in New York City. She agreed to meet Honoree and Bessie at the train station and assured him there would be a safe place for them to stay.

There were no balloons, streamers, or mistletoe to mark the beginning of 1926. Honoree was disappointed. She'd dreamed of her first trip to New York City and it included a cheering crowd of theatergoers shouting her name. But it was a dream. Although sneaking into New York City alive was better than never getting there at all, she supposed.

"Don't worry, Honoree," Ezekiel said. "You'll be on the train in a few hours, and this will be behind you."

"Trudy stopped by earlier today." This was her first chance to tell him.

He lowered his fork, setting it on his plate. "What did she want?"

"She wanted to let you know that Archie

has put his goons on you. He's telling them you killed Dewey." The rest of her conversation with Trudy, the part about the betting slips, Ezekiel wouldn't like, and she kept to herself.

Ezekiel glanced at Jeremiah. "That's what we planned. Remember. Pretending I killed him so that Gallo would get off Dewey's ass and Archie could keep making money."

An hour after supper, Ezekiel and Jeremiah left, promising to return shortly, but they had to take care of something. Honoree didn't want to know what they had to do or where they had to go. It was just something more to worry about.

"I'm going up, Bessie. It's nearly three o'clock in the morning. Might as well get a few hours' sleep. We won't get much rest on the train."

Honoree chose to have a last hot bath before climbing into bed. She filled the tub, scrubbing her body with the fragrant white soap in the bin. Once clean, she applied talc powder and perfumed toilet water, removed the hair net keeping her short bob in place.

She put on the cotton chemise and returned to Ezekiel's boyhood bedroom. Waiting in the room, seated in the rocking chair, was Ezekiel.

"You're back? I'm glad. I was worried."

"You were worried about me?"

"Absolutely. Positively."

"I wanted to wish you a happy birthday."

"You remembered?"

"I'm a few hours late, but yes, I remembered, Honoree." There was a breathlessness in his voice. As if speaking her name sent a shudder down his legs. Or were those her legs shaking?

His gaze moved over her body like a gentle stream in spring.

The waters rushed into her, warming her bones, her thighs, and her shoulders. She slipped out of her chemise. He rose swiftly from the rocking chair and placed a hand on her shoulder, preventing her from exposing her bubs.

"Are you sure?" His voice was hoarse.

"I wouldn't be taking off my clothes if I wasn't sure."

There was a desperation to their kisses. An urgency to feel more, to touch more, love more than two lovers had ever loved. She clung to him, to his touch, to his every caress, whether soft or hard or painful.

The walls closed around her, and the weight of him made her sad, but she needed to feel his large hands caress the flat bone between her breasts. Feel his mouth pressed against her mouth, kissing her lovingly, soulfully, wholly.

She wrapped her arms around her waist, the bubble of nerves in her stomach bursting. His beautiful eyes trailed over her as if she was precious. A remarkable treasure he wanted to swallow whole, but she wanted more than for him to look at her. She wanted to be touched, touched by him.

She let her arms fall to her sides.

No words were required between them. Not for this.

Why she wanted him now, she couldn't answer. Whatever it was, she tried to forget and remember at once. He stood in front of her, his knees slightly bent, and his shoes, socks, all his clothing were gone.

She rested her hand on his bare shoulders to steady herself. Her fingers dug into his flesh, and he paused.

"No. It's okay. I'm fine."

He stroked her arm, his fingers moving tenderly over her skin; the electricity of his touch soared through her. He touched her throat, and she moaned, for no other reason than the sudden rush of anticipation that filled her chest.

It had been too long.

"Did I ever tell you how much I love your face?"

He moved his hand through her hair and

closed his eyes and kissed her. They made love until dawn.

The words she couldn't utter choked her, and she buried her head against his shoulder.

"I swear to you, Honoree. I will rid myself of Tony Gallo and Archie Graves." He pressed his lips to her forehead, mouth, throat, and mouth — again. "No matter how long it takes, I will find you because I can't survive without you. I love you too much."

When she awoke, she was in Ezekiel's arms, her body curled into him, her breath in rhythm with every breath he took.

Ezekiel's earlier words clung to the soft waves floating around her. He had said he loved her, and she believed him.

"Ezekiel? Are you awake?"

He stirred. "Yes."

She moved up on the bed, tucking her legs beneath her, and looked at him, her eyes pleading with him. "You should leave with us today. Both you and Jeremiah."

He stroked her cheek. "I want to, but I can't."

"What if I become famous and open my own nightclub? You could stop operating a policy wheel and go back to medical school."

Ezekiel sat upright in the bed; his muscular arms folded over his broad chest.

"I want to join you in New York, but I don't know if leaving Chicago is in the cards for me."

"Why? I don't understand."

He kissed her bare shoulder reverently as if to make his words easier to hear. "All the years, I never thought we'd find a way back to each other. My only thought was revenge and Gallo and guilt. How could I deal with the life I'd taken? And for you to want to be with me after that — I never imagined."

She swung her legs to the floor, grabbing her chemise as she stood. "Then come back to New York with me now. Put the revenge and hate behind you."

"I can't. Not yet, but I will, I promise."

She touched his cheek. "I'll hold you to it." She bent forward and kissed him.

"I love you, Honoree." He kissed her eyes, her throat, and her mouth — again. "No matter how long it takes, I will make this up to you."

Ezekiel and Jeremiah loaded the pickup truck first thing in the morning. But when Honoree and Bessie climbed into the cabin, Jeremiah wasn't there.

"Where is he?" Bessie asked.

Ezekiel waved off her question with a shrug, but the muscle clicking in his jaw told Honoree something was off.

"Don't worry about Jeremiah," Honoree said to Bessie, wanting to calm her fears. "He'll show up before we board the train. He wouldn't miss saying goodbye."

The drive to Union Station was slow and cautious. The windshield wipers jerked back and forth, doing little to rid the glass of the blinding white powder. Ezekiel might do better without the wipers, Honoree thought. Then as if reading her mind, he turned them off.

Cranking down the driver's window, he swatted the snow from the glass with his gloved hand and the sleeve of his overcoat.

"Don't look so worried. We'll get there on time. You won't miss the train, Honoree. I won't let that happen. I promise."

She winced because he didn't understand. "I don't want to leave. I am desperate to stay. The city is home. I grew up here." Unshed tears roughened her voice. "I know I can make New York home, too. I just wish all the things that happened had happened to someone other than me."

"I deeply wish the same thing," Ezekiel said. "But you leaving Chicago is what has to happen now."

The engine sputtered, and Ezekiel pushed down on the gas pedal, his fist fighting the gearshift. When the engine revved, he smiled at her. "That is if we don't get stuck in the snow."

He drove west and then north, avoiding State Street and Halsted. Too many people on those streets might recognize him and his automobile, and one could alert Archie or Gallo's men that he was on the move.

The ordinarily short ride, even in bad weather, ended up taking an hour. Ezekiel parked on a side street several blocks from the train station's main entrance. "It'll be better to leave the car here and blend in with the other travelers on the sidewalk."

Honoree glanced at the bags and the large box in the trunk. How would they carry everything in one trip without Ezekiel's brother?

"I thought you said Jeremiah would be here." Bessie hugged her coat around her belly.

Honoree had a decision to make. There was too much to carry and too much to leave behind. But she had so few possessions left, it felt like giving up parts of her body. "We should leave the sewing machine in the car," she said. "You can bring it when you meet us in Harlem."

"We can take it with us now," Ezekiel said. "I'll carry it."

The three of them hoisted shopping bags onto their shoulders and loaded their arms. Then they hiked to the station.

The new Union Station had a shiny polished look and towering doors, and vaulted ceilings, so high birds nested at the top of the iron columns. They walked as quickly as their burdens allowed, through the vast rotunda toward the waiting room for colored passengers.

"We're here an hour early, aren't we?" Bessie's head tilted upward. "Do they have someplace for coloreds to eat?"

"What about the food you stuffed into your bag?" Ezekiel asked.

"It takes nearly two days to get to Harlem. I ain't touching that basket until we're on the train."

Honoree was cold and nervous, not hungry. Walking through the station had her imagining all sorts of calamities. Every white man who passed by might pull out a tommy gun and shoot them down.

"I'll find something for you two to eat once we get settled," Ezekiel said. "You will love New York. I promise."

"It'll take some adjustment, but everything

will be jake soon enough." Her attempt at a lighthearted tone sounded false to her ears and likely to Ezekiel's as well. He found a spot for them in the colored section, and they sat on a long wood pew. "I'll be right back."

Bessie snuggled up close to Honoree, her head resting on her shoulder.

A few minutes later, Honoree spotted Ezekiel, his hands empty, running toward her with Jeremiah on his heels.

"What is it?" Honoree asked. "Ezekiel?"

"Oh my God." Bessie sat up beside her. "What's wrong? Does Archie know I killed his brother? Is he coming for me?"

"Hush," Honoree said, placing a calming hand on Bessie's shoulder. "Let him talk."

"Crazy Pete —" Ezekiel swallowed. "He was shot dead this morning."

The world spun on its side in front of Honoree's eyes. "Oh God. Did Archie kill him? Why? He wasn't there. He'd gone to the store to buy lemons." She closed her hand into a fist and pounded her thigh. "He couldn't have heard a damn thing, anyway. Why would they hurt him?" The tears came fast, and she could feel the blood in her veins pounding, pounding, and asking why. "Jesus Christ."

Ezekiel sat on the bench and picked up

her hand, cradling it in his large palm. "All I know is that Pete's dead, and someone gunned him down this morning. Outside that motel where he lives."

Honoree grabbed his arm. "Now we all have to leave town. Archie has lost his mind if he's killing people who had nothing to do with anything."

"We don't know who shot him. We just know he's dead."

"Who else could it be? No one other than Archie."

"We just don't know," Ezekiel insisted.

Jeremiah stood stoically. "We have a good idea."

"Quiet, now," Ezekiel replied. "What we have to do is make sure Honoree and Bessie are on the train. Until that happens, nothing else matters."

"Don't be foolish, Ezekiel," Jeremiah said. "It doesn't matter if it was Gallo or Archie who killed Pete. If it was Archie, it's because he thinks you had something to do with his brother's death. If it's Gallo, he'll tell Archie you killed Dewey, and then they'll both come after you. Nobody is looking for these young ladies."

"Except Gallo," Ezekiel said solemnly. "He wants Honoree."

Jeremiah grunted. "And you'll be no help

534

to her floating facedown in the Chicago River."

Honoree squeezed her arms around her stomach.

Ezekiel sat on the pew, his elbows on his knees as he lowered his head into his hands. "Goddamn. Goddamn."

"Ezekiel." Honoree put her hand on his shoulder, but he jerked away.

"Give me a minute, Honoree. One minute."

"You don't get any more minutes. You need to get on this train. Whatever beef you think you need to handle with Gallo or Archie, or anyone in this town, you can walk away. If I'm walking away, you can, too."

CHAPTER 47
HONOREE

Friday, January 1, 1926

If the train had left on time, everything might've worked out differently.

Honoree strolled through Union Station, absorbed in her troubles and with little thought to what Bessie might be feeling, or what crazy ideas brewed in her childish mind. What tormented Honoree was Ezekiel and his stubbornness.

He had decided to remain in Chicago to wrap up matters with Archie and Gallo, a plan Honoree criticized as foolhardy and a death wish.

The four of them, Honoree, Ezekiel, Jeremiah, and Bessie, walked in a straight line, carrying suitcases and boxes, toward the platform where the colored passengers boarded the train.

"He thinks I'll wait for him in New York City," Honoree said with no interest in holding back her opinion.

A few feet ahead, but within earshot, Ezekiel marched with his head cocked, listening.

"I waited for him once," she continued. "I won't wait for him again. I also won't be in Chicago to read his obituary in the *Defender* after he's been shot dead." She took Bessie's hand. "He wants revenge for his father's death." Honoree's voice cracked. "He shouldn't bother."

Ezekiel spun around. "I can hear every word."

"I know," Honoree said unapologetically.

They had reached the loading platform and Ezekiel and Jeremiah swooped up the women's shopping bags and battered suitcases and showed the conductor their tickets. Ezekiel said something to the Pullman porter about helping the ladies with their belongings and keeping an eye on them during the long trip. He might've given the man a fistful of cabbage to ensure his attentiveness.

"It'll take some doing and a bit of time, but I'll make it to New York City, I promise," Ezekiel said, leading Honoree and Bessie to their seats. "Wrapping these things up should only take a few days."

"I want to believe you, but that would be a mighty dangerous thing for me to do."

Honoree ushered Bessie to the window seat. She sat in the aisle seat and stared at her hands, folded primly in her lap. "I am sorry if I have caused you more trouble than you caused yourself."

Ezekiel kissed her forehead. "I'm not sorry. It gave me a chance to fall in love with you again."

Honoree rested her head against his chest, listening to his heartbeat. "I love you, too." She looked at him. "Do me a favor and don't stand on the platform, waiting for the train to pull off. Just go."

They were settled in their seats, with Honoree swapping seats with Bessie to sit next to the window. She wanted to watch him until he disappeared. A moment later, Ezekiel and Jeremiah had vanished into the crowd.

Next to her, Bessie stared straight ahead, dry-eyed and silent. They remained that way until a Pullman porter walked into the car and bellowed, "Something wrong with the engine. We'll be sitting here for a few minutes."

"At least Ezekiel and Jeremiah didn't stay and wait for us to depart." Honoree's sob interrupted the rhythm of her words. "Couldn't stand it if they were still on the platform. I'm not used to long goodbyes."

She held Bessie's hand. "How about you?"

"Y'all wouldn't be in this mess if it weren't for me."

"Not true, Bessie. Archie would find something else to be mad about if Dewey weren't dead."

"You saved my life. If you hadn't done what you did, I'd be dead or worse." Bessie's breathing came in short pants. "Did I have to kill him? You been thinking the same thing. I saw it in your eyes."

"Don't get yourself all excited. It won't do the baby any good."

"I told you I don't give a damn about this baby."

Honoree hugged Bessie's shoulders. "Don't say that." She grabbed one of the bags of food and removed a ham sandwich. "Here, calm down and eat something. You'll feel better. This train will soon be on its way, and we'll put all this trouble behind us."

The train didn't move for two hours, and at some point, Honoree dozed off, and when she woke up, Bessie was gone.

Everything she owned was on the train. The Singer sewing machine, the heart-shaped basket, a couple of dresses Bessie had managed to save. Honoree left all of it and ran.

Bessie had gone to tell Archie, the coppers, whoever might listen about the broken broom handle she'd shoved into Dewey's back. Foolish girl. Her confession wouldn't save Honoree or Ezekiel or Jeremiah; only muck things up even more. Bessie had to be stopped.

Outside Union Station, a snowstorm raged, and the headwind took Honoree's breath. Somehow, she caught the attention of a kind cabdriver and arrived at Miss Hattie's thirty minutes later. It was eleven o'clock in the morning, and the chorus girls, Miss Dolly, the cook, and anyone else who had worked the night before were likely still at home in their beds. The cafe's back door was unlocked, and she walked right in and immediately smelled Archie's cigar. They must be in his office.

Honoree paused outside his closed door and listened to his smoke-charred baritone shouting about his dead brother and the soon-to-be-dead woman who had bumped him off.

"Hello, Honoree."

She turned. "Trudy, what are you doing here?"

"I dropped by to pick up my things. I have a new job at the Plantation Cafe."

"Good for you. I guess." She glanced

540

anxiously back at the office door. "I can't talk to you now. I need to get into his office." Archie's voice had grown louder and angrier.

"I understand. I just wanted to say I delivered the envelope to my friend on the North Side."

"You did it?" Honoree placed a hand over her heart. "Thank you." She wanted to say more to Trudy, but angry voices drew her attention back to the happenings in the office. "Who else is in there with Archie?"

"Other than Bessie? Ezekiel and Jeremiah."

Honoree felt sick. "Damn it." She raised a fist to knock on Archie's door.

Trudy backed away. "I can't be here for this."

"I wish I weren't here for this." She paused with her hand on the door. "Thank you, Trudy."

"You already thanked me once. That was enough." She tipped her head to the side, smiling. "I'll see you when I see you."

Honoree opened the door to a room full of frightening things. Archie's tommy gun was pointed at Ezekiel, and behind Ezekiel, Bessie stood, a small, trembling whisper of a girl, clawing at his shoulders to let her pass. Jeremiah was a few feet away, blocking the view of one of Kenny's paintings. Standing as tall as Honoree had ever seen him stand in life, he held the Colt that Dewey had kept under the bar and had it aimed at Archie's head.

"Come on in, Honoree," Archie said. "Your boyfriend is trying to stop me from drilling holes in the bitch for killing my brother."

"Dry up, Archie," Ezekiel said. "Honoree, why don't you leave?"

"She should stay," Archie's voice boomed. "My gun has a hair trigger, and when your brother's bullet hits me in the head, my finger will squeeze off at least one round. I guarantee somebody in front of me will be shot dead."

"Honoree, Bessie, ladies." Jeremiah's dangerous baritone chilled her blood. "You need to leave."

Archie waved the barrel of his gun. "I said I want her to stay. She had something to do with Bessie killing my brother. The sow wouldn't have thought of it on her own."

"Don't worry, Archie, I'm not leaving, no way," Honoree replied. "You're right. I was there when Dewey died, and I don't know what Bessie told you, but he was trying to hurt me, and she stopped him."

"God, I wish you'd be quiet, Honoree."

Ezekiel held Bessie behind him with an arm. "Archie, you can't shoot Bessie. You'd be killing the last of your family."

Archie flinched. "What do you mean?"

"She's pregnant with Dewey's baby."

Honoree stepped farther into the room. "Didn't Dewey ask you to give her a job? Didn't he mention the girl he'd been messing around with? I bet he'd bragged about her. You know it's true."

Archie pointed the gun at Honoree. "I don't know a damn thing about her and Dewey. She's nothing more than another lost colored girl I took pity on. Just like I did with you."

"Archie, look at her." Ezekiel pulled Bessie to his side. "Open your coat. You can tell she's with child." He pushed her back behind him, shielding her with his body. "Let the women go, and we can settle the beef between us. I'm the one who threw his body in the river."

"Why don't we all go home?" Honoree pleaded, and if begging could work and stop what was about to happen, she'd drop to her knees and never stand on her feet again. "Please. There is no point in any more killing. Two men are already dead. Please."

Bessie started to move away from Ezekiel, giving Archie a clear shot.

"Stop," Honoree's pinched voice called out. "Stay still."

Jeremiah stepped toward Archie, pistol aimed, his finger cocked on the trigger.

There would be no convincing Archie to lower his gun. Either Ezekiel or Bessie would die, and Jeremiah would kill Archie.

"My God, Ezekiel," Honoree whispered. "You're going to end up dying today."

He lifted an eyebrow at his brother, and something passed between them. Then gunfire shattered Honoree's eardrums and ripped her heart into pieces.

CHAPTER 48
SAWYER

Sunday, July 12, 2015

"What happened at the shootout in Archie's office? Who survived? Who died?" I am behaving as if someone had rudely turned off the movie reel in the middle of the big battle. On pins and needles, I ask again, "What happened?"

Her laugh is a dry, pained cough. I pick up a swab with an ice chip and place it on her lips.

"The only person to die was Archie Graves. Jeremiah shot him in the head. No jail time, though. Jeremiah was arrested, but Trudy Lewis came to his defense. A favor to Ezekiel, I imagine. They had a strange relationship I never understood."

"I thought she'd left."

The woman I will always think of as Honoree smiles at me. "Trudy was on her way to the other side of town when the shooting started but swore on a Bible Archie

545

fired the first shot. The coppers believed her. They weren't interested in making a fuss over a bunch of coloreds killing each other at a juice joint like Miss Hattie's. Not like there was anyone important in the room. Other than, well, other than Honoree." The old woman taps her chest and coughs. "I need a glass of water."

The ropy veins in her hand bulge as she tries to grip the cup. I end up holding the drink to her lips.

"Now, Ezekiel, he got hurt bad. He wasn't dead but close. And Jeremiah, Lord, he moved like lightning." She pauses to swallow. "He came to check on me, I mean, me — Bessie. I was covered in blood, too, but it was Ezekiel's blood.

"Jeremiah had been shot, too, but it didn't slow him down. He saw I wasn't hurt and dropped to his knees next to his brother. I don't remember much of what happened next. Ezekiel was talking a lot between groaning and passing out. Jeremiah had to keep his brother alive on his own. He stuffed a piece of torn shirt into Ezekiel's wound and kept him from bleeding to death then and there, I believe."

Her breathing starts to sound wrong, like taking a breath underwater.

I touch her hand and massage her knuckles. "Are you comfortable talking about this? We can finish later."

"I ain't got many *later*s left, Sawyer." Her face darkens into hues of brown and gray.

"Okay. Tell me the rest, if you want. I'm all ears."

"We girls stood there. Didn't even scream — didn't have time, everything happened too fast."

"Did he die? Did Ezekiel die that day?" The question sounds heartless, but I need to know. "We found a death certificate for every member of the Bailey family, except for Ezekiel."

"You can rest assured he's dead now. That man couldn't outlive me."

She had a point. It seemed she had an endless stream of points. "How about Honoree? Did she die? Now, we didn't look to see when she passed since we didn't realize you weren't her."

"I didn't let anyone talk about her around me once I changed my name. It didn't matter much. Everyone who knew her had died or run away, anyhow."

I searched for a sign of sadness or a hint of sorrow in a quivering cheek. Bessie Palmer had made up her mind long ago; regret would never be her friend.

"Lula and I found only a few news articles

about the shooting. The first story in a black newspaper ran in February. The article was about the police search for Bessie Palmer. They wanted to question her about the murder of Dewey Graves. No mention of Ezekiel or Honoree." I pause to let that settle in.

"They stopped looking for me after that. Women were never that important. If a man, white or Black, said they saw something or done something, they'd be believed before a colored woman, most of the time."

"We found Jeremiah's name in an AME church record. It was his obituary. He died unmarried but with a fiancé. That was you?"

She stirs in the bed. "That was me. We never married. He was kind, and things might've been different if he'd lived longer and helped raise Margaret. He was such a young man when he passed."

She groans, and I gently squeeze her fingers. "You want to stop and take a nap?"

"I don't want to stop. I want to stay awake for as long as I can be awake." Her eyes darken, making a point of looking me in the eye like I anchor her to this world.

"Dewey's murder was never solved, from what Lula and I could find."

Honoree laughs out loud. "The police were looking for the wrong girl."

"They had an eyewitness. Someone saw her commit the crime, according to the article, but they never mentioned who."

Honoree looks at me, eyes wide and bright. "The coppers were looking for a girl who looked like me, but I was a blonde by then, a colored girl with bleached hair. Like Trudy. She dyed my hair." Honoree smiles. "The coppers weren't looking for Trudy, though; she was working at the Plantation Cafe. Under the protection of Capone's gang. But most likely, she was spying on him for Hymie Weiss." She shakes her head slowly. "We might've been best friends if I wasn't Honoree's best friend."

"So, is that why the police didn't know you?"

"Coppers didn't care about finding who killed Dewey. They had their hands full with Capone. He went crazy in 1926, and every police department in the city, even in Bronzeville, was busy fighting mobsters."

Honoree smacks her lips, creating a loud popping noise. "The folks who worked at Miss Hattie's moved to another speakeasy a block over from Miss Hattie's. Even Miss Dolly relocated. Miss Hattie's had been her mother's place before Archie came along, but after Archie died and Honoree vanished, the joint wasn't what it used to be."

The wretched coughing drags through her body; even her legs lift beneath the sheet as she gags, the color vanishing from her face, her eyes blood-soaked from the pain.

"Should I get the doctor?"

She pants for a few horrific seconds, catching her breath, holding out a pleading hand. "Don't leave me, Sawyer. Stay. I'll be okay. Just tired." She squeezes the railing of her hospital bed.

"Let's get someone in here." I move toward the Call button.

"Don't bother. I'm almost done," she says; the finality in her words tears through me. "We were all broken, Sawyer. Broken hearts, broken bodies, broken dreams." She laughs. "You never know how shit will work out, though. I did live to be one hundred and five years old. That's something, ain't it?"

Chapter 49
Sawyer

Tuesday, July 14, 2015

I am in the hospital room, seated in the corner, watching her rest. She should be in hospice but begged me to let her die at Cook County. A place with a bit more action than a hospice, she claims.

I don't argue when Honoree's doctor takes me aside. "It won't be long now," he says. "She'll soon make the transition."

Transition. "Why do you use that word? I don't like how it sounds. Could she transition back, if she doesn't like being dead?"

I recognize his type. After the accident, I spent a month in the hospital. Doctors can be a pain in the ass, waiting for them to figure out how to keep you alive. Or, in the case of Honoree, figuring out the most merciful moment to let you die.

The doctor stares at me with an expression crossing neatly between sympathy and dread, and I can hear his mind working, like his fabricated smile. "I'm sorry, son. It's her time."

I am not a religious guy. Church and I don't mesh, although Maggie prays for me every day when she remembers. The most important lesson I learned was from Azizi — death shouldn't be romanticized. It comes because it is inevitable; sometimes it's soon, sometimes it takes too long, but it happens. Always in its time. Nothing more. Nothing less.

"I'm thankful," I say. "I'm thankful we met and talked and got to spend some time together."

Honoree opens her eyes. "Don't start thanking me. I'm not dead yet." Her smile whispers through the room. "There is no reason to rush the conversation. Oddly, I have more time to talk, finally."

We even accept the gloom on the doctor's face, but the only sound is the rattle in Honoree's chest, struggling to draw oxygen into her lungs.

"I can't see you." The strength in her voice is gone.

I scoot a chair close to the bed, sit down, and take her hand. Her smooth skin wrinkles like tissue paper beneath my touch. "You need to rest."

"Not enough rest in the world will make

me a day younger."

I drop my chin into my chest, unable to look her in the eye. There is too much I want to say. "I'm a little tired, too."

"Why you staring at me so hard?" She raises a hand weakly to her brow. "What that woman do to my hair?"

"The nurse combed it wrong," I say. "I can fix it if you don't mind."

I touch the thin curl at her brow. She likes her wispy bangs to kiss her forehead.

"I guess with all those long braids, you gotta know something about hairstyles."

I reach into the drawer, remove a small comb, and move a few thin curls onto her forehead.

"Sawyer?" Her voice is the barest whisper. "If something was wrong, not with me, but if something were bothering you, you'd tell me, wouldn't you?"

"Yes, I would." I squeeze her hand. "Truthfully, I'm sad. I'll miss you."

Her chin trembles. "I can't live forever, but I did live pretty damn long. More than a hundred years, and considering the things I've done in my life, it makes me wonder if hate is as powerful as love in keeping the breath in your lungs."

Honoree died that Tuesday. Burned to ashes

on Thursday. I left for Paris Friday afternoon.

CHAPTER 50
SAWYER

Five months later

The knot in my throat loosens as I wait for Lula to arrive. I'm at the coffee shop across the street from the Sage Fool's Pub, and I'm early. I want to see her the moment she walks in. See her smile, her walk, have a moment to enjoy our reunion before I open my mouth, and risk spoiling it.

"Sawyer, you're here already?" She walks toward me wrapped in wool and scarves and a knit hat she swiftly removes. "The temp is so cold outside."

We hug. It's not awkward, and relief fills my chest. "Yeah, I noticed. Paris wasn't this cold."

I help her with her coat, and she doesn't stop me. Why would I think she would? My nerves are on high alert, and I should chill, but I'm happy to see her. "You look great, by the way," I say.

With a shyness I don't recall, she sighs

and slips into her side of the booth as I ease into mine.

I pass her a menu. "I'm starving for a fried USA breakfast. One more buttered baguette, and I'd lose a significant number of brain cells." I laugh and feel infinitely better when she does, too. "Forgive me for my lack of manners. Paris. Jet lag. How are you? How have you been?"

"Not too much different from what I covered in my last email, Sawyer."

The waitress arrives, a young woman with large-framed blue glasses, striking against her winter-pale skin and dark red hair. "You ready to order?" She glances at the unopened menus. "Or do you need more time?"

"He's starving," Lula says. "He's been dreaming about this breakfast for a while."

I laugh. She's right, and I go for it. "Two eggs with bacon, wheat toast, hash browns, orange juice. Black coffee. Do you have grits?"

"Yes, sir. We have grits."

"I was right. You are starving." Lula turns to the waitress. "Two scrambled eggs and coffee. Thank you." She passes the menus to the waitress.

"How's your dad?" A flash of concern fills her eyes, which I appreciate.

"He's on this self-prescribed twelve-step program, but I'm the only person on his guilt list." I chuckle. "He checks in on me often, and he does care about my well-being, but other than that — it'll take time." I lower my voice. "We still don't talk about Azizi, but the last month in Paris was decent."

She nods; her closed-lipped smile is comforting. "The whole rebuilding-relationship thing takes time."

The waitress arrives with water and coffee.

"Are you returning to Berkeley? Did you finish your thesis?"

I only answer the question that matters. "Yes, I finished the thesis." We do a fist bump. "I have my doctorate."

"Congratulations, Sawyer. Great news, exactly what you wanted."

"Thank you, but I've got better news. I submitted it to the Santa Monica Film Festival, and it was selected."

She places a hand over her heart and smiles. "Sounds like you are on the path to win a few Oscars."

"No, but if it happens, I'll dedicate my first Oscar to Black film legend Oscar Micheaux — and Miss Honoree. I mean, Bessie."

Her eyes cloud. "I miss her. The facility is different without her."

We both glance down, harnessing emotions, recalling Honoree's rough voice challenging my identity, my wit, my emotional consciousness. "I only knew her a few weeks, but I miss her, too." I gulp down some coffee. "How about you? How are things at Sage Fool's Pub?"

"I have news, too. The band is recording an album."

The waitress arrives, balancing a tray loaded with plates of food expertly. She one-hands the tray and fills every spot with some kind of dish.

"Excellent. Excellent." I bite my lip. "You mind if I dig in?" I gobble down some orange juice and a forkful of eggs, pausing when I sense Lula watching me. "God, I'm sorry."

"Don't apologize." She pauses. "Toast looks good."

I shake my head and laugh. "Here." I push my plate of toast toward her. "Let's share."

"You're a good man, Sawyer Hayes."

"Working on it."

"You are welcome." Lula butters her toast. "Deidre wanted to make sure I thanked you for convincing your grandmother to donate her collection. It is fabulous, and she is ecstatic. The opportunity to dig into Maggie's box — it's a once-in-a-lifetime project. We thought for sure it would end up in the California library system."

"I think Maggie figured she owed Chicago. She and her mother could never see eye to eye, and Maggie never forgave Bessie Palmer for hating her." I tilt my head and sigh. "I mean, Miss Honoree. I can't think of her as Bessie, but Maggie couldn't see her as anyone other than Bessie."

Lula takes a bite of her toast and washes it down with a swig of water. "I can't call her anything else but Miss Honoree, too. Did she tell you why she did it? Pretended to be Honoree Dalcour."

"It wasn't as calculated as I thought. Most of what Bessie did, however, was calculated, but not with Honoree. She loved her and missed her, and ultimately wanted to be her."

Lula nods. "I get it." She takes a sip of coffee. "Oh. Deidre had some updates. Remember Jeremiah Bailey was questioned about the shooting at Miss Hattie's?"

"Archie Graves. We found that in the *Defender.*"

"An article in another newspaper in January 1926 reported Dewey Graves's body washed up on the banks of the Chicago River."

I shake my head and smile. "Bessie and Honoree ran with a wild crowd."

"The *Crisis* article also said one of Capone's henchmen —" Lula pauses. "You like that word, right?"

I laugh out loud. "It works."

"Anyway, a Tony Gallo was also questioned concerning Dewey's murder. A year later, the same Tony Gallo was shot and killed on January 17, 1927." Her grin is outrageously broad, which makes me smile, too. "Do you recognize the date?" Her eyes widen. "Come on. Guess."

I am grinning, tickled by her enthusiasm. "Capone's birthday."

"One of his own gunned him down."

"I wonder if he knew what happened to Honoree and Ezekiel."

"Ezekiel remains a mystery," Lula says, wiping her mouth. "Still no death certificate. Nothing in the US or Europe that we can find. Deidre says he probably traveled to Baton Rouge after the shootout, but he was messed up. He moved in with Jeremiah and Bessie for a year or two. Then he disappeared."

"Miss Honoree, I mean Bessie — she never answered the question of what happened to Ezekiel, did she?"

"I don't believe she knew, or if she did, I don't believe she cared. He likely left Baton Rouge around the time his brother died and never returned. By then, everyone she cared about was in Baton Rouge."

"Until Maggie left her."

Lula props her elbows on the table, her hands closed into a fist beneath her chin. "What if Ezekiel is alive and living in a beach house in Jamaica?" Lula laughs. "Stranger things have happened."

"He's dead, Lula. Trust me. Otherwise, he'd be pushing one hundred and fifteen." I pause.

A gleam brightens her eyes. We are in that giddy place where we can't help but smile at each other. "The Santa Monica Film Festival is in April. I'd love it if you could join me for the premiere."

"I'll be there."

She answers so quickly I choke and clear my throat to avoid losing all my cool points. "You'll come to Santa Monica?"

Lula smiles that big, beautiful smile. "What did I just say, Sawyer?"

My smile feels uncomfortable on my face, but I trust Lula's words. Hers is a promise I can count on. "I'm excited. It will be fantastic having you there. Miss Honoree will love that."

Lula blushes, and her smooth black skin glows. "You're right. She will be there."

"Stop with all the smiling," she playfully complains. "You can't charm me with that cute grin of yours. You'll get yourself in trouble."

"I could say the same about you." I lift her hand from the table and cradle it in my palm. "Have I ever told you how much I enjoy talking with you?"

"Let's save that conversation for after you've spent some time back in California." She releases my hand and takes a sip of her coffee. I close one eye. "Should I worry?"

She sighs. "No, Sawyer. Nothing to worry about."

"I have something to show you." I pull out my tablet and show her the footage of three chorus girls dancing in a nightclub in 1925 Chicago. "The restorers cleaned up another section of the reel. See, that girl — Honoree Dalcour, the original. Now, that one —" I point at the round-faced girl at the end of the chorus line. "See the scar on her arm. That's —"

Lula's eyes light up. "Bessie Palmer."

I inhale deeply, filling my lungs with gratitude. "My great-grandmother."

EPILOGUE

Honoree hadn't thought about Archie Graves, Tony Gallo, or Bessie Palmer, or her last day in Chicago since she moved to Paris in 1926. Not even Ezekiel played through her thoughts until she received his first letter in '29, and she blamed Trudy Lewis for telling him how to reach her. How she ran into Trudy in Paris was another story altogether.

Honoree didn't throw his letter away, but she didn't pay it much heed, either. She buried the letters in the nightstand drawer next to her bed, but they came so often, she purchased a burr cedar box and placed them inside. Ezekiel's love letters were a diary of his adventures — entertaining, tragic, and hopeful. He wrote about loneliness and the memories that broke his now brittle heart.

563

After the shootout in Archie's office, it took years for Ezekiel to heal, and most of those years he spent in Baton Rouge with his brother and Bessie, and Bessie's baby girl, Margaret Rose. She was named after the sister the Bailey brothers lost to the Spanish flu in 1918.

Once he was able, he went to sea, became a merchant seaman, shoveling coal in the boiler room of a ship. Honoree liked to think of it as his penance. He called it remorse for his stubbornness that kept them apart for a decade. Each letter was another piece of his heart, the feelings he couldn't stop.

She never replied to his letters. The time for love — youthful, blindly passionate, irresponsible love — was behind her.

She lived in the Montmartre neighborhood, and after a few years of dancing in cabarets and Paris revues, she had opened a jazz club where she was the star attraction. The cafe was small, barely held fifty people, and her jazz band comprised half a dozen journeyman musicians. The club was profitable by 1930, and she had enough to buy a sturdy old French building. Tough enough to withstand the Germans and World War I with only a few broken windows and a dozen or so cracks in the ceiling. Nothing that couldn't be fixed with a hammer and a nail.

Her nightclub was one of a few jazz spots in Paris featuring colored musicians, despite the Third Reich's ban of "Negermusik" in 1935. Honoree had learned in Chicago that whiskey and pretty girls dancing on a stage had a way of attracting a crowd. She named her nightspot, aptly, Danseur Noir Cafe.

In the summer of 1938, before World War II began in Paris, Honoree was standing on the sidewalk outside her cafe when Ezekiel Bailey arrived and claimed his life was not worth living without her.

Dramatic, but the look on his face when he spoke those words made her heart tumble inside her rib cage, giving her a forgotten joy and a passion she hadn't felt since the night they made love on the roof of the tenement building in Bronzeville.

She didn't bring him to her bed right away. Love was one thing, forgiving and forgetting was another. He slept in a room in one of the buildings she owned, and industrious Ezekiel found a job working in a clinic shortly after that, helping doctors care for the sick and elderly. No longer a young man, he nonetheless dreamed of returning to school to study medicine.

Finally, the man she had loved since she

was twelve was a man she could love at thirty-eight. They married in 1941 during the height of the war in Paris. She'd been indulgent and self-absorbed in her youth, and Ezekiel, bitter, tragic, and vengeful, but his strength, his desires, his selflessness charmed, and strangely, freed her soul. Love was better the third time around.

The city was aglow in the fall of 1945. The Allied Control Council in Germany had repealed the Nazi laws. Honoree was ending her last performance of the night at the cafe with Ezekiel standing in the wings, as he always did. Another man, however, was at his side, a stranger.

The crowd was enthusiastic, and Honoree hated to disappoint an audience. The band, all Caribbean musicians, played swing, and the number of patrons was larger than usual for a Friday. Everything in Paris lately seemed louder, gayer, and bigger since the war ended. Pounding feet, clapping hands, whooping, and hollering, the partiers and jazz enthusiasts all would joyfully continue their revelry until dawn, except for the ordinance that mandated the club to close by midnight. The war might be over, and the Germans defeated, but fear took time to subside.

On a stage, Honoree could find the best

light blindfolded. She drew every ounce of magic from every moment. A swing of her leg and a swirl of her hips, and the spotlight was her heaven. She felt ageless.

As the band played the last tune, she danced her final set of the evening, and Honoree got a better look at the man standing next to Ezekiel. A young Negro soldier in a US Army uniform.

She spun across the stage, her jade-and-gold-feathered costume circling her body with a soft but audible swish. The audience shouted, "Bravo!" She bowed and bowed again. Then she raced from the stage.

"Oh, darling, what an audience! Simply divine." She kissed Ezekiel on the mouth like they hadn't just seen each other that morning. When she pulled away, she smiled at the young man at Ezekiel's side.

"Who are you?" Honoree said, catching her breath. "Shouldn't you be out at one of the cabarets on the Champs-Élysées?"

"Hello, ma'am." Tall, but not as tall as Ezekiel, he squared his broad soldiers, showing off his uniform proudly.

"He's come a long way to meet you, Honoree," Ezekiel said, then turned back to the soldier. "I haven't even asked your name."

"Sergeant Norman White of the 761st

Tank Battalion." He extended his hand to Ezekiel and removed his hat, before bowing to Honoree. "You don't know me, but my mama was Cleo Dalcour's best friend, and I was asked to bring you a letter, ma'am." He held an envelope in his hands.

"Would you like me to read it, Honoree?" Ezekiel asked, his tendency to protect her from pain a gallant, but also an obtrusive, trait.

"I'm fine. I can read a letter addressed to me, Ezekiel."

"I couldn't give it to you, anyway, sir. I promised to hand-deliver the note to Ms. Dalcour. I mean, Mrs. Bailey."

Ezekiel shook his head. "Honoree didn't take my last name. Hers is still Dalcour."

"Oh. I — I guess that sort of thing happens every day in France."

Honoree smiled. "The French are a wild bunch." She splayed a hand over her heart. "Cleo Dalcour, you say. That's my mama's name."

"Yes, ma'am. We call her Aunt Cleo. She helped raise my two sisters and me after my mama passed. Learned you were in Paris a while back, and when my sister learned my battalion was near Paris, she asked me to find you and give you this letter." He handed her the envelope.

"Aunt Cleo told me to look for a Negro dancer who wasn't Josephine Baker," he said with a small laugh. "When I heard about the Danseur Noir Cafe, I figured that would be the first place to look."

Honoree's hand was steady as she held the envelope to her bosom. "You say your name is Norman White, and you live in Baton Rouge?"

"Yes, ma'am. Well, right outside, ma'am, in Livingston. My folks were sharecroppers when they were alive. Now my sisters live in Baton Rouge and teach school."

"You're a soldier," Ezekiel said.

"Yes, sir — at least until the war ends. Then I'm returning to California with my bride to play professional baseball."

"My father's name was Rufus, his middle name Norman." Honoree tilted her head.

He nodded, grinning. "Aunt Cleo told us all about him."

"Did she now?" Honoree opened the letter but held it in her hands without looking at what was written. "Are you on leave?" she asked.

He nodded. "I'll be heading back home in a few days. My tour in Paris is about up, and I'm just glad I found you — and Mr. Bailey, or there would be hell to pay when I returned."

Honoree bent her head, reading the letter slowly, digesting each phrase, and understanding what the blank spaces in between didn't say. She wiped a tear from her eyes. Her mother would never change.

I'm sure you're living the kind of life you daydreamed about. I kept tabs on you while you remained in Chicago but lost track after you left New York City. Years passed before I received a letter, a letter from Ezekiel Bailey, letting me know he'd found you. I'd almost forgotten I had a daughter. Still, I expected to hear from you soon. But that was a decade ago.

I never understood why you couldn't just come home. What was it that made Chicago and that dirty apartment so important? You never could let anything go. Like your father. Even after Ezekiel and his family abandoned us, you stuck to what you wanted and ignored the things you needed, like seeing your mama.

Perhaps that's a gift. I hated new things. I hated losing my baby. I hated your father for making me leave Baton Rouge. I did love you, though. But unlike you, I fear what I don't know. You grab on to it like it's a shining star from the Lord himself. I don't understand that kinda thinking. I don't understand that kinda love.

Must say, I surely never knew how much a mother's ways could harm a child. Though I like to believe you're stronger because you had to figure out how to get by on your own.

I'll never set eyes on you again, but I did my best, considering who I am and what I had to endure. I did my very best. I believe you have done everything possible to live a happy life. I guess happiness is a good thing. You take care.

Love, your mother
Cleo Dalcour

She stopped reading and battled the surge of forgotten anger and hurt. "How is my mother these days? She's getting up there in age."

"Celebrating her sixty-fifth birthday soon. She keeps busy. An old friend of yours is her next-door neighbor. Her name is the same as yours, Honoree, but her last name is Bailey."

"She took Ezekiel's brother's name, but they never married. Her maiden name is Palmer, Bessie Palmer."

"Right," the soldier said. "But she'll tell you in a heartbeat that Bessie Palmer died in a bar fight in 1926."

"She's right. We all died that afternoon, but then we were reborn. If I never set eyes on her again, I know everything there is to know about her."

"She says the same kind of things about you, except she doesn't talk to me much anymore." He wrinkled his nose. "Not since I married her daughter."

Ezekiel gave Honoree a tender glance. "So you married Bessie Palmer's daughter?"

"No, sir, I married Honoree Bailey's daughter," the young soldier said with a laugh. "She's the sweetest girl in the whole wide world."

"I'm sure she is," Ezekiel said.

"Would love to catch up on you and the folks back in Baton Rouge, and, of course, your young bride." Honoree took the young soldier's elbow. "By the way, what's her name?"

"Maggie Bailey." His cheeks flushed. "Oh, I mean, now, Maggie White."

Honoree smiled. "Well, Norman, I want to hear all the news from Baton Rouge. You must join us for dinner."

"Yes, please do," Ezekiel added. "My wife is a wonderful cook." He touched her cheek.

"My darling Honoree makes the best can of pork and beans in Paris."

"Thank you, Ezekiel, but I'm a much better cook than I was in the old days."

AUTHOR'S NOTE

I love books, music, dancing, art, and history. Frankly, I am a fan of any creative discipline designed to entertain, educate, or engage our minds, emotions, and hearts.

My journey to writing *Wild Women and the Blues* was influenced by several factors, dating back to my connection to the 1920s.

My Jamaican-born maternal grandmother, Ella Elizabeth, arrived in New York City in 1923. A twenty-three-year-old island girl, she had traveled from Montego Bay with a ticket purchased by her lover (and future husband), a merchant seaman named George Edward Joseph. But when she arrived at the Port of New York, expecting to live her life in the glamorous city, he wasn't there to meet her. The man with whom she'd been corresponding for the prior two or so years (they'd met and fallen in love while his ship was docked) sent someone in his place to meet her. That man escorted her to a small town in Ohio where George now lived. They were married for fifty years, raised five children, with my mother being the youngest.

Another inspiration for *Wild Women and the Blues* is also personal. While dancing in New York City in the 1980s, I had a job as a waitress (as many professional modern/jazz dancers tend to do) at a club called the Cookery, owned by Barney Josephson, founder of Café Society in Greenwich Village. Café Society was one of New York's first nonsegregated nightclubs.

One of the headliners during my tenure there was Alberta Hunter. The then-octogenarian had revived her career as a blues singer and was the featured weekend entertainment. At the time, I wasn't up-to-speed on the history of jazz and knew little about Miss Alberta or the jazz scene of the 1920s and after. Nonetheless, I was able to form a bond with the artist. My "special assignment" on the nights she performed was to bring her tea, during which we shared our fondness of Chicago (my hometown) and love of performing in front of an audience.

Then I watched a video about Alice Barker, 102 years old, being shown a video of herself dancing as a young woman, and my "what if" took flight.

The main characters in both the 2015 and the 1925 storylines of the novel are fictional. Historical figures from the jazz scene and Chicago's Bronzeville inspired several fictional characters in the story. The locations and some of the events were taken from news articles and advertising I found in the archives of the *Chicago Defender* and *Chicago Tribune,* along with numerous other resources.

My research also included several nonfiction books. They helped me set the stage for *Wild Women and the Blues* and included (but are not limited to):

- *Chicago's New Negroes: Modernity, The Great Migration, and Black Urban Life* by Davarian L. Baldwin
- *Images of America: The Chicago Outfit* by John J. Binder
- *Chicago Jazz: A Cultural History 1904–1930* by William Howland Kenney
- *Louis Armstrong: Master of Modernism* by Thomas Brothers
- *Hear Me Talkin' to Ya: The Story of Jazz As Told by the Men Who Made It* by Nat Shapiro and Nat Hentoff
- *Kings: The True Story of Chicago's Policy Kings and Numbers Racketeers:*

An Informal History by Nathan Thompson

- *Oscar Micheaux: The Great and Only* by Patrick McGilligan

I also wish to acknowledge the assistance of the librarians and curators at the Harold Washington Library Center (Chicago), Library of Congress (Washington, DC), and the Schomburg Center for Research in Black Culture (New York City).

Chicago's Black Belt's history in jazz and the arts, as well as the community's economic strength (the Stroll) during the 1920s, isn't as readily recognized as the Harlem Renaissance. Still, the City of Big Shoulders and its Second City moniker was something I wanted to examine.

Some of those notable 1920s landmarks of Chicago's Black Belt included the "Stroll"; the Dreamland Cafe at 3520 South State Street, which was wholly owned and operated by Bill Bottoms (but fictionalized and renamed Buttons in this story); the Plantation Cafe; and the home owned by Louis Armstrong and Lilian Hardin Armstrong.

Policy gambling's role in the South Side of Chicago's economic stability is touched upon in the novel as well, but this "illegal lottery" was an integral aspect of Black life throughout the country for decades.

It was a pleasure exploring this period and featuring this part of Chicago's past as the backdrop for my novel about Honoree Dalcour, Sawyer Hayes, and Bessie Palmer.

ACKNOWLEDGMENTS

My journey to publication has been long but rewarding in so many ways, but mainly because of the people, authors, readers, and publishing industry professionals I've met and had the opportunity to get to know.

I owe an enormous debt of gratitude to my friends and colleagues who have supported me. Many of you have listened to my ramblings about writing fiction for a decade. Well, here it is, and I can't express how much each one of you has contributed to helping me achieve this goal.

Specifically, I would like to send a thank-you to my excellent, patient agent Nalini Akolekar, and the most outstanding editor this book could ever have, the fantastic Esi Sogah. Your encouragement and guidance have been instrumental in making this book better. Also, thank you to Krista Stroever for your expert helping hand. You women are the best!

Thank you, Kensington. I sincerely appreciate the opportunity to work with such a team of professionals. Special thanks to Vida Engstrand and Michelle Addo and the publicists and marketing and sales team who helped this book reach readers.

Thank you, Reggie Stovell (my wonderful son as well as the entire Stovell and Joseph crew), Sharon Shackelford Campbell, Veronica Forand, Alicia Rasley, Patricia Birmingham, Pamela Prince-Eason, Tin House, Mat Johnson, Nancy Johnson, and my Saturday at the Pool team, Nina Crespo and Michelle Arris, and Lori Ann Bailey — and Diana Gaston for her encouragement so many years ago.

Another huge thank-you to the Dreamweavers, the 2014 RWA Golden Heart® class.

I'd also like to recognize two of my favorite writing teachers — Margie Lawson and Donald Maass.

I cannot express how fortunate I am to have such incredible beta readers as Nadine Monaco and Eliza Knight — your comments and encouragement and friendship have been extraordinary.

And to my critique partners, who have been in the trenches with me and this book for several years, thank you, thank you: Pintip Dunn, L. Penelope, and Vanessa Riley. You three women helped keep me sane enough to write this novel. Thank you!

■ ■ ■ ■

A READING GROUP GUIDE:

WILD WOMEN AND THE BLUES

DENNY S. BRYCE

■ ■ ■ ■

ABOUT THIS GUIDE

The suggested questions are included to enhance your group's reading of Denny S. Bryce's *Wild Women and the Blues*.

DISCUSSION QUESTIONS

Wild Women and the Blues uses dual story-lines, but a large portion of the novel is set in 1925 Chicago. During the Jazz Age (1920s–1930s), Chicago was the epicenter of music, entertainment, and policy gambling.

Here are a few questions that your book club or reading group might find useful to kick off the discussion about the book, the characters, and Chicago's Bronzeville, a.k.a. the Black Belt, community during this time in history.

1. When was the Jazz Age, and who were your favorite jazz musicians from the period?

2. Oscar Micheaux was one of several black filmmakers who produced "Race films." These films starred black actors and actresses who portrayed characters that

weren't featured in Hollywood's racist stereotypes. How might these race films of the 1920s, '30s, and '40s have set the stage for the Blaxploitation films of the 1970s (*Coffy, Shaft, Cleopatra Jones, Super Fly*)?

3. In 1973, a film starring Paul Newman and Robert Redford, *The Sting,* reawakened interest in ragtime (1895–1919), a form of music that might be called a predecessor to jazz. A celebrated composer of the musical style was African American Scott Joplin. While the Jazz Age helped define the Roaring Twenties, what other music forms helped define a generation?

4. Was Honoree Dalcour a "New Negro" or naturally resourceful and stubborn about what she valued about her life in Chicago?

5. What did you think of Honoree taking in the homeless Bessie Palmer? Was it an act of kindness or frustration with the other chorus girls at Miss Hattie's Garden Cafe?

6. Toward the end of the novel, did Honoree feel genuine affection for Bessie or more of an obligation to her roommate?

7. In 2015, Sawyer's depression was a

complicated response to the loss of his sister and his estranged relationship with his father. Does his sister haunt him because of his guilt, or his grief at the loss of his connection to his family? Would he be better able to deal with his grief and guilt with a more supportive family?

8. Oscar Micheaux made more than forty films, but many were lost. In the novel, Sawyer finds a reel of film that is confirmed as a lost Micheaux. However, the most recent "find" in terms of Micheaux's lost films happened in 2017. One of Micheaux's films, *Within Our Gates,* was released in 1920 and called by some a response to D. W. Griffith's *The Birth of a Nation,* a film cited as heightening the visibility (and acceptance) of the Ku Klux Klan while promoting a negative image of African Americans. What film(s) would you credit as impacting public opinion about an individual/group or political issue? (Think about *Reefer Madness,* a 1936 film, or propaganda films of World War II, for example.)

ABOUT THE AUTHOR

Denny S. Bryce is an award-winning author and three-time RWA Golden Heart® finalist, including twice for *Wild Women and the Blues.* In addition to writing for NPR Books and FROLIC Media, the former professional dancer is a public relations professional who has spent over two decades running her own marketing and event management firm. A member of the Historical Novel Society, Women's Fiction Writers Association, and Novelists, Inc., she is a frequent speaker at author events and lives in Northern Virginia. Visit her online at DennySBryce.com.

The employees of Thorndike Press hope you have enjoyed this Large Print book. All our Thorndike, Wheeler, and Kennebec Large Print titles are designed for easy reading, and all our books are made to last. Other Thorndike Press Large Print books are available at your library, through selected bookstores, or directly from us.

For information about titles, please call:
(800) 223-1244.

or visit our website at:
gale.com/thorndike

To share your comments, please write:

Publisher
Thorndike Press
10 Water St., Suite 310
Waterville, ME 04901